IT'S IN THE CARDS . . .

The Queen of Heaven: On a throne suspended in the air sits the crowned Queen of Heaven. Her expression is detached, her eyes raised, one hand across her chest, the other trailing down. At the hem of her skirts crouch three supplicants: a man, a woman, and a calf. *Meaning:* Forgiveness; selflessness; giving of one's substance to succor others; also, detachment.

The Archer: In a winter forest, a naked woman draws her bow, aiming at an unseen target. *Meaning:* Revenge; purpose which must be carried out; justice.

Lord Death's Progress: Lord Death, mounted on a stallion, leads a parade of the doomed: a weeping woman holding a child in her arms walks beside him, one hand gripping the trailing end of his fine robe. *Meaning:* Death, but also conception; a sundering from old ways, but also the beginning of new; barrenness, but also the suspended power of growth.

The cards sent them through the Gate; only the cards can see them home again . . .

W9-BYK-781

ALIS A. RASMUSSEN

THE LABYRINTH GATE

'Tis a gift to be simple, 'tis the gift to be free,
'tis the gift to come down where we ought to be;
and when we find ourselves in the place just right
we'll be in the valley of love and delight.

THE LABYRINTH GATE

This is a work of fiction. All the characters and events portrayed in this book are fictional, and any resemblance to real people or incidents is purely coincidental.

A Baen Books Original

Baen Publishing Enterprises
260 Fifth Avenue
New York, N.Y. 10001

First printing, December 1988

ISBN: 0-671-69793-5

Cover art by Larry Schwinger

Printed in the United States of America

Distributed by
SIMON & SCHUSTER
1230 Avenue of the Americas
New York, N.Y. 10020

For J.E.S.
(who claims he wrote half of it anyway)

ACKNOWLEDGMENTS

E. P. Thompson, The Making of the English Working Class. *New York: Vintage Books, 1966;*

Eric Elliott, who illustrated the Gates for me;

and finally, everyone who helped babysit 3R-S—thank you!

PROLOGUE:
THE MIDWIFE

She turned the first card over with a deliberation that frightened the boy.

"To the east, the Heiress," she said in a voice made colorless by great effort. "Who is she?"

"The Princess Georgiana, your highness," he said through his fear, because he could not stop himself. He saw only her head and chest and her pale hands moving in the circle of light on the table; the rest was shrouded in darkness and broad skirts like the veil of night.

"Ah." It came out halfway between a sigh and a moan. She rocked slightly, her eyes shuttered. "Heiress by decree, not by law or by nature. She is innocent and unsuspecting. She will not remain heiress for long, not when my claim is stronger. Not once I gain the power to remove her." She turned over the second card. "To the south, the Hunter."

The boy whispered now, afraid to speak louder. "The Earl of Elen, your highness."

Her eyes opened fully and she stopped rocking. "The Earl! Here's a dangerous turn. By the cards, companion in some way to the central figure. That he will aid me I cannot believe. I know he seeks power as well. He must be my foe." She seemed to recall something and began to rock again, a rhythmic pattern, a wisp of a satisfied smile on her face. "In the heavens . . ." She turned the third card, frowned slightly, puzzled. "The Paladin. Who can this be?"

The boy's forehead furrowed with effort. He shivered, for the first time feeling the cold drafts of winter infiltrat-

1

ing the closed, shuttered room to chill his bare skin. "I cannot name him, your highness. He is not of this land, but he is pure."

"Another virgin, like yourself? That purity?"

"No, highness. No—purity of vision." His voice trailed off. She rocked. "Somehow he will aid the Hunter, he will aid—" His voice, faint already, faded to nothing as he mouthed a word. "He is the bringer of aid to those whose last hope is past. That is all I can see, but his trail leads to the next card—"

"Best to know your enemies," she muttered, "though I had not expected them from that direction. Ah." She shifted her seat beneath the dark skirts and seemed better satisfied. "Heaven leads to the Underworld." She turned the fourth card, and gasped. "The Labyrinth! Nastagmas!"

A thin, bent man appeared from out of the shadows. Unlike the boy, he was clothed, in plain, dark clothing that absorbed the little light left in the room. "Your highness." His voice was thin as his face.

"These were to be sorted. Nastagmas. Face cards, figures, only. How did this card get in here?"

"I assure you, highness." He bobbed. "I assure you. It was done."

Suddenly she smiled. "A powerful card then, and perhaps not unexpected. For I see it is here that I must search for the knowledge that will give me the power for my plot to succeed. Where is it, boy?" She resumed rocking with a passion that stirred the skirts around her. She gasped slightly, regained control of her voice. "Where is the labyrinth?"

Now he would have shrunk away from her, from the terrible intensity of her desire to know, but the old man Nastagmas stood just behind him, and he could not, in any case, move at all. "Only through the labyrinth gate can a path be found to what is sought," he gasped, the words forced from him by power far greater than his ability to resist.

"The labyrinth gate! An old legend to write pretty tales about!" Her voice rose with anger.

Nastagmas took two steps forward. "Yet your spell binds to truth, highness. Consider."

"Indeed. Indeed." She considered. "If there is truth to

the old tales—if the labyrinth gate existed, if it could be
found and opened to give up its fabled treasure. Such
power! Then tell me where it is, boy."

"There is one person who knows. I cannot see him." He
shivered again in the cold air. "But the Hunter can lead
you to him. The Hunter seeks the labyrinth as well."

"Ah," she said. "Then I have only to follow him." She
appeared content. "So to the north." She turned the fifth
card. "The Seeker—but here in isolation. Who is this?"

"A foreigner. I see, I hear music. She will aid the
center. She is linked to the Paladin. That is all, highness."

"So she will aid me." She sighed. "Perhaps as antagonist
to the Paladin. As well, as well. The strength of the
patterning grows. Now, to the west. Ending, changing, and
death." She rocked to her words as to an incantation, and
turned the sixth card. "The Crusader."

The boy whispered. "He is a poor man, highness, of no
higher station than myself. A laborer."

"A peasant!" Her voice was half scorn, half amusement.
"Perhaps it *is* you boy. How old are you?"

"Fifteen, highness."

"Indeed." Now her voice took on satisfaction, and in the
half-light he saw her examine him with a thoroughness
that terrified him as much as if he saw his own death
before him. She rocked. "If I can gain such power, I will
then have more use for your purity than just its truth-
fulness—" Her hands closed in fists on the table. Her eyes
shuttered again. He tried desperately to move his arms in
order to cover himself, could not. "For the final act of the
princess' transformation, I need only the true source, the
strongest source, of power." Her lower lip jutted out and
for an instant her face spasmed into an expression he had
not enough knowledge to read.

Behind him, Nastagmas said urgently, "The center,
highness."

"Yes," she groaned. Her hand unclosed and moved with
effort as she rocked forward to turn the seventh and last
card, the center. "The Dark Queen," she sighed, obviously satisfied. "The Mistress of the Underworld."

The boy stared in awe and terror at the picture of a
young woman running blindfolded through a forest of
nightmare.

"Who is she, boy?" she demanded, but there was a note of surety in her voice.

He could not speak.

"You must talk, boy. You are bound to it by the spell. You must talk."

"I do not know." His voice came out choked and rasping.

"Do not know!" Her anger emanated like the force of the spell that held him fixed in one spot. "Is it not me? It must, it shall be."

"She is veiled." A strangled whisper. "Veiled, or not here yet. I do not understand. But all power is hers. She is the wheel, the center." His recitation sounded clearly now as if another spoke through him. "The treasure of the labyrinth is hers alone, and will come to her as it has always meant to."

"No," she gasped. "The treasure must be mine. The power must come to me." Her rocking became violent. Her eyes shut, and her hands gripped the table edge as if in a convulsion. Her gasps receded in strength and she ceased at last to move. For a long moment only silence held in the room, until finally her hands relaxed.

She opened her eyes to look at the cards laid out in the seven directions on the table. "Forewarned, forearmed," she said in a low voice. " 'She is veiled.' It could be Madame Sosostris—she has powers enough to know of and to seek this treasure. But if my efforts are the greater, than I shall gain it first, and succeed to the Dark Mistress' power, and to my rightful place as Queen. Nastagmas!" The old man slipped forward another pace. "Two watchers. The first to track the Earl, for he will reveal the labyrinth. And the second on Madame Sosostris, since she will certainly attempt to recover the treasure for herself."

The old man coughed, a slight sound. "Then you believe, highness, that the old writings are indeed true. That ages ago the Mistress of the Underworld left a treasure of great power in her labyrinth, before she went into hiding from her sister."

"Church stories," she replied, scornful. "These church-goers are fools, calling the Dark Mistress the daughter of the Queen of Heaven when in fact she is Her elder sister, and the greater in power, though the Queen and Her Son eclipse her now. They cannot believe she was once worshipped in her own right as Queen of the Depths. But that was not the legend I was referring to, Nastagmas."

"Do you refer, highness, to the legends of the Princess Sais and the fall of Pariam? She, too, was said to have sealed a magnificent treasure in the labyrinth of Pariam before she and the city died together."

"Sealed behind the labyrinth gate." She frowned. Her gaze shifted, and fastened on the boy, seeing him as if for the first time.

He took a step back from her gaze and, surprised that he could move, reflexively shifted his hands to cover his groin.

"Give me the deck," she snapped. Nastagmas hurried to hand her a small pouch. "I will seal him to silence. Then get him out of the city. I will see that he is safely guarded on the journey. He must be lost. Thoroughly. But in a safe place, Nastagmas, where his—ah—innocence will stay intact and where he will remain comely. If my plans can indeed be brought to fruition, I will have use for him later. No dungeon."

"Yes, highness." The old man bowed once again.

"Well! Have it done." There was a shifting under her skirts. "Have it done!" Her irritation broke into the room like the draft as Nastagmas went to the door, sheparding the naked boy before him. "Send one of my women, immediately."

"It will be done, highness." He closed the door behind himself.

"It will be done," she echoed, standing. The vast skirts raised slightly, but otherwise did not move. She swept the cards together, picked the Heiress up from the pile, and thrust it into the candle flame. The card burned with satisfying brilliance. "Before one year has passed, it will be done."

When the flames touched her fingers, she opened her hand and passed it, palm down, through the last flare. "Flames seal innocence to silence," she said.

She spread the seven cards back out. The Heiress lay whole and unmarked among them. As the door opened to admit two of her waiting women, she placed the gold circlet of the Regency on her head, and smiled.

CHAPTER 1:

THE GATEKEEPER

"Say you drew a series of scenes from the wedding," said Chryse to her newly wed husband, "and a stonecarver replicated those drawings in a long relief, a—what are those Parthenon marbles called?—a frieze."

They stood under a pale *Exit* sign, the double doors behind them open to the cold night beyond. In the hall, friends and relatives moved in the slow, half-chaotic movements of the final cleaning up.

"Metopes," said Sanjay.

"And say those reliefs were buried for two thousand years, and then dug up by whatever distinguished archaeologists the future might produce—what do you suppose they would make of them?"

"I think," said Sanjay, gazing at an oblong white box being carried out the far door by the best man, "that we should have taken some of the leftover cake with us."

"Exactly. They'll think the cake was an offering to some beneficent goddess and the champagne toast the benediction, in human blood, perhaps, of the sacrifice of a virgin—of course, depending on whether it's a patriarchal or matriarchal culture, the virgin will be female or male—and the exchange of rings . . . Well, maybe that part of the stone will be damaged so that they only see the hands and therefore reconstruct the scene entirely differently. Say as part of the celebratory dance."

"Is that a gift over there?" asked Sanjay. She followed his gaze. On one of the bare folding tables lay a small velvet bag, its cloth as brown as good soil, tied at the top with gold strings. Sanjay set his top hat down on the picnic

6

hamper and walked over to the table, returning with the little pouch. A strip of parchment attached to the string read, in fine calligraphed letters: *To the Newly-Wed Couple.* "Anna must have overlooked it when she loaded the presents into her van."

Chryse shrugged. "Why don't we just take it with us?"

For a moment the hall and the bitter chill of outside faded as they regarded each other in silence. Chryse's smile surfaced first. With Sanjay it was a slower process: his happiness touched his eyes before his mouth. They both leaned forward, and kissed.

"Well," she said at last, mouth still a light brush on his. "I think we should find a more private setting for the rest of this conversation."

He smiled and picked up the hamper, and they let the exit door cut the hall off behind them.

"It's freezing!" she exclaimed as they walked towards the car. Their footsteps slipped in quiet crispness over the concrete walk. Behind, the low voices of last guests at the front entrance faded away into the stillness of late night.

"It's a beautiful dress," said Sanjay, hamper in one hand, the little velvet pouch in the other. "Especially with you in it."

"Madame de Pompadour would have been proud, although I'm not sure she would have chosen such a penetrating shade of green." She smoothed her hand down over the emerald brocade of her bodice. "But when Marie and I saw this fabric in the store, we couldn't resist—a real solstice green. White is so insipid, especially with my complexion in December. It's just too bad we had to mismatch our centuries, but you look so gorgeous in top hat and tails I can't complain."

"I could have worn a djoti."

"Or some kind of regimentals. Though the English weren't in India in the mid-1700s, were they? No, I suppose they were." She laughed. "Oh, the look on my father's face when you handed out the 'World Peace' buttons for the men's lapels instead of boutonnieres."

He sat the hamper down by the car, turned to grab her by the waist, and swung her around. "I love you," he said.

She tightened her hold on him, for once saying nothing, just holding.

After a bit they separated. He fished the keys from the

hamper and unlocked the passenger door. "I take it I'm driving," he said.

"I don't think I fit under the steering wheel." She eased herself into the front seat. Skirt and petticoats swelled around her. "Sanjay!" she cried as he handed her the velvet pouch. "Let's open it now. Our first gift."

"You mean, you'll open it, while I drive."

"Don't worry. I'll let you open at least two of the other presents when we get back from our trip."

Their eyes met—brown in a dark face and, startlingly, brown against pale skin and blonde hair—and they both grinned.

There wasn't much traffic. The car traveled through pools of diffuse light, marking street lamps and the occasional signal. She undid the strings and slipped her hand inside the velvet. It caressed her skin, soft as fur. Inside, something harder, flat-surfaced, with the barest grain of texture. She fit it into her hand and drew it out.

"Oh," she said.

"What is it?" He slowed the car to a halt at a red signal and turned on the dome light.

"Oh," she repeated, flipping through them. "They're beautiful." She handed him one.

A card. In the background, a desert landscape, stark and barren. A young man, armed and outfitted, rides a horse on a path only he can see. His eyes are fixed on a single star that pierces the haze of night, as if it guides his quest. On the back of the card, an heraldic animal.*

"What is that?" Chryse asked, leaning to look.

"I think," he said, tentative, "that it's a newt."

In the intersection, the light turned green.

"Look at this one," said Chryse.

Half-light, dawn and dusk. At the gates to a walled town, a cloaked figure turns away from the lighted gates to follow instead a dim road that leads up into dimmer mountains. Hidden in the hills, the suggestion of a castle. On the back, a wolf.

She handed him more cards. At least half were of a central figure, a person: a cross-legged woman levitating, a child dressed in rags, a naked archer, a man in chains.

* A description of all cards in the "Gates" deck appears in the Appendix.

Others were of places, a temple of stones backed by a
marshland, a fine, high hall backed by burgeoning fields;
or of scenes—

"A wedding feast," said Chryse. "It's got to be, the
bride and the groom at the head table. Look, her dress is
green."

Sanjay examined a card with a stone gateway. On its
back the same gateway, but of living birch trees. "There's
something about these, almost like there's another dimen-
sion underneath the flat drawing. I almost feel that if I
could just see it from the right angle, I could step through
it into somewhere else." He shook his head and realized
that a car was pulling up behind them, pausing, and then
passing on through the intersection. He gave the card
back to Chryse and started the car forward. "I don't know,"
he finished. "It's probably my imagination."

"Do you think someone—there's no signed card, of
course. It must have gotten misplaced—did them 'spe-
cially for us? Who could it be?"

"Especially for us? I don't think so."

"Here's a grim one. A woman in her nightshift running
through the forest. But what a forest! Snakes and bugs and
horrible little faces—it's a nightmare. But she can't see
any of it because she's blindfolded and—yuck—she's stepping on a snake."

"That's nice. What's on the back?"

Chryse gave a little laugh. "A nightmare, of course. A
black mare. I wonder how many there are—"

She began to count. By the time they reached the hotel
she had triple-checked: fifty-two. Sanjay maneuvered into
the underground garage and found a parking space.

"Well," he said as the motor died. "We really did it."

She laughed. "You're giving me that 'now what' look.
What did we get married for, anyway?"

"So you can support me in the style to which I should
be accustomed, wasn't it?"

"And I thought it was to assuage your broken heart."

Watching her, he reflected that it was this quality as
much as any other that made him love her: an ability to
take both the failures and triumphs of life with a grain of
salt, a quality that some might call light cynicism if they
did not recognize that it sprang from a true and deep love
of life. He shrugged. "After all," he said, "if I have to give

up my professional freedom in two weeks, I might as well give up my other freedoms as well."

"Oh, Sanjay." Her voice took on the half-disgusted tone of one about to embark on long, familiar, and overused arguments. "You didn't have to apply to the master's program in architecture, and once you got in, you didn't have to agree to go. You're such a martyr to your parents' wishes sometimes. And I hate to see you get so depressed about the prospect of three more years sitting in a classroom drawing suburban tract homes and urban office boxes when you really want to be hacking through the jungle with a machete uncovering some marvellous old city that you can draw."

"Don't forget to mention the picturesque native inhabitants whose portraits may, as my father says, strike a chord of humanity in all of us, but won't pay the rent." His tone was uncharacteristically, if softly, caustic. "I have to make a living somehow."

Chryse laughed ruefully. "I don't know. We're making enough to live on from my job."

"You can't work there forever. You know it's not what you want to do—even what you should be doing. You're the one who should be going back for a master's, not me. You know you can get into the music school at the university."

"And do what? It's no good getting a performance degree—there's no future for me there." She blew out her breath on one sharp gust. "What can I do with my music? I feel like that year we spent travelling around Britain as itinerant folk musicians was the apogee of my music career."

"Chryse," he said with some exasperation. "You've been in music since you were a girl. I think you're just afraid to make the real commitment to it now."

She made an impatient movement with one hand. "I don't want to talk about it. What I should do is smash every camera in the world."

"What?"

"Then you'd have a profession. Before cameras they needed professional illustrators for archaeological digs and geological sites and newspapers and magazines."

His hands were still on the steering wheel, the high lights of the garage shading their length in the kind of detail he might have drawn into a sketch of the scene. "Like Catherwood at the Mayan sites. All those beautiful ancient images coming into the light again."

"Listen to us." She leaned across to kiss him on the cheek. "No wonder we got married—it was supposed to take our minds off our trivial problems for at least one night. I for one would like to get my dress off."

He smiled. "So would I—your dress, that is."

"Shall I leave your hat in the car?" she asked as they got out of the vehicle.

"No! I want to wear it." He took it from her. She rolled her eyes, and he laughed. "You're right. I'll just forget it in the hotel room." He set it down on the passenger seat and shut and locked the door.

Their footsteps echoed in the deserted cavern of the garage as they walked towards the corridor labeled *Exit* and *Elevator*. He had their coats and the hamper, looking almost like a Victorian gentleman on an outing. The overnight bag clashed culturally with her 18th-century gown. She held the bag awkwardly, out away from the stiff circle of her skirts. In her other hand she still held the cards and the pouch.

"Why are you bringing those?" Sanjay asked as they went up a dim hallway and stopped by the elevator to the lobby.

"I thought we'd lay them out on the bed, see what we've got."

He smiled. "Then I'll tell your future. I think it starts with kissing the handsomest man in the room."

The elevator arrived, opening for them with a light chime.

"They're going to think we're in a masquerade," said Chryse as they entered the elevator. "Here, let me put your 'Peace' button in the suitcase before you forget you're wearing it and leave it on the tuxedo."

As the doors shut, Sanjay set down the hamper and coats and took the suitcase from her. A shudder signaled the beginning of the elevator's ascent. With a movement almost startling in its abruptness, he embraced her, this time letting one hand caress her intimately.

Chryse gasped and started and laughed, and dropped the cards. They fluttered down around the couple, like the pattering of hard, slow rain, and as the embrace tightened, she let the last card, still caught in her hand, go as well, and gathered her husband closer to her.

The card struck the floor with a light tick.

The lights went out. Dead black, without a trace of light. A barely perceptible shuddering vibrated through the floor.

For a little while there was only soft laughter and the rustling of cloth and half-heard whispering.

"I'm dizzy," said Chryse finally into the blackness.

"I know," said Sanjay; and before she could retort, "so am I."

Her petticoats rustled down around her as she crouched and began to count, picking up cards.

". . . ten, eleven—Sanjay. Was the floor of this elevator wood?"

He had crouched as well. "It is strange," he said. "Here's ten more. Let me see—"

She had gotten to forty-three when with a snap a tiny flicker of flame wavered to life. It was hardly enough to illuminate more than a face on a card: an old woman's face. Hooded and cloaked, she sat on a bench, or an old log; behind her the gateway, sinister, yet inviting; a lamp stood, unlit, by her feet.

"Henry and Margaret," said Sanjay, reading from a white matchbook cover. "November 19. And to think I thought it was a silly custom."

"Forty-four," said Chryse. The match snuffed out, followed by a *snik* and a new, brighter flare—two matches. "Five. Six. Seven. Over there—thanks. Eight and nine. Fifty."

The flame went out, catching her in darkness as she reached for the fiftieth card and slipped it with the others into the velvet pouch.

"Chryse," said Sanjay suddenly in an odd tone of voice.

She looked up. He struck two more matches. Centered in the dim light was a brass door handle. He lifted the matches, tracing up from it, outlining, instead of an elevator door, an old, thick wooden door reinforced by heavy crossbeams. For the first time they realized that the slightest nimbus of light, the barest of diffuse glows, edged the door as well. And that a sound came from beyond, a low blending of voices in a kind of hymnal chorus, unfamiliar and eerie.

The matches dimmed and died. For a long moment, drawn out in silence and in a force as strong as physical tension, they stared at each other through the darkness.

"Do you ever get a feeling," said Chryse in a faint voice, "that the ground beneath your feet has suddenly vanished, and you're just waiting for the realization to hit you before you fall?"

Sanjay knelt. "We'd better find those last two cards."

New matches revealed a floor of old wood, split and shrunk to reveal gaping cracks beneath which they could detect nothing at all.

"Lift up your dress," said Sanjay. Immediately the light found a card, the gateway, just before the match smouldered and failed. He tucked the card into his suit pocket and rose. "Just one. The other must have fallen through."

"Sanjay," she said. "What's going on?"

He handed her her coat, put on his own, and picked up the hamper. She buttoned the pouch into the inside pocket of her coat and picked up the overnight bag. First they kissed; then he opened the door and stepped through.

The light was inconstant enough that it took some moments to fully distinguish their surroundings, to separate wall and window, floor and furniture, into discrete parts. They stared: at a high, vaulted ceiling of carved wood; at patterned windows that lanced up into darkness; at a ring of candles standing in tall sconces that illuminated an altar of white stone, a large portrait of a serene woman who, seated on a throne, held a haloed child in her arms and, below the portrait, a stone effigy of a young man pinioned in death.

Sanjay put out a hand blindly and gripped the nearest thing that came to hand. It proved to be a long wooden bench, first in a row of benches. "Now I'm falling," he murmured.

Chryse simply gaped. Her face had lost several shades of color.

For a space there was only their breathing.

"This is not—" began Sanjay finally. He broke off to turn back abruptly, and Chryse spun as well, as if fearing what might be behind her.

There was nothing. No door—however impossible that was since they had moments before come through one. In the mellow glow of lantern light they could discern a mural, a painting of figures larger than life that stretched along the long wall, easing into shadow at its height.

A woman and a man dressed in exotic, unfamiliar clothing handled, or constructed, a series of small, rectangular objects.

"Sanjay." Chryse's voice died away into the vast stillness of the air. The chorus they had heard so faintly had vanished as utterly as the door. "Those are our cards—the same pictures on them—"

He began to reply. Broke off at the sound of soft footsteps.

From down the dim aisle between the benches came a silent figure holding a light. Sanjay put out a hand, found Chryse's, and gripped it, hard. But the figure metamorphosed into an elderly woman clothed in a severe habit of unbecoming lines, like the clothing worn by members of religious orders.

"It is a fine set of murals," the woman said. The very ordinariness of her voice seemed somehow the greatest shock of all. "The only remaining sixteenth-century murals that can be conclusively traced to Master Van Wyck's studio when he resided here during the reign of Queen Catherine the Eighth. The subject matter is perhaps a touch heathenish for a cathedral, but none of the bishops has had the heart to order them painted over with a more pious tale. And I have always maintained that one can gain moral instruction even from such legends as the fall of Pariam, for the princess Sais certainly did the honorable and Christian thing in offering to sacrifice herself to save the city, although the skeptical might opine that as she only did it out of her illicit love for her sister's husband, who was the cause of the whole thing and ought to have given himself up for the death he was marked for—which I'm sure he would have done had he been a godly human and not of the unnatural blood of elvinkind—" She halted and lifted the lantern a little higher. "But perhaps there is some way I can help you. We don't usually get visitors at such a late hour."

"We're lost," said Chryse without thinking. "And I'm beginning to think that we're far more lost than we think we are."

"Ah." A reassuring smile lit the woman's features. "Spiritually or physically, I might ask."

"Both," said Sanjay abruptly.

Chryse began to speak, but thought better of it.

The woman examined them a space longer, and at last lowered her lantern and moved away, gesturing at them to follow. "I fear it is beyond my powers to help you," she said rather cryptically over her shoulder. "But I can show you to the door." She led them down the aisle toward a large set of double doors at the far end of the cathedral.

"But where are we?" asked Chryse as she and Sanjay followed helplessly in her wake.

"In the church of St. Cristobal of the Gates, patroness of travellers. Of course." She reached the end of the aisle and set a lined hand on the latch of a smaller door set into the right half of the great carved pair.

"But—"

The woman shook her head. "I am the keeper here, nothing more. You must find your own way." Her tone was kind, but final. She lifted the latch.

From beyond the door they could hear, muted, a rumbling roar of sound punctuated by an occasional penetrating human voice.

"Fare you well." The woman pushed the low door gently open. "And may Our Lady be with you."

"Thank you," said Sanjay reflexively. He looked at Chryse, she at him; together they looked back into the gloom of the great church interior that lay behind them. What they wanted to know, what they needed to ask, seemed unknowable and unaskable in the face of the overwhelming strangeness of their surroundings and the implacable, if gentle, determination of their companion.

"Thank you," Sanjay repeated, as if it was the only phrase he could remember.

Having at last accepted that she was not in fact dreaming, Chryse found herself too stunned to speak.

The woman opened the door a little wider, and smiled once again.

Chryse and Sanjay had no choice but to turn and walk outside.

CHAPTER 2:

THE WANDERER

They came out onto snow. For an instant they could believe it was the parking garage corridor, the dirty white concrete, until they looked up and saw stars, cold and silent in the night sky. Buildings rose on either side, close and high. Where the snow had melted or been cleared away, cobblestones showed through.

The noise came louder here, recognizable as a rabble of shouting and cries and the roar of humanity massed and agitated. Far down, at the end of the alleyway, torches flared and gathered and separated. In the flare of light shapes moved.

A single, tenuous piece of light split off from some corner of the turmoil and began to grow as it approached them.

Both of them stepped back instinctively towards the wall. Sanjay stopped so that he stood a little in front of Chryse. He put down the hamper.

The light resolved into a smoky torch, carried by a small, cloaked, long-skirted figure.

"Trouble, trouble," it muttered in a voice dry as an old woman's but somehow altered. "They'll be callin' out the troops 'fore long."

The figure halted abruptly, seeing Chryse and Sanjay. A hood shadowed her face. "Bless me, Mother," she wheezed. "Nobs, ain't you? Come down to Goblinside to get yer fortune told after a fancy-dress, I reckon. You chose the wrong night, lovies. You'd best be running back to St. Solly's."

She shifted her torch to survey them. The smoky light fell for an instant on her face.

Chryse gasped.

The old woman turned and fled onward, up the alley.

Sanjay reached back and gripped Chryse's hand. Cold fingers entwined together.

"Sanjay," said Chryse in an unsteady voice. "She wasn't human."

"Did she say Goblinside?" asked Sanjay in a voice no steadier.

In that brief glimpse they had seen a face vaguely mouselike, but leathery and pouched and punctuated with two alert, inhuman eyes.

"Maybe there was something in the champagne." Her fingers tightened on his to the point of pain. "Let's go back."

Sanjay turned, hesitating as he set his hand on the door latch, and then opened the door. In the inconstant flare of distant torchlight, they saw, not the vast interior of a great church, but an empty room no bigger than three meters square. Its dim, dusty corners flickered in and out of view in the unsteady illumination.

Sanjay dropped the hamper abruptly and took three tense, angry steps into the middle of the tiny room. He swore, words Chryse did not recognize.

"Maybe there's a secret door," she said quickly, but her voice shook. "There must be." With her free hand she pounded a circuit all the way around the dark room, rattling old, decaying boards, even prying one loose, but it was obvious there was nothing beyond, except, perhaps, more tenement rooms as decrepit as this one.

Halting at last, her fist sore, Chryse grabbed a fold of skirts into her hand and clenched it tight, as if its thick texture gave her strength. "This isn't possible, Sanjay."

As if a hint of fear in her tone had penetrated his anger, he turned and held out his hands to her. She let go of her skirts and their overnight bag and gripped his hands.

"Maybe it's not possible," he replied, "but we're here."

She took in a deep breath, let it out, released his hands. "And we're together." She picked up the bag. "I guess there's no choice but forward now."

"Is there ever?" he murmured. He got a good grip on the hamper with one hand. "I suggest the alley over the riot." They looked at each other, and walked together out of the room and up the alley.

It gave out onto a wider street, snow swept off the
cobbled surface by the passage of small groups of people
hurrying all in one direction, toward the swelling noise of
agitation. A wagon drawn by two oxen passed, carving its
path through the scattered traffic. Faces fled by them,
many commonplace in their humanity, others altered but
still strangely familiar. Men in overcoats and top hats
made their way down the street, women in long skirts,
shoulders draped with shawls. Glass windows shot warped
glimpses of lamplight reflecting back on the streets,
unshadowing the surfaces of shop signs: Haberman's Lock
and Key Emporium; Master Bitterbrew Hearth Spells and
Gates Tellings; Mistress Penty's Bookshop and Seeing Eye;
Meriwisp & Daughter Tobacconist. A child stood huddled
against a lamppost, barefoot, clothes in tatters, a little cap
forlornly askew on a wealth of dark hair that framed a
pointed face. *Truly* pointed—ending in a whisker-tipped
snout.

Sanjay and Chryse were still staring when the flow of
traffic, like the tide's reflex, suddenly reversed and began
to pour back in the other direction. They were pressed
back against a shop window as the flood increased. Inchoate shouts and warnings swept through the press:

"Troops out."

"Damn the Regent for her bloody ways,"

"Old Devina's gang broke in at the goldsmith's—"

A trio rushed past bearing a tattered cloth sign that
folded itself just as they came through enough light to
illuminate the letters: *Universal Suffrage.* More shouts
and a sudden explosion from away down the street.

"To the Daughter with the damn landlords and the
House of Nobles with 'em!" shouted a man as he ran.

"Votes for all!" cried a woman, hidden in the crowd.
"Free and equal!"

Closer, incongruous by its nearness and its complete
opposition to the rising hysteria and flight, came laughter,
light and slightly uncontrolled. An instant later a man
collided with Sanjay.

"Forgive me, sir!"

Torn from their hypnotic appraisal of the street, both
Sanjay and Chryse turned to stare at a well-dressed gentleman. He doffed his hat. "Monsieur, I am clumsy. Please,

again, forgive me." His eyes strayed to Chryse. "Madame!" he said appreciatively, and bowed.

"Bloody hell, Julian, can't you hold your liquor?" A second, slighter gentleman collided with the first, stumbled, and straightened to reveal a woman rather than a man. She was dressed in the same dark coat and trousers, waistcoat and white shirt and cravat set off against the darker colors. Several muffled reports sounded from farther up the street, punctuated by a scream and the shattering of glass. "Come on," she said, sounding abruptly more sober. Her gaze took in Sanjay's dark coat and trousers and Chryse's rich gown. "Slummers like us?" she asked good-naturedly. "Troops are coming. They've got quite a lather up from the riot in the square—there'll be a few heads broken tonight."

The man called Julian, with a smooth maneuveur unhampered by the obvious smell of spirits, took Chryse's arm and steered her along the walkway. "Really, Kate," he said over his shoulder, "how are we to remove ourselves from this charming neighborhood? I fear that I am not as well acquainted as you are with such haunts and am therefore utterly lost."

"Like bloody hell you are." Kate laughed again as the crush of the traffic grew worse and cast an eye, as obviously appreciative as Julian's, on Sanjay. "You must have connections with the East Seas Trading Company. Turn down this alley, Julian."

Chryse looked once at Sanjay; by unspoken consent they let themselves be led through a maze of small streets until at last their companions came to a stop by a carriage in a deserted square.

At their approach, the figure walking the horses pulled the animals to a halt and bowed briefly. "My lord. Miss Cathcart." He moved to open the door into the carriage. "An uneventful trip, may I hope?"

"You may hope, Abbott," said Julian. "But as usual Miss Cathcart does not live by such uneventful rules. Madame." He turned to face Chryse. "If you will allow me to hand you and your companion into the carriage, I would be honored to deliver you to anywhere in the city."

Chryse and Sanjay looked at each other.

"We thank you for the trouble—" began Sanjay.

"No trouble at all," interposed Julian smoothly.

"—but unfortunately," said Chryse, with a small lift to her hand that she hoped would signal Sanjay to silence, "not only do we not know where we are, but we shouldn't even be here."

There was a short silence. Julian and Kate regarded each other. Sanjay coughed slightly. The groom Abbott made himself busy with the horses.

"That didn't come out quite as I meant it to, did it," said Chryse.

Kate began to laugh. "Are you runaways or refugees?" she asked. "I smell an adventure here."

"Kate," cried Julian as if in despair, but he surveyed Chryse and Sanjay with a new light in his eyes. "Are you in trouble?" he asked. "Perhaps we can assist you."

"We can't ask you to go to so much trouble for us," said Sanjay quickly. He moved to put an arm around Chryse, realizing that she was beginning to shiver.

"I think Julian has put our case incorrectly," said Kate. "We're not saints. We're just bored."

"No, Kate. Not *just* bored. Excruciatingly, numbingly bored. Indeed, your troubles would undoubtedly provide us with a much-needed diversion. Why else would you have found us in the least savory area of town? I fear that we had simply run out of anything else to do."

"Now, Julian, that isn't quite true. I did want to visit Master Cardspinner, but how was I to know that he'd left the city after reading the coming riot?"

"In any case," finished Julian, "it will be warmer at Vole House. Permit me to introduce myself." He bowed slightly. "Julian Haldane, Lord Vole. This is Miss Sophia Cathcart."

"Sanjay Mukerji." Sanjay put out his hand. After the barest hesitation, Lord Vole shook it, followed by Miss Cathcart, who was still smiling.

"I'm Chryse Lissagaray," said Chryse, repeating this ritual.

Lord Vole handed her up into the carriage, and the rest followed after.

It was a quiet ride. Chryse attempted an explanation. Julian assured her that morning would be soon enough. The carriage clattered over the streets, the steady rhythm of the horses blending with a second set as they met up with another carriage, then a third as the thoroughfare grew wider and better lit.

That they had reached the wealthier districts was apparent by the many fine carriages and broad, clean, and well-lit house entrances. At last the carriage halted in a quiet square and they walked up the steps of a large, well-proportioned house, set in a line of others like it.

The door opened before them as if by magic.

"My lord. Miss Cathcart." The individual responsible for this sleight of hand was evidently the butler. His eyes registered Chryse and Sanjay, but the rest of his face showed no reaction whatsoever.

As they came into the grand entrance hall, a rustling sounded from above. An apparition descended the gilt staircase. In one hand she held a lamp; the other held on to the curved railing.

"She is lovely, Julian," said this figure, resolving into an aged lady of small stature and formidable presence. "And he—well, were I but forty years younger—" She halted at the second-to-bottom step and regarded them with an aristocrat's hauteur, dignified by an ornate purple dressing gown that could easily, to Chryse's eye, have passed for a ball gown. "But I am surprised that you now bring your trifling pleasures openly to your respectable home. Are there not other places for this sort of activity?"

"You mistake the matter, Aunt Laetitia," said Julian without any sign of deference to her sharp tone. "Madame et Monsieur are foreigners, lost and robbed. Miss Cathcart and I saved them from unfortunate circumstances and now I offer them the hospitality of Vole House."

"Hmph," stated Aunt Laetitia categorically. "You forget that I am your sainted grandmother's sister, not some married-in poor relation. If your mother and father were still alive—"

"Alas," said Julian, "but they are not."

"I'm sorry," said Sanjay automatically.

Julian bowed in acknowledgement. In the light of his aunt's lamp, Chryse could see a slight smile on his face and she realized that he was enjoying himself. Miss Cathcart was silent. "I thank you for your concern," he said, "but it isn't necessary. My mother died some years ago. I believe she expired of exhaustion after delivering her twelfth child. And my father—died of a fever."

"He died of drink," said Aunt Laetitia.

"How uncharitable of you to say so, Aunt."

She made a sound indicating her disdain. "How my niece married herself to such a wastrel neither your sainted grandmother nor I could ever understand. And I must say that you are following well in his footsteps. Though I daresay your Miss Cathcart outdoes you in that department." She cast a disparaging look at Kate, who simply offered her an elaborate bow in response.

"Kate is not *my* Miss Cathcart," said Julian. "And I must protest that her capacity for drink certainly does not exceed mine."

"Bloody hell it don't," muttered Kate.

"And what sort of language is this, young woman? In *my* day a woman knew her place. And it was certainly not drinking to all hours of the night in this rakish and dissipated manner."

Chryse, unable to help herself, laughed. "Where was her place?" she asked. "Ma'am."

"Between the sheets, I expect," muttered Aunt Laetitia's great-nephew ungraciously.

"You are drunk, Julian," Aunt Laetitia said without heat. She regarded Chryse with a penetrating but distinctly non-hostile eye. "A young woman of good birth and manners was taught to manage her estates and to hunt. These days, of course, such accomplishments as embroidery, sketching, and trivial conversation are considered sufficient. It is no wonder that Miss Cathcart has taken to drink."

"Fortunately," said Chryse, beginning to like Aunt Laetitia quite well, "I'm not good at sketching, but my husband is."

"Ah," said Aunt Laetitia, lifting her lamp a trifle higher to examine the couple more closely. "You are married. Julian!" This in a voice long accustomed to command. "Introduce me. And then call Mistress Housekeeper and have her show them to the Gold Suite. We can discuss their predicament in the morning, when *we* are rested and you and Miss Cathcart are sober."

"Yes, Aunt," said Julian meekly.

CHAPTER 3:

THE EMPRESS OF BOUNTY

She dreamed of music. She often did, and woke pensive at having lost it or laughing at its awfulness. But here she dreamt of music as she never had before—a purity and simplicity of line that was so close to the truth she felt she should be seeking that she ached.

And woke pressing herself close to her husband in an unfamiliar bed in a strange room.

"Sanjay?" she said, sitting up startled and a little frightened before she remembered with a kind of vague unclarity the events of the night before. "Where are we?"

Sanjay stirred and pulled her back down against him in a movement made smooth by much practice. "In bed on our honeymoon."

"This is not our hotel."

"No," he agreed. He smiled, caressing her. "Although that didn't seem to bother you last night."

She kissed him, lingering, finally disengaged herself. "I was too shocked to protest last night. I needed some kind of reassurance." She paused. "I had the strangest dream," she continued. "And beautiful."

Now he sat up. "So did I. I was on an exploratory expedition of some kind and we came on a—not quite a ruin—it was a forest with a city so perfectly intertwined with it that—I almost hate remembering it."

"As if," she said slowly, "all those classes you took in archaeology and ecology and art and culture fit together perfectly."

"Yes." He regarded her for a moment. "How did you know?"

"Because I had the same dream, I think—except of music—and it had a forest in it, too. Sanjay, where are we?"

The soft light of morning had penetrated the curtains, scattering beams across the bed. The room was furnished as if from an antique store, but the pieces had a look of well-polished newness about them. Above the fireplace hung a painting, a rather studied, sentimental pose of a mother and child, each with a halo. A fire burned in the hearth, but it was mostly coals, and dying.

Chryse tested the floor with a foot and found rug. On a beautifully carved chair next to the bed lay draped a fine woven dressing gown. She slipped it on.

"It's cold," she said, padding across the wood floor to the window. She leaned forward to look out. "This is not our hotel," she repeated at last. "If I had to make a guess, based on these rooftops, and what I can see of the streets, and the carriages, I'd say a century or more ago. Well?" She turned to regard Sanjay a little belligerently, as if daring him to come up with some explanation.

He was now sitting up, examining first the dressing gown of white lace and frills that lay on the chair on his side of the bed, then the dressing table beyond. "Whatever do they use all those drawers for?" he said to no one. He turned to look at his wife. "I don't know, sweetheart. And I'm not going to make a guess until I've got more evidence."

"Said just like your father," said Chryse, but with humor. "I *know* we're not dreaming, but it's impossible— isn't it? Last night I thought we would wake up and discover that your sister had played an elaborate practical joke on us. I think that's the only reason I was able to act with any degree of outward rationality. My other choice was catatonia."

"An unusual state for you."

She made a face at him.

"I do know one thing, though," he added.

"Which is?"

He lifted up the lace dressing gown. "You put the wrong one on."

They both began to laugh, cut off when a knock sounded on the door. Sanjay sat back under the covers. The door opened silently and a girl's face appeared.

"Begging pardon, Madame— Oh!" She looked surprised.

"And Monsieur. I brought your chocolate. An' Betty's here to stoke the fire up."

Sanjay grabbed the bed curtains and quickly pulled them shut.

"Please come in," said Chryse, feeling at a loss. The first girl entered bearing a tray with cups and two steaming pitchers. A second girl, younger and just as neatly dressed, followed and went directly to the fire after offering a brief curtsey to Chryse.

"Shall I pour for you and Monsieur, Madame?" asked the first girl.

"Oh, ah, thank you," replied Chryse. She walked over to the door to her dressing room, half recalled from the night before. Opening it, she found a huge space. Her gown had been hung up, and her suitcase's contents unpacked and hung up as well. In the vast space, the few outfits looked meagre. Sanjay's clothes were, she presumed, beyond the door on the other side of the bedroom.

"If you're wishing to dress, Madame," said the first girl tentatively, "I can help you, or Lady Trent's dresser, Miss Botherwell, can be called. She's ever so good. Oh, and Lord Vole's valet for Monsieur."

Chryse turned around rather quickly. "No, thank you. I think we can manage for ourselves, if—ah—" She faltered. "Thank you."

The girl curtsied, a slight smile on her face as she glanced once quickly at the closed bed curtains, and she hurried the other maid out in front of her.

"Are they gone?" asked Sanjay from behind the drapes as the door clicked to.

"Coward," said Chryse.

The curtains opened slowly. "Perhaps I've just woken up in one of my previous lives, as a rajah." He offered Chryse the elegant lace dressing gown in exchange for the one she was wearing. "Imagine needing someone to help you dress."

"I had to have help getting into my wedding dress. Good lord, this is almost obscene, with all this lace. I'm afraid to sit down." She did so anyway, next to the tray of hot chocolate. "Do you want a cup? It's very good. Do you know, somehow I don't suppose they have showers here. But they've left us a pitcher of hot water and some towels,

and there's a basin over there. Oh well. I'm just glad I
only drank one glass of champagne last night."

"Why?" Sanjay had gotten up and was now examining the
contents of his dressing room.

"What are those hallucinations you get when you drink
too much? Delirium something?" She gave a slight laugh
and poured herself another cup of cocoa. "Worse, imagine
having to face this with a massive hangover."

"Chryse," said Sanjay rather plantively from the closet,
"do you think I can wear my jeans?" There was a brief
silence, broken by his voice coming from farther away.
"There's a whole second bedroom in here."

"Aunt Laetitia did call it the Gold *Suite*, didn't she?
Maybe we're supposed to sleep in separate beds. And I
don't see what choice you have but to wear your jeans."
He wandered back in, clothes in hand, looking bemused.
"What I don't understand," she continued, "is if we went
back in time why are there people who don't look human,
like that old woman—"

"She might have been in an industrial accident. Scar
tissue."

"But I saw other people like her, even a child. And if
we went somewhere else entirely, why does everyone
speak English?"

"Maybe they don't speak English," said Sanjay as he
dressed. "Maybe we just perceive whatever they speak as
English. Maybe they're really speaking Hindi."

"Or Urdu?"

"In any case, you know this is all your fault."

Chryse laughed. "I didn't until you reminded me. Why?"

"You're the one who said you wanted our honeymoon to
be an adventure."

"But you're the one who said we should go somewhere
completely different."

They both grinned.

"I feel so guilty," said Chryse finally.

"Guilty?"

She shrugged. "Last night I was too stunned to think.
But now it's morning and we're safe—I'm excited, Sanjay.
We haven't the faintest idea where we are, and I'm not
sure I care. It really *is* an adventure."

"But why guilty?"

"What about Anna? She has all the presents, and she'll expect us to pick them up."

"Not for two weeks. No one will expect to hear from us for two weeks."

"And when the two weeks are up? Anna will call your parents, they'll call mine, and mine will call the police."

He sighed and sank down on the bed. "You're right. We'll just have to find out where we are, how we got here, and how to get back."

Chryse sighed, an echo, and sat down beside him. "Maybe finding out how to get home means we can get back here again." With one foot she traced the bright geometric pattern of the carpet morosely. "It seems a pity to have to leave before we have a chance to explore."

"We'll have to do what we can in the time we're here," said Sanjay, working one hand up the sleeve of her gown. "For instance, they should have put the lace—" He shifted it on her so that a different patch of skin showed through. "—there."

She pulled him down on the bed.

This time, when a knock interrupted them, Chryse hid behind the bed curtains and Sanjay stood. The door opened to reveal a young man in clothes that resembled a uniform.

"Begging pardon, Monsieur," he said. "When you and Madame are ready, I'm to show you to the breakfast room."

"Certainly," said Sanjay. "We'll be out in a moment."

"Is he gone?" asked Chryse as the door shut.

"Coward," said Sanjay.

"I take back everything I said about having servants. You never get any privacy."

"What did you say about having servants?" he asked as she went into her dressing room.

"I don't remember," she called. "But I'm sure I said something."

After a few minutes Chryse reappeared in a calf-length skirt and a sweater and boots. "Not very nineteenth-century." She regarded Sanjay's jeans and shirt. "But we're neat and clean. Good thing I brought a skirt."

"Kate—Miss Cathcart—was wearing trousers."

"I'll take bets that isn't usual. I'm starving."

"Madame." With an elaborate gesture he offered her his arm. "Shall we go down?"

Aunt Laetitia and Kate were already in the breakfast room, arguing good-naturedly over something to do with a regent, a succession, and a possible royal marriage for an heir.

"Ah," said Aunt Laetitia as the butler showed Chryse and Sanjay in. "I hope you rested well." She lifted a monocle to her eye and examined their clothing, but mercifully said nothing.

"Very well, thank you," said Chryse. "Good morning, Miss Cathcart."

"Hell in a basket," exclaimed that woman. "Call me Kate, please. I only endure the other title from Lady Trent because I daren't offend her by demanding she call me anything else."

"I am relieved," said Aunt Laetitia, "that your education at least included the basic respect for one's elders that was expected in my youth and is sadly lacking in young people today."

Kate merely grinned. She still wore men's clothing, but her suit was less formal than the unrelieved black and white of the night before.

"We can't thank you enough for helping us last night," began Sanjay.

"Good gracious," said Aunt Laetitia. "Please eat your breakfast first. I never advise serious talk on an empty stomach. It only leads to hasty decisions."

Chryse and Sanjay acquiesced gratefully. The sidetable was lined with an abundance of food: meats, breads, fruits, and sauces. They had almost finished when Lord Vole entered. He looked distinctly under the weather.

"Ah, Julian," said his aunt. "Tell me if I'm speaking too loudly. Mistress Cook has prepared your favorite meat sausages."

Had he been able to turn green, he would have. "Perhaps a thin slice of bread and some tea, Aunt," he said in a strained voice as he sank into a chair.

"Never could hold his liquor," said Kate to the room at large.

"Good morning," he continued weakly, inclining his head as slightly as possible towards Chryse and Sanjay.

"Sorry to see you're not feeling well," said Sanjay. "My mother has a recipe that she often gives to people suffering the after-effects of drink. If I could—"

"Is she a healer?" asked Aunt Laetitia. "Let me call Master Butler and he can convey your recipe to Mistress Cook."

Sanjay hesitated. "I could just as well—" faltered, and finished. "—of course."

When the butler returned some minutes later, glass in hand, both Kate and Lady Trent examined the contents of the glass with interest.

"That looks utterly disgusting," said Kate with satisfaction. "Drink it up, Julian."

By the time Aunt Laetitia ushered them into the parlour next door, Julian had recovered most of his usual complexion, and Chryse remembered that she had thought him very attractive on their first meeting.

"Now," said Aunt Laetitia as they disposed themselves on the sofas and chairs that ringed a small table in the center of the room. "That you are foreigners I can certainly believe. Monsieur Mukerji's coloring is obviously that of a native of the East Seas, and most likely Indhya. Madame Lissagaray I cannot place so easily, although her height and the extreme lightness of her hair—I have heard that across the Western Ocean in the Vesputian colonies the women grow as tall as the men, and the men as tall as giants. An unlikely tale, but in any case." She paused to clear her throat. "Perhaps we should start by asking what brought you to Heffield."

"Heffield?"

Even Julian, still recovering, regarded Sanjay in some astonishment. "You're in Heffield."

"I see," said Sanjay slowly. "This city."

"Evidently we shall have to start at a more basic level." Aunt Laetitia's tone was amused.

"Of course," said Chryse suddenly. "Sanjay! What brought us here?" He looked at her and nodded abruptly. "Excuse me a moment." She rose. "I must get something that I can only hope will explain what we cannot."

She returned, carrying the velvet pouch. "I believe these brought us." She removed the cards from the pouch and spread them out on the low table.

"Did you get the—" Sanjay began.

"Yes." She lay the Gate down on top.

"May the Son bless us." Aunt Laetitia put a hand to her bosom.

Kate stood up and bent over the table. "That's a remark-ably fine set," she breathed, overcome with an emotion Chryse could not identify. "May I touch them?"

"Of course."

Kate knelt before the table and with an obviously expe-rienced hand collected them together and dealt them out on the table so that the cards fell into a pattern. "Bloody hell," she murmured under her breath as she examined each card, both sides, before placing it.

"That's the finest deck of Gates I've ever seen," said Julian, leaning forward to watch Kate's movements.

"SACU, or UCAS," said Aunt Laetitia in a low voice. "It is double-sided, Julian." She examined Chryse and Sanjay with a new light in her eye. "I have heard of double-sided Gates, but never seen one. It is said to contain so much power that even unused it is dangerous."

"What does *sacu* mean?" asked Chryse. "And what 'gates' do you mean?"

This question brought her the immediate attention of all three.

"Oh dear," said Aunt Laetitia.

Julian merely looked startled.

"I think," said Kate, laying the last card, the Gate, out between two others, "that we will have to start from the beginning." She looked at Aunt Laetitia, who nodded.

"This deck is called the Gates," said Kate. "Or, academ-ically, the SACU. I've also heard of the UCAS, the other side, but never known anyone who has seen a set." She swept her hand, palm open, over the cards. "It starts here, with the Gate set between the cards of Dawn and Dusk, beginning and ending, youth and age. These three cards are the centerpiece, the hinge, of the deck."

"Out from the hinge is the round, the wheel of the year, known to most of us as the eight holidays. These eight cards are set in a circle, so. They begin and end with the Festival of Lights, the Winter Solstice—"

"Yesterday!" said Chryse.

"Exactly. And progress through the year: The Festival of Lights, Twin's Faire, Sower's Day, the Feast of Somorhas, High Summer's Eve, Hunter's Run, the Harvest Faire, Lord Death's Progress, and back to the Festival of Lights.

"Below the circle of the year lies the journey, the thir-teen months. These thirteen cards form a progressive line:

the Hut, the Village, the Road, the Town Square, the Temple, the Tower, the Harbour, the City, the Great Hall, the Garden, the Barrow, the Labyrinth—" Here she paused, staring for a moment at the card, a maze of walls in which a tiny figure, perhaps a child, was about to lose its way. "—and the Castle."

"And the face cards," said Chryse, "they're above the circle."

"The days of the month," said Kate. "But you're missing one, the Sinner, the fifth day of the first week."

"Ah, I see," said Aunt Laetitia. "The card properly called the Queen, or Mistress, of the Underworld. This must be a very old deck. I see cards here that are archaic, medieval. Your archer is naked, while we always see her clothed. And this card of a child in rags, the Beggar, is certainly medieval, or older."

"Yes," said Kate. "That should be the Monk."

"Not 'should be,'" said Aunt Laetitia. "'Is now,' but was not years ago. I have seen a medieval deck. You see, the days of the month are most changeable. The four weeks: the Queens, the Kings, the Knights, and the Magi, combine with the seven directions to identify the twenty-eight days of the month."

"*Seven* directions?" asked Sanjay.

"Of course," said Kate. "East, South, Heaven, the Wheel, Underworld, North, and West. So you have, for instance, the King of the West who is the Hunter, the Knight of the South who is the Crusader, and the Queen of Heaven."

"What direction is the wheel?"

"The center. The most powerful card of each week, each suit. Here is the Empress of Bounty, ruling over the Queens, and the Emperor of Reason over the Kings. The Master of Waters over the Knights, and last, the Angel of War."

"Ruling over the Magi," said Sanjay as Kate touched a card with an armored woman advancing, sword out, light radiating around her.

"And so on for the other days," said Kate.

"I know which one is missing," said Chryse suddenly. "I showed it to you, Sanjay. The blindfolded woman running through that grim forest."

Kate and Julian merely stared at her, uncomprehending. But Aunt Laetitia crossed herself. It was a movement so instinctive and quick, but so identifiable, that all the others recognized it.

"Aunt?" said Julian. "I'd never taken you for a devout churchwoman before."

"I've never heard of a blindfolded woman," said Kate. "The card you're missing is the one called the Sinner. The repentant knight kneeling before an image of Our Lady, pledging her service for her sins. I always thought it was based on those old medieval stained-glass windows of Saint Maretha's legend."

"Some things it is as well not to know," said Aunt Laetitia. "But when I was a girl the cult of the Daughter was stronger than it is now. The young bloods who were rich and bored took to her worship, as a kind of game, instead of to drink. Had they truly understood what they were doing, that it was no game, they *would* have taken to drink. The woman in the forest is Her card, the Dreamer, the true Queen of the Underworld, Mistress of the Labyrinth. The Sinner came much later."

"Bloody hell," breathed Kate.

"Well, Aunt," said Julian expressively. "I see there is a great deal more to your past than even Grandmama told me."

"Your sainted grandmother," said Aunt Laetitia severely, "was well able to keep a closed book, thank the Lady. In any case, *that* card is just as well lost, to my mind."

"Except that it leaves the deck incomplete," said Kate. "And therefore lessens its power."

"We're just looking at one side," said Chryse. "You said a double-sided deck of Gates is more powerful, both—what was it?—SACU and UCAS. What is the difference?" She picked up the last of the face cards, a woman burning at the stake, and turned it over to reveal a bird rising from the flames.

Kate shrugged and looked at Aunt Laetitia. "I'm out of my depth. I've only learned the minor arts of the Gates."

Aunt Laetitia extended her hand, a patrician gesture, and Chryse gave her the card she was holding. "The UCAS is the wild magic, the ancient seed, all of nature. It is forgotten now, and best left so, except by the northerners, whose name we do not speak and whose lands remain wild and untamed. I do not know how the UCAS is used, but I do know that unlike the SACU it is impossible to control.

It is said that centuries ago, before the coming of the Mother of All Peace and Her Son, an old and terrible civilization ruled on this island, and the SACU were formed to control magic. But that control also limited the amount of power any one mage could use."

"Do you really believe that old legend of Pariam's fall?" asked Kate. "The destruction of the city by famine and plague and of the princess who killed herself to save a man who didn't even love her?"

"I do," said Julian unexpectedly. "Perhaps not all of it, or even all the destruction and sickness part, but there *was* a civilization here, before ours. I've introduced you to Professor Farr, haven't I?"

"That old cracked pot?"

"He's a scientist, Kate."

"Who digs in the ground?"

"Yes. He's found fragments of old writing and pieces of ancient paintings, and dug up part of an old city in the Midlands that he claims is part of that old civilization. He even claims to know where the original city of the labyrinth is."

"And the treasure of the labyrinth, too, the one she supposedly hid?" retorted Kate, openly skeptical now. "Why doesn't he just go dig it up and bring it back? He'd be rich."

"An expedition of that kind can be very expensive, and prolonged," said Sanjay.

"You know of his work?" asked Julian. "I find it fascinating."

"Not of Professor Farr, but I know of the kind of work he does—exploring for ancient cities and artifacts. Digging up the past, really."

"Exactly!" said Julian. "And Farr has proof that a civilization we no longer know of once flourished here—farther north really, but on this island."

"Smoke leads to fire," said Aunt Laetitia. "Really, Julian, I hadn't realized that you extended yourself to such strenuous intellectual activities. I am pleased."

"Thank you, Aunt," he murmured.

"Of course he hasn't mentioned the niece and the daughter of Professor Farr, has he?" said Kate. "I met them as well. The daughter is a trifle serious and scholarly to be of *that* sort of interest, but the niece—quite a beauty."

"Quite indigent," interposed Julian. "As is Farr. Had I less money entangled in my estates after the fiasco of Father's debts, I would fund his work gladly. As it is, I help him with his papers."

"What?" cried Kate. "Did that handsome young fellow who was his secretary leave, then?"

"He got a very good position with Lord Felton's ministry."

"Ah," said Aunt Laetitia, seemingly at random. "A good choice."

Julian chuckled. "That's right," he said. "Wasn't Lord Felton one of your suitors, after Uncle Trent died?"

"Your sainted great-uncle was not a man who could be replaced," said Aunt Laetitia repressively.

"Of course," said Julian. "I beg your pardon, Aunt. It must have been my imagination that you prefer widowhood to the constrictions of marriage." He grinned, and coughed discreetly as his great-aunt raised her monocle to examine him with a frown. "As I was saying. For that reason, I've been assisting Miss Farr with the secretarial duties. As a favor."

"Assisting Miss Farr?" Aunt Laetitia gained a sudden gleam in her eyes.

Julian chuckled. "Don't try to marry me off, Aunt. She's a perfectly respectable female, not unattractive, but Kate summed her up: serious and scholarly, and quite devoted to her father. I thought you wanted me to marry Lady Wentwith's daughter."

"I will settle for any respectable young woman at this point, Julian."

Kate laughed. "I'll sing at your wedding, Julian. Very sweetly."

"You would," said Julian.

"Which leaves us," said Aunt Laetitia, "with Monsieur et Madame still without help. You say the cards brought you. Is there someone here that you wish to see this deck?"

"I meant it literally," said Chryse. "They brought us. We were in another country entirely, our home, and I dropped the cards and then we were here."

A short silence followed this statement. Kate's movement broke it finally as she leaned forward to pick up the central card, the Gate. "You're quite serious, aren't you?" she said slowly. "You didn't mean to come here. Do you have any idea where you are? Besides being in Heffield, of course."

"No." Sanjay shook his head. "And we don't know how to get back, either."

"Kate—" began Julian.

"I've heard that magi with great powers can use the Gate to move, from place to place, over great distances. I've *seen* Master Cardspinner do it from one side of the street to the other. Perhaps you triggered these cards, without knowing it."

"Perhaps the cards, double-sided as they are, cast the Gate themselves," suggested Aunt Laetitia.

"Is that possible?" asked Julian.

"Like a machine," said Sanjay, considering.

Julian chuckled. "Like one of the great factories of the Midlands?"

"You're too literal, Julian," said Kate. "You know the Gates don't work like that." She frowned. Her short, dark hair framed a face made pale by late nights. "But could they really have brought you from as far as—"

"As Vesputia?" Aunt Laetitia's voice was firm. "They could."

Kate swore. Lady Trent rose, beckoning to Chryse and Sanjay. "There is a globe in the library. Let you and I go there. If you will excuse us, Miss Cathcart, Julian." It was more command than request.

The library was a room made dim by many books. Aunt Laetitia led Chryse and Sanjay to a tall, standing globe and spun it slowly. "We are here, in Anglia." She pointed to a large island off the western coast of a continent. "And here—" She traced a line across the western ocean to a continent almost half a world away. "—is Vesputia. Of course, although I remember them as colonies, they are recently become a sovereign nation. That is where you are from."

"Well, it isn't really—" began Chryse.

"That you are from much farther away I have guessed," said Aunt Laetitia kindly. "None of us, I fear, truly understands the full power of the Gates. But it is where you shall say you are from. It is fitting, and comprehensible."

"You don't seem surprised." Sanjay twirled the globe, studying the fall of land and water, strange, yet vaguely familiar.

"At my age, one is rarely surprised. But I do confess to being curious. Later, when we are more settled, I shall expect to have a very long conversation with both of you. Now, shall we go back to the parlour?"

"You'll have to see Madame Sosostris," said Kate as the three of them entered the room. "She is the most powerful mage in Heffield—"

"The most powerful?" interrupted Julian. "Kate, you neglect such notables as the wicked earl and your Master Cardspinner, not to mention our beloved Regent."

"And while I am present," said Aunt Laetitia, "*that* woman, princess of the blood though she be, will not be mentioned."

"But Lady Trent," said Kate, "at breakfast we were discussing her proposal for—"

"At breakfast, Miss Cathcart, we were not in mixed company. And neither will the Earl of Elen be a source of conversation in *this* house. Master Cardspinner I have never heard of, though I take leave to doubt if he is any more respectable."

"Strictly hedge," agreed Kate, turning her attention back to a curious but bemused Chryse and Sanjay. "You *must* arrange to see Madame Sosostris. Perhaps she can help you."

"I will have one of the footmen take a message to Fenwych House immediately," said Aunt Laetitia.

"I didn't know you knew Madame Sosostris, Lady Trent."

"One does not *know* Madame Sosostris, Miss Cathcart," replied Aunt Laetitia with dignity, "but one does on occasion consult her. After all, she is quite the fashion these days."

"I think—" Sanjay looked at Chryse for confirmation. "—that perhaps we should go back to the place you found us last night. Surely there must be some—"

"Yes," said Chryse. "Some link that brought us there. Or some one. We were in a church, called—St. Cristobal's."

Kate shrugged. "Never heard of it."

"Ah," said Aunt Laetitia, as if something had just been confirmed for her.

"Do you know where it is?" asked Chryse.

"No. But I know of it."

"Kate?" asked Julian. "I don't suppose *you* remember where we were?"

"I doubt you do, besotted with drink as you were," retorted Kate. "But doubt not that I can find it again. And Goblinside is a better place to be by day than by night."

"You will not," said Aunt Laetitia abruptly, "go out of this house without proper dress. Julian, surely your sister Lucy's gowns would fit Madame Lissagaray well enough, with a little lengthening. My dresser can see to it. And you and Monsieur Mukerji are much the same build. Miss Cathcart and I will frame a suitable missive to be sent to Madame Sosostris."

"Perhaps that won't be necessary," said Sanjay. "If we can find the church."

With a practiced gesture, Aunt Laetitia swept the cards into a neat deck. "The Gates brought you here without your willing it. I think it unlikely your unpracticed will can return you." She slipped them into their pouch and handed it to Chryse. "And in any case, when one is dealing with these levels of power, it is always advisable to consult an expert."

CHAPTER 4:

THE EMPEROR OF ORDER

"There is Parliament," said Julian as they rattled along in the carriage over the streets of Heffield. "Built originally as the fortress at the confluence of the Tens and the Bishop Rivers by Queen Caroline the First before she was beheaded. Converted to its current use as Parliament by Queen Jasmina the Second. The current heir's great-grandmother," he added, glancing at Chryse's somewhat perplexed expression. "Of course, the Princess Georgiana is in a peculiar position, being the first undisputed heir to descend from the male line—from her father, brother to the previous queen. Am I confusing you?"

"Not really," said Chryse. "It just takes a moment for me to get my history straight. Bishop's a funny name for a river, isn't it?" Across from her, Kate lounged beside Julian, with a single booted foot braced carefully by the door to absorb shocks.

"From my research," replied Julian, "the name doesn't actually come from bishop, the church title, but from some form of 'bissoff,' an archaic word whose meaning is now lost. Undoubtedly, in medieval times, devout city folk began to render it as bishop." He clasped his hands together, as if warming them against the chill of winter that surrounded them. "Heffield itself is a shortening of the medieval name Hefenfelthe—Heaven's Field. That is the name this city had in medieval times. And if there was an earlier city, it probably had an entirely different name, one we don't now know."

"Bloody hell, Julian," said Kate. "This is supposed to be a guided tour, not a lesson in languages. There's St. John's

38

Palace. Princess Georgiana—the heir—lives there with a chaperone and her younger brother and sister, Prince William and Princess Jasmina. The Regent—that's their aunt, you remember, the younger sister of the princess' father—lives across the Tens in Blackstone Palace."

"Let me get this straight," said Chryse. "Queen Jasmina the Fourth died childless, leaving her younger brother next in line, but he had already died, leaving his three children, all underage, so Jasmina's youngest sister, Blessa, was appointed Regent until Princess Georgiana turns sixteen. Which will happen in one year. Do I have that right?"

"Very impressive," said Julian appreciately.

"Blessed Lady," swore Kate. "Took me years to figure it out. Of course, some say it shouldn't pass down through the male line, that the crown should have gone to Princess Blessa, as the sworn daughter of Jasmina the Third, but—" She shrugged. "Politics. I'd rather drink."

"Kate," said Julian, "you'd always rather drink."

"You slander me, Julian. I can think of at least two things I'd rather do than drink. Unfortunately, my parents— bless their noble and small-hearted souls, if a soul can have a heart—forbade me from studying to be a physician, and disowned me for indulging too openly in my taste for men. So what was left me but drink?"

"Gambling," offered Julian.

"Easy for you to say, Julian. You have the devil's own luck with cards. I wish you'd pass a bit of it on to me."

"You would have better luck if you didn't play so impulsively."

Kate's expression changed abruptly, and a certain tension sprang into being between her and Julian, charging the carriage air.

Chryse glanced at Sanjay, but he was staring out the window, seemingly oblivious to the conversation. "Why would your parents forbid you from studying medicine?" she asked quickly.

Kate waved a deprecating hand. "Why, our line can be traced back to the Conqueror's. A daughter of an aristocratic house should not be engaged in a trade, a *profession*. No matter how impoverished." Her voice, always a little raw, took on a deep bitterness.

"I'm sorry," said Chryse. "It's terrible to have to give up something you've always wanted to do."

"Oh, I suppose I could have disowned myself and gone ahead and done it anyway, but they scared me off it. It was right at the time that the Earl of Elen became notorious—rumour had it he was raiding cemeteries for bodies and raising the dead and performing horrible rites on sick and injured people. Appalling things. Later I realized it was just to scare me that they told me such tales. And at my tender and innocent age, I was taken in."

Julian coughed.

"Then the tales weren't true?" asked Chryse.

"Who knows. They probably were. Probably still are, from what I hear. But there are good and decent physicians, even surgeons. It shouldn't have stopped me." She lapsed into silence.

"The Earl of Elen." Chryse felt again that it was up to her to change the subject. "He's one of the people you said might be able to help us, if we can't find anything on our own today."

Julian shook his head. "Even if you could interest the Earl in your predicament, which I doubt, I can assure you that you would not want to pay the price he would demand."

"Which would be?"

"I don't know," replied Julian, face somber, "but whatever it would be, you would not want to pay it."

"Is he so awful?"

"Only," said Kate out of her silence, "if you think slaughtering infants in bloody rituals in order to add the power of their innocent souls to his sorcery is awful. Or raising the dead. Or buying an entire brothel for his—ah—pleasures, and then personally dismembering everyone afterwards, while they were still alive, so they could never speak of his—ah—" she coughed, "—unnatural tastes. Although it is also said that one young girl escaped, almost dead from whipping and cuts, and that underneath the fresh scars were uncounted numbers of healed-over scars."

"Surely those stories aren't true." Chryse felt an impulse to laugh at the absurdity of such tales. "Surely there are laws protecting people from—" She halted. Now it was Kate and Julian's turn to look perplexed. Chryse looked out the carriage windows. They had moved out of the more fashionable areas and into a neighborhood whose

dilapidated housefronts and rag-tag of street loiterers
betrayed slow decay and the first descent towards those
slums where the simple struggle for survival might over-
whelm any better and more abstract goals. "No, I don't
suppose there are," she murmured.

"Chryse!" Sanjay's hissed exclamation and his hand gripping her arm startled her. "Look at that carriage!"

Her gaze followed his. Kate and Julian turned as well.
Their carriage had slowed and now stopped, caught in
some flux of traffic, and for a moment they had a full view
of a black carriage drawn by four splendid bay horses that
also sat at a standstill, impeded by a cart piled high with
vegetables being pulled by an emaciated cart horse.

Chryse looked at the carriage, black and blank, windows
shuttered, not even a crest to mark it. The horses, true
beauties, were more interesting. But Sanjay continued to
stare in some combination of awe and horror at the vehicle, so rapt a stare that the two hard-faced, armored men
seated in front both turned suddenly and began to look
towards him.

Julian jerked forward and slammed close the shutters.

"Bloody hell," swore Kate. "Holy Lady damn me to the
pits of the underworld."

"Sanjay—" began Chryse.

"What was it?" he asked, and it was not a rhetorical
question. "It was a—" He examined Chryse as if she could
provide the answer.

She shrugged. The carriage jolted and started forward
again. "It was a carriage and four beautiful horses."

"It was one of the Regent's carriages," snapped Julian,
exchanging a sharp glance with Kate, "if I don't miss my
guess. I've seen those horses before. Let's hope those two
drivers didn't recognize my crest."

"A griffin!" said Sanjay triumphantly. "That's what it
was." There was a brief silence while the other three
merely gazed at him. "On top of the carriage." He hesitated. "That's what the creature sitting on top of the
carriage was." Another pause. "A griffin."

No one replied.

"But you must have—" He faltered. "Chryse, even you
couldn't have failed to notice something that *big*."

"Sanjay," she said quietly. "I didn't see anything on top
of that carriage."

"Lady bless us," muttered Kate.

"Did *you* see it?" Sanjay asked, very tentative now.

"I don't have that kind of sight," said Kate.

Chryse realized, watching Kate and Julian, that, like her, they had seen nothing, but that, unlike her, they both believed and were impressed by Sanjay's vision.

"You don't suppose it was the Regent herself?" Julian leaned forward and pushed the window shutter open slowly, but any sight of the black carriage was lost to a turn in the street.

"I doubt it," said Kate. "It seems to me that if she were going somewhere secretly she'd use neither the bays nor one of her own carriages, and if she were going openly, she'd go in more state."

"Then there must be something valuable in that carriage, or she wouldn't have protected it in *that* way." Julian fingered the buttons on his waistcoat. "I wonder—" he mused. "It could be headed Westside, or across the Tens—"

"Or there's the toll road for the Midlands, past Keep Bridge," said Kate.

"Sanjay," said Chryse, almost accusing. "You really did see something on top of that carriage, didn't you?"

He shook his head. "You never believe me. Let me see the cards a minute."

She handed them to him mutely. As he flipped through them, examining both sides, she regarded Julian and Kate skeptically. "And you believe him," she finished.

"Why shouldn't we believe him?" asked Kate, now regarding Chryse with the disbelief that Chryse felt should be reserved for Sanjay. "Neither of you told us Monsieur Mukerji is a seer."

"A seer!"

Sanjay, still flipping through the cards, grinned at the tone of his wife's voice. "You never appreciate me," he said, not looking up from the images.

"He isn't a seer."

Kate shrugged.

"This one." Sanjay handed a card to Kate, who looked at it together with Julian. Chryse craned forward to look as well.

Julian whistled.

"Whatever is in that carriage must be very valuable,"

added Kate, "if she's protecting it with a summoning of this power."

"It was as big as one of the horses," said Sanjay, speaking now mostly to Chryse. "With gold headfeathers and a gold beak, and golden wings folded in on its back. And it was crouched, like a lion waiting to spring. And brilliant eyes."

"It *saw* you?" asked Julian.

Sanjay blinked. "That's funny," he said. "Of course it saw me. It seemed natural that it would look at me since I was looking at it."

"Weren't you scared?" asked Kate.

"No. Should I have been? We just looked at each other."

Julian whistled again, shaking his head.

"What's the figure on the other side?" asked Chryse, taking the card from an unresisting Kate and examining first the stylized beast on one side, then the person backing it.

"The Emperor," answered Kate automatically. "Seated on his throne. The most powerful of the kings, but also the most conservative."

"But my real question," said Chryse, frowning first at the card and then lifting her eyes to examine her husband, "is why could you see this, and we couldn't? Since I have no reason to believe you're kidding me."

"I'm not, sweetheart. And I have absolutely no idea. It was there."

Three quick raps sounded on the roof of the carriage. All four started. Julian laughed self-consciously.

"Coachman needs your directions, Kate. You'd better get up with him."

Kate got out, and now they watched as the streets around them took on an even poorer cast. The inhabitants stared at the carriage. Children, some of their faces imprinted with features not wholly human, raced along behind and beside it. Kate's voice could be heard now and then, sometimes cursing, sometimes directing. They passed through a square, a dilapidated, moss-encrusted fountain gracing its center, a mass of indeterminate litter strewn across it as though a tearing wind had swept through. Julian leaned forward.

"We must be coming close," he said as the carriage veered sharply down a narrow street.

"There!" said Chryse after a few minutes. "This must be—" The carriage pulled up sharply, throwing her forward. Julian caught her, one hand on her shoulder, one hand on her waist, and after a brief pause, she pulled away from him. " 'Master Bitterbrew's," she finished, reaching out to touch Sanjay's arm. "I remember the name. We came out of the alley somewhere here."

The carriage door opened to reveal Kate. Several children crouched a safe distance away from her, eyeing these unfamiliar visitors.

"Goblinside." Kate swept an elaborate bow. "At your service." As the other three clambered out she tossed a coin to the largest of the waiting children, a hollow-faced girl. "Another if you keep good watch," she said.

They were greeted with passing stares, but no one accosted them. It was the same mix of folk they had seen the night before—but in the daylight the shabbiness of their dress and the gauntness of their faces showed more clearly. A child stood huddled against a lamp post; with a strange feeling of familiarity in a land completely removed from her own, Chryse recognized the skewed cap and pointed face of the child who had stood there last night. Two bright eyes met her own across the narrow expanse of street. A cart blocked her view. When it had paused, the child was gone.

"Madame." Julian offered Chryse his arm. She looked around to see that Sanjay and Kate were already wandering up the street, peering into dark openings.

But they could find no alleyway, no narrow corridor between the close buildings that would lead to an old, rickety door hiding behind it a cathedral that could not possibly be disguised amongst these tenements. They found alleys, certainly, but much too far in either direction from those few landmarks Chryse and Sanjay recalled and Julian and Kate could second.

At last they found themselves back across the street from Master Bitterbrew's and Mistress Penty's and the solitary lamppost.

"There," said Chryse with a sudden decisiveness that caused her companions to look first at her and then to follow her fixed gaze. "There's that child again. I know he was there last night." She stepped out onto the street.

"Chryse—"

The child's brilliant eyes fixed on hers. Chryse slipped around a wagon and pony and came up beside the lamppost. Crouching, her slender skirts caught and curled under her bent legs.

The child stood no higher than she crouched. This close, the unnatural shine of its eyes gave it a feral look, but one compounded by a child's intelligence. It was not a human face, yet neither animal—the mouth and nose came forward snoutlike, but above the tufting of fur that arched over dark eyes rose a high, broad forehead.

"I know where you be looking for." The child regarded Chryse with a street-urchin's calculation. "But I got to have coin 'fore I tell."

Chryse looked up. Sanjay had arrived, both concerned and wondering. Behind him stood Julian.

"Do you have a penny?" Chryse asked Julian. His eyebrows rose, surprise.

"Tuppence," squeaked the child.

Julian chuckled, fished in a pocket, and brought out a silver coin.

The child's mouth—or was it snout—wrinkled up in an almost doglike fashion. "Lady!" it swore. A tiny hand, four-fingered with the suggestion of claws, grabbed the coin out of Chryse's hand. "You be looking for St. Crist'hell But she's gone now. You can't get back in there."

"Where has she gone?" asked Chryse.

The child shrugged. Its eyes left off scrutinizing Chryse's yellow hair for a moment to squint at the silver in its hand. It hissed something inaudible, looked up again. "You only come out o' St. Cee's," it said. Chryse wondered abruptly whether it was a boy or a girl, or as indeterminate as it seemed. "You can't go back in, not by that gate." The bright gaze shifted from Chryse to her companions, quick and measuring. With the speed given hunted animals, the child darted suddenly away and before Chryse could do more than call out in surprise and rise, it had vanished in the constant flow of traffic.

Two women brushed by them. Chryse felt Sanjay's hand on her back, a warm, comforting presence. She turned.

"Did you hear what the child said?" she asked.

He nodded. His face was grave. Behind, Julian and Kate reappeared from the direction in which the child had run. They were alone.

Sanjay's face was still, hiding his feelings, but Chryse's eyes held the brilliance that presaged tears. She sniffed and made a disparaging face.

"Look at me—this won't get us anywhere," she said. "I guess we're left with Madame Sosostris."

"We should have gone back that night," said Sanjay in a fierce undertone.

"How could we have?" she replied. "We did look for it. We can't blame ourselves."

For a moment he said nothing. "At least we have two weeks," he said at last, quiet. "Come on." He took her hand and looked at Julian and Kate. "Shall we go back?"

No one spoke much on the return trip, although Kate pointed out a few more sights.

Aunt Laetitia greeted them at the entryway to Vole House and directed them into the parlour. Tea and warm cakes awaited them on the sidetable.

"I see," said Aunt Laetitia once a decent interval had passed for them to warm themselves and drink and eat, "that your expedition met with little success. I have better news."

Chryse and Sanjay both looked up.

"Usually Madame Sosostris only grants appointments months in advance," continued Aunt Laetitia, looking pleased by the hopeful and attentive expressions on her guests' faces. "But in this case, she writes that seeing the importance of a visit connected with such a rare deck, and given the delicate and urgent nature of the request, she has agreed to see you in only five weeks." She smiled, benignly aware of their great good fortune.

"Five weeks!" cried Chryse. "We can't possibly wait that long." She turned to Sanjay, grasped his hands. "They'll think we're dead."

"Surely if we went to this woman's house she would agree to see us right away," said Sanjay.

Aunt Laetitia frowned. "It would not do to offend her. Indeed not. No, you have been given every consideration. You must not ask too much or she won't see you at all."

"But then—" Chryse began. "You mentioned some others." She met Kate's sympathetic but unhopeful eye, and gave a little laugh. "No, I don't suppose the earl would be a good choice."

"And frankly," added Kate, "you can't possibly get an

audience to see the Regent. She isn't very—ah—open to petitions. It would be easier, in a manner of speaking, to see the heir, but she can't help you."

"Wasn't there another one? Anyone else?" Chryse asked, feeling now as if she were grasping at straws.

"Chryse," said Sanjay softly. "Maybe we're just stuck."

"I know," she said, lowering her voice to match his, "but we've got to make sure we've tried every avenue. Otherwise we'll keep feeling as if we might have done more."

"There are other mages, to be sure," said Aunt Laetitia. "But none others of sufficient power who live in or near Heffield."

"If you meant Master Cardspinner," said Kate, "I'm afraid that that was a bit of a joke. And in any case, he's left town, as I found out last night."

For a long moment Chryse and Sanjay simply gazed at each other. The others turned their attention elsewhere. Finally Sanjay shrugged and Chryse gave him a rueful smile and released his hands.

"It seems Madame Sosostris is the only choice left," said Sanjay.

"But we haven't any money," Chryse said to him. "Or suitable clothing. Or a place to stay. How can we wait five weeks?"

There was a moment of silence. Aunt Laetitia regarded first Kate and then Julian. "Yours are reasonable concerns, Madame Lissagaray," she replied finally. "But it appears to me that the matter of clothing has already been settled. And as chatelaine of my *bachelor* nephew's establishment, I see no reason why you cannot continue to stay with us. It must be obvious to you both that we have ample room and staff and little enough occupation."

"But we couldn't impose—" began Sanjay.

"Why not?" said Kate. "I do." She laughed at his stricken expression. "Don't worry about insulting me," she continued. "My parents disinherited me years ago in favor of my cousin Miranda. I've lived on my wits and charm and my aptitude for gambling ever since. But mostly on Julian's charity."

"Yes, and a damned nuisance you are, too," said Julian, helping himself to a biscuit from the tea tray. "And have been since I've known you."

"Which since we were born only five days and two miles apart has been a bloody long time."

"And in any case," added Julian, looking now at Sanjay, "I think I may have a solution, if it is acceptable to you. My acquaintance Professor Farr needs a secretary, as I mentioned before. He could employ you, and you could continue to stay at Vole House."

"Of course," said Aunt Laetitia. "That will serve very well."

"But what am I to do?" asked Chryse. "I suppose I could take in sewing."

"Certainly not. No gentlewoman would stoop to such an occupation."

Chryse shrugged. "There must be a school of music in this city. I can teach piano, voice, and recorder, and perform."

Aunt Laetitia raised one finger. "A gentlewoman may perform for the pleasure of others, but never for money. She may, however, teach—there is no shame in instruction. And there is a pleasant and neglected music room here. You will of course teach privately. I will tell my wide acquaintance that you are a noted musician from Vesputia who is willing in her short stay here to accept a few select students. That should be enough to send them thundering to your door. But both of you must realize—" Here she examined them with a stern glance. "—that although you will be treated as family in this house, the fact that you are employed for pay means you will not be able to go out in society."

Chryse laughed. "We're overwhelmed already. I can't imagine we'll *want* to venture into society."

Sanjay shook his head, looking somber. "How can we possibly thank you? Under our circumstances, your generosity is—" He broke off, unable to find words.

"If they can't throw me out," said Kate, "they certainly can't throw you out."

"Don't fool yourself into thinking that it is generosity," scolded Aunt Laetitia. "It is pure selfishness. I find Julian's youngest siblings tiresome and callow. His sisters Lucy and Emily, with whom I remain in charity, are married and live elsewhere. It is obvious to me that you will enliven this house. Therefore, you will stay."

Julian smiled, waving one hand negligently. "And obedient nephew that I am, I would never dare oppose my aunt's wishes."

"Great-aunt, Julian. I'll have you give my age the respect it is due."

CHAPTER 5:

THE HUNTER

"Charity," said Maretha Farr from her desk, where she carefully rewrote her father's scrawled notes into a readable and coherent form, "when you're done fixing your hair, could you walk with me down to the booksellers? There's a package come in I need to pick up for Papa."

"Of course, Maretha." The young woman who turned from the dressing table bore a striking resemblence to the soft-eyed Queen of Heaven who sat holding her ruddy-cheeked baby Son in the painting above the fireplace. "But I hope you mean to change and do something to your hair before we go out. It is possible for you to look quite presentable, Maretha, even though we don't have a maid. If only you'd try."

"Is it?" asked Maretha, not looking up from a list of the evidence compiled by her father, written here in his crabbed handwriting, supporting his theory of the existence of Pariam, the city of the labyrinth.

"You know I will help you whenever you wish. You and Uncle Raymond have been so good—"

A light chime sounded from the corner of the room. Maretha sighed and set down her pen.

"Shall I go down?" asked Charity quickly, setting down a ribbon she had been about to braid into her hair.

"No," said Maretha. "You should finish dressing. It can't be Papa ringing, since he's in the study with the new secretary, so it must be Molly to say there's a visitor. I'd have to see them in any case." She examined her inkstained fingers with some dismay, cast a brief glance at herself in the mirror, sighed again, and left the room.

As she walked down the narrow stairs, she considered Charity. She was fond of her, as sweet and good-natured an impoverished cousin in an already impoverished house as anyone could wish. But Maretha, who had never been brought up to think about her looks, had in the last three years gained a vivid impression from Charity: that though, with a little more effort, she, Maretha, might be pretty, could in fact be desirable and attractive, underneath was that constant, unspoken assumption that beauty like Charity's could never be hers.

And why should it? she thought in anger. You never thought twice about it before she came, because you were too busy with your father's scholarship and with maintaining a house on no income. And now—

But Molly stood at the bottom of the stairs. The housekeeper's face was ashen with fright.

"Why, Molly," Maretha began. "Whatever—"

"Hush, mistress," hissed the woman. "I didn't know what to do, so I put him in the library. And I daren't go bother Professor Farr. He's that put out if I disturb him with the new secretary, seeing as they're setting all in order finally. But I daren't turn *him* away."

"Never mind, Molly." Maretha walked past the woman to the library door. "I'll see the visitor."

Molly's face flushed red and she reached forward like a drowning person grasping for line. "No, miss. You mustn't—"

But Maretha had opened the door. With a warning glance for Molly, she stepped inside.

And halted, struck motionless from surprise and sheer, instantaneous horror.

Of course she knew who he was, though she had never met him, had only had him pointed out to her once from a great distance. Impossible to forget.

"You are Miss Farr," he said.

He was beautiful, of course. Any human with so much sorcerous power, gained by foul means or fair, must surely choose to be handsome. But behind that beauty—a chill. Deep and unfeelingly cold. She felt it immediately, even as she stared at him: hair so rich a yellow that it seemed unnatural, especially set against skin almost as pale and fine as Charity's—though this paleness suggested that cast of skin touched by night and moon's glow more than by sun. He looked younger than his reputation. Surely a man so innured to unspeakable diversions should look as dissipated as those rakes who merely drank themselves to death, or at least be not as slender and well-formed as the perfect fit of his conservatively dark coat and trousers showed him to be.

But it was impossible to be taken in by his fairness. "My lord," she said at last, knowing she was staring and that he was scornful of her inability not to stare. She met his eyes now, steeling herself, knowing what she would see: eyes so dark as to be black. Enchanter's eyes—all color lost, drained away.

He took off his gloves, a careful, deliberate process that revealed white hands. She waited, sure he did it to test her; it took her full complement of courage to stand quietly until he finished. He examined her, his expression unreadable, and at last placed his gloves at a precise angle on the high booktable.

"Well, Miss Farr," he said, his voice as cold as his face, "are you finding it difficult to believe that I murder infants and violate girls and boys whom I buy off the streets from their destitute parents?"

"No," she said.

His smile was as chilling as his eyes. Now she saw clearly that he was amused, but for a reason she could not possibly fathom. "Very good," he said softly. "I see I came to the right place."

"My lord," she said, more deliberate now, or perhaps made rash by a combination of plain fear and, worse, admiration for his beauty. "I cannot imagine you came here simply to mock me. Whatever business you might conceivably have with my father or myself could not possibly interest us."

"It will." His conviction silenced her. "In any case, has it not occurred to you that by angering me you might be endangering yourself?"

"No." It had indeed not occurred to her. "Even you could not harm or enchant a respectable young woman of good birth with impunity."

"It is true," he said, "that it is more difficult to meddle with those whose birth and wealth in some measure protect them. That does not mean it is impossible. Now I suggest you call your father, since my business is primarily with him."

For a moment she wanted to refuse, but she knew it would be both futile and foolish. "My lord," she said stiffly, acquiescing; but the door opened before she could move, and her father and the new secretary entered.

"Maretha." Professor Farr's voice was slightly peevish, a tone Maretha recognized—he hated to be interrupted. "Molly says there is a visitor—" He paused, blinking in his absentminded way at their guest.

"My lord," she said, surprised at the calm in her voice. "May I present my father, Professor Farr. And Monsieur Mukerji. His lordship the Earl of Elen."

Professor Farr bowed, but it was obvious that he was not quite sure who this personage was and why he should recognize him. "My lord," he said.

Mr. Mukerji bowed as well, but said nothing. His eyes met Maretha's briefly, a questioning look, and she saw from his expression that although he recognized the name and reputation, he, too, was at a loss to explain the earl's presence.

The earl inclined his head to acknowledge the two men, but his gaze lingered longer on Mr. Mukerji: whether because of his foreign looks or because of some other quality he saw with whatever sorcerous sight he possessed, Maretha could not tell.

"Please sit down," said Professor Farr.

The earl glanced at Maretha, eyebrows lifted, and as soon as she sat, seated himself. There was a moment of silence.

"I see you own a Gobella," said the earl finally, nodding towards the wall next to the window, which bore, not bookshelves, but a magnificent old tapestry.

"Yes, yes," said the professor, "a fine original. I identified it immediately when I saw it. You see that it gives the ten scenes of the Life of Saint Maretha, but it can be dated to the troubador period by the rendering of scene four—of course historically she rejected the Prince of Fronsai's offer of marriage, but due to the romanticism of the period she is seen here accepting it. He then dies, in some versions while defending her brother when he was martyred, as is depicted here in scene five, but as is appropriate leaving Saint Maretha free to dedicate herself to the

Knights Guardian in the service of the Queen of Heaven—
scene six of course is always constant in all depictions."

"Ah," said the earl. His eye lit for an uncomfortable
moment on Maretha. "And perhaps you named your daughter after the esteemed saint?"

Professor Farr appeared, for a moment, flustered.

"I believe," put in Maretha quickly, "that it was my
mother's choice of name."

"I see," said the earl. "Professor Farr. I have read a
number of your monographs. I am here today because of
my interest in your work on the Pariam, or as you call it,
the Pariamne civilization."

"Indeed!" The professor flushed slightly. "Indeed, my
lord, I must inform you that amongst my colleagues my
work on Pariamne is dismissed as erroneous, ridiculous,
and completely unfounded in fact."

"And by some as fraud," said the earl. He lifted a hand
to forestall Maretha's comment. "But I must assure you
that I am not one of your detractors. Quite the contrary. I
have conducted researches in my own branch of—ah—
expertise, and it is quite clear to me that Pariamne not
only existed but flourished on this island some millennia
ago."

Maretha recognized instantly her father's change of expression. Whatever confusion he might have felt concerning the earl before vanished now. He had found a partisan.
She managed to stop herself from frowning.

"Of course," cried the professor. "The evidence is overwhelming. The two settlements, which I can by no means
yet classify as cities, that I have had opportunity to study in
the Midlands were obviously not of Latanic origin, although that of course is one of the main points disputed by
my colleagues. But there are a number of structural and
architectural differences, and beyond them the indisput-
able evidence of the fragments of writing and the frescos."

"But isn't that exactly the evidence that is most disputed?" said the earl.

"Only because they do not understand its importance!
The frescos are the key. They are the depiction of the
great rituals that fueled the civilization. You have read of
course my monograph regarding the fragments from the
throne room of the site near Eppot-Staw, which I have
tentatively restored and interpreted."

"Indeed," said the earl, a cold flatness in his voice that caught Maretha's attention, "that particular paper has been of great assistance in my own investigations."

"Then you know that I propose that at the heart of the primary ritual event of the Pariamne year was a sacrifice—"

"Of course," said the earl evenly. The chill in his voice made Maretha shiver, as if the window were not sealed against drafts. "At the center of every ritual is a sacrifice."

"But the frescos at Eppot-Staw and at Mantion are too fragmentary to prove my theories. I have been working to decipher the writing, but as you know if you have read my monograph on the use of symbols, that although one sees a certain correlation between the Gates and various of the writing and symbolic gestures at the sites, I do not have the key to link them definitively. I must have more writing."

"Where will you find it?"

"This past year I have studied exclusively the problem of the site of Pariamne itself—a word incidentally which I believe derives from the root Topo Rhuam—a root I interpret as holding several symbolic meanings: including a reference to the Consort of the Queen of Pariamne, but primarily which I translate as 'the labyrinth of the Queen's sacrifice.' "

"Yes," said the earl. "I have read your latest monograph. You even claim in it to have deduced through your research the location of Topo Rhuam itself. And if you could find and catalog Topo Rhuam, all your theories would be proven."

"Yes!" exclaimed the professor. "All those legends of the ancient treasure of the labyrinth have been dismissed as nonsense by those who only read the fables of the princess Sais and the fall of the city. Even the church simply equates the Queen of the Underworld with the Daughter of the Queen of Heaven, with the Mistress of Sin. But they do not recognize the historical perspective, the actual existence of the Queen of the Underworld as a pre-catholic deity in her own right, existing as the primary deity, with her consort, the Hunter, of the Pariamne civilization, which by all our moral lights today would seem a very violent and brutal one—something which the frescos bear out, incidentally. And there is every reason to believe that the tales of the princess Sais and her sealing of the labyrinth gate before the destruction of the city and her death

represent some lingering remnants of actual events of
those days. Of course, the common understanding of 'treasure' is usually in our devalued times merely one of gold
or some moveable wealth—scientifically speaking, the key
to both the writing and to the true and perhaps complete
and earliest version of the great ritual frescos would be at
Topo Rhuam—"

"Father," began Maretha.

The earl lifted one hand, and Maretha was silent. "Why,"
he asked, "if you believe that you know the location of
Topo Rhuam, why don't you travel there, hire laborers,
and uncover both it and its treasures?" He was very still,
waiting.

"Father," began Maretha again. "Surely it is inappro-
priate—"

"My dear," the professor said, interrupting her with one
of his rare decisive looks, "we are clearly in the company
of friends here, and Monsieur Mukerji is already aware of
the state of our finances."

"Ah," said the earl. Had he been a more expressive
man, Maretha thought, he would have leaned forward
now, revealing both eagerness and satisfaction. "You cannot afford such an expedition."

"I fear that I have to support a daughter and a niece,
although neither of them are accustomed to luxury, and
indeed help greatly in the economic running of the house-
hold. But my previous expeditions have been—" The professor halted suddenly. "Maretha, my dear," he said, a
trifle more gently, "it is an open secret that we are
destitute—that we can ill-afford this house and Molly to
keep it and a secretary for myself, and that you and
Charity must do all the rest. Are you ashamed of that?
There is no sin in being poor in one's search for the truth,
only in being rich in falsehood."

Maretha said nothing.

"In fact," said the earl, "you have spent your entire
inheritance, and your daughter's inheritance from her
mother, on your work, and since your recent theories have
met with disdain and ridicule from the members of both
the Royal Geological and the Royal Historical Societies,
you have been unable to obtain any funding at all."

Maretha stared at her hands, brown from working in the
garden. She had not the discipline of Charity, who bathed

hers every night in milk and linden oil to keep them white and who also steadfastly refused to work outdoors at all, for the sake of her complexion.

"That is true," said Professor Farr.

"Very well," said the earl. "I am offering you that funding. For an expedition to Topo Rhuam."

For a long moment Maretha was convinced she had not heard him correctly. Then she looked up, and saw the dawning joy on her father's face.

"My lord!" he exclaimed. "If your interest extends so far—" He stopped, too overwhelmed to continue.

"There must be a price." Maretha turned to look at the earl.

"Don't you believe that I might simply be a generous benefactor?" he said, mocking her. "Of course there is a price. I must go with the expedition. I will not interfere with your work, Professor Farr, but neither will you interfere with my investigations."

"Of course," said the Professor. "Of course. That is eminently reasonable, my lord. And a full share in the credit for the discoveries we make will be yours as well, as you know."

"That's all?" asked Maretha flatly.

"Why, no, Miss Farr. That isn't all." He examined her again, that chill amusement back in his eyes and in his demeanor. "There is one other stipulation." Now he stood. "Professor Farr. I wish to marry your daughter. When the appropriate papers sealing the engagement and the date of the wedding, to take place before we leave Heffield, are signed, I will settle on you the funds necessary to mount your expedition."

Maretha was too stunned to do anything but look at her father. But meeting his gaze, she saw not outrage or any intent to deny, but instead appeal. "Mother in Heaven," she breathed, soundless but to herself.

"My daughter is of age, my lord," said the professor slowly. "She must say yes or no to your proposal of her own will." He looked at her.

"Father!"

"Perhaps," said Monsieur Mukerji quickly, "you would like to talk it over with Miss Farr in your study, Professor. I will gladly remain here with his lordship."

Maretha cast him a grateful glance as she left the room,

forcing her father to follow her out. She turned on the professor as soon as they reached the privacy of his study.

"You can't expect me to marry him, Father!"

"But Maretha." His expression was one of gentle confusion. "Any father would wish such an eligible connection for his only daughter. A title. Wealth. And he is well educated as well, will enter into your interests."

"Holy Lady. Perhaps I can enter into his as well, and we can slaughter infants together. He is a sorcerer, Father. You *know* his reputation."

"Need I remind you of *my* reputation, my dear? Shall we listen to the common run of gossip, which has not even the sense to accept my many years of research? I hope we are above such talk, and can approach life from a rational and orderly perspective."

"But, Father—"

He turned, pointedly, to gaze with that vague fondness he occasionally displayed at the portrait of his young wife that hung over his desk. The action alone silenced her. "Your mother would have wanted you to have this opportunity. She would know how important it is to my work, Maretha. Have you not the same care for me? I know you will do what is right, my dear."

She could only stare at her father's profile, absentminded but obstinant. For the first time she recognized truly how selfish her father's single-minded obsession with Pariamne had made him since her mother's death; recognized that her unqualified love and support had only fueled his self-absorption. Finally she turned away from the damning portrait and without a word returned to the library. Her father did not follow her. Monsieur Mukerji, with a quick, comprehensive glance at her face, left the room.

Maretha sat down in a chair, unable to support this illumination of her father's character. Instead, she stared at the wall opposite, the tapestry of Saint Maretha—at the final scene, her martyrdom at the hands of the worshippers of the Daughter of Darkness, eldest child of the Queen of Heaven—and shuddered. So selfish had he become that he was willing without a second thought to sacrifice his only surviving child.

The earl remained silent.

"Surely," said Maretha at last in a low voice, still not

looking at the earl, "surely with your wealth and your title you could easily marry a young woman whose fortune and background are far better than mine."

"Surely?" he mocked. "When you yourself acknowledge the—ah—potency of my reputation. Be assured that I have tested the waters, that I would prefer a gentlewoman whose noble lineage matched my own, rather than a gentlewoman whose birth is merely respectable. But for some reason, the parents of these eligible young females seem to believe that any wife I take will come to a very painful and tragic end. My wealth and title are of no good to her, or to her parents, if she is dead, are they?"

She lifted her head to glare at him, a better response than admitting her fear. "Then surely you can buy some girl off the streets, if that is all you have in mind for your wife."

"But isn't that what I've done?" he asked. "It is self-evident that the Countess of Elen must be a woman of good birth."

"And my father is destitute enough, and desperate enough, to agree to it."

"Exactly. And you are too dutiful a daughter to refuse. I am very thorough in my research."

Since there was nothing to say, she did not reply.

Into their silence, the door opened. Charity walked in, halted, looking prettily confused. "I beg your pardon," she said in her light voice. "I had no idea you were still in here, Maretha." Her eyes remained fixed on the earl.

"My lord," said Maretha. "May I present my cousin, Miss Charity Farr. Charity, may I present the Earl of Elen."

Charity curtsied with elegance. The earl inclined his head slightly.

"I won't interrupt another moment, my lord," said Charity, and swept out.

"There," said Maretha, succumbing to bitterness. "She is a dutiful niece, of equally respectable birth, destitute, a beauty in the bargain, and preserving herself in that state, as you can see, for the best marriage she can possibly make. She would be *eager* to marry you."

"Tempting," he said, "but Miss Charity Farr lacks a vital qualification which, despite your lack of—ah—eagerness, you possess."

"I can't imagine what it might be."

"Then I won't enlighten you. Well, Miss Farr, what is your answer?"

She had to look away, at first. Despair and anger mingled equally within her. She forced herself to face him, finally, because she would have despised herself if she did not. "You must know," she said, her voice tight, "what my answer has to be. You judged the price correctly. But never believe that under any other circumstances I would ever choose to marry you."

He smiled. "I have always found it expedient to determine my circumstances, Miss Farr, rather than to endure them. But in any case, I grant you fully the right to hate me. After all, it will only enhance my reputation. My secretary will arrive tomorrow morning with the preliminary agreements." He picked up his gloves.

"But why?" she asked, spurred on by his movement to leave. "Why do you want to marry?"

"Society will say," he paused, pulling on his gloves, "that I need an heir. That is the usual reason given. Now I bid you good-day, Miss Farr."

She scarcely noted him leaving the room. An heir. It was, indeed, the obvious reason for his sudden decision to marry.

At this moment, the thought of what she would have to do, with him, to produce a child, was so horrifying that she succumbed to an urge she had not felt since the age of ten, the day her mother and two younger siblings had died and left her bereft, with an absent father.

She flung herself over the pillows of the sofa, and wept.

CHAPTER 6:

THE MAGE

"No," said Sanjay. "I don't think you would like to meet him. But I also don't think he's necessarily—what is the phrase—as black as he's painted." He shook his head. "Don't ask me to explain that."

"So, Julian," said Aunt Laetitia. "The wicked earl, whom Monsieur grants to be wicked, but not perhaps as wicked as he ought to be, has stolen your bride from beneath your nose. You shall have to settle for the beautiful but impoverished niece."

"Please do," said Kate.

"*Please* don't abet her," said Julian to Kate. "Although I will admit I am as astonished as any of you. When did you say it happened?"

"The final papers were signed today. And the wedding itself set for six weeks from Sonsday. Oh, and—where is Chryse? Still at lessons?"

"Her last pupil today is the Countess of Gosson's youngest."

"My, Lady Trent," said Kate. "You do move in exalted circles."

"Of course."

"I'll see if she's finished yet." Julian rose. "The rest of you can finish your tea." He left the room before anyone could respond.

"It is a peculiar business," said Aunt Laetitia. "Very peculiar." She took another slice of cake from the tray. "Tell me again where this expedition is going."

"That is the one piece of information Professor Farr has not told anyone, except perhaps his daughter," said Sanjay.

"But I've looked over his maps and his notes, and I can make a guess."

Kate grinned. "But the question is, will you?"

"No," Sanjay replied. "I feel it is only right to show a certain measure of loyalty to my employer. However, be assured that you will be the first to know once the professor allows the location to become public knowledge."

"Will he?" asked Lady Trent. "Despite Julian's claim that the professor's work is considered nonsense by his esteemed colleagues, I frankly imagine that an announcement of an expedition to the lost city of Pariam would create quite a stir, and perhaps interfere with the professor's plans."

"Oh, I don't know," said Sanjay. "I suspect it isn't the professor we need fear disturbing. I suspect it is the earl."

Upstairs, Chryse turned her head as the door into the music room opened quietly and nodded to Julian as he came inside, but did not stop playing until she came to the end of the piece.

"Is your pupil gone already?" he asked.

"This hour or more," she said. "I was playing for myself, really."

"I hadn't realized you knew Bach." He walked forward to look down at the manuscript paper on the fortepiano.

Chryse was caught speechless for a moment. "Why, yes," she said finally, standing up and moving to one side. "I transcribed that particular set of pieces from memory. They're good for the younger students."

"May I?" When she nodded, curious, he seated himself, flipping the tails of his coat out over the back of the bench with a practiced gesture, and played a few bars. "Of course not everyone has heard of her," he said. "This is the Notebook she wrote for her husband, isn't it? She is growing in stature now, of course, and being recognized for the fine composer she was. She was never appreciated in her own time."

"No, no," said Chryse. "I suppose—ah—she's been neglected, until—ah—Mendelssohn—" She hesitated.

"Yes, Fanny Mendelstochter." He stopped playing and turned to look up at her. "Imagine finding the manuscript of the Saint Miriam's Passion used as butcher's wrapping paper."

Chryse laughed suddenly. "It strikes me, Lord Vole," she said, "that you are particularly interested in finding things—Professor Farr's studies in old cities, the origin of the name of Bishop's River, and now, old manuscripts."

"Please, Madame Lissagaray," he said, standing now to lend his words a more formal bearing. "After more than a month at Vole House, I would hope we could descend to a less formal mode of addressing one another. I notice you and Kate have long since dispensed with such formalities."

"With Kate it's rather difficult not to." Chryse smiled.

He smiled back at her. "Then perhaps you will call me Julian. And you are right. Having been at a loss for any other occupation since I came of age and inherited my position in society, I have occupied myself with looking for things that are lost. That is why I agreed to accompany Kate on that ill-fated expedition to Goblinside where we found ourselves *not* at Master Cardspinner's, whoever he may be, but in the middle of a riot for emancipation."

"But you did find something that was lost, did you not, Julian?"

He smiled again, and gave her a little bow before he opened the door and offered her his arm to escort her downstairs. "That I did, Madame Lissagaray."

"Chryse," she said.

"It is a beautiful and unusual name," he said. "The lament of the ocean."

"The lament of—?" She laughed. "I see. Cry-sea. I hadn't thought of it like that. It's actually an old family name, although I'm not certain how it got into the family since it's a different nationality entirely. Some scholarly connection, I think."

"Yes," said Julian smoothly. "Both your parents are associated with a university, are they not? Professors, I believe."

"Not quite." Chryse felt inexplicably that he was testing her in some way. Sanjay had always been more easygoing than she, not extroverted exactly, but certainly more convivial; she usually felt more restraint with people she did not know intimately. "They are both university educated, like me, but only my mother teaches at that level. My father teaches younger students."

"Like you?"

She shrugged. "I've done some teaching before, but it

isn't my profession. I'm not sure I really have one." She considered. "You look for things that are lost. I just seem to be looking, but I'm not sure what for, except that it has to do with music." She coughed suddenly, and looked a little embarrassed at her loquaciousness. To cover her embarrassment, she went on. "Your title is rather unusual. The name, that is."

He smiled. "It is an old name. Originally Voler, from across the Channel, of course, but it was shortened in time as such names usually were. The Haldane branch of the family picked up the title after the unfortunate demise of a third, a second, and a first cousin in the great Heffield fire of Queen Caroline the Second's reign. But the title has passed down unbroken since the Conquest."

She laughed. "No wonder there are so many portraits in the family gallery."

Julian stopped, and because she held his arm, and because it would also have been rude to go on, she halted as well. On the stairwell, curving down below them, they seemed to stand close together; she realized how close in height he was to Sanjay, although for some reason he had always seemed slighter to her. "If I may be so presumptuous as to offer a personal observation," he said, looking down at her with a curious and unreadable expression, "it has been obvious to me for some weeks now that you and Sanjay come from a quite different society than my own."

"What is it that makes it so obvious?"

He reflected that when she was curious she was at her most attractive. "For one thing, your complete lack of deference."

Chryse's interest turned to puzzlement. "Lack of deference? For what?"

He smiled abruptly, a smile both charming and, at base, satisfied. "I'm not sure I can explain it." He continued, with her, down the stairs.

"Then I won't ask you to," she said as they reached the bottom of the stairs and he ushered her into the drawing room.

Sanjay rose immediately to take her hand and kiss her on the cheek. When she sat, Aunt Laetitia offered her tea.

"I have had an interesting day," Sanjay declared as soon as Chryse had taken a mouthful of cake and a sip of tea. "Not only have all the arrangements been completed for the marriage of the earl and Maretha Farr, but in addition I had a private conversation with the professor concerning his daughter and you, Chryse." Here he paused for the announcement to have its intended effect upon his audience.

Chryse coughed behind her hand. "Are you sure this is a topic suitable for mixed company?"

He smiled. "It seems the professor is concerned that since his daughter is about to enter a new state in life, she enter it not completely unprepared. Since he knows that I am married, he asked if my wife would, as he put it, instruct his daughter into the—ah—intimate duties of married life that will be expected of her."

Kate choked back a laugh.

"Very commendable, I'm sure," said Aunt Laetitia.

"Poor girl," said Chryse. "But Lady Trent, perhaps with the respect due your wisdom, you would be more qualified than I."

Now Julian smothered a laugh. "Please, Aunt. I've heard stories of the various forms of induction into intimate duties that were fashionable when you were a girl. If any of them are half true, I'm not sure that you would be at all a suitable choice."

"Is this how you show respect for your elders, Julian?" asked his aunt. "I find Madame Lissagaray to be infinitely better schooled, and you to be as tediously strait-laced as your mother and father. My only consolation in being old is that I was not born into this generation of tiresome conventionality and prudishness."

Chryse smiled. "I'm afraid you've aroused my curiosity now."

"My dear," said Aunt Laetitia. "This is a conversation definitely not suitable for mixed company, especially in such puritan times as these, but someday when we are alone, you might find that I am not immune to the temptation to reminisce."

"Kate," Julian warned.

"Don't accuse me," retorted Kate. "Even I find Lady Trent's reminiscinses scandalous."

"Indeed. But I notice how well you attend to them."

Kate sketched her the thread of a bow. "I must get the inspiration for my rakish and dissipated ways somewhere."

"Well," finished Aunt Laetitia, "you shall invite the Misses Farr to tea, Monsieur Mukerji. Once a suitable period of acquaintance has been accomplished, then Madame can arrange a more personal encounter with Miss Farr. I find that the custom these days of leaving young persons in ignorance of natural desires only leads to terribly confused and dissatisfied marriages. Would you not agree with me, Madame Lissagaray?"

"Oh, entirely," replied Chryse, managing not to smile as she looked at her husband.

"Then we must set a date for inviting them to call," said Aunt Laetitia. "Next week, perhaps?"

"A week from today?" Chryse suggested. She reached out to brush Sanjay's hand briefly. "A week from tomorrow we see Madame Sosostris."

"Ah." Aunt Laetitia looked away. "I had forgotten."

Chryse thought she saw regret cross the elderly lady's features, but it was only a momentary expression.

"So had I," said Julian.

Kate said nothing, merely took another sip of tea and crossed her legs in a gesture made masculine by the cut of her gentleman's attire.

Kate, indeed, was the only one to attend Chryse and Sanjay as they settled into Lord Vole's town carriage for the appointment with Madame Sosostris the next week. Aunt Laetitia pleaded an uncharacteristic headache, and Julian had disappeared to his club.

"Well," said Kate, "I enjoyed the Misses Farrs excessively."

Chryse smiled. Excitement and a certain strange sense of reluctance filled her in equal parts as they rattled along the cobbled streets. "Only because you enjoyed shocking Charity Farr by your dress and speech. I thought Maretha was charming, and very interesting. How could her father let her marry such a monster? It's obvious she's hiding behind indifference, but whether it's because she loathes the earl or fears him, I can't decide."

"I expect," said Sanjay slowly, "that Charity Farr would have taken the earl. But that's just a guess. Maretha is much the better educated—which undoubtedly is what makes her more interesting."

Kate grinned. "Then you aren't a man to be taken in by a pretty face?"

"Certainly not," said Sanjay.

"I beg your pardon!" Chryse hit him in the stomach.

"I meant—" Sanjay gasped, not entirely feigned. "—not by a pretty face alone."

The carriage slowed to a halt in front of a well-kept townhouse in one of the well-to-do but definitely not aristocratic districts. "Here we are," announced Kate. "Fenwych House."

There was a hesitation as Sanjay and Chryse simply sat, staring out the carriage window at the clean classical front of the house.

"I'll wait here," said Kate abruptly. "Abbott will need someone to help him walk the horses."

Chryse leaned forward suddenly and grasped Kate's hand. "Whatever happens, Kate—thank you."

Sanjay bowed his head a moment. "We can't really thank you enough." He lifted his gaze to look at her. "Without your help, and the others, I don't know what we would have done."

Kate flushed. "You'd better go. You don't want to be late."

Chryse smiled and released her hand and let Sanjay help her down out of the carriage. Together they went up the walk to the entryway.

The door, plain and white, without knocker or other adornment, opened just as they reached it. A woman of indeterminate years, dressed in somber grey, ushered them inside.

"You will be Madame Lissagaray and Monsieur Mukerji," she said in a voice unaccustomed to disagreement. "Come this way."

The entry hall was spacious, but empty. A filagreed staircase led up to the next floor. The woman led them past it, to the first door on the left. Here a young man dressed in equally somber attire stood still as if molded in stone. At their approach he shifted, and opened the door deftly and with a minimum of movement. The woman halted, nodding that they were to enter. On the stairs behind, a flicker of movement betrayed a grey-garbed girl going about some task in efficient silence.

Entering, they found themselves in much brighter surroundings. A broad window overlooking the street, shaded by a thin curtain, let in light from the outside.

But the immediate sensation was of flowers turning to

the sun: as Chryse and Sanjay halted, seven heads turned to peruse them.

Chryse's first thought was: This is worse than the doctor's office. But as the eldest of the seven rose, she realized that it was nothing of the sort.

The eldest was a young woman scarcely younger than Chryse herself—she laid down a skein of knitting on a neat sidetable and came forward. Her face bore a certain vague familiarity, as if Chryse had seen her once in a crowd and then forgotten. Behind her, six females ranging in age down to girlhood set aside their tasks—here a book, there embroidery, farther back a careful sheet of calligraphy—and examined the couple with alert and interested faces. All bore that stamp of familiarity, unplaceable and mysterious. They wore neat, conservative gowns in pleasant but not overwhelming colors.

"How do you do?" The eldest extended a hand to shake with both husband and wife. "Mama is indeed expecting you, but I fear it will be a few minutes. I am Ella. Would you like tea?"

"Thank you," Chryse managed.

"Chasta," said Ella, waving them towards seats. "Please pour for our visitors."

A younger woman, with an adolescent face but a woman's confident gaze, rose and poured two cups of tea into plain but finely-made porcelain. Two girls, scarcely younger, identical in face but mercifully not in clothing, each took a cup and saucer and brought them forward to Chryse and Sanjay. They presented the tea with neat curtsies.

"Very good, dears," said Ella with an amused smile. "Madame, Monsieur, let me present the family, although I fear you will not be able to keep so many names straight all at once." She smiled again. She was fair, light-browed and light-eyed, bearing herself with that air of assurance that eldest children often have.

"Sara is after me." The young woman holding the embroidery nodded. She had a plump face, evidence of enjoyment of the more sensuous pleasures of food and drink, and an expression of great good nature; even her hair, much the color of Chryse's, bore some suggestion either of ripe corn or of gold. "And Chasta next, sort of." Chasta was darker-haired than her elder sisters, as if their fairness was being slowly diluted with some Eastern strain.

"And the twins, Helena and Ursula." The twins had deep brown hair, and Chryse saw that while one had highlights in her hair that lightened towards gold, the other had coloring that shaded towards black. "And Nora our scholar." There was a slight giggle among the sisters. Nora, just into adolescence, had a serious, dark-complexioned face that must have seen a good deal of sun, and hair of deepest brown. "And finally, Willa." This youngest girl was barely out of childhood. She was quite dark, in stark contrast to the pale, fair looks of her eldest sibling.

"You are all Madame Sosostris's daughters," said Chryse, trying not to make it sound like a question.

"Of course," replied Ella. "All seven of us."

Sanjay set down his cup. It chimed lightly as it touched the saucer. Every head turned to gaze at him, but he looked merely puzzled for a moment. "I'm sorry. I just had a passing thought, but it escapes me now. Have you lived all your lives in Heffield?"

"Oh, no," said the youngest. "We travel a great deal." She had a high voice, not fully formed, but a certain inborn solemnity of bearing.

"You must have seen a great many interesting places, then." Sanjay favored her with a smile.

"Oh, yes," said the girl, "and at the oddest times, too."

"Now, Willa. Don't confuse our visitors." Nora turned dark eyes to regard Sanjay with a serious and somewhat withdrawn expression. "Certainly we've seen a good many places. It comes from the nature of Mama's profession, you know. And it has proven to be an excellent source of education for all of us."

Sara, the plump one, laughed. Her voice had the infectious and rosy tones of one at ease with the world. "Don't frighten them, Nora. Travel can be entertaining as well. You are travelers yourselves, I believe."

"Yes. We've come to consult your mother about a matter of—" Chryse hesitated, but a quick perusal of the sisters' faces convinced her that there was little these young women did not know about their mother's work. "A matter of transportation."

"Of course," said Ella. "It is one of Mama's specialties."

"Indeed." Chryse exchanged glances with her husband.

A bell-like sound rang suddenly through the air, though there was no evidence of a bell.

"There we are." Ella rose. "If you'll come this way, please."

Chryse and Sanjay followed her through a set of double doors and into a tiny anteroom. As they passed through it they heard scraps of conversation from the parlour behind them.

"How very agreeable—"

"Mama assured us all along that we had nothing to be ashamed of in *that* quarter."

"—such a pleasant voice, so mellifluous."

"—obvious where Willa got her—"

Ella opened a second set of doors and waved a hand. "If you'll enter, Mama is waiting."

"Thank you," said Sanjay, and Chryse echoed him.

As soon as they entered the room the door shut behind them and they found themselves in half-darkness. A single table and two chairs sat in the middle of a featureless room. Facing them was a third chair, and in this chair sat a woman, veiled, in a gown that caught glitters from two lamps set in the wall. The corners of the room remained shadowed.

"Please be seated." The woman's voice was resonant. "Madame Lissagaray. Monsieur Mukerji." She inclined her head, directing them each to a chair. "I am Madame Sosostris. You have come a great distance to see me." It was more statement than question.

Sanjay reached out to touch Chryse's hand, signaling that she should speak.

"Yes, we have. As far, we think, as from a different world entirely. Do you understand?" She hoped her voice was steady. Sanjay gave her a little nod, encouragement, half lost in the gloom.

"I must see the cards."

When Chryse laid the deck on the table, the veiled form shifted forward. She placed her dark hands on either side of the deck and contemplated it for a long moment. Sanjay shifted in his chair.

"The deck is incomplete," said Madame Sosostris abruptly into the silence.

"It wasn't when we got it," said Chryse. "There were fifty-two cards. But only fifty-one after we—" She faltered. "After we found ourselves here."

The veiled head lifted as if to study them. "I am relieved

to hear that it was complete when you received it." There was a quality to her comment, a dry irony as if at a joke they had missed. She laid one hand on the deck and with a deft and practiced movement spread the cards out over the table. "I must cast you first. Please shut your eyes and pick three cards each."

Sanjay looked at Chryse and shrugged, shutting his eyes and leaning forward. She did the same.

"Excellent," said Madame Sosostris, though no noticeable change of expression sounded in her tone. She swept the remaining cards into three piles. "Now, Mr. Mukerji." She extended a hand. "Your cards, please."

Without a word, he handed them to her.

"I cast the Hinge—your basic nature, between the forces pulling you downwards and the forces pulling you up."

With a deliberate, precise turn of her wrist, she laid the first card. "Ah, of course." There was, for the first time, expression in her tone: pleased amusement. "The Paladin. You possess purity of soul. This quality gives you the privilege of pure sight and the burden of interpreting it correctly."

She placed the second card. It showed a scene, a cluster of huts. "You are pulled back by the Village, by conservatism, by others urging you to traditional courses, from goals that have been followed for many generations by your family. This stifles you, and yet you find it difficult to break away from it."

Chryse smiled slightly, but Sanjay's face remained focussed and impassive.

"Last." Madame Sosostris placed the third card. An armed woman advancing, sword out. "The Angel of War. The strongest of the fire elementals, the wheel of the magi. This card pulls you upwards. You desire not strife, but a goal that will consume you entirely, that burns from within." She paused, and then as if with hesitation, turned the card over. A silver dragon, twined and in profile, wings open. "You desire dragons," she said. "For just as they embody the purest of magic, they embody the purest of desire."

There was silence again, disturbed only by the sound of their breathing, and a faint rustling from one of the corners.

"Madame Lissagaray."

Chryse handed the woman the three cards that she held.

"First." Madame Sosostris placed the card on top of the Paladin. "Ah. The Seeker. She searches for an answer, an understanding, a grasp of that calling to which she has dedicated herself. Although it has so far remained elusive, she feels that it is almost within her reach and will be if she continues the quest. Her nature is solitary, and she is burdened by a restlessness that can cause her to leave behind all that is familiar and loved."

She placed the second card. A man lay, like a discarded toy, half-frozen and limp on a field of ice. "The Wanderer. A second card from the north. This reveals the danger of lost purpose, of wandering aimlessly, of stagnation and indecision in the pursuit of one's goal. This fear pulls you down, endangers your ability to continue your search."

Chryse had clasped her hands on her lap. Sanjay was frowning, but in concentration, not disapproval.

"Last." Madame Sosostris placed the third card. "Yes. The Castle. Ringed by a moat. Impregnable, except by knowledge, in its seat on a high hill. Here one can find the synthesis of what is known and what has yet to be known. Here is the source." She turned the card over. The reverse side showed a peaceful dell, at the center of which bubbled a spring. "You see," she said. "The double-sided deck speaks both languages: the molded, the hand-formed, the controlled magic of humans, and the clarity of the natural forces, uncontrollable but purer. It is the melding of such a deck as this that produced the power to bring you here."

"Then you can help us get back?" asked Chryse.

"Is that, at this moment, the greatest wish of your heart?"

Chryse frowned and met Sanjay's eyes. She knew, with the instinct that comes from long intimacy, that he felt the same reluctance she did at having to leave this adventure—perhaps, now, as abruptly as they had come.

"But our families—" began Sanjay.

"The worries of your families, however deep and sincere, I can do nothing about," said Madame Sosostris smoothly, "and neither, while you are here, can you. There is no profit in *that* sort of speculation. In any case, with an incomplete deck, I cannot help you."

"Do you mean there's nothing you can do?" Chryse reached out to grasp Sanjay's hand.

Madame Sosostris lifted one hand imperatively. "I did not say there is nothing I can do. However, you must bring me a thing I cannot get for myself. With it, I can help you."

"What is that?" Sanjay's hand tightened on Chryse's.

Madame Sosostris's head lifted beneath the veil in such a way that one might imagine she was smiling. "Bring me the treasure of the Queen of the Underworld," she said. "The treasure sealed beyond the labyrinth gate."

"Impossible," said Sanjay.

Chryse gasped.

"Impossible?" said Madame Sosostris. "Why is that?"

"For one thing, there isn't a treasure."

"How do you know?"

"Professor Farr says—"

"Does Professor Farr know everything?"

Sanjay did not reply.

"And what about the—" Chryse stopped abruptly. "Might there not be others," she began again, "who also want and feel they are entitled to this treasure? If it exists."

"Bring me the treasure, and I will be able to send you home."

"How will we even know what it is?" asked Sanjay.

"You, at least, have the gift of sight. That should be enough. But I can also tell you that it will be the one thing in the city of the Queen that will be familiar to you."

"Then you believe the Pariamne civilization, the lost city of Topo Rhuam, really existed?"

"I know they existed."

"Then why," asked Chryse, "don't you get the treasure for yourself? I thought no one knew where the old city really was."

"I have many reasons, which I do not choose to disclose," replied Madame Sosostris. Her voice remained even, untouched by impatience or anger. "If you wish to call it the fee for my services, then do so. The treasure is my fee."

"And if we do get it," said Sanjay, "what guarantee do we have not just that you *will* help us, but that you *can*?"

"Do you still doubt my power?" she asked, sounding

more amused than offended. "That I *will*, you have only my word. But that I can—"

She lifted her hands, crossed them, palms facing towards her body, in front of her throat. For a long moment only the faint rustling in one corner disturbed them. The doors behind opened abruptly, soundless but for a light click, and her seven daughters filed in.

The lamps flared slightly, showing their faces: Ella interested and curious as she went to stand in one corner, Sara with a smile that seemed to say she was enjoying herself as she walked to a second corner; Nora serious and Willa somber as they took up places in the last two corners. The twins, heads bent so their faces remained shadowed, knelt on either side of the table, like twin saints, or sinners, praying. Chasta stood behind her mother: her face had the same rapt clarity of the paintings of the Queen of Heaven that adorned Aunt Laetitia's sitting room and Chryse's bedchamber—intent and wholly removed from mundane concerns.

"Chasta." Madam Sosostris's voice deepened in resonance. "The Feast of Somorhas."

The girl reached around her mother, stacked the cards neatly by the center of the table, and laid on top a scene of a wedding feast, bride and groom at the head table, the groom in black, the bride in green.

Chryse tugged on Sanjay's arm. He flashed her a look, nodded to show that he recognized the card.

"The Gate," said Madame Sosostris.

From somewhere in the deck Chasta pulled out the Gate and laid it crosswise on the Feast of Somorhas.

"Now," said Madame Sosostris as Chasta stepped back behind her. "From each of you, I need a symbol of your wedding."

"Our rings?" asked Sanjay.

The veiled head inclined, approving.

They slipped them off, simple gold bands, and laid them on the table. The twins moved forward and lifted their arms so that their hands rested, palms down, a finger's breadth above each ring.

The veiled head lowered until the top of the veil was almost touching the hands open at her throat.

No one spoke.

There was, not a humming, but a suggestion of a sustained, single note, like the aural equivalent of a beam of light.

Behind her mother, Chasta stood with eyes closed. Her sisters in the corners were too shadowed to make out more than the dark outlines of their figures. But the twins' heads lifted slowly—their eyes were open, augmented by a smile on one, by a frown on the other. Their gazes were focussed, but not on anything in the room.

Sanjay's grip tightened convulsively on Chryse's hand. She glanced at him, followed his stare.

A blur of darkness shadowed the table, resting like an ominous cloud over the deck of cards.

Then, a picture snapping suddenly into focus, it solidified. The humming stopped. The twins closed their eyes. Chasta opened hers. Sighs sounded from the corners. Madame Sosostris lifted her head to survey the table.

A plain black top hat sat in the center of the table, covering the cards.

"May I?" asked Sanjay quietly.

A nod.

He rose, retrieving first the two rings, giving Chryse hers, and bent forward to pick up the top hat. As he turned it over, Chryse picked up the cards and tucked them into their brown velvet pouch.

Sanjay smiled. "Boot's Rental Company," he read from a tiny white label on the inside of the hat. "Albany, California." Chryse made a slight noise and looked up at him. "Yes," he agreed. "It's mine. I wonder what the late charge is going to be."

Because he remained standing, Chryse stood as well, smoothing out her gown as much to do something with her hands as because it was wrinkled.

"The treasure of the Queen of the Underworld," said Madame Sosostris.

"For our passage home." Sanjay extended his hand. The mage rose as well, a majestic figure a little taller than Chryse, and shook first his and then Chryse's hand, bargain sealed.

Ella, with a smile, showed them out.

CHAPTER 7:

THE CRUSADER

"There." Charity Farr finished draping a shawl over the shoulders of her silent cousin. "That looks much better, much more fashionable. After all, when one calls on a gentlewoman as notable as Lady Trent, one must look one's best." She frowned, sitting back to survey her handiwork. The carriage they rode in, sent by Lord Vole, slowed to a halt at an intersection, lurched, and started forward again.

"I think it's quite marvellous," she continued, now tucking a stray wisp of Maretha's hair back into the loose braided bun that Charity had insisted Maretha wear as befitting an engaged woman, "that Lady Trent should so honor us with her notice. This is the fourth time she has asked us to call. Do you know—" Here she paused. A tiny frown creased her delicate features. "Perhaps Lady Trent would condescend to advise us on your bride clothes. After all, the earl agreed that you might go to any dressmaker in town—surely you may as well go to the most fashionable."

"And the most expensive?" said Maretha abruptly. "No. Thank you. My church dress will surely be good enough."

"Maretha! You've had that dress for years. Why, this will be a great society wedding. I'm sure most of polite society will be there—"

"To stare," muttered Maretha.

"And in my case," added Charity, her expression changing, "much as I hate to—" Her pause spoke eloquently of a reluctance to say what she meant to say next. "The truth is," she continued in a subdued voice, "that this may be one of the very few chances I have of being noticed, so that I might—" She broke off again. Even in a simple gown, old by several years and dressed up now with ribbons and lace purchased from an inexpensive emporium, she looked charming. "I haven't your education, Maretha," she said quietly. "And certainly no fortune at all. After you marry you know I will simply be a burden to your father. My only hope is that I can contract a respectable marriage. Don't deny me this chance."

Maretha stared down at her hands. She felt, first, a rush of guilt for not considering Charity's predicament—Charity, who never complained, did work that gentlefolk hired servants to do, put up with the professor's odd humors. But following on this as quickly was a swell of annoyance at herself.

Since that day she had accepted the earl's offer, knowing that she really had no other choice, she had lapsed into a passivity that she could only despise in herself. Only on those handful of occasions when she had faced the earl— the final negotiations; the signing of the betrothal agreement; the awful gathering where the betrothal had been formally announced—had her spirit asserted itself: she refused to let *him* believe that she was so fainthearted. But at home she went about her tasks listlessly. Her own father, she thought bitterly, had not noticed the change— but then, he was so consumed by preparations for the expedition that he could hardly be counted on to notice anything so far outside his immediate concerns.

"Very well," she said at last, with that rush of energy and confidence that a burst of resolve engenders, "we *will* ask Lady Trent to recommend the most fashionable, and expensive, dressmaker. You and I will get the finest dresses we can order."

And, she added to herself, spend as much of *his* fortune as is humanly possible before— But farther than this thought she was not willing to go.

"Oh, Maretha!" Charity cried, her gratitude completely unfeigned. "Oh, just imagine. After all," she nodded, trying now to appear judicious, "he is quite, quite rich. A few dresses won't make a ripple in his income—not if he can fund Uncle's expedition without blinking an eye. I helped Monsieur Mukerji copy out some of the lists of provisions— though I haven't as good a hand as you—they're even going to hire some of the laborers here in Heffield and take them all the way to the site. Imagine the expense!"

"Laborers aren't paid *that* much, Charity," said Maretha. "But it is much cheaper to hire local labor—there are always poor folk about any place who are eager for a day wage." She shrugged. "But the earl insisted. Undoubtedly he has his reasons. Keeping them beholden to him in a place far from their own homes, for instance."

"Surely not. You don't think he would—"

"Charity." Maretha sighed. "You don't suppose he's doing this out of some whim of generosity, do you? Monsieur Mukerji and I are to go down to Hutment today to hire some foremen. After tea. Perhaps you would like to come as well?"

"To Hutment?" Charity hesitated. The carriage, as if in echo of her feelings, slowed to a stop. "I'm not sure. Isn't that a terribly poor district? With all sorts of unfortunate people? And criminals?"

The carriage door opened. "Vole House, miss," said the uniformed individual who had helped them in.

"Of course it's a poor district," muttered Maretha as they descended. "That's where you get labor cheapest."

Lady Trent and Chryse were waiting to receive them. After the usual pleasantries, Charity ventured the topic of the dressmaker, and soon she and Lady Trent were deep in a close discussion of the merits of various modistes in the city. Chryse moved to sit next to Maretha.

"I understand," said Maretha, "that it has been arranged that you and your husband will accompany the expedition."

"Yes." Chryse smiled. "It should be quite an adventure."

Despite her own misgivings about the expedition, Maretha smiled back. She had liked this light-haired woman immediately, the first time they had met, and their further meetings over tea at Vole House and Farr House had only confirmed her first opinion. "I'm glad to have the company, too," she added, diffident now.

"Yes," said Chryse thoughtfully. "I should rather imagine you are."

Their eyes met in understanding. Maretha flushed slightly.

On the other side of the room, Lady Trent had unearthed

her stack of current fashion plates, which she and Charity now perused with great concentration.

"I've hesitated to mention this before," began Chryse slowly, lowering her voice, "but Sanjay mentioned that your father had asked if I would—" She faltered. "That as a married woman, if you had any questions—if I would talk to you about—oh dear. Now I'm embarrassed."

But Maretha smiled, and Chryse managed a weak chuckle.

"What my mother would have done," said Maretha, "had she been alive. To instruct me in my marital duties."

"It seems rather foolish, doesn't it?" said Chryse, but to this Maretha frowned.

"No." She lowered both her voice and her eyes. Her hands, clasped on her lap, tightened. "Of course I know the—the mechanics of—" Rather than flushing, her face had gone quite pale. "I don't think Father was being progressive. I know it's the fashion now to keep young people in ignorance of the procreative functions until they marry, but Father simply considered it another branch of natural science. But you see—" Now her eyes lifted, giving her pale face an expression of appeal. "—knowing the mechanics doesn't make me know the—the process any better."

"Oh dear," murmured Chryse. Without thinking she reached out a hand to clasp Maretha's. "Are you so very frightened?"

Maretha could not reply.

"I'm sorry," said Chryse. "I'm sorry you have to face something so—" She made an impatient movement with her free hand. "I'm afraid that any word I use will be trite. It should be something to look forward to, not something to fear."

"With any other man," said Maretha in a voice barely audible to her companion.

"They are just rumors. Surely—" Chryse stopped herself, refusing now to say those trite words Sanjay had used: Surely he's not as black as he's painted.

"What if he is?" asked Maretha as if Chryse had voiced the thought aloud. "He is a sorceror. Such power does not come free. It must be drawn from somewhere, from oneself, from natural forces, from other people. There is always a price. I don't know much about magic, but I have heard that it is easiest to steal that power from others. But perhaps that isn't true."

"I don't know. I just don't know. But I am a musician—have even done some composing, on and off, when I had the courage and the commitment to do it. And it *is* easiest to steal from others, when you're composing, or creating any art. But it seems to me that the strongest art, the truest art, the most difficult to create, comes from oneself. Maybe that holds true for magic as well."

Maretha bowed her head.

"Surely—" Chryse began, distressed by Maretha's sudden passivity. "Surely as his wife, he would treat you with more respect than a—than some poor soul bought off the streets."

Maretha winced. "How different am I?" she asked bitterly. "Bought and sold? But it is true—it is true that he mentioned having an heir."

"Then he must know that he has to take care of you, if you are to bear a healthy child."

Maretha's hands tightened in a convulsive grip around Chryse's hand. "But then I have to lie with him," she whispered.

"Then for goodness sake," said Chryse, trying to brace up her voice even as she grimaced at the pressure of Maretha's grip, "you'll just have to make it clear to him that he's better off making it a pleasure for you than a—than otherwise."

"Can it be?"

"Of course it can! It can be glorious. It can be uncomfortable for the woman at first, but if the man is gentle and if you—ah—convince him to take as long about the first part as possible, before—" She realized that her face was flushed, but Maretha was still looking down. "—then there is no reason it shouldn't be pleasurable. And Maretha, all else aside, remember that in one respect at least it could be worse. He *is* attractive."

Maretha's hands relaxed and she raised her head. "He's beautiful," she breathed, and then blushed to the tips of her ears.

And as if that admission alone broke the tension, they both sat back and laughed. A little unsteadily, true, and with perhaps a touch of resignation, but it was laughter.

"Well." From across the room, Lady Trent lifted her

grey head from the plate Charity was exclaiming over, "If you two have nothing better to do than gossip and laugh over frivolities, then you had better join us here in choosing some gowns." But her gaze met Chryse's for a moment and she gave a little nod, in approval.

"Thank you," Maretha murmured as she and Chryse rose. "Whatever course I choose, I need to remember that despair only leads to defeat."

"I think it's something we all need reminding of."

"Then I shall resolve to be resolute," replied Maretha, with a sweeping gesture of one hand, a parody of bad dramatics that almost tipped over a vase. She and Chryse both giggled, but composed themselves quickly when Lady Trent cast a stern glance in their direction.

"Now," Aunt Laetitia demanded as the two younger women seated themselves on the sofa next to her, "you will of course want a gown in the traditional green—"

"If I may," ventured Charity, a little hesitant, "Maretha's coloring has never taken well to the greens."

"Nonsense," declared Aunt Laetitia. "Girls these days feel free to take any liberty they please with honorable traditions."

Charity colored immediately, and shrank back into her chair.

Chryse laughed. "What do *you* want, Maretha?"

"Oh, I don't know. Perhaps a hairshirt like my name-sake was said to wear when she went to her martyrdom."

"Good Lady," said Aunt Laetitia. "I have never under-stood why a woman of Saint Maretha's obvious intelligence would wear such an uncomfortable garment under armour."

"But she was a *saint*, Aunt Laetitia," said Chryse. "I'd never heard that saints were concerned with comfort."

"One would, however, expect them to be concerned with practicality. She was a Knight of Our Lady, and surely it behooved her to uphold Our Lady's honor by wearing apparel most conducive to victory in martial endeavors."

Maretha laughed suddenly. "Of course you are right, Lady Trent. I'm sure we can find a suitable pattern, and a *shade* of green that will suit even my coloring."

"Of course," said Lady Trent decisively. She gave Chryse the barest of winks as the four women settled themselves in for the task at hand.

They had provided, on paper at least, Maretha with
bridal clothes and an additional wardrobe fit for a countess, and Charity with an attendant's dress and a handful of
other gowns, by the time Sanjay arrived. He had Julian
and Kate in tow.

"We have good information," he said after greetings
had been made all round, "that one of these so-called
correspondence societies is meeting this evening at the
Crusader, an inn in Hutment, and that two of the people
Professor Farr has worked with in the past will be there."

"Just as I'd hoped," said Maretha.

"What?" asked Julian. "Are you really going to hire
those radicals, Miss Farr? Isn't that dangerous? I was
almost caught in one of their emancipation riots. They're
hot-headed, proud of it, and don't seem to care a whit that
their activities could bring them a stiff prison sentence. I'd
think it would be a chancy proposition."

"That very pride you mention makes their work all the
better," answered Maretha. "And don't you agree that
there is some substance to their grievances, and to their
demands?"

"Certainly not," said Aunt Laetitia with feeling. "I say
that that kind of hooliganism is what comes of wasting
education on classes unable to absorb it rationally."

"But Lady Trent," said Kate. "You yourself insist that
your servants be taught to read and write."

"So they can read the Bible, Miss Cathcart. I'll have no
truck with these radicals—they are merely a wild rabble,
inspiring mobs to violence."

Chryse leaned towards Sanjay. "Correspondence societies?" she whispered.

He shrugged. "Working-class people, usually craftsmen,
the sort who have had a bit of education, who write to
their professional counterparts in other cities and towns."

"That's all?"

"—I can see," Maretha was saying, "that it is a subject
we cannot agree on, Lady Trent, so I won't say any more.
But the expedition must have workers, and supervisors to
oversee them, and these men are experienced. They worked
with my father at Eppot-Staw." She rose. "Only Monsieur
Mukerji and I need to go on this business, but any of you
are welcome if you are interested."

"I certainly am." Chryse rose as well.

"I certainly am *not*," said Lady Trent with asperity.

But Kate and Julian, applied to, proved eager to go, and Charity quickly, with less enthusiasm but a surreptitious glance at Julian, followed suit.

"Hmph," said Aunt Laetitia when Julian, the last to leave the room, had paused to take his leave of her. "Young people these days have no respect for the law of the land. Lawless and unruly mobs who have not a scrap of permanent property interest in the land cannot be allowed to rule. It is unseemly to hold such notions."

"Are you speaking of Miss Farr, Aunt?" asked Julian. He smiled.

"A good sort of girl, but no daughter of mine was ever allowed to cherish such radical leanings. She ought not to have them."

Julian raised his eyebrows, giving him a musing look. "I don't suppose she will, much longer." He paused. "She is marrying the earl, after all. You can't imagine he has any tolerance for even the mildest of reform politics."

"Oh dear," murmured Aunt Laetitia, looking now concerned rather than outraged. "I hadn't thought of that. Poor girl."

"Indeed," said her nephew. With a bow he left the room.

It was twilight by the time the carriage pulled up outside the sign of the Crusader, a large inn in the district of Hutment. The wooden sign, its bright colors dimmed in the gathering dusk, depicted a knight in medieval style riding his caparisoned horse towards a distant and faintly-seen city, shield hung by his leg, sword in his free hand.

Lights showed through shuttered windows. Two nondescript men paused to stare at the rich carriage and went into the inn.

Inside, a pall of smoke from the two great hearthfires hung over the room. Many glances turned their way as the party entered to stand as unobtrusively as possible in the back of the room. The speaker, however, did not falter.

"—and at the trial of Mr. John Hardin for distributing pamphlets, the Justice herself asked 'What right have these ignorant country people, these lower classes, to representation? A Government,' she said, 'should be just like a corporation—and in this country, it is made up of the

landed interest, which alone has a right to be represented.'
Then she sentenced Mr. Hardin to ten years in prison. I
ask you, citizens, is it for *this* that we sweat and toil and
starve?"

A general clamor rose from the seated and standing
listeners. The speaker, raising one hand, quieted them.

"We have been abused in the Parliament, calumniated
in public, persecuted in private, and forced out of public
houses, yet we continue to meet, we continue to receive
addresses from new societies of working folk in other cities,
new correspondence from others who have combined as
we have—for our rights—"

"Hear, hear."

In the resulting chorus of approving response, Maretha
leaned toward Sanjay. "There, just to our left: the middle-
aged woman in black and the young man beside her. Those
are the two we want to speak to."

He nodded, whispering back. "I think our party is too
conspicuous. I'll get the others outside; perhaps you can
bring those two out there."

"But let me ask you for yourselves, the question." The
woman at the front of the room continued, once the shouting had died down. "The question, which is the only
requirement of admission to membership in our order, of
which we are agreed that the number of members *shall be
unlimited.*" She was dark-haired, small and vital. Sanjay,
looking from the young man of the pair Maretha was now
moving toward to the woman speaker, saw at once the
family resemblance—an older sister, perhaps. "Are you
thoroughly persuaded that the welfare of these kingdoms
requires that all adult persons, in possession of their reason,
and not incapacitated by crimes, should have a vote for a
Member of Parliament?"

In the tumultuous acclaim that followed this query,
Sanjay herded the rest of the party out.

"I can see," said Chryse in an undertone to her husband
as they came out into the cold evening air, "that you and I
had better not enter into any political discussions, all
things considered. What a good deal we take for granted."

"To be sure," agreed Sanjay, squeezing her hand.

"Now I understand," said Julian, "why the Regent and
her cabinet are so set on outlawing the correspondence
societies."

"Of course." Charity added quickly in her small, agreeable voice, "They had better go back to their work and let those who are qualified to know the laws make the laws."

"That isn't quite what I meant," said Julian gently. "Frankly, as long as I have enough income to support myself and my dependents, I don't particularly care *who* votes for Parliament."

"But Julian." Kate grinned. "How are you to maintain your income if your own tenants can vote for members who might institute radical changes?"

"Quite," said Julian.

Charity lowered her eyes to gaze at her hands and said nothing.

"Here is Maretha," said Chryse.

She came up to them with two companions. "I've persuaded them to listen to our proposal." She stopped by Sanjay. "Lord Vole, may I present Madam Thorwell and Mr. Southern."

Julian inclined his head slightly.

The elderly woman, a broad-faced, sharp-eyed individual, dipped a brief curtsey, but Mr. Southern morely narrowed his eyes and inclined his head in return. Julian frowned, looking for a moment very much the displeased aristocrat, but said nothing.

"And Miss Cathoart and my cousin Miss Farr," Maretha hurried on. Kate tipped her hat, insouciant, to which Mr. Southern offered an ironic sketch of a bow. But for Charity he bowed indeed, and when she tentatively extended her hand, he took it and brought it to his lips. Chryse noticed with some surprise that Charity did not flush, but rather kept her eyes a moment longer on Mr. Southern's face before gently pulling her hand away.

"I am Monsieur Mukerji." Sanjay extended a hand to both individuals. "I am Professor Farr's secretary. This is my wife, Madame Lissagaray." Chryse shook their hands as well. Mr. Southern had a firm and confident grip. "We'll both be accompanying the expedition."

"So there is to be a new expedition." Mr. Southern turned to Maretha. "Begging your pardon, Miss Farr, but how does the professor mean to finance this one? We came as close as ninepence to not having the funds to pay the day labor at Eppot-Staw."

"Yes, there is a new expedition, Thomas." Maretha's

voice was quiet but forceful. "The professor has acquired the funding from an interested party for the site of Pariamne."

Mr. Southern raised a hand to brush at his black hair. He had an air of suppressed vitality about him, as if he were holding in a great store of energy. "That's unexpected, miss."

"Glory be saved," exclaimed Madam Thorwell. "An' he's got his heart's desire at last, has he, missy?"

"Yes," replied Maretha in a constrained voice.

"We'll be needing experienced foremen," said Sanjay. "And we intend to hire a small force of laborers here in Heffield, to supplement those we take on at the site itself."

"And just where may that be?" asked Thomas Southern quietly. "I've my ideas, based on a few conversations with the professor. And unless I'm missing my guess, you'll need to do a great deal of convincing to get a good complement of steady and reliable workers."

"That may be true." Maretha looked from Southern to Madam Thorwell. "That is why I have approached you two first. You have the experience to recommend laborers and to suggest a fair wage for them, and to convince workers to hire on."

"Where is the place?" asked Madam Thorwell. "If it's a fair wage in these lean times, you'll not be wanting for workers. Midlands ain't so bad, even with them factories."

Julian coughed slightly and he and Kate moved away from the group, ostensibly to examine the horses.

"North," said Maretha in a low voice. "At the border, in the highlands—the area sometimes called the labyrinth gates."

A small cart laden with vegetables trundled past, slopping through half-frozen puddles. From the inn behind a chorus of sudden shouts rose and then ebbed into a confusion of voices that trailed back into quiet. The shop fronts around were all dark; an occasional light showed through shutters in the stories above.

"I see." Thomas Southern's face bore a fragment of a smile. "You'll have to offer very good conditions indeed to attract any honest help."

"You're crazy," snapped Madam Thorwell. "There isn't an honest laborer would take gold to work up there.

Everyone knows those parts are haunted—labyrinth gates, indeed. And next to *their* lands, to boot."

"*Their* lands?" Chryse glanced at Mr. Southern. "Who do you mean?"

Southern flashed a surprised glance at her, but Madam Thorwell was well begun now. "Them barbarians, with their cruel sorceries. Strange and awful things of their making haunt those borders, and especially the gates."

"Why is it called the labyrinth gates?" asked Chryse.

"Well may you ask," muttered Madam Thorwell darkly. "All those as wander in the hills called the labyrinth gates, whether for good purpose or bad, are lost and never be seen again. It's said the worst of it lies underground, where by rights no building should be, but wicked magic builds in wicked ways. Ay, it's a cursed place, whether or not the lost city of Pariam rests there as well, with its own ghosts of plague and treachery and death. A cursed place that guards the border to a cursed land. It's sheer foolishness to stir up trouble in a nest of vipers."

"Oh come now," said Maretha. "In this day and age haven't we risen above such superstition?"

"Call it superstition if you will." Madam Thorwell's expression was fixed. "An' you'll be as dead as the ghosts an' the other creatures—which I shan't name for it's bad luck—that inhabit those hills. They may be just tales, of what's hidden beyond and below the gates, but my father allus told me, where smoke rises you're sure to find fire. I shan't be going, not for any price, and neither shall you find laborers."

"Not even for two pounds a week for you, with meals and lodging in sturdy tents? And the same food and living, at five shillings a day for the common laborers."

Thomas Southern whistled. Even in the lamplight, one could see his eyes widen. "Those are handsome terms." He turned. "Come now, Madam Thorwell, not for such wages, and perhaps even a chance to find the lost treasure?"

"Treasure!" She snorted. "Any treasure will be sick and bitter with tainted magic, let me tell you, young man. What use are wages of any sort to a dead fool? I'll have no truck with this expedition." With a final contemptuous lift of her head, she disappeared back inside the inn.

"So, Thomas," said Maretha. "I suppose we've lost you as well."

"By no means, Miss Farr. I don't disbelieve the tales, but I have faith in Our Lady to protect me from the tricks of the Daughter—and faith in Her Son to grant me the mercy of a quick and painless death if I should be overcome. And I've family to support—younger siblings, mother and father both ill from the mines, and my sister's work with the correspondence societies."

"Yes," said Maretha quickly, "but I advise you to keep that particular interest quiet for now."

"Yes, miss," he agreed, not at all meek. "I can find plenty of honest men and women who are desperate enough for any wages that they'll hire on despite their fears. These are hard enough times. But the wages must be met regular, and the living conditions hold good. And good wages for the local help, though I wonder how many you'll find living up there willing to work so near the border."

Maretha considered. "It's poor country up there. Poorer than here, I've read."

He nodded. "But I must know, miss, two things. Who is this benefactor? I must have some surety that the people I hire will get their wages."

Maretha's gaze faltered a moment, recovered. "The Earl of Elen."

His eyes narrowed, and he crossed himself. His expression took on a look of intent calculation, somewhat at odds with the usual openness of his mien. "I see."

"What is the other thing you need to know?" Maretha asked quickly, not wanting the silence to stretch out.

It was a moment before he spoke. "The workers will need a guarantee, Miss Farr. A wage guarantee, that wages will be set at the same rate, and regularly, from hiring until the completion of the expedition."

Maretha blinked. "Be reasonable, Thomas. The wages being offered are excellent. A guarantee . . . that is radical talk, indeed."

The laborer shook his head. He had a fine-boned, handsome face, but Chryse saw now that the cut of his jaw lent it obstinacy. "Not when the workers may be at risk of their lives." He turned unexpectedly to Sanjay. "What do you say, Monsieur Mukerji?"

Sanjay shrugged. "I don't think it unreasonable, but I have no say in these arrangements. I doubt if the earl would agree to it."

"Then the earl can go to the prisons for his workers. He'll hire no decent folk unless he has me or someone like me to do the hiring. You know that's true, miss."

Maretha sighed. "Both the professor and I respect your judgment in workers, Thomas. That's why we came to you. But there's nothing I can promise. The earl is not—" She hesitated. "—not an easy man to deal with. I will do what I can." She extended a hand. "Can we consider you hired then, Thomas?"

He nodded and, with great seriousness, shook her hand. "You have always dealt fairly with us, miss. That's the only reason I agree."

"Come to Farr House tomorrow, and you can discuss with the professor and Mr. Mukerji the number and skills of the workers that we'll need."

"Very good, miss. When will we be leaving Heffield?"

But to this Maretha could not, for a moment, reply.

"The week after equinox," said Sanjay quickly. "After the holiday of—" He glanced at Chryse.

"Sower's Day," she supplied with a slight grin. She leaned toward Sanjay. "That is what they call the spring equinox here," she whispered.

"It's a very auspicious day for a wedding," said Charity.

"Charity!" Maretha's tone was sharp.

"I beg your pardon," murmured Charity.

Thomas Southern looked a trifle mystified by this exchange, but he shook hands with Sanjay and Chryse, and bowed again over Charity's delicate gloved fingers. "Tomorrow," he said. "And be assured," he added, "that Madam Thorwell and I will keep this business as quiet as possible. I'm sure that will prove best for the expedition."

"Good evening, Thomas." Maretha nodded, and he went back into the inn. Voices raised into song as the door shut behind him, a lively tune about "planting the tree of liberty."

"Well," said Chryse. "That's what I call an interesting young man."

Sanjay looked at her. "Ah, well." He grinned. "Too bad you married me."

"I don't know," retorted Chryse. "Perhaps polygamy is allowed here."

Maretha laughed. "He is a nice-looking young fellow, and well read, really."

"For his class," said Charity. "I can't imagine he's really *well* educated. And laborers soon lose their looks, I've heard."

Maretha shook her head. "Doubtless because of poor food. Do you know, he once told me that his dearest wish was to become a clergyman—not one of those wandering itinerant preachers, but a real, vested clergyman. Of course he has neither the birth nor the education *nor* the fortune to get a place in the church. But he's a very godly man."

"Then he'll enjoy working with the earl," said Julian, coming up at that moment with Kate, "for a more ungodly man than Lord Elen I have never met. Though this fellow I thought a trifle impertinent." He stopped suddenly, seeing Maretha's stricken expression. "I beg your pardon, Miss Farr." His voice was now soft. "It is not my place to speak of your fiance."

"No, no." Maretha turned away to go to the carriage. "It was nothing."

Chryse hurried up beside her, taking her by one arm. "I did have one question, though." She made her voice bright. "Who are these barbarians that Madam Thorwell was so horrified to contemplate?"

Maretha's hand tightened gratefully on Chryse's arm, a brief squeeze. "The northerners. You've seen the maps. The far northwest is their country. The region is called Herelf Ismor-ef, the Forgotten Lands."

"But surely, on an island like this, that would have been—well, if nothing else, conquered by now."

"Oh, it's never been conquered, though many have tried."

Chryse shook her head, pausing to let Maretha climb into the carriage before her. "Then the men and women living there must be terribly fierce, or have as powerful a magic as Madam Thorwell implied." She mounted the steps and settled herself by Maretha. The interior was dark, Maretha's face shadowed. By the door, Charity had paused, waiting to let Julian hand her in.

"Oh, they're not human," said Maretha in a soft and matter-of-fact voice that penetrated the darkness easily. "They're elves, or what's left of them. I don't really know. But it's quite true what Madam Thorwell said—people no longer go there, to the gates, and those that do don't come back."

CHAPTER 8:

THE MERCHANT

"Have it brought before Parliament as soon as they convene," said the Regent to one of her cabinet ministers. "I want these correspondence societies outlawed and participation in them punishable as sedition. As treason, if possible. This rabble is absorbing influences from across the Channel that must not be allowed to proliferate in this country." She frowned and swept the sheaf of papers in front of her to one side with an impatient movement. "The notion is in itself ridiculous, in any case. Our Holy Mother ordained our stations in life. We must be content with what She has seen fit to gift us."

A general murmur of assent ran round the long table. The Regent eyed her ministers with a gaze both penetrating and tinged with contempt. The look faded when her scrutiny came at last to rest on her niece.

The heir sat at the far end of the table. The girl, dressed neatly and soberly, stared thoughtfully at a paper laid on the table before her. Her eyes, the best feature in an unremarkable face, lifted to return her aunt's gaze. The Regent recognized at once the girl's disapproval, but the small mouth merely tightened and the clear eyes dropped again to peruse the document.

Such a prim little thing, thought the Regent. It's a miracle my profligate brother produced someone of her temperament. She allowed herself the briefest of smiles. After all, the girl was so dutiful that she never corrected her elders in public—or at least would not until she gained her full rank as queen. If she gained it.

The girl pushed the document aside and scanned the next one. Her plain face brightened.

The Regent coughed, to gain the assembly's attention. "I believe," she said in her clear, well-modulated voice, "that our final business is of better cheer than most." This elicited a few smiles. "His Highness, Prince Elberic of Alsetz-Orray, has graciously accepted in all particulars our final negotiations for the marriage of his son, Prince Frederick, to—" Here she paused to let the ministers cast surreptitious glances at the Princess Georgiana. The girl's cheeks bore a faint but becoming flush. "—our future queen."

Another murmur of pleased assent flowed around the table.

"Your Highness." One man interrupted the undertone. He was examining the list of articles under the agreement. "I understood that Prince Elberic originally asked for the wedding to take place this summer. But in the final articles, I see here that it is fixed for midwinter instead—that, indeed, it is to be held concurrently with Princess Georgiana's coronation."

"Have you an objection to this course, Lord Felton?" The Regent glanced quickly towards the heir, but the girl's face was impassive. "Surely the hasty preparations that would be necessary to present a summer wedding would not allow us to do justice to the importance of the occasion. While by combining the wedding and the coronation, we will have ample time to present a setting and spectacle fitting to Princess Georgiana's rank and person."

"Hmph." Lord Felton's mouth held a disapproving line. "I'd have thought it best to get the wedding over and done with, the new-marrieds acquainted and an heir on the way, all before the coronation."

"Indeed, Lord Felton," replied the Regent in her smoothest voice. "All reasonable concerns. But it is true that we are in general blessed with good health in this family, although my brother's constitution, sadly, was never strong. And also, that Princess Georgiana had some hand herself in choosing Prince Frederick. They are acquainted, as you know. We are past medieval times, I hope, when royal children were forced to marry sight unseen. Is that not so, your highness?"

"Indeed, Aunt." The girl retained her composure under

this attention. "It is my duty to marry as will benefit my realm. I am grateful that some choice was allowed me in a prospective consort. Our Lady was gracious enough to have allowed there to be a field of several candidates." A brief chuckle greeted this remark. The Regent frowned. "I know," continued the girl, as deeply serious as if she was not aware of anything humorous in her comments, "that my father, may the Son bless and keep him, had only one choice of bride, and that you yourself, Aunt, had no eligible suitors at all available. I know I have been blessed in this matter."

Several of the ministers coughed. Lord Felton shuffled papers.

"Very true, my dear princess," replied the Regent when it was obvious the girl had nothing more to say. "We are all blessed in this contract. Now." She took on a brisker tone. "Lord Felton. As Minister of Ceremony, I will leave it in your capable hands to draft the initial preparations for the Festival of Lights wedding and coronation. I believe it will be an auspicious time, coinciding as it does with her highness's sixteenth birthday, and will prove to be a fine occasion for such spectacle as will please the lower classes."

"As you wish, your highness." Lord Felton bowed his head.

"Then." The Regent nodded to a servant, who moved forward quickly to pull her chair back so she could stand. The ministers stood as well. The heir remained seated. "With your leave, your highness, we should prepare for our private audiences."

"Of course." The princess inclined her head. The ministers collected their papers and, taking their leave of her in turn, departed from the chamber.

"I'm afraid, Aunt," said the girl when the others had all left, "that I've forgotten whom we are to see today."

"Only one. At his request." The Regent moved around the long table to stand closer to her niece. "The Earl of Elen."

Princess Georgiana rose abruptly, not waiting for a servant to help her with her chair. She crossed herself. "I will not receive him." Her voice held uncharacteristic passion. "That such a monster is a peer of the realm I can do nothing about. But I refuse to acknowledge his presence by receiving him."

"As you wish, my dear," said the Regent softly.

"What does he want in any case?"

"I'm not sure." The Regent paused. "One cannot simply refuse a request by, as you said, a peer of the realm. You will soon enough have to accept that he is one of your subjects."

"Then I will deal with him," said the princess stoutly, "as he deserves. But while you are, as is proper, my Regent and Protector, Aunt, I will abide by your supervision. If you insist I see him with you, I will."

"I do not insist," murmured the Regent.

"You are very good, Aunt. I would prefer not to see him."

"Then, with your permission, I will leave you, your highness."

The princess hesitated. "There is one thing else. I cannot like the harshness with which you propose to deal with these trade people. Surely you do not fear that all this letter-writing presages an invasion from across the Channel?"

The Regent sighed, a showy, dramatic gesture. "My dear. It is naive to believe that simple, poor trading folk could read and write so eloquently, that they have the education and the ability to present such arguments. They are simply pawns in the hands of an outside force, a mob to be swayed against us with clever slogans. *That* is the danger that must be crushed, once and for all."

"But—" The princess looked thoughtful for a moment, a curious combination of puzzlement and determination. "Do you not suppose that even the mildest of these grievances has perhaps some grounding in fact? In justice? That perhaps, as it says here—" She picked up again the document she had been examining earlier. "—their wages are too low for them to even buy food for their families?"

"My dear girl." The Regent pulled the document gently from the princess's hand. "When I was a girl there was never any of this sort of talk. The lower classes were perfectly content with the station that Our Lady had ordained for them. It is only the revolution across the Channel that has brought in spies and rabble-rousers who work to incite a few malcontents. Once that faction is erased, the people will be happy again. After all, remember that one of the basic tenets of these societies is universal suffrage."

The princess frowned. "Of course that is impossible. But surely a better method of poor relief—"

A liveried servant entered. "Your highness." He bowed. "The Earl of Elen awaits in the gold chamber."

The princess flushed, breaking off. "I will go now, Aunt." She turned away quickly. "I believe Mistress Wynne is expecting me for my mathematics tutorial." With a little flick of her skirts to avoid a chair, she hurried around the table and out a side door.

The Regent put down the document she held with a satisfied smile. Really, that girl wore such conservative clothing that it was almost laughable. She had no style at all.

She straightened her own dress, a low-cut, fashionable gown that made her handsome figure apparent without flaunting it. One had, after all, a certain appearance and decorum to maintain.

She nodded to the liveried servant and let him precede her to the gold chamber. At the door to that room, she paused a moment, silent.

The earl sat in a finely-brocaded chair, legs stretched out negligently before him, ankles crossed. It amused her that his dress was, like her niece's, elegant but quite conservative. He stared, all fine-boned intentness, at the fire wavering in the hearth. Following his gaze, she discerned shapes moving within the flames, like creatures gesturing in some arcane wordless language. Abruptly they dissolved into mere fire. She turned to see that he had now risen, and was regarding her with the cold arrogance that characterized him.

"Your highness." He punctuated the title with a brief, but correct, bow.

"Speaking to friends?" she asked as she passed in front of the fire.

"There are many who can speak," he said softly, "if one knows the means to communicate with them." He clasped his hands behind his coat, regarding her with an entirely neutral expression. "But you know that as well as I. To what do I owe the honor of your summons?"

She smiled, stopping now at a window that overlooked the great central courtyard. "No pleasantries, Lord Elen? No polite conversation before the business at hand?"

When he did not reply, she turned to face him. That he

was so handsome was a pity, she thought. She had sufficient confidence in her own attractiveness that she had
never felt the need to augment it by sorcerous means.
That *he* used magic to cover his true features she did not
doubt—she sometimes wondered what he really looked
like. Her brother, before his unfortunate demise, had
once told her of an interview he had conducted with a
servant girl who claimed to have been raped by the earl.
He had appeared to her, the girl had said, as a hideous,
deformed monster. What her brother's interest in the girl
had been she had not inquired after too deeply.

She coughed slightly. The earl's expression, under scrutiny, remained carefully polite but obviously disinterested.
"I must congratulate you, Lord Elen, on the announcement of your betrothal. I believe the wedding is to take
place in but a few more days."

"Ten days, your highness."

"To a titleless young woman, I believe. Her father is
some sort of academic."

"A professor."

"Ah. A professor. Yes, I remember now." She touched,
lightly, the back of a gold-embroidered chair. "One can
only hope she is prepared for your—ah— tastes, Lord Elen."

His face remained closed. "My tastes, your highness?"

"Girls. Boys. Young, old, violent, persuasive. Broad, so
I have heard. I hope she is a flexible girl."

The barest of smiles, completely undecipherable, touched
the earl's face. "I am certain she will suffice for the purpose." His voice was as calm as the stillness before a storm
breaks.

"You have decided at last that it is necessary to produce
an heir?"

"That is the general opinion of society, yes. But I feel
sure that you did not summon me here in order to felici-
tate me on my betrothal."

"Indeed. It has come to my attention that you are
undertaking the financing of an expedition to the fabled
city of Pariamne."

"Indeed," he echoed, not moving.

"I see no reason," she continued, "why our interests
cannot combine in this instance."

"I was not aware we had any interests in common, your
highness."

"There is no need to play the simpleton, Lord Elen."

"I was not. You refer, I collect, to the obvious truth that we have both ventured deep into the magical arts. But our ultimate goals I doubt in any way intersect."

"Do they not? Let me be frank, Lord Elen."

"Please do." He let the comment escape with less sarcasm than she imagined he intended.

"I want a share in that expedition. I can offer you a great deal for a portion of any treasure found, and for access to all the discoveries you make and the conclusions you and Professor Farr draw from your investigations."

"Under the agreements I signed with the professor, I am not at liberty to assign any portion of treasure or disclose anything he has or will confide in me regarding his researches."

"By Our Lady!" she swore, losing her composure. An instant later she had controlled it again. Her anger seemed to radiate uselessly against his chill disdain. "He is not even a noble. I have said I will reward you."

"And with what," asked the earl, "do you mean to interest me?"

She let a long silence fill the gap while she paced across the room to halt before the fire. "The Princess Georgiana," she said flatly. "Her betrothal arrangements are not yet final. I can arrange that she marry you instead."

"I am intrigued, your highness, by what I can only deduce from that proposal must be your opinion of me. As you know, I am already betrothed."

"To a chit of a non-titled girl with no connections—not even a beauty, I have heard. You know perfectly well that she can be disposed of quite easily."

"Of course I know it," he said. "It is one of her chief attributes. But let *me* be frank. I have no interest in the Princess Georgiana, and less in the throne. I do have an interest in Parlamne. My intended bride gives me complete leverage to indulge that interest. Try to harm her in any way, and I will use every means at my disposal to injure you in return." He sketched the slightest of bows. "Your highness."

She smiled. "Have we descended to threats already?" she asked. "Is there no middle ground we can agree on? Tell me the location of the city. You know I do not possess enough liquid funds to buy out your interest from this professor. Instead, I will send a few of my own people, discreetly. They will not interfere with your expedition in any way."

"As I said before, I am not at liberty to disclose any information about the expedition."

Her eyes narrowed, a look meant to pierce even the iciest hauteur. "Surely your duty to your Regent supersedes that to a mere professor!"

"Undoubtedly it does," he replied, unperturbed. "But it does not supersede my duty to myself. Do you not know the motto on the Elen crest, your highness? 'Build first thine own estate.' "

"Are we so different, Lord Elen?" Her tone became more soothing. "Are the sources of our power so utterly opposed? By joining forces we can gain the more."

The earl smiled for the first time, a grim expression indeed. "Somehow, I doubt you appreciate the source of my power—and might disbelieve it if you knew. I think there is no point in our joining forces."

"None at all?" she asked sweetly.

"None. With your leave, your highness—" He inclined his head.

"I had hoped for better, Lord Elen. But I must respect your refusal. You have my leave to go."

His bow was curt, but not disrespectful. He turned and with almost preternatural grace left the chamber.

She mused in front of the fire for some time, examining the flames again as if in hope of seeing those arcane creatures he had seemingly called from their depths. Nothing appeared.

At last she moved to the bell pull and rang it. A servant appeared immediately. "Send Nastagmas," she commanded.

The elderly man appeared within a few minutes, giving a low bow in the doorway.

"Ah, Nastagmas." She watched him make a careful circuit of the room, checking the two doors and the windows. "You were right. The earl has refused my overtures."

The thin face registered no surprise. He nodded merely.

"I must accomplish all the spell on my own, then, and in such a way that I am never forced to forswear myself and thus jeopardize my power."

"So the boy will be doubly necessary, then."

"Yes." She turned sharply to face him. "The boy *is* still safely disposed?"

"Yes, highness. The loyalty of the factory owner will not waver. The boy is safe on all counts, and easily retrievable, but not easily found should any seek him deliberately."

"Good. Now. I must find one person in this expedition whom I can bribe to act as my agent. I have, therefore, two tasks for you." She fingered the gold brocade of the chair again, relishing the sensuous roughness of the fabric and stitching. "First, find me one who can be bribed. Not the bride, I think. Unless she is stronger than I imagine, the earl will quickly penetrate all her defenses and control her easily. But her father, perhaps, if his obsession extends far enough. You said he has a secretary. Any others connected with the expedition—one of them has a price that can be met. Bring me that person."

"Yes, highness."

"Yes," she echoed. "Then, I want you to hire on as a laborer. Can it be done?"

He considered. "They are hiring laborers from Heffield, it is true, highness. Offering rich wages, but still not finding all the workers they need. I am strong, but perhaps they look only for younger folk."

"I can augment your strength and give you the illusion of youth, an illusion none but the earl will be able to penetrate."

"Then, highness, as a common laborer I will simply take care never to come to the earl's notice."

"Not a difficult task, I expect. I will arrange a means of communication. And order a troop of soldiers to be stationed in that area. All this I can accomplish—just find me an agent within the group accompanying the expedition. How soon do they leave?"

"Two weeks, highness."

"Then let us start without delay." She removed her hand from the chair. Her eyes seemed brighter—almost as if lit from within. "Bring two of the boys to my chamber. I will layer the spells on you, starting tonight—that will afford you better protection."

"Highness." He bowed and left the room.

She stopped before the window again, rubbing her hands together slowly. Outside, in the great courtyard, the Princess Georgiana walked sedately along one of the paved pathways. Her two young siblings, followed by their elderly governess, trailed behind. Georgiana held in her hand a book. Her face was serious; her lips moved. She seemed to be reading aloud.

"A disgrace." The Regent stared down with a dispassionate eye on the domestic scene. "That after so many years, the succession should pass out of the female line. It is impossible that those bovine children are William's seed. I always suspected that that little cow of a provincial princess got her children by other men. A disgrace!" She jerked away from the window. "Passing through the male line, indeed! What a ridiculous notion. This would never have happened in my grandmother's time. Well." She paused in front of the small glass above the mantelpiece and examined herself critically. Not a beauty, but she had good features augmented by a fine figure and an air of authority and sensuality that was absorbing, to both men and women.

"And my mother's features." Her voice was soft. "None of which I see in those children. They must not inherit." She turned from the glass, thinking of the task she had set herself for this evening. "Ah, well," she sighed, letting her tongue moisten her lips in anticipation. "By one means or the other I will gain the treasure of the labyrinth and with it the power to dispose of Georgiana without incriminating myself." She smiled, sly and satisfied. "And without even killing her. There will be no broken oath on which to break my power. And once Georgiana is gone, and I remain in a position of trust, I will have many years to determine the fate of the other two. And to cover my tracks equally well."

She smoothed out her skirts a final time, and left the room.

CHAPTER 9

THE SACRIFICE

It was more spectacle than wedding, but when such an event involves the most notorious nobleman in the realm, that must be expected.

Folk from all walks of life lined the streets leading to the church, eager to see the parade of fine carriages and rich clothing of those holding invitations to the event itself.

There was at first a good deal of speculation on whether or not the Church would allow the wedding to be held within its sacraments. After all, it was well known, depending on whom you spoke to, that the earl was an active worshipper of the Daughter or that he believed in Heaven and Hell not at all. In general, it could not be decided which was worse.

But when the carriage bearing the boss of the bishop of Heffield passed, there could be no doubt: the Church had, either out of coercion or of generosity and hope, sanctioned the marriage. In general, public sentiment sympathized with the bride, whom it was commonly felt must have been forced into the match by horrible and unthinkable means.

"I feel like we're in a procession," said Chryse as their carriage made its slow way down the final avenue that led to the church of St. Lucias the Fallen. She watched the crowds as the carriage inched forward, suppressing a wild fancy that she should be waving.

"And so it is, my dear." Lady Trent adjusted her gloves for the fourth time. "So are all weddings, though only the largest ones betray it so obviously." She regarded the massed faces that in their turn regarded these half-concealed forms inside the passing carriages. "Ceremony is what binds us together. Isn't that true?"

Kate yawned. "Lost again," she said to no one in particular. "I had good money riding on whether they'd approach St. Lucias's by Mexton Street or Eberton Square."

Chryse choked back a surprised laugh. "Kate! you gambled on which *street* the procession would take?" She exchanged a glance with Lady Trent, but it was only disbelieving on her side. "I hope you didn't lose much."

Kate did not reply, but she looked morose.

Lady Trent cleared her throat discreetly. "Miss Cathcart's debts are not, I believe, a proper subject for conversation on such an occasion. Miss Charity Farr looked well, don't you think?"

"Quite beautiful," agreed Chryse. "Although I still don't understand why Maretha chose to ride in that awful grand carriage rather than with her father and cousin. I would think the journey would be hard enough for her without doing it alone. I even offered to ride with her."

"It is an old custom," Lady Trent explained. "The bride, having chosen, must then make her way solitarily out of the house of her mother—the church has sanctioned the custom forever, although like the high church holidays I believe it a holdover from pagan times. But the church has always proved adaptable at absorbing those customs that folk are least likely to be willing to cast off when they embrace a new religion."

"Rather heretical of you to say so, Lady Trent," said Kate.

"Is it?" asked Lady Trent. She smiled in such a way that one could but speculate on what heresies she might have indulged in and cast off in the span of her very long life. "Tell me, Madame Lissagaray. I was curious to know who was that man you were entertaining in the parlour day before last. It quite slipped my mind, what with all the fuss."

Chryse had to think a moment before she could remember. "Oh yes!" She shook her head. Lady Trent's dresser had put her blonde hair up in a style called La Hellenika; a few light curls hung down over the shoulder of her gown. "Rather a case of mistaken identity. I thought at first he was the elder brother of one of my students. But then he seemed more interested in the expedition to Pariamne, and it was quite the oddest thing—I almost thought he was—how do you say it—just skirting the issue of whether or not I could be bribed to reveal some information about the expedition. Evidently he decided I couldn't be, for he soon excused himself and left." She shrugged, a movement copied from her husband.

"Ah." Lady Trent smiled. "I did wonder."

"What?" Chryse laughed suddenly. "About my entertaining strange men? But I'm married."

"Well," continued Lady Trent, "it *is* understood amongst our class that marriages are usually contracted for practical rather than romantic reasons. Such—ah—entertainment is neither unusual nor frowned upon, as long as it is discreet."

"Oh dear." Chryse grinned. "How exhausting. Would it be unfashionable of me to admit that ours was a—how would you call it—a love match?"

"Quite unfashionable. You must not spoil the illusion by revealing that particular fact to anyone else."

Kate laughed.

"I assure you we will attempt to be discreet," replied Chryse. "But it was a strange visit. Sanjay told me later that he had also been approached, quite openly, by an elderly man about acting as an agent, for some third party, to give them information about the expedition. So obviously someone else is interested, but not quite in an open way. Do you suppose there really is a fortune in gold there? That would explain it."

"Wherever *there* is." Lady Trent regarded Chryse thoughtfully. "Only remember to keep it in mind when you are travelling. The very word 'treasure' turns many a good soul into a bad one."

Kate laughed suddenly. "If there is a fortune in gold," she said, "perhaps I ought to go. Recoup my losses. Julian is all up in the trees to be going, now. Although he really hasn't had a direct invitation from the earl yet. But I'm sure he'd frank me. Good old chap that he is."

Lady Trent turned her shrewd gaze on the younger woman. "The earl or my nephew?"

"Bloody hell! Julian, of course."

Lady Trent smiled again at some tidbit of knowledge only she seemed aware of.

Chryse stared out the carriage window. A sea of faces stared back; not really specifically at her, but the very number of them overwhelmed her. The carriage began the long loop that led into the square fronting St. Lucias's.

Lady Trent and Kate had lapsed into an extremely disrespectful conversation regarding the possible chance of attendance by any of the royal family. Chryse considered them with half her attention. Not for the first time, she wondered how she and Sanjay could possibly find and claim a treasure that uncounted others, known and now unknown, were also seeking. A treasure that was not only more legend than fact, but one that they had only a mage's word existed at all. She sighed and wondered how Sanjay was getting on in his part in this wedding.

"Heaven help us." Julian took another sip of brandy. "I'd swear this must be foreign. Probably smuggled in from across the Channel."

"Julian," said Sanjay slowly. "Am I drinking too much or is there something moving in the fire?" He lifted one hand, palm out and open, cautionary. "Lean forward slowly and look."

"You've scarcely drunk a third of your glass." Nevertheless, Julian did as he was told. He shook his head. "Fine flames, but not a thing more. We'll have to work on your head for liquor."

But Sanjay continued to examine the fire that shot up in the large hearth. It was the eyes, really, that had caught his attention first. In the lick and spit of flame pinpoints of darkness formed and held. Eyes, peering out at him, or perhaps seeing some other sight entirely, one human eyes could not hope to see. As each pair of eyes, black and intelligent, shifted, he began to make out a form as well: here the lifting of a tiny red-gold hand, there a claw tipped with scintillations. He became aware, too, of whisperings, a hush of speech as if spoken just under the breath, blending with the snap of the fire.

All at once he saw, quite clearly, a shape curled in the embers, underlying the main flush of flame. It glowed with the same bright heat as the fire. Its long tail curled in and around itself. Brilliant eyes stared unblinking back at him.

"Bloody hell!" swore Julian suddenly. He set down his glass with an abrupt jar that jerked Sanjay's attention from the fire. "It's a damned salamander," Julian hissed. He stood up. "This whole bloody house must be infested with magic." Quick, nervous strides took him to the door where he halted, turned, and paced back to his chair. He downed the rest of his brandy in one gulp.

The salamander sat utterly still in its haven of flame. The other creatures continued to whisper and move.

"What I don't understand," said Sanjay softly so as not to disturb them, "is why the earl asked you and me to accompany him. I understand that a bridegroom customarily has two male attendants, but why us? Doesn't he have any relatives? Or old friends I don't know from growing up, from school? Surely he can't be so solitary a man that we two, scarcely two months met and with just the Pariamne expedition in common, are the closest comrades he can find?"

There was a silence. The fire whispered and crackled.

Julian finally shrugged. "Maybe we are. Who that is the worse for I can't say. I just hope he agrees to let me go along with the expedition."

"What made you decide you wanted to go?" asked Sanjay, standing up now as well and venturing closer to the fire. The salamander's tail flicked slightly, almost like a dog's tentative wag.

Julian picked up the bottle of brandy from the sideboard and considered it and his empty glass a moment. With a sigh, he set the bottle down again still stoppered. "The looming prospect of boredom," he replied. "Crossed with the usual spur of curiosity. A formidable pair."

The salamander flicked its tail again, and disappeared.

"Look," said Sanjay. "It's—No. Now they're all gone."

A noise at the door. Both men turned, a little quickly, and the door opened to admit the earl.

He was dressed so faultlessly in dark coat and trousers, brilliantly white cravat and perfect coiffure, that for a moment the costume took all attention from the utter coldness of his expression.

"Lord Vole. Monsieur Mukerji." His voice was toneless. "You honor me with your acceptance of my request."

Julian bowed.

Sanjay ventured a smile. "The honor is ours," he said with his usual good humor.

Humorless eyes turned on him, but for an instant Sanjay thought he spied an expression in them: curiosity. It lasted, however, only for a moment. "Is it?" The earl's gaze shifted to Julian, who looked uncomfortable. "Lord Vole," he said softly. "I understand you wish to accompany the expedition. I have no objections."

Julian bowed again, in acknowledgement, but did not trust himself to speak.

"Now," continued the earl, pulling on spotless white gloves. "Shall we go?"

They went outside without speaking. A silent servant opened the door into a well-made but featureless carriage, not even the Elen crest on the outside to mark its ownership.

Sanjay, last to get in, glanced back at the earl's house. In a high window, a curtain moved. He paused. A face, white and inhuman, insubstantial as a wraith's, fluttered for a moment at the glass. Vanished. So brief it could have been merely a trick of the light.

As he settled into the seat beside Julian he felt the earl's gaze on him, and turned his own to meet it. The earl's eyes reminded him quite suddenly of the void of space, absorbing all light, or perhaps concealing depths so great that light simply diffused into nothing within it.

"It is as well," said the earl quite suddenly, "that you and I are working together on this expedition, Monsieur Mukerji."

Sanjay blinked and cast the briefest of startled glances at Julian. At the same moment, he recalled the old man who had approached him just the day before with a proposal very similar to a bribe. "Are you of the opinion that another person is seeking the city and its treasure?" Sanjay asked, thinking simultaneously of Madame Sosostris.

"More than one, I don't doubt," said the earl smoothly. He tapped the front of the compartment with his cane. The carriage started forward. "But today I have more immediate matters to consider." He sat back against the cushions and shut his eyes.

Julian shrugged expressively and mouthed, to Sanjay, "Poor girl."

Sanjay raised both his hands in a gesture of helplessness, but his thoughts were not really on the "poor girl." Her fate was out of his hands. Instead, he wondered how he and Chryse were to gain the treasure for Madame Sosostris, when the earl wanted it as well. He sighed and, not for the first time, touched the pocket of his coat where he carried their deck of cards. Since the meeting with Madame Sosostris, either he or Chryse always carried it on their person. As a precaution. Against what, neither were quite sure.

She heard someone say it plainly. "Poor girl." But she willed her face to show no emotion at all as she climbed into the open carriage provided by her future husband as fitting for his bride's procession to the church.

Even here, before the modest front of Farr House, folk had gathered to stare and wonder and talk.

"Poor girl," said a different voice. It, too, faded into the crowd.

She sat still as death, hands clasped motionless in her lap, while the carriage moved off through the crowd. Against the dark wood and dark leather seats of the vehicle, the brilliant green of her dress shone like the hope of burgeoning spring, fresh shoots rising from deep soil. She repressed a shudder.

Professor Farr and Charity had gone ahead to wait for her at the church, as was fitting. The carriage, with the shuddering jerk she had not allowed herself, started forward. She stared straight ahead, willing herself to see nothing, hear nothing. She looked well, she knew that. Even Charity had admitted it, although Charity looked so beautiful in her attendant's gown that it was no great generosity of spirit for her to compliment Maretha. The gown suited her. Her hair was done in the traditional Bride's Night, an elaborate style meant for the groom's hands to unravel.

Her hands tightened on the little handbag she carried, closed on a familiar, hard shape. That alone gave her reassurance. She had had a great deal of time to think, these past weeks, on what few things the earl had said to her, and what he had not. She concentrated on her grip on the bag, as if it alone gave her the resolve to go through with the event.

The ride, the greetings from her father and Charity on the steps of the church, the procession in, the wedding itself: it all passed in a numb blur. She knew she said her own name, as she voiced the vows; what he spoke she did not hear. She could not even have recognized the bishop, though she stood scant paces away from that worthy official.

But one moment stood out with brilliant clarity: the moment they had to touch to exchange the rings of binding, of matrimony. She had never touched him before.

His hands were cold, as if the chill in his eyes permeated his entire body.

Sometime later they were at the wedding feast. She ate nothing.

Later still her father, still glowing with excitement at the prospect of his life's dream come to fruition, handed her into the closed carriage in which she would go to her new home. Bitterness swelled within her: had a young man of background and circumstances equal to her own, *her* choice of partner, been now her husband, he would have come to live in *her* home.

The flash of emotion quickly died as the earl climbed in and settled himself opposite her. She clutched her handbag.

"You look quite lovely, Maretha," he said as the door closed behind him, shuttering them in dimness. His voice was as expressionless as his black eyes.

She did not reply.

In silence they arrived at the monumental front of his town mansion. In silence the door opened to let them into the huge entry hall. It was empty of servants. He offered his arm; she had to take it. He led her up the wide stairs to the next floor. Lamps lit the broad corridor, illuminating rich paintings and thick, patterned carpets. The house bore a hush so deep that they might have been entirely cut off from the city, or drowned beneath fathoms of water.

"Your chamber." He halted before a door that opened soundlessly. "I will send someone to help you undress."

"No," she said abruptly—the first word, but for the service, that she had spoken all day. She felt with sudden certitude that she and he were the only humans in the house.

"As you wish." He relinquished her arm, gave her a stiff bow, and motioned her into the room. She went.

The door shut with a slight click behind her. She stood in a sitting room furnished with great richness and sumptuousness—couch and chairs but also a desk and behind it, a bookcase filled with the volumes she used at her father's house—ones that must have been newly purchased for her to use here. It was a kindness she thought her father incapable of, but perhaps Charity—

In the lamplight she saw a gorgeous triptych, depicting the marriage of Saint Maretha to the service of the Queen of Heaven, hanging above the fireplace. A fire burned, low and steady. Other pictures, cloaked by shadows, adorned the other walls. Across from her, a door opened.

She went, reluctantly, into the bedchamber. Bed, wardrobe, dressing table, all of the finest quality. A large window let in the glow of the moon. She walked across to it, looked down into a secluded garden, walled in. She thought she detected movement, shapes gliding along well-manicured paths, but she could not get a clear view. She sighed and turned away.

A night dress lay on the bed, laid out for her convenience. It was white, frothy with lace. She did not remember seeing it when she had entered the room. Lifting her eyes from it, she stared across at the far door—the door that would lead to the earl's suite.

She turned abruptly and walked back to the sitting room door. The handle did not move: she was locked in. She stood for what seemed an eternity, unable to act. At last, gripping her handbag, she went back to the bed and the nightdress.

She did, in truth, need help undressing, but she managed it in ungainly stages. By the low light above the dressing-table mirror, she examined herself. The nightdress fell along her body in graceful, attractive lines. The lace at the front revealed the white fairness of the top of her bosom without being immodest. What would it be like, she thought, to be awaiting a man I loved and desired?

The realization came to her with that sudden harshness that characterizes unwanted truths: I do desire him. She clenched the back of the dressing-table chair. Her reflection blurred into tears.

A noise behind her. The turn of a key.

She whirled and ran to the bed, flinging her wedding gown to the floor in her haste to find her handbag. She fumbled in it as the door opened and *he* entered.

He was brilliant in his beauty, cold as if spring and sun never warmed him. He wore an elaborately embroidered dressing gown. Gold and silver threads glittered in the lamplight.

"Maretha," he said.

She straightened, lifting her arms to aim the little pistol she had hidden in her handbag.

In the silence, the fire snapped and whispered like a thing alive. He stood perfectly still, said nothing for so long that she began to wonder if he was merely an illusion. She continued to hold the pistol on him with a steadiness that belied her fear.

"If you intend to shoot me," he said at last, "I suggest you do so."

"I will—" she began, but stopped, her voice was so hoarse. "I will hold to our agreement as husband and wife." Her voice was low and full with emotion. "In name. In everything in name. But I know a sorcerer's word bonds him, and I have never heard you say that you, *you*, want an heir."

His gaze did not waver from her face. He had not once looked at the gun. She had thought his face expressionless; now she saw it chill to some emotion much harder than before. He said nothing.

Because she had to force herself to say the next words, they came out with biting clarity. "Then never believe that I will let you touch me again."

There was a pause.

In her hands, the handle of the pistol was suddenly scorching, burning. She gasped, flinched, and dropped the gun. It landed with an empty thud on the floor.

They faced each other across the expanse of floor.

"Never believe," he said, his voice as soft as slow death by freezing, "that you can stop me, if I choose to."

"I may not be able to stop you," she breathed, "but I will fight."

"No need." His expression did not change. "You have made your choice, now. So be it."

It was a sentence, but what its terms were she did not know, knew only with piercing lucidity how completely he owned her. He drew from his pocket a key and, inserting it in the lock on her side, he left the room. The door shut behind him with quiet finality.

She ran to it and turned the key, locking him out. Went quickly to the sitting-room door. It remained locked from the outside. Went to the window, reaching for the casement latch.

A hiss, a breath of warmth, startled her. Curled on the casement lay a red-gold creature. Burning eyes regarded her, unblinking. It hissed again. The crest along its elongated neck rose. A tiny, thin tongue, almost glowing, flicked in and out of its snout.

She backed up two steps. It shifted slightly, tail arching up on one side of the window. She had an idea what it was: more lizard than miniature dragon, a creature called from fire by sorcerous means to do *his* bidding. Her guard. It stared at her with its fiery, unwavering gaze. It did not hiss again.

Maretha felt, like a weight, the sudden onset of weariness. There was nothing more she could do, prisoner in the house. She turned back to the bed, pulled back the covers, slipped in. The sheets were cold.

The lamps extinguished themselves.

She lay huddled in a darkness broken only by the low gleam of the dying fire. Awake, she listened for any sounds of the city beyond, but nothing penetrated these walls. She might as well have been alone in a chartless waste. Her feet were cold.

A rustling like paper stirred at the window. A moment later she felt a light pressure on the bed, and then warmth at her feet. The creature circled twice, nestled finally over and around her feet and ankles. Despite herself, she relaxed by imperceptible stages until finally, lulled by the creature's warmth and by a strange, tuneless humming that emanated from it, she fell asleep.

CHAPTER 10:

THE BEGGAR

"Maretha," said Chryse, looking up from the table, "are you sure you don't want some tea and cakes? You aren't eating enough."

Maretha stood at the window, staring out at the stand of trees that hid a clump of factories from the view of the inn. A pall of smoke rose behind the sparse greening of leaves. Smokestacks showed here and there from beyond the woods like huge, petrified trunks shorn of life. Closer, a few cottages huddled around the village common and its shallow pond.

"Can't be that fascinating a sight," muttered Kate when Maretha did not answer. She sat next to Chryse, shuffling the deck of Gates into different patterns on the table. "Lady Trent says this used to be beautiful country, the Midlands, before the factories."

"I worry about her." Chryse kept her voice low. "She hardly eats, and I don't think she sleeps well at night, either."

Kate turned up the Lover, placed in the middle of the wheel of cards, and gave a little snort. "Would you, with that monster in the room?"

"Shh." Chryse leaned closer to the other woman. Maretha still stared out the window, seemingly oblivious to them. One of her hands lay perfectly still on the curtains; what she watched was not apparent to the two women sitting in the little inn parlor where they had halted this late afternoon. The three of them were alone—the men off on other pursuits, Charity still up in the bedchamber she shared with Kate, presumably attending to her dress for dinner.

"I don't think," said Chryse in the barest whisper, "that the marriage has been consummated."

Kate raised one eyebrow, disbelieving. "I thought he wanted an heir," she replied in an equally quiet voice.

Chryse shrugged.

"Well." Kate swept the deck into one pile and turned up three cards one by the next. "I can't believe he has any scruples about her maidenly modesty. Now this pattern is called the Hinge. It can read the immediate future, or the central hinge of a life or work, or, if you know how to channel magic, work a spell. For instance, I could move you from one side of a room to the other. See, here it shows the Town Square and—" she paused, "well, this is a wasteland, but on the other side, the SACU side, it would be the Garden, hinged by the figure of the Beggar."

"*Move* you?" Chryse examined the three cards with immediate interest. "What do you mean?"

"Transportation," replied Kate. "I've seen it done. But short moves, like from one end of a room to the other, nothing like the distance you and Sanjay must have covered to get here from Vesputia. It depends on how much skill you have at channeling the power of the cards, and how much power your deck itself has." She looked up suddenly, examining Chryse's face. "You don't believe me, do you?"

Chryse looked a trifle sheepish. "No."

"How can you *not* believe me?" Kate set the main stack of cards aside and pushed the tea things to the far end of the table. "I don't have much skill, but these Gates are powerful. Now, let me see if I remember this." She placed her hand, palm down, over the Beggar, and shut her eyes.

"Can you only work magic through the cards?" asked Chryse.

Kate opened her eyes and frowned. "True mages, who have studied, can use their arts in ways I can't even comprehend. The Gates act as channelers, augmentation, and also help the unskilled tap into the source of power. *But*," and she shut her eyes again, "one needs to concentrate."

"Oh," Chryse grinned. "I beg your pardon." She folded her hands on her lap and waited.

Kate sat very still. Nothing happened. By the window, Maretha turned suddenly and walked back across the parlor to stand by Chryse.

"Do you see the runes on the cards?" she said in a low voice. Chryse bent forward to look. "There, in the Town Square, you can see what we would call the consonant 'F', hidden in the panelling in that doorway."

"Oh, I see."

"I believe," continued Maretha, "that those runes, our letters now, are direct descendents of the writing of the Pariamne culture, although they would have had different values, different connotations, then. Unless my personal theory that the Gates themselves are also a relic from that time proves true. There is one tale in the Sais legends that explains how she bound power into the cards in an effort to save the city, which corroborates my idea, although one can't take old myths as an accurate guide. But I'm doing some work to correlate the runes and the symbology embodied in each card as a way of translating the written language fragments that we have recovered."

"Between the two of you," said Kate, opening her eyes, "it is impossible to focus my mind at all."

"Here." Chryse leaned forward. "Let me try." She placed her hand over The Town Square. "Now what am I supposed to do?"

Kate removed her hand from the central card. "Concentrate on the essence of the card. That's why those who study magic are much more successful."

"Well," said Chryse, "since I have no expectation of success, I won't be disappointed."

Kate rolled her eyes, but said nothing.

Chryse lifted her hand to look at the card once again: a few buildings, a common green, a pond—the medieval version of the village they were in at this moment. Embedded in the fine tracery of the inn door's panelling she made out a letter-like figure 'F'.

Shutting her eyes, she tried to concentrate on the inn itself, the room they were in now, but her thoughts kept wandering back to that rune. She thought of faces in the windows of the buildings, of flowers growing up on the grass of the common, of the fluidity of the water in the pond.

That image stuck with her, the gentle lap of water on a gradual shore, the heavy lulling swell of deeper water, the smoothness of the water itself— She began to feel as if she could not catch her breath, as if she were running up a steep hillside or swimming many strokes.

A sudden gasp from Maretha startled her out of her concentration, and she opened her eyes.

Kate was gone.

Chryse looked up at Maretha. Maretha ran to the window and, with no warning, began to laugh. Chryse followed her.

There, in the middle of the village pond, sat Kate, immersed up to her shoulders. As they watched, she stood up. The water came over her knees.

By the time Chryse and Maretha arrived on the green, Kate had slogged her way out of the water and stood dripping and bedraggled on the grass that edged the pond. Her sodden clothes clung to her body. Chryse and Maretha, coming up to her, could not stop laughing, although they tried.

"Bloody hell," swore Kate. Her coat, perfectly tailored, now stuck to her in creases. "I've never been so surprised in my life."

"Oh, dear." Chryse wiped a tear from her cheek. "I'm terribly sorry. I had no idea it would work. Oh, Kate, you do look funny."

"Thank you," replied Kate with a grand bow. Water dripped into puddles around her boots. She laughed. "Now I understand why I was the kind of child who was always getting broken bones and burns and bruises. However did you do it, Chryse?"

Chryse could only shrug, helpless. "I don't know. I'm still not sure I believe it. Are you sure you didn't just run out here while my eyes were shut and throw yourself in?"

Kate shook her head. "It isn't a matter of belief," she said, serious now. "It just is."

"We'd better go in," said Maretha. "People are staring."

A few villagers had, indeed, gathered near the inn to look. But Chryse, touched by an instinct she could not name, looked only briefly at them. Instead she turned toward the wood that separated the village from the hulks of the factories. A path emptied onto the far side of the green between two cottages. A small figure stood there, poised on the edge of the trees.

"I would swear," said Chryse slowly, "that I recognize that—" She began to walk away from the other two.

"Chryse!" Maretha called after her.

By its stature, it was a child, clothed in tatters, a little cap askew on its dark-curled head. Chryse went across the green as if drawn, vaguely aware of Maretha and Kate following in her wake. She knew she would see the pointed face and bright eyes before she was close enough to recognize them.

"Penny for a poor child," it squeaked as she neared, then backed away as if it feared her presence.

"You recognize me, don't you?" said Chryse.

The child retreated. "Just a penny," it repeated. Its dark eyes glittered like glass catching the light of the sun.

"Chryse." Kate's voice, behind her. "I'm sopping wet. If you stop to interview every beggar child between here and our destination, I'll never get changed."

The child retreated up the path into the wood. Chryse followed.

"How on earth did you follow us here?" Chryse was walking faster now but coming no closer to the child. "I don't believe this is chance."

The child turned and ran. Chryse hiked up her skirts, gripping them tightly in one hand, and pursued.

"Chryse!" Maretha cried from behind, but Chryse was intent on her quarry.

She lost sight of the urchin once in a dim patch in the middle of the wood, but a glimpse of cloth, a quick movement, caught her attention and she ran again. By the time she came out of the wood she was out of breath and had to stop.

The child, halfway down a long slope, paused to look back up at her. But Chryse's attention had gone past the urchin, focussing on the ugliest building she had ever seen.

It was a huge, hulking block. Tiny windows pierced dark walls in layers, demarcating three stories. Smokestacks jutted upward at all corners, spouting fumes and dark smoke into an already overcast sky. A high, grim fence encircled the vast structure. A single gate, one carriage wide, allowed access. In bold, iron letters over the archway, she read: *Crudebelch's Mattress Works.*

The child ran down to the fence, slipped through a gap in the metal railings, and disappeared through a tiny door into the interior.

"What in bloody hell!" Kate startled Chryse as she came up beside her. "What was that all about?"

"I'm going after that child." Chryse started down the slope. "I saw that child twice in Heffield. It can't be coincidence to see it here, too."

"Good Lady," swore Kate, squelching along behind her. "You're not going in *there*, are you? I hope Maretha finds the men soon. I think you've gone off your head."

"I think," Chryse muttered as they came down to the gap in the fence, "that I've been dreaming a very long and complicated dream for the last four months. Can you squeeze through here?"

"Why should I want to? Chryse, respectable gentle-women do not traipse unescorted through factories."

"Kate, I only see you and me here. Come on."

Much struck by this point, Kate followed without a word.

The ground surrounding the factory was red clay, packed down by much traffic, though now they saw no one at all. Behind the building, winding away into a hazy distance of fields and woods, lay a small river. A constant racket swelled from the factory in counterpoint to the fumes spewing out above.

"I'll never get clean," said Kate cheerfully as dust dulled the black sheen of her bootleather. "And my skin's begin ning to chafe."

"You can go back." Chryse stopped in front of the door through which the child had disappeared. Heavy iron bands ribbed the stained and cracked wood; the door hung slightly ajar.

"And miss an adventure? Oh, no."

Chryse, with her hand on the door, paused. "Are there trespassing laws here?"

Kate regarded Chryse for a moment with a puzzled look. "Some upstart mushroom of a factory owner wouldn't dare charge you or me with any crime. And if they did dare, the appearance on the scene of a peer of the realm would—" She moved her hand across her throat in a cutting, final gesture.

"Oh, yes." Chryse pushed the door slowly open. "I'd forgotten about that."

They stepped into a vast cavern of a room crowded with dozens of square machines twice human height. Chryse's first sensation was of overwhelming heat. Her second, of an incessant racket of moving parts that in a strange juxtaposition of sense drowned out, obliterated, the human figures who worked beneath and around the machines. For a long moment she simply stared. Beside her, Kate swore, seemingly under her breath, though for all the noise she might well have been shouting.

"This way," shouted Chryse, pulling Kate to the left.

They hurried down an aisle of machines. Men, women, and children stood hunched over clacking teeth and huge webs of tight fabric. Sweat shone on thin faces, trickled down bare arms, pooled in stains around bare feet. The din made by the machines made speech impossible.

At the end of the aisle a door shut slowly, as if someone had just gone through, leaving it to swing closed. Chryse tugged Kate to it.

They entered a second room, larger than the first. As the door shut behind them the noise level dropped, but it was also, as if to compensate, considerably hotter. Chryse felt sweat begin to permeate the back of her dress.

Huge structures, like looms, filled the room floor to ceiling. There were no windows, only flickering, sooty gaslight to illuminate the work. Women with drooping shoulders ran bolts of thick thread across the fronts of the machines. Higher up, hidden behind growing nets of fabric, smaller figures could be seen, like ghosts moving amongst the workings.

"This is awful," said Chryse.

Not fifty feet from them, a slender girl swayed and fell in a faint at the base of her work station. The girls on either side of her looked hurriedly around and dragged her back up, shaking her until her eyes opened again. The loom clattered on, and thread began to tangle.

A shout, and a broad-shouldered, hairy man appeared at the end of the aisle.

"Come on," Kate said.

"But that girl—"

"*Come on.*"

They hurried to the next aisle, and the next.

"There!" cried Chryse. A tiny figure in tattered clothes scurried away up one of the aisles. They followed, though there was scarcely enough room between the workers, the machines were crowded so closely together, to squeeze through.

The room seemed to stretch on forever, aisles branching into dimmer aisles of massive cacophanous machinery that dwarfed the fragile human figures tending it.

"I'm lost," said Kate eventually.

Chryse stopped, panting. She was now as thoroughly soaked as Kate looked in those places where the cloth of her dress touched her body. Swatches of her skirt clung to her legs. "This is a maze. How do these people find where they work? There!"

And they were off again, coming at last to a far wall and a door, ajar.

"I hope you know where you're going," said Kate as Chryse laid a hand on the doorlatch.

"No," admitted Chryse. "But I have a distinct feeling someone else does."

They came into a hall. It was empty, narrow, and dark, seeming tomblike and cold in contrast to the room before. It led straight on into dimness. Torches hung at long intervals along the wall, but they gave off little light. There was no sign of the beggar child.

Chryse shrugged, starting forward. "There is only one way."

The hall seemed to extend forever, as if it pierced a straight line into the heart of the factory. Their footsteps scarcely sounded on the hard floor.

At last the corridor branched to the right and ended in a small door. Chryse unlatched it and pushed it open.

They came into a small chamber, silent except for the labored breathing of four children chained to a block of metal embedded in the center of the room. Tubes led out from it in four directions, like the vessels of a mechanical heart.

Each child perched on a high stool on one side of the block, bent over a flat surface where they laid down and picked up in an unceasing circle the cards of a deck of Gates. With their cropped hair and emaciated faces, it was impossible to tell whether they were boys or girls. One was not even human: it had the pointed face of the Heffield urchin, but its eyes, like the other children's, had the dull languor of terminal illness. The youngest of the children could not have been more than five. Each bore, on its right ankle, a manacle appended to a chain that fastened into the metal square.

"Bloody damned heaven and hell," swore Kate in an undertone. In the hush of the room, the oath startled Chryse. She turned.

Kate was white, her expression appalled. "I heard rumors, but I never believed—"

She rushed forward suddenly and swept the cards out from in front of the nearest child. They rained in a spattering fall to the floor. The child shuddered and slumped forward into a faint. An ominous rumbling sounded, far away.

"Kate!"

"Don't you see what they're doing?" cried Kate, circling the block to the next child. "They're using the Gates to suck the life from these children in order to power the factory!" She cleared the cards from in front of the child with a single, violent stroke of one arm. This child, too, fainted.

The third child, the youngest, faltered and paused, its eyes lifting to stare at Kate. The great block of metal, a deep, reddish-copper color, faded abruptly several shades darker, and an obvious pulse began to run through the tubes that lanced out from it. The fourth child labored on, oblivious. Chryse stared. The rumbling increased.

Kate went to the third child and pulled it from its stool. It grasped her tightly and began to whimper. She pulled a small knife from her pocket and hacked at the manacle.

"There are keys on the wall," said Chryse abruptly, and she started forward.

"Stop the last one," said Kate.

"Let's undo the others first." But she paused by the fourth child. It was working feverishly now, eyes sunk in, face far too pale, attention focussed utterly on the wheel of the cards: the slight *tick* of each card as it was placed corresponding exactly to the strained breathing.

And above it, almost inaudible, a whisper.

"Help me."

Chryse looked around.

"Help me."

She looked up.

Directly above the center of the block a grate had been set into the ceiling. Two slender hands gripped the metal lacing. A face, a youth, a boy with a visage that might have been that of an angel peering down from on high, stared down at her.

"Where are those keys?" demanded Kate from the floor.

The tubes pulsed more strongly now, in time to the fourth child's gasping breath. The rumbling sounded louder. In the distance, muffled by doors and length of hallway, Chryse heard voices, shouting alarm.

"I'm being held prisoner," whispered the boy. "Please help me."

CHAPTER 11:

THE PAGE

The heart of the factory shuddered and beat to the labored rhythm of a small child's breathing as Chryse stared up at the face above her.

"The keys!" Kate's hiss, full of an anger that was not directed at her, shocked Chryse into action.

She ran to the wall where the heavy ring of keys dangled from a hook, far out of the reach of the children bolted to the metal block in the center of the room. Grabbing them off their hook, she hurried back to Kate and knelt beside her.

"There's so many." Chryse chose one at random. It didn't fit.

"By direction," said the youth from behind the grate. "They're each set to a compass point."

"Kate?" asked Chryse.

"Of course!" said Kate. "Give me the keys. There are runes." She took them, studied each one. The child still clung to her. "Do you remember the layout here?" she asked. "Ah, here's one."

"Haven't a clue." Chryse glanced at the four doors. "But they'll be here any moment."

"You're east," said the youth from above. "I remember that much."

"Yes." With a deft twist, Kate unlocked the manacle. It dropped away and struck the floor with a high, hollow sound. The child stopped weeping, and when Kate extricated herself from its grasp and stood, it simply sat and stared about with a bewildered expression.

Kate quickly unlocked the two children who had fainted.

As soon as the manacles separated from their ankles, they began to stir weakly.

"Here." Chryse reached for the keys. "I'm taller. I'll unlock the grate."

"Above," said Kate. "Heaven's rune." She paused and stared up, getting her first good look at the youth. "Good Lady," she swore. "A vision. Heaven, indeed. Here."

Chryse climbed up on the block. Touching it, she felt a humming throb course through her, as though the metal were indeed alive. The fourth child labored on, but its breathing grew more ragged.

The grate unlocked at four spots, lowered off. Kate had climbed up beside Chryse, and together they helped the youth get down. He was slender, in their hands, but unlike the others' it was a natural slimness, not emaciation. He stood just a hair shorter than Kate. His eyes, this close, had the brilliancy of the midday sky.

"Bloody hell." Kate stared at him.

One of the doors opened. A man and a woman, burly, broad-faced people, stepped into the room.

"Back the way we came," cried Kate, jumping down to face them.

"But which door—" Chryse shook her head and scrambled over to the last child. She kicked the cards into disarray as she climbed down beside it. "Damn! I don't know which key—"

A hand touched hers. "Let me," said the boy.

"—and I'll have you know," Kate was saying in a loud, bluff voice that echoed strong and ringing in the chamber. There was no other sound; the metal block had ceased to beat the instant the last cards were scattered, and a thick hush shuttered them. "—that we are protected by a peer of the realm. Lay hands on me, and you'll hang for it."

The man and woman hesitated, whispering, and the woman backed up and ran out the door they had entered.

A bell began to ring, a harsh, insistent clamor.

The fourth child, freed from the manacle by the youth, still sat on its stool, its hands, empty of cards, continuing to deal them out in a circle of air as though it were unable to stop. Chryse grasped it by the shoulders and jerked it to its feet. It stood, limp, blank-faced, hands still moving.

The youngest of the children was now standing and ran quickly to the snout-faced child.

"Come on, Pin," its tiny voice cried. "Got to gets up."

Kate was backing up slowly.

"Can you carry this one?" asked Chryse of the youth. The sound of shouting came suddenly nearer, too fast. She did not wait for the youth's assent but hurried to the last child, picking it up. It was shockingly, horrifyingly light.

"Not that door," said the youth from behind her as she gathered up the child called Pin as well. "Here, take my hand," he added, a strange aside until she realized that he spoke to the smallest child. "This door." Carrying her two burdens with precious little effort, Chryse followed him. "I think," he finished, but they were at the door.

It opened easily and a long hallway, lit with torches, stretched out before them—empty, silent.

"Kate!" cried Chryse.

Kate turned and bolted for the door. The man dashed after her and, in the instant Kate passed through the opening and they threw the door shut, more people entered the room, an amorphous group surrounding a huge, broad-shouldered figure. His roar reverberated, shuddering through them, until the slam of the door cut its volume in half.

"It's got a lock! Chryse, help me hold it shut." Kate flung herself against the door, bracing. The youth let go of the child's hand and fumbled at the keys. Chryse set down her two children and stationed herself next to Kate, gripping the door handle.

They felt the impact of many people. The handle clicked and began to turn. Chryse strained against it.

"Kate!" she gasped.

The youth fumbled with the keys, trying one after the next. Kate grasped the handle, but it continued to turn, inexorable.

"The one with the sign of the road," said the smallest child, suddenly. "That's what you wants." A snuffling sounded on the floor. "Here, Pin," the tiny voice continued, seemingly oblivious to Kate and Chryse struggling to keep the door closed and the youth examining each key with urgent keenness. "Don't cry, mittens. We'll be right fine now."

"Got it!" The youth's cry was triumphant. The key turned with a satisfying click in the lock, and with it a second roar shook the door.

"Lord." Chryse gathered up Pin and another child. "What was that?"

"That'll be Crudebelch," piped the small child, trotting alongside the youth and Chryse. Kate brought up the rear, dislodging each torch as they passed so that the lights guttered out on the floor to leave the length of hall behind in darkness. Shouts and pounding faded as they moved forward.

"But what an awful sound," said Chryse, puffing a little.

"Well, yes," replied the child, quite matter-of-fact. "But he's an ogre."

"Clearly." Chryse nodded. "Any man would be, imprisoning you here like that. Lord!"

"Now where?" The youth had reached the end of the hall. Three doors offered exit.

"Bloody hell." Kate came up with the last two torches, one in each hand. The hall lay in blackness behind, the darkness like a cloak muffling sound.

"Where do you wants to go?" asked the child in its tiny voice.

"Out," said Chryse. "Out of this place."

"Oh," said the child, as if this possibility had never occurred to it. "Out!" It glanced up, awe-struck, at the blonde woman. Dark eyes examined Chryse as if she were a saint made flesh. "Out! Hear that, Pin!" The snout-faced child stirred in Chryse's arms with a weak reply that sounded more like a squeak than words. "Bless Her lady." The child pointed to the middle door. "Then we wants that way."

Kate breathed a deep sigh of relief. "Good girl," she said as the youth started forward to open the designated door.

"Boy," retorted the child. "I'm a boy. Name's Mog. Pin here's a girl, though."

"Come on," hissed the youth, impatient.

They entered a vast storeroom. Piles of rough fabric lay heaped in long rows that stretched out to the ends of the room. The tones of the bell, still insistent, clamored around them; otherwise the place was silent.

"You're our scout, Mog," said Kate. She still held the two torches. "Get us out of here."

He skipped on ahead of them. Chryse attempted a jog behind him, but the two children, however thin, weighed more and more heavily in her arms. The youth panted along beside her, Kate in the rear.

Mog led them into a second storeroom, this one lined with row upon row of mattresses, each neatly stacked atop the next. "Along here." He pointed to a row of double doors at the far end, clearly enjoying himself.

They had not reached the doors when the sounds of many people in pursuit burst into the room behind them. The bell's loud ringing tolled above, accompanying the cries and a low, rushing sound that grew louder as they neared the end of the room.

"Damn," swore Kate as two people rounded a corner of mattresses and, spying them, began to shout for reinforcements. She looked abruptly at the torches in her hands and stopped.

"Kate!" Chryse and the others had reached the first set of double doors and Chryse set down the now-struggling Pin to help Mog and the youth tug one open. Kate had moved away from them, back toward the pursuers, but she halted by the closest stack of mattresses and thrust the torches into it. One faded, smoldering, but the flames of the second began to lick at the coarse fabric.

A party of some ten people appeared, running towards them.

"Kate!"

Now Kate responded to Chryse's cry, turning to dash for the doors.

"Lady!" she gasped as she came into the space.

They stood on a long wooden platform that sided a small canal. Water rippled alongside, jostling boats. At one end a waterwheel pushed around and around, drowning out the noise of alarm behind. At the other:

Light, and a door open to the outside; the stream burbled out beside it through a great culvert in one wall.

"Run!" cried Kate.

They ran. Kate paused to grab a pair of long poles with boathooks attached to the ends, but caught up easily with the others. Chryse waved the youth through the outside door first, followed him, herding the two conscious children before her. But Kate, coming up behind, collided with her as she pulled up short. The youth cried out in fear and surprise.

" 'Cor," said Mog, more resigned than afraid. "We're in for it now."

About a dozen sour-faced persons, armed with thick staffs and knobbly cudgels, advanced slowly towards them on their left, along the fence perimeter.

"Hell," Kate muttered under her breath, the more vehement for its softness.

"No, wait!" cried Chryse. "They're not going for us. Look!"

" 'Cor," said the unperturbable Mog. "Nobs."

"Sanjay!" Chryse yelled. She waved one hand wildly.

"Bless that woman," said Kate, and she too began to shout. "Julian! Julian, you deaf idiot, look over here."

And he did. He and Sanjay and Thomas Southern stood just inside the fence some ways down and to their right. Julian had a pistol and Southern a shovel. Sanjay was unarmed. The factory party on the left hesitated, unsure now of what action to take. The three men quickly ran toward the factory, avoiding the larger group. "Thank God," said Chryse as Sanjay stopped beside her. "Don't ask. We've got to get these kids out of here."

"Now see here." Julian's voice was loud and commanding. "You had better get the owner here before you attempt anything violent. I am Lord Vole, and I assure you I will have you prosecuted—"

"Not bloody likely if you're bloody well dead," growled one of the burly men. He lifted his cudgel in a hairy hand. "We've our orders, from the top—beating first, talk later—if there's any left."

Julian shot him. The crack of the report shattered through the air, and with a cry the man fell, writhing, to the ground.

"Kate," added Julian companionably, keeping his pistol raised as he drew a new slug and a small powder flask from the pocket of his spotless jacket. "What *have* you gotten into this time? I suggest we all retreat inside."

"Julian," began Kate.

"The boats," said Chryse.

Thomas Southern picked up Pin, balancing the shovel in his other hand.

"Boats?" asked Julian, pressing the others back through the door onto the dock.

"Of course." Kate caught Sanjay's eye. "Here." She

handed him a boathook. "You'll need it. Pursuit behind as well."

They turned to see a smaller party gathered at the far end of the docks.

"Good." Sanjay scanned the boats that lay tied up along one side of the wooden platform. "They think they've cornered us. Get the children in one of the boats."

They backed up until they stood at the edge of the dock. Both parties facing them now hesitated, as if waiting for some signal or some one.

"Get them in." Sanjay held the boathook like a pike, the hooked end out in front of him. Julian had reloaded his pistol and stood now beside Kate. Thomas Southern put Pin down and balanced the shovel in both hands. Chryse set down the child she held and climbed into the largest boat, reaching back to receive the child the youth held.

In her arms, this child lay completely inert, as limp as cloth. She caught her breath, seeing no breath at all, but she laid it down gently in the bottom of the boat and stood up to take the second child, this one stirring slightly. Mog and Pin, both tiring now, Pin trembling, she helped into the boat as well. She looked up to see the smaller of the two factory parties closing in.

From the next boat, moored beside the one they now occupied, she grabbed the oars and thrust one into the hands of the youth.

Julian fired. The shot hit a woman in front, who staggered and cried out, but the others hesitated only a moment before they rushed in.

Sanjay thrust the first one right in the abdomen, the hard metal curve of the boathook knocking the man's breath out. He bent double, gasping. Kate's aim was not as good, and now she grappled, the pole held like a quarterstaff in front of her, with one of the others. Thomas Southern lay about himself with the shovel, holding off three while Julian struggled to reload his pistol. The youth waited, uncertain, grasping the oar in one hand. More of the factory people closed in.

"Get in the boat," yelled Chryse, clambering out and shoving the lad into the vessel. He tripped, dropping the oar on the dock, and stumbled in beside the children.

" 'Cor," piped young Mog, eyeing this disturbance with great interest. "Just wait 'til the guvnor gets here."

Sanjay snaked his pole between Kate and her adversary and with a strong tug hooked the man and jerked him off his feet. The man screamed. Blood seeped from his shirt where the hook had sunk in.

"Sanjay!" cried Chryse. She swung her oar at the woman advancing on her husband. He battled the man on the floor, trying to dislodge the hook. The oar felled the woman with a blow to her head, but another followed behind her. Sanjay got his hook loose and struck at her companion.

Kate had turned slightly to join Southern as he fended off his attackers. Julian, as he finished reloading, picked up the fallen oar and aimed his pistol.

A roar, huge and penetrating, shook the melee to a brief halt, like an instant's freeze into a tableau.

"Bloody hell," swore Julian, looking beyond Kate and Thomas to the figure approaching them from the double doors.

"Told you," said Mog, undisturbed by the fact that no one but a shivering Pin was paying him any mind.

The youth went dead pale and began to untie the boat with trembling hands, getting the rope tangled with those of the next boat. "Help me!" he cried, and Mog quickly went to aid him.

"Get in the damn boat!" shouted Julian.

The factory people began to back away.

"Dear Lady," breathed Thomas Southern.

Chryse and Sanjay turned. Chryse gasped.

"Get in the boat," hissed Julian, grabbing Southern's arm and pushing him towards the vessel. It was completely untied now, and a thin line of water grew between it and the dock. "Kate!"

The largest person Chryse had ever seen was striding towards them, mouth open. A roar so loud it seemed to shake the floor itself burst out of—him? A shock of unruly hair, coarse and thick as rope, crowned the head of a creature fully one meter taller than herself. Its face seemed horribly scarred, until she realized that that was its natural visage. It used one huge hand, tipped with yellow nails as sharp as claws, to shove aside those workmen who impeded its path.

"Good Lord," she gasped. "I thought what Mog said was just a figure of speech."

"Chryse!" Kate's voice.

Chryse turned her head. Kate was in the boat, children huddled at her feet. Julian straddled, one foot in, one out, barely able to hold the boat, which was rocking unsteadily with the waves, against the dock.

The ogre roared. Behind him he dragged a burning mattress. Like a discus, he flung it at the boat, but Sanjay struck at the bulk as it passed above him and it struck the edge of the next boat instead, setting up a heavy wash of water. Julian tumbled backwards, and their boat separated from the dock and drifted off into the current.

"Chryse!" Kate tossed her boathook towards the dock. Chryse dropped her oar and caught it, turning.

Sanjay, pole out, was facing down the ogre.

"Get in the boat, Chryse," he said, retreating step by slow step.

The ogre charged. A shot, wild, from Julian's pistol.

Sanjay sidestepped and swept at the creature's face with the hook, scoring a cut down the side of its cheek. It roared, stumbled, and turned ponderously around.

"Behind you!" cried Chryse, and parried a blow meant for Sanjay's head. She thrust at the man wielding the weapon, missed, but forced him two steps back.

"A second boat's loose," Kate shouted, and then the first boat was swept out beyond the wall by the current. About ten of the factory hands ran outside, following.

"Straight back," Chryse called to Sanjay, seeing now the boat that had drifted loose from its mooring.

The ogre charged. Sanjay sidestepped again, but his sweep, grazing the ogre's side, caught in the tough hide, and the creature grabbed the pole. They grappled. Sanjay was lifted off his feet entirely; he hung, dangling, in the air. Chryse chopped her boathook repeatedly into the side of the ogre's head, but it seemed to have no effect on him at all.

Then Sanjay kicked, twisted, and was free. The pole snapped, and the ogre flung it at him, striking his shoulder.

"The boat!" yelled Sanjay, one hand holding his injured shoulder.

Chryse jumped into the vessel and began to push it away from the dock. The ogre, face contorted with rage, roared again and stamped. The entire dock shuddered, as if an earthquake shook it. Sanjay fell backward into the water. He flung out his arms and grabbed the edge of the boat just as the current caught it.

The ogre, with a deep growl, leaped into the water after them, but the wash created by his mass picked up the boat and, with Sanjay clinging desperately to the wood, pushed it speedily out the culvert. They were far past the factory wall by the time Sanjay had, with Chryse's help, dragged himself on board.

On the bank about twenty people ran, pointing and gesturing. The ogre appeared in the doorway. Water pooled off him. Ahead, the stream widened and branched into two channels. The first boat was already in the left hand channel.

"Sanjay," said Chryse softly as the current pulled them to the right. "We haven't got any oars."

CHAPTER 12:

THE MASTER OF WATERS

Julian and Kate waved at them, but there was nothing they could do. The current dragged them on, and the boat began to turn around in the water, like a sluggish top.

Already they had lost sight of the other channel. The factory receded until only its smokestacks, fumes a mere trickle now, were visible. The current grew stronger, pulling them inexorably towards some unseen goal. The boat steadied finally into a slow turning pattern, and Chryse moved to kneel beside Sanjay.

"Are you hurt?" She kissed him and reached to touch with tender solicitude his shoulder.

He winced. "Just a bruise. What was that thing?"

"I think it was an ogre."

Sanjay could not reply for a moment. On the banks, woods and fields and pastures dotted with sheep drifted past them. "I had to ask," he said finally. He eyed the water and the bank. "I told you we should have taken up canoeing."

"Can we reach those trees with the boathook?" she asked. She balanced herself carefully at one side, but although it was only a small river, about thirty feet wide, the current carried them along briskly just out of pole's reach of the shore.

"We might as well drift awhile before we swim for it, get away from the factory." He leaned forward and embraced her. They stayed for a bit in this reassuring position.

"Chryse," he said at last, into her ear. "Why were you in there? Where did those children come from? Julian and I were in the stables, and Maretha had found Southern in

132

the inn—and she said—" He pulled a little away from her. "I'm very confused."

"So am I," said Chryse, "but I'll attempt to explain." She did so, recounting the events that had led them there. The boat rocked and turned like a slowly spinning cradle. "It's hard to believe what Kate said, using the Gates like that," she finished. "That dealing out that constant circle allowed the factory to actually run on those children's life force. Like draining their souls for energy."

"It's one of the things they say the earl does, to get his power. I don't know."

She sighed and hugged him tightly against her. "I'm just glad Maretha found you. Where is she?"

He gave her a weak smile. "She went to find the weapon of last resort."

"Oh," said Chryse, and then she giggled. "I'd like to see him face down that creature. I'll bet he wouldn't change expression one least bit. I don't think anything can break his composure."

"I beg your pardon," protested Sanjay, "if you feel I wasn't adequate to the purpose."

She smiled. "My sweet, you're *always* adequate to the purpose." Kissed him again.

The boat began to turn more quickly, with the rocking more pronounced. Now, in the distance, a low humming grew, sounding like the rush of wind at first, and building in volume and intensity.

They broke apart.

"Chryse—"

"Sanjay—"

They stared at each other. The river rushed them along. The noise grew louder, and, simultaneously, each knew that the other suspected the same thing: rapids.

"Swim for it," said Sanjay.

The boat jerked, throwing them both to the floorboards, and began to spin wildly. A hard, abrupt curve in the river kept them pressed to the bottom of the vessel, where they clung, attempting at once to gain the edge of the boat and yet to keep their grip on the thwart. The roaring of the river filled the air around them, and as they lifted themselves up, the boat hit the rapids.

They were both flung down again, Chryse hard enough to take her breath away, Sanjay directly on his bruised shoulder. The boat jerked and bucked and tilted high up, first to one side than the other. Water slapped over the side, wetting them.

"We'll have to ride it out," cried Sanjay.

Chryse began to nod, stopped. The noise of the rapids surrounded them, spray tipping off from the bow, but a lower, more ominous sound grew underneath the race of surging water. Even as their grips on the struts tightened, the bucking eased, but the vessel continued to pick up speed. They were being drawn as on the end of a string. She pushed herself up.

The world dropped away. It was the briefest of moments, poised on the brink. It seemed an eternity.

She cried out. Sanjay shouted her name. The trees ended around them, only to begin again below—far below.

And they plunged down. The boat was, mercifully, lost almost immediately. Surrounded, immersed, in water, she felt that she fell forever. Spray hissed and hung around her. She tried to twist her body, to absorb the impact of the pool beneath, but when she struck the water at the base of the falls, she blacked out.

Drowning was a strange sensation, like a waking dream. She felt the water close over her, that initial slap fading into a gentle caress. It was like a thing alive, comforting and safe. Some part of her knew that she would drown, that though her mind could function her body could not, like lying in bed in the early morning aware but not yet awake. Some part of her told herself *not* to take a breath, while another struggled to gasp.

She sank, and hands took her and gentled her as she descended. Not real hands, not Sanjay's or some other rescuer's, but fluid, mobile hands, like her brief vision of water when she had accidentally used the Gates to cast Kate into the village pond. She felt, abruptly, no urge to breathe at all, as if by some spell her lungs had refilled with oxygen of their own. The deep boil of the pool's water seemed to part before her, and she saw the shore approaching, a long, velvet strand of grass.

She slid onto it gently, felt a haze alternately rising and falling before her eyes. She thought she saw a figure, almost translucent, but as perfectly formed as any supernatural youth, standing before her—heard it speak a single word, and descend with fluid grace back into the pool, dis-

solving into spray along his skin, edged in rainbows. She
sank her head onto the soft grass and passed out.

"Chryse!" The voice shocked her awake. A hand, warm
but hard, shook her, and she coughed and lifted her head.

"Sanjay!" she cried, remembering, and sat up.

"Easy." It was Julian, pushing her back down. "He's
alive, and looking as drowned as you. By Our Lady," He
crouched now, laying an arm around her back to support
her as she gasped to regulate her breathing. "I can't believe you're both alive."

"Why—" She looked up and caught her breath.

The pool stretched out before her, placid here, but
foaming at its far end under the force of water falling from
a height of at least two hundred feet. Lapping at the
stretch of beach on which she lay were the splintered
remains of the boat, planks and struts in single boards and
shattered lacings.

For a long while she simply stared. Behind her she
heard, like a reassuring echo of the fall's roar, Sanjay's
voice as he spoke to someone else. Julian's arm remained
firmly about her.

"I had the strangest—" She broke off and shook her
head.

"The strangest what?" asked Julian, quiet.

"Never mind. Let me try to stand up."

He helped her, solicitous, and she turned to see Sanjay
sitting between Kate and Thomas Southern some way
around the pool. The river itself seemed to vanish in this
pool, as if swallowed by the earth.

Sanjay saw her. He, too, stood up, and they met halfway. When they embraced, the others looked away
discreetly.

"Do you remember anything?" she asked as she held on
to him. Their sodden clothes seemed to fuse together.

"No. I don't even remember hitting the water. I woke
up on the grass." She felt him shake his head, disbelieving. "Do you—"

"No, I just—" She paused. "No." Just hallucinations,
she thought, and she chuckled weakly, holding to him.
Just a vision of an impossibly perfect youth, not quite a
man, who stood protectively and lovingly over her and
called her "mother." "No," she finished, pulling away

from him. "I'm just glad we're both alive." She turned to the others. "How did you find us?"

Behind Southern she saw the five children they had freed from the factory. The youth stood, boathook in one hand, like a guardian angel over the others.

"We beached the boat," Julian replied, "on the opposite shore, and cut through the woods. Southern seems to think the road lies in this direction."

"I'm sure of it," said Southern sharply, with a brief glance at Lord Vole. "My lord," he added as an obvious afterthought, but Julian had gone over to the children.

Sanjay stripped off his coat and wrung it tightly to get rid of the excess water. "Then we'd better go." As if on cue, a dog barked in the distance, accompanied by a shout and an answering hail.

Julian and Kate had already each picked up one of the unconscious children and were heading into the woods on the far side of the pool. Mog and Pin trotted gamely after them, Pin lagging behind until Thomas Southern came up beside her and lifted her up into his arms. Sanjay picked up the protesting Mog, leaving Chryse to bring up the rear with the youth.

She paused at the edge of the clearing and looked back. The pool was bathed in the mild glow of late afternoon sun. The debris of the boat floated on the water as if a hand had flung it there. The falls shimmered; at the center the water seemed almost to coalesce into an insubstantial being.

"Thank you," she whispered, and then, embarrassed at herself, she hurried on to catch up, falling in beside the youth.

"What's your name?" she asked as they made their way through the underbrush.

He hacked at bushes with the boathook. "Lucias, ma'am," he answered.

"Wasn't he a saint?" she asked.

"Yes, ma'am." He flashed her a brilliant smile, fair as the dawn. "Fallen from grace because of his vanity at his own beauty, but redeemed by Our Lord in His mercy."

"I see." Chryse suppressed a smile.

Kate dropped back to walk beside them. The child in her arms stirred weakly and grunted, a tiny noise, at each step. "'Are you making the acquaintance of our escaped prisoner?" she asked. "Quite an appropriate name, Lucias, don't you think?" She grinned, gazing at the lad with undisguised appreciation.

"I'm afraid I'm not familiar with the story, Kate," Chryse said quickly, seeing that the boy was blushing under Kate's scrutiny. "But tell me, Lucias, why were you locked up there?"

He looked troubled. "I don't know, ma'am. Truly." He shook his head, frowning. He had rich, blond hair that tumbled in waves to his shoulders. "I feel that I should, but I don't."

A shout from ahead. They had found the road. It bent off into curves on either side, screened by trees.

"But won't we be in more danger on the road?" asked Sanjay as the group turned to walk along it.

"Yes," said Julian. "But Miss Farr said she would try to bring a carriage, and we won't meet it in the fields."

Dogs barked again, closer now, and they heard horses and the sound of wheels. Julian raised his pistol. Thomas Southern set down Pin and took his shovel in both hands. Mog, struggling, wriggled out of Sanjay's arms and ran over to Pin.

"Here." Lucias handed the boathook to Sanjay.

Around one bend drove a familiar carriage. Kate shouted, and Maretha's head appeared at the carriage window. She waved wildly, and called up to the coachman to stop.

Dogs barked, this time followed by a roar that reverberated through the air, and around the other corner came a wagon and about twenty of the factory hands, a dozen or so evil-looking dogs swarming at their feet. And striding alongside, Crudebelch himself.

Mog shrieked and Lucias huddled up against Chryse.

Julian levelled his pistol. "I wouldn't advise that you advance any closer," he called in a clear, firm voice. "I am Lord Vole, and these people are under my protection."

The ogre growled. Not a canine sound, really, but drawn out and brimful of a crazed anger. "Ye'll pay for this, my fine lord. Thieves must pay." His voice had a low edge like knives being sharpened. "Surround them."

His people fanned out, widening into a loose chain around the party. The coachman pulled the carriage to a halt with difficulty. The horses, catching the ogre's scent, were beginning to back and fight against their harness.

Maretha flung open the door and stepped out, a pistol in each hand.

"Stop, or I'll fire!" she cried.

Crudebelch roared and strode forward towards the carriage. Julian fired. Two more shots, from Maretha. All three bullets hit, one showing like a red spot between the eyes, but Crudebelch merely batted at his face as if at flies and lumbered on. Sanjay and Thomas ran forward, swinging, but the ogre swept them aside with ease, and with such force that they both landed sprawling on the hard surface of the road.

He reached Maretha, who was trying frantically to reload, and with one huge hand grasped her under one arm and lifted her bodily up into the air. His cronies closed in around the others. Pin began to cry. Lucias clung so tightly to Chryse that her arm hurt.

"Interfere with what is mine," Crudebelch growled. "This for you." He reached with the other hand towards the horses. They pulled back away from him, neighing and snorting; above, the coachman fought the reins, eyes on Maretha.

With a swift, violent swipe, Crudebelch raked his claws through the neck of the lead horse. Blood spattered Maretha. She was pale, eyes wide, but her face was controlled and she did not struggle in his grip.

The animal collapsed, pulling the other horses down in their traces. At the same moment, the earl rode into sight. The dogs ceased barking and slunk whining back to the wagon, huddling at the wheels. He pulled up his horse, his gaze raking the scene in a single, frozen instant, centering on the ogre and Maretha.

"Put down my wife," he said, his voice glacial. He was not armed.

Crudebelch laughed, a harsh, ugly sound. "You can't harm me," he growled. "Whoever you be."

"Is that so," replied the earl. His horse stood uncannily still beneath him.

"It is so," retorted the ogre. He brought a blood-tinged claw up to touch, tenderly, Maretha's throat. She shut her eyes. "I'll have you know that I am protected by one higher in state than any of you, mere commoner though I be." Could his features have managed a sneer, he would have sneered now. "You can't threaten me."

"Can't I?" said the earl, even quieter now. It was amazing his voice could be heard at all. "Put down my wife."

For the first time, Crudebelch hesitated.

"Put her down."

The factory hands had drawn back now, slinking away like the dogs.

Crudebelch's lips curled back. "Very well," he growled, and with a roar he flung Maretha aside, launching himself at a run for the earl.

The earl did not move, nor did his horse. The ogre, halfway to him, burst into flames.

His shrieks were terrifying. Everyone but the earl shrank back, covering their ears; some shut their eyes. The flames burned with vivid brilliancy, completely soundless.

Crudebelch threw himself on the road and rolled and thrashed about, but the fire only burned with more vigor, pulsing as if to the beat of his heart. He shrieked and roared until his vocal cords were burnt away. After that, he merely thrashed more and more weakly until there was too little of him to move. When he was reduced to blackened skeleton, the flames at last faded and died.

There was a long silence.

The people from the factory, and their dogs, were gone. Lucias had fainted against Chryse. The rest could only stare at the remains in horror.

The earl rode forward, with no change of expression, and prodded at the skeleton with his quirt. The bones disintegrated at its touch. No one moved.

Maretha, in a heap by the carriage, picked herself up at last and brushed off her hands and hair. She did not touch her dress. She limped over to Pin and Mog and shepherded them to the carriage. They were too terrified to resist, much less speak. She was, with Kate's help, loading the third child into the carriage when the earl turned from his silent perusal of the ashes and saw what she was doing.

"Maretha!" His voice cracked like the snap of ice through the air. She finished settling the child onto the seat before she looked at him. "You will remove those children. Gutter rats have no place in the Elen carriage."

"I will not," she said calmly, taking the last child from Kate's arms and motioning her away with a glance. Kate retreated as the earl approached, halting his horse beside Maretha. "These children are ill, perhaps with their death.

We are taking them to the inn." She turned and gently laid the fourth child, as dirty and tattered as the other three, on the plush velvet of the seat. Mog and Pin cowered against the far door.

"Remove them," he repeated. His eyes were as cold as his voice.

"No."

He lifted his quirt. "You dare?" he whispered. His hand tightened.

"Yes," said Maretha. "I dare."

For a long moment their eyes remained locked. Then the earl lowered his whip with a jerk, reined his horse around, and galloped abruptly away.

It was a quiet journey back to the inn, and they saw not a soul either on the road or in the village lanes. They buried one of the children in the village churchyard the next morning. By noon, they were well on their way north.

CHAPTER 13:

THE PHILOSOPHER

The second child lasted for almost a month before fading to a peaceful death. She was buried in the graveyard of an old abbey, attended by a handful of aged monks. Pin grew quite ill and lapsed into a semi-coma.

Only Mog flourished. Although he sat often by Pin with a concern that was touching in one so young, not even the graveness of her condition could dampen his spirits. He began to trail after Julian, aping his walk and, to the best of his ability, the way he dressed.

Chryse had some days ago given the little boy one of her white handkerchiefs to use as a cravat, and she was now helping him tie it into a poor imitation of the more elaborate styles Julian and Kate sported, when Julian walked into the inn parlor and stopped short, seeing them.

"Lady help us," he said, surveying Mog. "What do you call it?"

Chryse laughed, looking from the complicated tie of Julian's cravat, which, she had learned, was named the Waterfall, to the disorder at Mog's neck. "I call it the Futile. Mog needs your valet, I'm afraid."

"My dear lady," said Julian, looking shocked. "You don't suppose I let my valet tie my cravat, do you? Here, boy." He knelt and with a few neat twists formed the handkerchief into a simpler model of his own.

" 'Cor!" breathed Mog, standing on tiptoe in order to admire himself in the mirror that stood atop one of the sidetables.

"What do you say?" prompted Chryse.

"Thank you, your lordship." Mog completed the phrase

with a stiff little bow, spoiling the effect by immediately jumping around again to preen in the mirror. "Cans I go show Pin, ma'am?" he asked.

"May I go," corrected Chryse, but she nodded and he ran off.

Julian chuckled as the door shut behind the tiny figure. "Civilizing him?"

"I rather thought you might adopt him." Chryse rose from the well-worn sofa on which she had been seated. "Since he's doing his best to take after you."

She walked over to a window and gazed out. A light spring rain cast a smoothing mist over the landscape: low hills, a few cottages huddled in a vale. Green shone in the low trees that surrounded the tiny village; wildflowers lay scattered along the slopes of the hills. When Julian did not reply, she looked back at him. He appeared pensive, examining her. "Any luck in the town?" she asked.

"No." He came to stand beside her. Even so far north, in these half-wild lands, in shabby inns like the one they stayed in now, in the occasional manor house of some provincial squire whose children wore fashions a good five years out of date, Julian looked immaculate, as likely to be leaving for an evening in the most fashionable of polite society as travelling along dusty lanes in search of a mythical, buried city. "As Southern predicted, the folk round here are not at all eager to go farther into the highlands."

"You'd think they'd need the money, at least." She gazed out the window again. "Their homes look as if they hadn't been repaired in years, and their children wear rags. It makes me wonder if these are the sort of people who have to sell off their third and fourth and fifth child to factory owners like Crudebelch in order to feed the rest."

"I doubt if the factory owners need come as far north as this to buy children from the destitute."

"No." She frowned, pensive in her turn. "There are poor everywhere." By the stables she saw Sanjay emerge from a side door, speaking with Professor Farr and Thomas Southern. "But if we can't hire more workers, how will we be able to do the extensive digging the professor wants?"

"Southern, who seems to be an expert in these matters, and unusually well informed, evidently feels that given time laborers will come forward. Hunger is ultimately a stronger drive than fear."

"It's a terrible thing to think about in the spring." Chryse watched Sanjay until he disappeared into the small wooden village church together with Thomas Southern. The professor backtracked towards the inn. Charity appeared a moment later on the church porch looking, Chryse thought, a little flustered, and hurried after her uncle, avoiding the shallow puddles that dotted the lane dividing the inn from the church. Chryse turned away from the scene in time to see Julian smile.

"Do you know what day this is?" he asked. When she shook her head, he answered himself. "The Feast of Somorhas."

"Oh yes." Chryse smiled. "Speaking of food. The wedding feast. I remember the card." She glanced out at the church, but the door was shut and the lane empty. A thin, dark-featured girl clothed in a shapeless dress carried two dead, plucked chickens from the inn-yard to the back door of the kitchens.

"I wasn't thinking of food," said Julian. The tone of his voice caused her to look up at him. He reached out with one hand and, fingers soft on her cheek, he bent to kiss her, a brief touch on her lips. He had a certain, becoming light in his eyes and, looking at her, wore the barest of smiles.

"Oh," said Chryse. She felt heat rise in her cheeks.

"Somorhas is, as you may not know," he said in a caressing voice, "the ancient goddess of love."

"Oh." Chryse felt entirely, utterly, unable to move. She knew she was blushing.

"You must know," continued Julian, smooth and perfectly sincere, "how much I admire you."

She made a noise somewhere between *er* and *ah,* and that seemed to satisfy him.

"And I have long suspected that you are not devoid of a certain—ah—admiration for me." His fingers remained on her cheek, warm.

Since she could not deny it, especially now, faced with what was undeniably an attractive face and person, so very close, she said nothing.

"And of course," he went on, "it has long been the custom for those of our class to find our love outside of our amicable but, alas, arranged marriages. I would be vastly honored, Chryse, should you care to make me that object."

It was too much—she could no longer meet his eyes. But as she looked away her gaze caught her reflection in the mirror, and she gasped and raised a hand to cover her face. "Oh, Julian!" she wailed. "My nose is all red. Oh, I *hate* it when I blush."

There was a pause. After a moment he lowered his hand and took a step away from her.

Immediately she grasped his sleeve and, looking back at him, sighed. "What a terrible thing for me to say. I'm very flattered."

Surprisingly, he chuckled. "And you are about to say, flattered, but not interested. Perhaps I was mistaken—"

"But I do—ah—admire you, Julian. You must believe me. Only—" She suppressed a smile. "Well, I don't know quite how to put this. Sanjay and I didn't marry by arrangement or for convenience. We married for love."

There was a second pause. This time Chryse broke it with a laugh. "Oh dear. I'm afraid I've shocked you."

Julian's eyes had gone quite wide, giving him that appealing look that small children have. "How very—" He coughed discreetly behind his hand, controlling himself. "How very reckless of you," he managed.

She laughed. "I daresay it was," she replied, releasing his sleeve. "I didn't know it was so very unheard of. This isn't to say that under other circumstances—" She shrugged. He smiled. "But there it is."

"You are most gracious, Madame." With a flourish of a bow, he took her hand and kissed it. "I am defeated, but not utterly cast down." He straightened, releasing her hand. "Who knows when circumstances may change."

"Who indeed," said Chryse, turning now as the door opened behind them and Charity appeared in the doorway, looking somewhat lost. "Charity, are you all right?"

Julian moved to stand by the window, back to them, as Chryse walked across the parlor to the door.

"I was looking for Maretha," said Charity.

"You seem a little pale," said Chryse. "I believe she's up in your uncle's room, copying out some notes of his on that old map."

"Old map?"

"The one the vicar here unearthed from some old chest."

"Oh." Charity considered. "That's why they both—" She broke off. "We must be very close now," she said

instead. "Less than a week, Thomas—Mr. Southern says.
And that only because there are no roads to speak of up
there." She shuddered. "Do you suppose the old stories
are true?"

"I don't know," said Chryse.

Charity looked past her to Julian. "I'd better go find
Maretha," she murmured, and left.

"There." Chryse turned to Julian. "A pity she isn't
married."

"Why is that?"

"I would have thought she'd make a fine mistress. She's
quite beautiful."

"Ah, Chryse." Julian approached her and took her hand.
"Beauty by itself is no qualification in a woman. I have
only to remember my wife."

"Your—I didn't know you were married."

"To quite the most insipid creature you can imagine.
We were both much too young. It was arranged by our
parents."

"What happened to her?" she asked.

"Died in childbed within the year."

"And the child?" she asked softly.

"And the child," he echoed. "Don't be sorry for me,
Chryse. It was a long time ago, and I never loved her."

"I'm still sorry," she said. "For the child's sake, at least.
And yours, whether you want it or not."

He released her hand, a smile on his face that was both
gentle and perhaps self-mocking. "I seem doomed," he
said softly, "to have only friendship from the women I love
best."

"Why, Julian—" she began, a sudden light of speculation in her eye, but something in his expression made her
leave the rest of the thought unspoken. "I think it must be
time for supper," she finished. "Shall we go find the
others?"

"Julian was right," said Chryse to her husband.

"About what?" He turned in the saddle to look at her.
They rode up a narrow track, beaten down more by the
passage of the wagons of their party rather than by any of
the folk who lived near this area. Behind them lumbered
the remainder of their wagons and the mass of trudging
laborers.

"About hunger being a greater spur than fear. Something like that." She glanced back at the hundred or so workers plodding along in the wake of the supply wagons—about half of them had come the long road from Heffield under Thomas Southern's keen eye. The earl's fine carriages had been left some three days previous, when roads had disintegrated to little more than parallel ruts in hard ground, in the care of a provincial gentleman too frightened to refuse their keep. "I'm amazed the ones from Heffield stayed so long."

"How were they to get home?" Sanjay asked.

"Well, that's true," she conceded, "since their pay is contingent on work. But I'm more amazed that any of the local folk hired on. More than one of the innkeepers told me scraps of story that would stop braver folk than I from coming up here. Ghosts in the night. Unseasonable storms that swept strange spells in their wake. Girls lost and crying for their lovers who were never seen again. And of course," she grinned, her blonde hair bright and loose in the sun, "bloody sacrifice."

Sanjay smiled, watching his wife. These lands were moors, mostly, but here trees had begun to appear, growing in clumps like seeds of a forest that could not quite come together. Though it was spring, it was still a little cool, and though the sun shone bright and steady above, there was a chill to the air that seemed to him unnatural. "That's all?" he asked.

"Of the stories? No. But the ones that intrigue me most are the briefest ones—of what lies beyond the labyrinth gate—a haunted forest and wild magic, whatever that is. And *them,* of course. That's mostly what they're called, the people who live past the gate and the great lakes that separate the two lands. Them. Not human, they say."

"Chryse, my love, how can you sound so skeptical after everything we've seen?"

She grinned again. "I'm not skeptical. But it's such a fine spring day that I find it impossible to be apprehensive. And after seeing that site yesterday—it was plainly the remains of some placid old castle with not a bit of haunting in it."

"That was only the first of the proposed sights—based on the professor's research and the old map we obtained, and the suggestions of the guide."

"Will we reach the second site—"

"Today? I think so. This will be the site the guide reckons as the old city. He says it's the place known for generations as the Labyrinth Gate itself, because of the way it lies between two of the long rift lakes. It's the only bridge to the northern lands in these parts."

"What do you think?"

"I think," he said, "that I'll have to see it first." He turned further in his saddle to examine the ragged collection of laborers walking doggedly alongside the wagons. Thomas Southern, at their fore, was engaged in a heated discussion with one of the locals, hired at the last village. "But I'm rather surprised at Julian, for having such insight into a condition so very far from his own."

"Oh, Julian is full of surprises." Chryse laughed suddenly.

"What is that supposed to mean?" Sanjay eyed her with the suspicion brought about by long intimacy.

"Well." Now she hesitated. "I've been trying to decide how to tell you—it's no great thing, really—but I would hate to see you—oh, this is ridiculous." She grimaced.

Sanjay laughed. "Next thing, you're going to tell me that he propositioned you."

"Sanjay."

His expression changed. There was a brief silence, shot through with the sound of horses and the creak of wagons and the singing of the workers, a rousing tune about sowing the fields and planting a tree. Then they both began to laugh.

"Well," she said finally. "I was quite tempted, I must say."

"Then let's hope he left the offer open," he replied. "When you get tired of me, you can divorce me and marry him."

"But he doesn't want to *marry* me. That's not how it's done here."

"All right. Then if he can come up with a substantial sum perhaps I'll allow him to bribe me to remain wed to you, in name only, of course, while he—"

"I see." Chryse considered this with mock seriousness. "That is a possibility. How much would you accept?"

"There would be one stipulation," he added.

"Which is?"

He grinned. "You'd have to cheat on him."

She laughed and leaned across to kiss him. "What would I do without you?" she asked as she settled back firmly into her saddle.

But the comment brought an unwontedly solemn look to his face. "I'm glad we're here together, Chryse," he replied with great seriousness. "Adventures are all very well, but without a companion to share them with—" He shrugged.

"Sanjay, if I hadn't been with you, I would have been terrified the moment I set foot in this place, and every moment since."

His lips quirked up into a little smile. "So would I," he said softly. "But don't tell anyone else."

Chryse laughed. "I hope," she added slowly after an interval of silence, "that this won't affect what you think of Julian. I wondered if I should tell you that he propositioned me."

"My sweet buttercup." He smiled. "How can I dislike a man who has the same good taste I do?"

"How you flatter me. But not often enough."

"I wouldn't want you to become vain," he retorted.

"Yes," she agreed. "I'm in terrible danger of that. Now look there—" She lifted her chin in the direction of the wagons in front of them. "Here comes young Master Lucias. He looks in a bit of a rush. Lord, Sanjay, how could I become vain with a face like that hovering about?" She waved one hand. "Lucias!"

The youth reined his horse over to walk beside them. He had taken to riding one of the most spirited animals when it was found that no one besides the earl and Kate could handle it. That he had a long acquaintance with horses was apparent by his seat; he rode with an ease and mastery that was surprising for a person of his age.

"Madame. Monsieur." He nodded at them in turn, but his eyes, as he looked at them, bore a troubled expression.

"Is something wrong, Lucias?" asked Sanjay. He frowned, examining the boy with a perplexed expression.

"No," said Lucias quickly. His hair shone like gilding in the noonday sun. "It's just that I keep thinking you and Madame look familiar somehow."

"You still don't remember anything?" Chryse asked gently. "Except the factory?"

"No, Madame."

"Not even why you were being held there? Locked away like that?"

He shook his head. His face, even in distress, had an unearthly quality about it, as though he had been touched by some divine hand to bear the blessing of heaven to the mortal world below. "But it wasn't for what the other children were locked there for, I know that."

"And that's all." Chryse shook her head in turn.

"You know horses," said Sanjay. "That in itself is some kind of clue, however small."

"Oh yes." Lucias nodded enthusiastically. "I love horses. I know that I knew them before—but in a different way than—" He broke off. His complexion paled, and he abruptly reined his horse back and away. "I must go speak to— begging your—" He cantered off, down the line of wagons.

Chryse and Sanjay had barely time to exchange a glance before a second horseman pulled up beside them.

"Madame. Monsieur." The earl's tone held the same slight chill as the air of these highlands. His glance strayed past them towards the retreating figure of Lucias. "Interesting lad," he murmured. His cool gaze came to rest on Sanjay. "Wouldn't you agree?"

"He has a certain—" Sanjay paused, "—a certain cast to him."

"I thought you might see it, too," said the earl smoothly. "A generous touch of magic, wouldn't you say? Some spell imposed by another."

"I can't see so much as that. I haven't your skills."

"No," agreed the earl, without a trace of self pride. "But I haven't your sight. Tell me, do you recognize it at all?"

"Recognize it? The magic? No. I didn't know it could be recognized."

The earl cast him a strange glance. "Any mage leaves a trace of his self in his castings, but the more adept a mage, the more difficult it is to read."

"As each deck of Gates is individual," said Chryse.

His eyes slid to scrutinize her, an unreadable expression on his impossibly controlled face. "Indeed," he said. "Although the cards are only needed by those who manipulate the lower levels of power."

Chryse thought abruptly of Madame Sosostris and, as if the idea had leapt to her from Sanjay's mind, she turned to look at her husband. In his eyes and expression she saw immediately that he was thinking the same thing as she was.

"Which is not to say," continued the earl as if he had followed their glances like conversation, "that the more powerful do not use them as well. But the Gates are limited as a single source of power." His glance flicked over them both, penetrating and alert. "Even such a deck as yours."

"Indeed," echoed Chryse.

He inclined his head: an uncomfortable salute, to her mind. Straightening, he addressed Sanjay. "Monsieur. If you and Madame would ride with me—there is a sight I would have your opinion of."

Sanjay nodded, and they rode forward along the line of wagons, overtaking the lead wagon and following the track up along a narrow ridge. Ahead, they saw a line of people— the professor, Maretha and Charity, Julian, Kate—staring out at some vista or sight beyond.

Each stood with a posture so indicative of emotion that it was as if they spoke aloud: the professor enthused and excited, Maretha subdued and intent, Kate and Julian curious, Charity detached, turning even as they approached to stare back beyond them at the first wagon lumbering into view behind.

They dismounted and walked to the edge of the bluff. Beside them the earl seemed to be holding some deep emotion in check, like fire confined in a small space.

"Lord," breathed Chryse as the valley opened out before her.

"The labyrinth gate," said Maretha in a low voice. "That's what the locals call it. No one comes here anymore, they say."

A valley nestled between the tips of two lakes that arced away into the highlands, lost in the distance. Like the lakes, the valley was narrow, pierced by a few high, small ridges, and lifting at the farther end into a high bluff that rose behind into mountain.

"There's another name for it," said Chryse slowly, trying to remember. "I heard someone use it."

"The belly of stones," said Sanjay in a soft voice.

Scraps of water and the tumble of great stones lying amongst grass in a pattern that seem achingly familiar, something not quite nameable, rested below them in the deep, long hollow. Beyond, far beyond, lay the suggestion of forest, a great, dark wood.

"*Their* lands," said the earl in a voice so quiet that only Chryse and Sanjay could hear it.

"Is it really a forest?" she asked. "I hadn't thought—" She shrugged. "Not in these lands."

"Oh yes, it's a forest." The earl smiled, an uncanny and disquieting expression on his face. "My grandmother, when she was a girl, went riding in that forest on a dare. She was a wild young woman, you understand. She was gone for two months, given up for dead and the new heir invested in his duties. Then she turned up, pregnant, a little fey, as they said in those times. Her parents found a respectable older gentleman who agreed to marry her and raise the child as his own, and in time my father was born. All were relieved that he had escaped any taint of the alien blood." His eyes, examining the ruins below, bore the cold glitter of a steel blade.

"But they were not so lucky in the next generation," said Chryse, unable not to.

His gaze, shifting to her, seemed more amused than angered. "I have a younger sister," he said, a confidence that surprised her far more than the previous one. "She is as quiet and unfey a woman as I have ever met."

Chryse only smiled. The earl turned his attention to Sanjay.

"Monsieur." His voice was as soft as the touch of the cool breeze on their faces. "What do you make of it?"

Sanjay shuddered and put out a hand to touch Chryse's arm as he stared down. In a scatter of stones he thought he saw a movement, shadow moving in the ruins, animate, watching and aware. Sound seemed drowned here, smothered in some enveloping hush that surrounded this place.

"This is it," Sanjay said. "Topo Rhuam. I would know it as I know my own self."

Sun illuminated hollows and rises and a greater pattern in the ruins and the lay of the land around them, hiding the rest of the city, that radiated out from a center discernible only by Sanjay's instinct.

"Then we have arrived." The earl's glance strayed for an instant to Maretha before returning to the stones below.

"It has rested alone and untouched for a very long time," said Sanjay. "I'm not sure I want to see what happens when we disturb it."

The earl smiled.

CHAPTER 14:

THE TUTOR

"The boy!" The Regent threw her hand out in a gesture so abrupt that it knocked over one of the three lanterns that sat at the points of a triangle on the table. Her great billow of skirts rustled as she rocked wildly. A silent woman came forward and set the lantern back on the table. By its light, the wavering image of Nastagmas came more sharply into focus. It hovered a finger's breadth above the table, and one could see faint shapes through it: a chair, the far wall. "You told me that he was safely disposed! How could he have escaped?"

The tiny image of the old man, dissolving into nothing at its edges, seemed to shrink back a little. "But he was safe—he was. It is impossible that he could have escaped, highness, and more so that he would be found by the earl's party, but it has happened." The image was too insubstantial to show his facial expression, but his posture now straightened, as if with confidence. "But I will wager, yes, highness, that none here suspects him at all. The spell still holds. I have spoken with him and he remembers nothing, only his name."

"You spoke with him?" Her rocking was still agitated. "That was foolish—like recognizes like. Well, it is done. Do not fail me again, Nastagmas."

"No, highness." Almost indistinct, this murmur.

"Then your report. What progress? Any sign of treasure?"

"None."

"None? In more than five weeks? Nothing?"

"Highness." The image flickered in the light of the lanterns as the Regent swayed back and forth, eyes half

153

shut. "The city is vast. Even with a crew of one hundred laborers, only a small part can be uncovered at a time. And the professor is fickle. His wishes change daily as his mood alters."

The Regent shut her eyes, hands grasping the smooth edge of the table. "Fickle!" she breathed in an undertone of disgust. "Surely the Earl of Elen does not tolerate such inefficiency."

The image made a movement with its shoulders, fading into dark on the fringe. "The earl has his own business. He does not seem to concern himself with the excavation. But I have, highness, put a few innocent questions to the foreman, Southern, and from his words and actions it is clear that he heeds the orders of the professor's daughter above those of the professor."

"The daughter—ah—the Countess of Elen, I take it."

A nod.

"Interesting." One hand rubbed the grain of wood caressingly as she considered some thought. "Southern," she murmured finally, as if the name reminded her of something. Her rocking gentled and slowed and she released the table edge, opening her eyes. "You must remove the boy from that place. I would prefer to have him alive—he is too fine a material for the final spell that I would willingly throw him away—but if you cannot remove him alive, then kill him."

"It will be difficult, highness. He has attached himself to the earl's party."

She grimaced, rocking harder again. "One or the other. Do you understand?"

Even as he said, "Yes, highness," her rocking stopped suddenly and she gasped twice. The image flickered out of existence, leaving only the three burning lantern wicks to cast shadows across the room. Her skirts rustled about her, and she relaxed as her waiting woman came forward and helped her up and out of the chamber.

In her dressing room she washed and changed into a new gown, and afterwards went to her private receiving room to look over the written reports of her numerous agents. Into this calm the Princess Georgiana was admitted.

"My dear." The Regent rose and came forward to take the princess's hands in hers, a look of concern on her handsome face. "You still look pale. Are you feeling no better?"

The princess squeezed her aunt's hands, but could scarcely manage a smile. She sank down onto a couch and the Regent sat beside her, one hand still on her niece's sleeve. "No, indeed, Aunt," Georgiana answered in a voice more subdued than usual. "I seem unable to recover my usual vigor."

The Regent frowned. "Your father had these very same symptoms—but I will say no more. What does your physician say?"

Georgiana shook her head. Her eyes had a lackluster cast, and shadows ringed them. "My physician has had to return to her family home—her father is quite ill, and she wishes to care for him in his last days. So I asked for that man that you recommended, Aunt. He suggests a stay at the ocean. He says many a young woman approaching her wedding and coronation will feel a trifle under the weather. It was meant to be a joke, I believe."

"I feel sure it was," said the Regent, soothing. She coughed behind her hand. "I find his suggestion to be a sound one. A few weeks out of Heffield, the good summer sea winds, and you shall be right again in no time."

"I am sure you are correct, Aunt," said Georgiana in a low voice, but she did not look convinced.

"Indeed." The Regent stood up. "Now, there is no reason to delay. I will order your carriage to be ready tomorrow, and your maids to pack your things."

"Shall I take William and Jasmina with me?"

"No, dear." She helped her niece to her feet with gentle solicitude. "You will want to be quiet, to recover as quickly as you can."

"Oh, of course." Georgiana looked unsure and slightly confused. "I suppose I will."

"Then you had best be on your way. I will call—"

A footman appeared in the doorway. "Lord Felton, your highness," he announced, followed quite abruptly by the entrance of Lord Felton himself.

"Lord Felton." If the Regent's tone was less than welcoming, only the footman was in a state of mind to notice it.

"Your highness," Lord Felton began, stopped. "Your highness!" He bowed to Georgiana with obvious sincerity. "I had not expected to see you here."

Georgiana inclined her head, but she was already drifting towards the door, propelled by the light pressure of her aunt's hand on her back. "It is good to see you, my lord," she said, as though she meant it. "Forgive me. I was just leaving."

He bowed again. There was a short silence after she left as he stared after her.

"Lord Felton." The Regent sat again, clearly impatient.

His glance returned to her as if he had forgotten her presence. The firm line of his mouth tightened as he regarded her with far less respect than he had previously regarded her niece. "The princess looks pale, your highness," he said in a sharp tone. "Has a physician been called to attend her?"

"Of course, Lord Felton. It is a mild ailment, merely, but a lingering one. The physician is sure that it bears no relation to the disease that carried off my brother."

"Of course it isn't," said Lord Felton impatiently. "You and I are well aware that your brother died of his own excesses."

"Nevertheless, as a precaution he has recommended that her highness spend some time convalescing by the ocean. She leaves tomorrow. With a proper retinue, of course." When Lord Felton said nothing, she smiled slightly. "Does this displease you, Lord Felton?"

His mouth was still tight. "Do not forget, Princess Blessa, that I was privileged to serve as an advisor to your gracious mother and sister and that I have known you all your life, both as a member of your family's court and as tutor to yourself in the ways of statecraft."

She did not comment.

"I have often thought," he continued, slowly but with the vigor of a much younger man, "that it rankled that the inheritance passed to William's children. We both of us know that your brother had few principles and fewer wits. Indeed, I often felt that you received the greatest share of intelligence in your family, and I have often wondered if it would have been better for you to have gotten fewer wits and more complacency."

"This is plain speaking, Lord Felton."

"Your highness knows that my highest loyalty is to the throne of Anglia, and to its heir, her highness, Princess Georgiana."

"As is all of ours," she answered.

He coughed, a keen look in his lined and aged face. "Your highness also knows that I am a very old man, and have less to fear than a younger man would."

"Indeed." Her voice was a trifle edged. "Is that all you wished to say?"

He gave her the briefest of bows. "Only that I expect to see Princess Georgiana back in Heffield soon, your highness. I have been working closely with her on the matter of her wedding and coronation."

"Of course." She rose now and walked to the doors that opened on to a little balcony. The view looked out over the courtyard of Blackstone Palace, a pleasant garden of walks and shrubbery. "And your visit here today?"

He followed her to stand in the doorway. "Your highness, I find inexplicable this sudden decision to delay the arrival of the princess's betrothed and his family until a mere five days before the coronation. More than inexplicable—unreasonable!" His voice was low, but not at all hesitant.

The Regent had been leaning on the railing that edged the balcony. Now she turned. "Are you questioning my judgement?"

"Yes." He met her gaze. "You can have no good reason for this whim. Prince Frederick can scarcely be expected to—"

"Lord Felton!" Her voice cut through his complaint. "I have made the decision. You will abide by it. I do not expect argument." With a wave of one hand, she dismissed him. "You may leave."

"Your highness—"

"You may leave," she repeated, giving him no choice but to bow stiffly and retreat.

For a few moments she regarded the garden. Then her gaze wandered to a latticework that had been recently constructed on one side of the balcony. She walked across and ran her hands along it as though it were her lover. A single pot sat at its base, but no plant yet grew in it or climbed the trellis.

"Yes," she said in a pleased voice. "Once I have the power, no one will suspect your fate, my princess." A moment longer she caressed it; then she turned and went back inside and rang for a servant.

"Bring Colonel Whitmore to me," she ordered. She sat and perused her papers until the colonel arrived. He was a young man, handsome in a florid way, with that flush in his cheeks and eyes that betrayed a weakness for the pleasures of the flesh. He eyed her greedily but with some circumspection.

She rose after a moment and went to stand near him. "I have long known, Colonel," she said in a slow, husky tone, "how you wish to be of service to me."

"Your highness," he said profoundly, and offered her a deep bow. "It is my greatest desire."

"First, you will assign three of your most trustworthy men to report to me all the movements of Lord Felton. I suspect his lordship of certain—indiscretions."

He inclined his head but showed no emotion at this charge.

"Good," she said. "You, with the rest of your troop, will ride north. I must be apprised of certain activities that may be a danger to my person. And if you complete both these charges successfully—" She rested a hand on the sleeve of his military coat, letting her voice trail off.

"Your highness." He dropped to one knee. "I pledge to serve you, with my life if need be."

She smiled. "Don't be careless of your pledges, Colonel. Sometimes the full price must be paid." But she took him by the hand and raised him up. "Let us hope you find the reward worthwhile."

For a moment he forgot himself, and let his eyes wander over the curve of her figure.

She chuckled, and he dropped his gaze quickly. "I have great faith in your desires, Colonel. Now go, and report back to me when you are ready to leave. I will give you further instructions then."

He bowed and left.

She stood motionless for a long while. The colonel occupied her thoughts for only a brief moment: he was a pawn, to be used and discarded for what gain he could bring her—and she had no doubt that she would find him useful. He was a man of little imagination and great ego. He would serve to fuel her magic; that was enough. Lord Felton concerned her more. Immune to the lure of gold or flesh, he might well prove the greatest barrier to her plans. Silent and pensive, she rang at last for one of her waiting women.

"Bring my cards to me," she said when the woman arrived. "I will be on the balcony."

She simply held the cards for a time after they were brought to her. At last she set them down on the little sidetable that was the only furniture on the balcony. The summer sun bathed the cards in its mellow afternoon light as she regarded them, flipping through them one by one. She stopped finally when she reached The Heiress.

"Yes." An expression of great satisfaction crossed her face. The card was brown at the edges, as if it were deteriorating slowly, and a trace of the decay also showed at the very center. "It progresses well, indeed," she muttered, and laid the card on the table. The Heiress, young and clear-faced, gazed into a mirror, seeing the clarity of her face reflected within. And in the reflection, so that one knew it stood on the wall behind her, arched a latticework on which climbed a thick-leafed, blooming briar-rose.

CHAPTER 15:

DUSK

Chryse rose from the table at which she sat transcribing to greet her husband with a kiss. Above their heads, the canvas ceiling stirred, brought to life by a dusk breeze; the heavy material of the tent muffled the wind's eerie call across the valley. The kiss prolonged, metamorphosing into an embrace.

"Would you put that thing down?" asked Chryse finally, shifting so that she could speak. "It's incredibly uncomfortable."

Sanjay chuckled and pulled away from her. He laid the sketchbook which had been pressing into her back down on the table and, as he removed his coat, examined the lined sheets of paper she had been working on. "Oboe?" he asked as he draped his coat over the back of her chair. "Are you composing?"

"Sanjay!" She picked up the coat. "Would you please hang this up? I get really tired of telling you." She held it out.

For a moment he did nothing; finally he took it. "Don't worry," he said as he went to the makeshift wardrobe in which their clothing was stowed. "I get tired of you telling me too."

There was a brief silence.

"Maybe we should change the subject," said Chryse. "Yes, I am." She sat down at the table and gazed pensively at the music sketched in on the staves. "You know I've been collecting the songs the workers sing, and it has been becoming increasingly clear to me that they fall into three categories: rhythmic work songs, the kind of thing that

helps pass the time in tedious labor—here—" She shuffled
the papers and brought out a sheaf with dark notes scrawled
across the page, small words written around and underneath the stave, "and what we would call folk songs in
general—"

"Is that two categories?" He stood now with his hands
on her shoulders, leaning to gaze over her head at her
work.

"No, that's the first one. Work songs and folk songs and
sad romances set to music. All very familiar in content and
style. The second category is hymns—A Mighty Fortress,
high-church stuff, you know the thing."

"Well, actually, I don't, but I'll take your word for it."

Chryse turned her head enough to make a face at him,
but immediately rummaged back through the papers to
withdraw four sheets of manuscript paper that were starred
at the top: "And then there's this." She held up the
sheets, shaking them as if their presence in the air was
explanation enough. "It doesn't match anything I'm familiar with—and god knows I had every survey course the
university offered."

"Yes," said Sanjay, musing. "You used to say you were
looking for something."

A perplexed look crossed her face. "I did, didn't I?" she
murmured. "Because, Sanjay, I think I've found it." She
spread the four sheets out before her, a few lines of sparse
notes, a few words penciled in below. "Fragments, that's
all I get. These two were being hummed by two of the
laborers. One of them said it was just aimless humming,
but look at this correspondence here—" she began to
point.

"You know I can't read music. Why don't you sing it?"

"It's so strange," she said. "But exactly right for what it
is. Now this, what he hummed—" She began to sing. She
had a clear mezzo, carefully trained and quite precise. It
was a peculiar little tune, never quite resolving into a
definite cadence, but not quite meandering either. "And
this," she continued, "is what I heard one evening while I
was out watching the stars." She sang again, using a slightly
different color in her voice. "Do you see the correspondence?" she asked when she had finished.

"Chryse, what do you mean, you heard it one evening?"

"Exactly that: as if some person, or some *thing*, were

just over the next rise. Maybe it was an echo. Or a ghost. Not quite a voice, but not any instrument I've ever heard, either."

"Have you seen anything strange here?" he asked suddenly, moving to sit in the other chair.

She shrugged. "Other than that it's a strange place—no." She looked up abruptly from her paper to examine him carefully. "I suppose you have." It wasn't a question.

He nodded, looking a little sheepish. "Not anything I could really explain or even describe to you, but other—" He opened his hands in a gesture of helplessness. "Other presences."

She rubbed the end of her pen along one corner of her mouth. "It strikes me that we're not much surprised by things anymore." Not waiting for an answer, she went on. "This third one—another little song, but with nonsense syllables. The woman singing it said it was, and I quote—" She read from a note penned at the bottom of the sheet. " 'A song to keep the demons away, miss, me grandpap were a witch and knew such things.' And this fourth one—it had lyrics—half nonsense and half a fragmented tale of two lovers, a hunt, and a murder—not exactly a murder—a sacrifice, perhaps. The man who sang it said it's an old song passed down in his village, which is the nearest habitation to this place, for what that's worth. His grandfather had it from a wandering sorcerer, who had it from who knows where, and he said it's a powerful charm." She frowned suddenly.

"What are you thinking?"

"Don't laugh at me, love." She stopped, grinned self-consciously. "As if you would, being where we are." She traced a finger across the notes. "I don't think it's human music. It's really caught me—it's almost as if I'm compelled to compose, using—not any one of those tunes, really, but—" In the yellow glow of the lanterns hung from the crosspiece of the tent, her face held an intent, serious concentration. "It's all an organic piece, like a circle, or—or a long series of spirals. It doesn't really have an end or a beginning."

"Sing it for me," he said, taking her hand in his.

"No." She shook her head, withdrawing the hand. "I can't. I don't dare. Not until it's finished. It's too strong. I think it's going to be a symphony, but I don't have any control over it at all." She grimaced, with a swift, determined movement sweeping the papers into a neat stack. "What have you done today?" she asked in a totally different voice, brisk and curious.

"Funny you should mention spirals." He opened his sketchbook. Page after page of beautiful, precise illustrations revealed themselves as he flipped through the volume. Half-ruined walls rising from earth, graced by faint traceries in the stone and the rumpled form of a sweating laborer with a pick-ax; a delicate flower, detailed even to the finest suggestion of texture; a three-story building of a slightly alien cast traced over a sketch of rubble, the construction of his artist's imagination.

"This is my favorite." Chryse stopped him for a moment. It was a sketch of Maretha, gazing intently at a low wall of undecipherable writing, one hand busy copying the shapes into a small notebook; behind her, hiding in a tumble of stones, one could see Mog and the recovered Pin, like two guardian cherubs, and much farther, on a distant rise, the sinister figure of a black-garbed man on horseback. "It will go down in history as Professor Farr the younger at her first major discovery. Maybe you should render scenes from Maretha's life to parallel those saint's tapestries of her namesake. I wonder why she never went to university?"

"Money, I expect. I don't suppose they have scholarships. And I don't suppose her father could have spared her from his work."

"You sound a little cynical."

"I think she's put upon—at the beck and call of one self-absorbed man after the next."

She cocked her head to one side, examining him with a speculative gaze. "That's harsh, coming from you. You're usually so tolerant."

"Self-absorbed in different ways, but alike in their absorption, in their willingness to use others to gain their own ends. Although personally, I think the professor is the more selfish man."

"Than the earl? What about the murdered infants?"

He considered, thoughtful. "It seems to me that blood would show."

"That's a cryptic statement."

He shrugged. "Here. I went back to the south ridge

today. Maretha asked me to do some sketches of the entire site. Since that tentative identification of the central area of the city, she wants to get a larger view, to see how what we've uncovered fits into the overall pattern."

"Sanjay." Chryse leaned forward, lips pressed tight, staring at the sketch in front of her. It covered both pages. "That's not what it looks like."

He smiled. "No. The sketches of what it looks like follow. This is my *impression*."

The lay of the ground was fairly exact in the sketch, but over it he had superimposed a series of concentric rings, like the ripples thrown out by a stone dropped into a calm pool, that bled a pattern onto the stone remains of the city. "Compare this," he said, flipping back and forth between this sketch and the next one, a more formal and exact rendering of the valley and ruins, and the haphazard digging that dotted the area. "Circles, yes, causing the ruins to fall into a form that has shape, but not exact circles. You see by this slope, the bend of the curve that I perceive here, that in fact it forms a spiral."

"And, in fact, a spiral centered precisely on that area where Maretha has had Thomas assign the largest number of laborers this past week."

"Exactly," said Sanjay. "She had a great argument with her father this morning over it. He wants to put most of the workers on that building we're uncovering up on the western ridge."

Chryse smiled slightly. "What is it he calls it? 'The Evening Palace of the Great Sovereign.' It sounds so grandiose. How does he even know it's a palace?"

"I suppose one gets an instinct for things like that—sees patterns, correspondences—"

"Like you do?" She shook her head. "I'm afraid that I believe the professor's instincts only go so far. I was up there about three days ago helping Maretha look over the walls for glyphs and frescos for her catalog. It could be a police station as far as I'm concerned. It's in a perfect position for observations of the rest of the city, plus the forest north and both lakes."

Sanjay shrugged, flipping forward another page to a sketch detailing the distant structure. "Well, evidently the professor believes it's the endpoint of the procession—"

"Procession?"

"Didn't you read his monograph on—you know, his interpretation of the frescos from Mantion and Eppot-Staw. The ritual procession of the great sacrifice, in which a young virgin priestess of the ancient goddess, or the Daughter, as they'd say now, is led to a sacred place and killed, for her—I suppose her life force—to enter and strengthen the power of the city itself."

"Like Persephone dragged down to Hades?" Chryse asked.

"More a fertility ritual, I think. Death and rebirth."

"Well, she married the King of the Dead, didn't she? And spent half the year underground."

"Maybe I was thinking more of Kali. You Westerners are so genteel." He laughed as Chryse rolled her eyes. "In any case, that monograph got the earl interested in the professor in the first place."

Chryse made a face of disgust. "Men always slaver over the thought of a nubile virgin, female of course, being sacrificed, as if it were some sort of sexual ritual as well."

"Isn't it?" He grinned and, pulling his chair closer to her, let a hand caress her waist. "Don't women slaver over the thought of nubile young men?"

"Like our angel Lucias?" She laughed. "Of course we do." She leaned forward to kiss him; her arms slid around him, pressing him close, his coat opening so that only the light cloth of his shirt and her gown separated their skin. "But this sacrifice business is nonsense—men are much more use to us alive."

As reply, he laughed, gathering her closer to his embrace and letting one hand go free to unbraid her hair until she could shake it loose to tumble down around her shoulders.

"Sanjay," she said in a low voice, "we're almost out of—" Giggled when he whispered in her ear. "If we do this many more times, we're going to start running the risk of starting a family, and I'm not sure—"

He prevented her from continuing with a long, extensive kiss. "Considering the alternative, it's a risk I'm willing to take," he murmured.

"Easy for you to say."

He began with great concentration and precise thoroughness to undo the row of tiny buttons that ran down the back of her gown.

"How long until dinner?" she asked.

He pulled back from her, smiling, his eyes lit by equal parts of mischief, desire, and need. His hands cupped her face, and he brushed his lips against hers. "We can be late."

CHAPTER 16:

THE ARCHER

"You're late," said Kate as Chryse, her hair braided neatly and coiled like a spiral at the back of her head, pulled out a chair and sat down beside the older woman. "And somehow, given the look on *his* face—" a glance here towards Sanjay, who sat across the table from them, next to Charity "—I don't imagine it was Maretha's catalog that kept you." She grinned.

Chryse could not help but grin back as she accepted a plate of chicken and vegetables from one of the cook's helpers. "I see Mistress Cook has outdone herself today."

"Yes. We almost had a riot when Mog and Pin discovered that their favorite hen—filthy creatures, if you ask me—was one of the chosen sacrifices for dinner."

"How was it averted?"

"Julian." Kate chuckled. "He threatened to stop tying Mog's cravats every morning." She cast a glance towards the head of the table, where the earl sat attending to his meal in disapproving silence while the professor, at his right, outlined in great detail the work accomplished on the Evening Palace. "By the way, you've thrown off the seating arrangements this evening. A mortal sin."

Chryse leaned closer to Kate. "Is it true there's to be a bonfire tonight as part of the celebration of midsummer eve, and that they're burning an effigy of His Blackness on it?"

Kate took a bite of food to smother her chuckle and succeeded only in choking. She quickly took a deep gulp of wine, but Julian, ever alert, caught her eye from his place at the earl's left and managed to convey with the

merest lift of an eyebrow his disdain at their levity. He
spoiled the effect immediately by allowing his lips to quirk
upwards as he turned his gaze in response to a quiet
comment from the earl.

"A bonfire is quite right," said Kate, recovering. "I
believe the men are out right now, building it up. The
locals made the effigy. Evidently it's a northern tradition."

"Pierced by an arrow," said Maretha suddenly from her
seat at Chryse's right. "Although I never have understood
where that fits in. And clothed in the skin of a deer—the
effigy, that is. The locals quite insisted on it, though some
of the Heffielders complained to Mr. Southern, saying that
it was godless superstition and quite unchurchlike."

"And what did Mr. Southern do to quell *this* latest
revolt?" asked Chryse.

Now Kate chuckled openly. "He's leading a prayer service." She paused, listening. "There, I thought so. When
the wind drops you can hear them singing."

It was one of those moments when all conversation,
bidden by some imperceptible command, lulls to silence.
The four lanterns hung from the tent crossbeam cast a
subdued glow on the eight figures seated at table, shading
into gray on the three cook's helpers who waited expectantly at the corners of the tent for their services to be
called for. In the fourth corner, a smaller table sat with a
single lantern placed in its center; over the earl's protests,
Maretha had installed Lucias and the two children here,
and now even Mog had, by some unknown prompting,
fallen silent.

The voices, mostly deep with a scattering of high harmony, seemed more a trick of the breeze than a human
gathering, heard through the fluttering canvas from such a
distance. 'Let goods and kindred go, this mortal life also;
Her Son they may kill, Her truth abideth still—'

"Which leads me to believe," Professor Farr continued,
drowning out the hymn, "that the writing at the evening
palace contains a detailed description of the ritual procession and sacrifice—"

"An' then," piped up Mog from the other direction, "I
saw another one, truly I did. Only he were no bigger'n
you, Luke, peering at me from t'other side of the water.
With a halo just like the Baby Jesse. Well, I think it were
a halo."

"Hell to pay now," murmured Kate.

Maretha turned in her chair to regard the small table with a quelling eye. "Master Mog." Her voice was stern. Mog's gaze shot to her, his eyes widening as he realized that he had been caught out. "Haven't I told you *not* to wander too far north, and *certainly* not as far as the river?"

Mog was silent. Pin and Lucias stared at their plates with an intensity the food did not merit.

"Lord Vole, I beg of you to take our young Master Mog firmly under your wing, since he appears to admire you so."

Julian started, surprised more by Maretha's addressing him from down the length of the table than by the request, but he swiftly inclined his head in a gracious assent. "I am sure," he said smoothly, "that Master Mog and Mistress Pin would be well served if they learned a bit about surveying techniques."

" 'Cor." Mog regained his spirits quickly once he had seen that no physical punishment was to ensue. "Just like a real foreman."

"Indeed," said Julian so repressively that Kate and Chryse both smiled.

"Rankles, don't it," said Kate to Chryse, but loud enough that Julian could overhear her, "being compared to a commoner."

"But it also," continued Julian, his gaze fixed on the far table, "means that you will have to attend to your morning lessons with Miss Farr, and show me daily progress in your letters."

"Aw." Mog's glance towards Charity, who had flushed slightly, taking this comment by Lord Vole as some sort of encomium, revealed clearly that not only did he consider her of little account, but that this opinion had worked to prevent his progress at these very lessons. "Why can't—" He stopped, wincing. "Ow, Pin. Why'd you kick me?"

Her hissed whisper, meant to be hushed, reached at least as far as Chryse's ears. "Be polite, you knobhead. Ain't her fault she's dull, an' allays sending us off so she can—Lady knows—anyways, she's nice 'bout it. *An'* she's pretty. Could be worse. We could have *him*." By the emphasis, it was clear *him* referred to the earl. "Count yer blessings, 'stead o' complaining." Spoken with all the sagacity of an ancient.

Chryse, Kate, and Maretha met each other's eyes and burst out laughing. Sanjay, who up to this point had been entirely silent, eating his supper with a smug air of satisfaction, hurriedly engaged Charity in a nonsensical conversation about the supplies brought up from the nearest village two days ago, together with several goats and another crate full of chickens. The professor continued to talk, oblivious to all else. Julian considered Pin and Mog thoughtfully. And the earl, raising his glass, sipped at his wine while his black eyes surveyed, one by one, the assembled company, pausing for the longest time on Lucias and, of course, his wife.

By the time they finished their supper, the prayer service had evidently finished as well, because as Sanjay, Chryse, Kate, and Julian strolled out into the warm evening breeze, there was no sound of singing to accompany them as they walked slowly over to the laborer's camp, where the bonfire had been built.

"One forgets how long it stays light this far north," said Chryse. "It must be going on ten and I can still see."

"It turns back from here." Sanjay took her arm as they made their way along a path only in the past weeks beaten down through the grass that covered the ruins. He laughed abruptly. "The year is like that. It just came to me."

"Like what?" asked Kate.

"Like a spiral, turning in, and then turning out again. Strange how something so obvious comes as a great revelation."

"Truth always comes as a great revelation," said Julian. "But it only arrives if you are ready to receive it."

"You're philosophizing again, Julian," said Kate. "I'm not sure I trust you in this mood."

"*Again?*"

"Yes. It's becoming a habit with you these days."

"Lady help me," he said with feeling. "I sincerely hope that I am not becoming a bore."

Kate merely laughed.

"Well, *I* didn't think of it," said Chryse. "Spirals and the year, that is, or you becoming a bore."

Sanjay grinned. "Maybe you thought of it first, my love, and I just chanced to be the first to say it out loud."

"Before me? Not likely."

Behind, they heard Charity's high voice as she chattered to her cousin about some aspect of housekeeping brought to crisis by the exigencies of the polite life lived in the confines of a wilderness camp.

Out of the half-light several figures appeared. They halted, and Thomas Southern materialized from amongst them and came forward. "My lord," he said, a little curt, acknowledging Julian, and greeted the other three in turn. "Where is—" Maretha and Charity and Professor Farr caught up to the others, Lucias and the two children tagging along at their heels. "Your ladyship." Southern inclined his head to Maretha, including the professor and Charity in the gesture as well. "The workers have asked that you light the bonfire."

"Why, thank you, Thomas," said Maretha, trying to hide what she considered to be an irrational surge of pleasure at this tribute. Seeing his face, she smiled. "You look as though you don't approve."

The tautness of his expression softened abruptly. "Of the honor they mean to give you I approve most heartily, my lady. It is the heathenish practice itself I cannot, as a good churchman, condone."

"I think it all rather exciting," said Charity, a little wild, and with a hint of challenge.

"Ladies are, of course, allowed their diversions, Miss Farr." His voice was level, with only a brief glance at her. "I would not presume to forbid them."

"How very sober of our Mr. Southern," said Kate in an undertone. "He reminds me of that horrible vicar who used to prose on so when we were children. Do you remember, Julian?"

"Judge not, lest ye et cetera," replied Julian. "Quite put one off religion, not that we Haldanes have had any bent in that direction in any case. Rakes, heretics, and black mages, every one."

"Black mages! Julian, this is a tale I've never heard."

"And High Summer's Eve is scarcely the time to tell it, Kate," he answered, reprovingly. "It was the second cousin of the fourteenth of our line, back in King Henry's time."

"How far back does your family go, Lord Vole?" asked Charity, coming up alongside the others. Maretha had gone ahead with her father, together with Southern and his companions.

Julian raised one eyebrow in that quelling way he had
perfected. "Why, to the Conqueror, of course."

Kate laughed. "A bit more hauteur, Julian. It lacks that
edge of scornful arrogance."

"Does it? But then, I should hate to usurp the earl's
place."

"I hadn't realized, your lordship," continued Charity in
a louder voice, "that your lineage was so very—" She
paused, glancing at the group in front.

"So very long-winded?" finished Julian, amused by her
obvious efforts at flirtation. "I fear it is, Miss Farr. Distinctly tedious."

"Oh, I am sure it is not—"

Kate fell back, letting Chryse and Sanjay lag with her. "I
feel no need to subject myself to this," she said.

They trailed along at a leisurely pace, arriving at the
edge of the worker's campsite in time to see the assem-
blage gather. The last sticks were placed with careful
precision around the edge of the stack, and the effigy itself
brought forward. It proved to be a large burlap sack stuffed
with old rags, with a smaller sack tied on above to symbol-
ize a head, and it was, indeed, pierced by an arrow through
the chest and wrapped in a rather tatty-looking deerhide.
A worker climbed laboriously to the top of the stack and
set the effigy up against a pole set there for that purpose.

When he had climbed down and gotten clear, Maretha
threw the first torch. The fires licked this way and that
along the stack, finding a path up the line of the driest
tinder. Soon the bonfire blazed merrily, roaring and spark-
ing, the deerskin effigy lost in smoke at the height. The
gathered workers applauded, as if Maretha herself was
responsible for the cheerful flame.

Suddenly, as if the effigy had come to abrupt, terrified
life, a long, drawn-out scream cut through the night. In the
hush that followed, every person there seemed paralyzed
by surprise or fear.

A chittering like the migration of hundreds of small
beasts broke the hush, starting far away, swelling until it
seemed to surround the camp, and fading as it passed
beyond. The alien nature of its very sound, touched by
unspeakable magics, set into relief the stark humanity of
that first scream.

Chryse found that she was gripping Sanjay's hand so

tightly that her fingers ached when he shook free of her and strode forward into the close glare of the bonfire.

"Mr. Southern!" he called. That man, followed closely by Maretha, hurried up to him. "I suggest we make a quick accounting of who is missing."

"The earl," said Maretha instantly, but Thomas Southern was already calling out to his two group foremen to have all the laborers assemble in neat rows.

"The children." Chryse came forward, too, but behind her Kate answered, "I've got them," and Chryse turned to see Mog and Pin huddled against her legs.

"What's that?" cried Charity, starting violently and grasping Julian's arm.

"What? What?" asked Professor Farr, standing next to his niece with a look of befuddlement on his face.

The sound rose high on the breeze—the rush of water that one hears in the distance as one nears a stream, but accelerated, until the stream indeed seemed to be coming to them, nearing, like a wave, or a river diverted from its course. It rushed, growing in intensity, and with a roar poured over them. Some cowered, some clung to their neighbors, but all, regardless of fear or determination, hunched down, bracing for the onslaught.

Not a drop of water touched anyone, not a breath of high wind, just the thundering roar. The bonfire went out. Hissing, abrupt, as if it had been drenched and drowned.

Silence.

Steam and heavy smoke curled up from the remains of the fire. As people straightened, they felt at their clothing, tentatively at first and then with disbelief as they discovered that they were bone dry. A murmur combined of fright and speculation ran through the assembly.

A sharp, hard break, the snapping of split stone, shuddered the air. The crowd's murmuring ceased abruptly. A low grating grinding followed, as if stone were being moved across stone, and then a gasp, like air, that exploded into a heavy shattering, some massive object fallen to earth, that reverberated in echoes and distant skitterings of tiny avalanches across the valley floor.

Silence again.

"Where is Lucias?" asked Julian. His voice sounded twice its normal volume, although the sibilance of his syllables betrayed that he spoke scarcely above a whisper.

He pried himself free from Charity's grasp and attached her to her uncle. Charity was too terrified to object as Julian left her and came forward to stand by Sanjay and Maretha. A few deep embers in the bonfire had found enough fuel to lend an eerie luminescence to the proceedings.

"Does anyone have any idea what's going on?" Sanjay asked of his immediate companions. There was no reply. "I was afraid of that," he muttered.

"If we're going to search, we'll need lanterns." Maretha turned to Thomas Southern, but he was shouting order into the laborers, using the simple task of lining them up to his command to calm them down. They quickly counted off in the same order as they were paid, and Thomas ordered ten to get lanterns and turned back to Maretha and Sanjay.

"It appears we are missing four people," he said. "We'll check again in the tents, but I think all are here that are in camp. A local girl named Daisy, a couple of Heffield lads, Hawthorpe and Billy, and an older man, Tagmoss."

"Teams of four," suggested Sanjay, looking at Maretha for confirmation. "Two lanterns per group, ten groups. The rest stay here, in case we have to search in shifts."

"Yes," said Maretha. "That sounds best. Kate, can you take the children back to—"

"Ain't going to the tent, ain't going to the tent," shrieked Mog, clutching Kate as if he would drown and burn all at once if she escaped him.

Kate shook her head. "They can come out with me. I don't think they'll stray, under the circumstances, and they know these ruins as well as any of us."

"That's true," said Julian with the ghost of a grin.

"I'll go with you, then." Chryse went to stand beside Kate, taking a lantern when Southern's people returned with them. Two of the laborers, a heavy-set young woman and an older man, joined them.

A number of the laborers were grumbling, unwilling to foray into the night. A few had begun to discuss the prospects of setting out that moment for home when Southern pushed in amongst them and, after a brief exchange, convinced them to return to their tents. Four he set to rebuilding the bonfire, a task which they could only accomplish by digging out the still-dry middle.

"Each group works as a pair," Sanjay was saying. "Don't get too far from the other group. And be back in one hour." He hefted a lantern high in one hand. "Thomas, perhaps it would be best for you to stay here at camp—ah, keep order." Southern looked up, meeting Sanjay's eye, and nodded. "And Chryse, could you escort the professor and Miss Farr back to their tents before you go out?"

"No," said Charity quickly. "I refuse to be alone. We'll stay here. Please, Uncle."

"Of course, my dear." Professor Farr patted her absently on the hand. He moved forward to peer through his spectacles at the damp fire. "Fascinating," he murmured. "Quite fascinating."

"We'll take that direction anyway," said Chryse.

"And we'll go that way as well." Maretha had marshalled a group of three workers. "There's nothing to fear," she said in a softer voice to one of the men.

"That's what Hawthorpe said," he replied, clearly unconvinced. "He said it were a load of superstitious rot."

"Well, then, he's quite level-headed, I would say." Maretha signalled to Chryse and Kate to lead the way.

"And mayhap dead, too," mumbled the man to his fellows as they followed her. "My missus told me it were better to leave what's sleeping lie, and damned if I don't agree with her now."

"Shut up," growled one of the others, but his voice shook.

Ahead, Chryse and Kate forged into the night. Mog clutched Kate's hand, Pin Chryse's. Beside them, the two laborers now each held a lantern, high aloft.

"I recollect now," said the heavy-set woman. " 'Bout Daisy. She and Billy were courting these past weeks, but she complained near every night that there weren't enough privacy. Some warned her it were an ill place for courting, but Daisy had no truck with them as took the old legends as truth. Which isn't to say she won't now."

Chryse fell back to walk beside her, lifting each foot carefully as she picked her way along the tumbled ground. The lanterns shone a faint nimbus around their party; far to one side, two lights like will-o-wisps betrayed Maretha's group. Otherwise, all was dark, but for the stars brilliant overhead.

"Surely," began Chryse as they came up to the large

tents that housed the earl's party, "you don't think they
would have gone out alone just to—"

Mog yelped. It was a brief, horrified cry, cut off by
Kate's voice.

"Bloody burning hell. Turn the light away, man. The
boy's seen enough."

"Kate?"

"You'd best see this, Chryse, but the girl doesn't need
to."

Pin refused to be detached from Chryse, so the expedient of burying her face in Chryse's skirts had to suffice.

"Good Lord," said Chryse under her breath as she came
up beside Kate and could see what the diffuse glow of the
lantern revealed. She felt bile burning in her throat.

The two chicken coops sat before them, cage doors shut
and latched. Inside lay carnage: some wave of destruction,
some beast or beasts, had swarmed through, raking and
biting and shredding and chewing until little was left of
the several dozen chickens brought up two days before
from the nearest village. Several were headless, a few
ripped quite in half. Feathers lay strewn about, lifting in
the breeze and drifting out through the coop mesh. Blood
pooled amongst droppings.

Chryse stumbled backwards, wrenching her gaze away.
"I feel sick. Oh Lord. The goats. The horses!"

"Blessed Lady," said Kate softly. "We'd better check
the stables."

Mog began to cry, and Pin, her little pointed face still
thrust in amongst Chryse's skirts, snuffled sympathetically
with him.

The stables were a makeshift of heavy canvas roof and
rough wooden fencing to contain and stall the horses and
other livestock. As they neared, slow and hesitant in their
approach, they began to hear the snuffling and shifting of
restless animals, disturbed, but not frantic.

"Thank the Lady," began Kate.

"Help! No, no—" A splintering, like wood cut through
with an axe. A startled neighing, followed by the same cry.
"Help me!"

"That's Lucias!" said Chryse. "Lucias!" she shouted.

"Damn." Kate wrenched Mog's hand from hers and ran
for the stables, Chryse and the workmen at her heels.

The noise from the horses increased, whinnying and

stamping. A cow joined the chorus, deep and worried. Goats bleated. A cry from Lucias, a second, splintering crash.

"Lucias! This way!" yelled Kate, reaching one side of the fencing. The canvas roof flapped and rustled in the night wind. In the light of the single lantern, they could see nothing but shapes of darkness within, an occasional animal head illuminated as the workman moved forward.

The cry again, the sound of axe splitting wood.

"He's moving off the wrong way," hissed Kate. "Come on." She charged down the center aisle. "Chryse! Quick! There!"

They came out at the other end of the stables. By some strange trick of the night, the moon had now begun to rise, faint, and faintly ominous. A single thin cloud streaked its curve.

Out on the flats beyond the stables, they saw the two figures: the slender, smaller form of Lucias, stumbling out across the ruins towards a man-high tumble of rocks; behind him a burlier figure, axe in hand.

Kate did not even swear, but ran. Chryse followed, feeling dread swell up in her, knowing that they were too far away.

Lucias stumbled hard, fell to his knees, groped to rise; his pursuer reached him and lifted, all in eerie, silent triumph, the axe for the kill.

The arrows came as silent, but sharply as a scream for their utter unexpectedness. Light streaked them, as if they had been dipped in moonglow. They pinioned the attacker even as his axe stroked down for the kill, hit him hand, shoulder, and throat. He crumpled. The axe fell harmless beside Lucias.

By the time Kate and Chryse reached the youth, he was gasping, half able to speak.

"What the bloody damned whoring hell happened?" Kate's voice was husky with the suppressed emotion of the night's strange events.

He let her and Chryse help him to his feet. "I don't know. I thought—" His voice shook with the effort of articulating. "I just had a notion of checking on the horses, there being something in the air tonight, and then—" His hands trembled in theirs. "I thought I heard Lord Vole calling me, that he wanted to talk to me, so I went to see,

and there was a man there, he began to ask me questions.
Wanted me to go with him, but I refused. I got fuzzy-
feeling, talking to him, and scared, and I ran, and he—"
He shuddered, a deep tremor that convulsed his entire
body. "He tried to kill me."

"You're sure it was a man?" asked Kate.

"Sure as I am one."

"No one could have shot arrows in this direction without
us seeing them," said the heavyset woman with conviction. "Not on such ground."

"Lucias." Chryse tried to keep her voice calm. "Can you
think of any reason someone would want to kill you? You
were a prisoner—someone who followed us? Someone
suspicious who has talked to you? What questions did this
man ask you?"

"I don't remember." He shrugged. "But I've not done a
thing, Madame. In the mornings I've lessons with Miss
Farr, and Mog and Pin, and sure we talk at times, sometimes about *that* place," a tremor, quickly stilled, "and
about my memory, and Mr. Southern I usually help in the
afternoons, or you, or Miss Cathcart, or her ladyship—"
He paused. In the dim gleam of the moon, his face took on
a wary look, quite at odds with the usual openness of his
expression. "The earl. He's suspicious of me, though I
can't say why."

"You aren't possibly suggesting that it was the earl—"

"Madame." It was the workman. "Look."

By lantern and moon the flat stretch of ground they
stood on lay stark and unbroken by shadow or stone for
some distance, The workman hefted an axe—it was one
used by the cook's helpers to chop wood. But it was not
the axe that drew their attention.

All else around him was clear—grass and ground and
ruins beyond—too far beyond for any, much less a mor-
tally wounded man, to reach in such time as they had
stood talking.

Of the three arrows and Lucias' pursuer there was no
sign at all.

"This is impossible," said Julian to Sanjay as they paused
in the lee of a high wall. Stones as broad as a man's
armspan had kept it at such a height despite centuries of
nature's depredations. "We don't even know what direc-

tion that scream came from. Or even if it was a man's scream, considering what else we've encountered tonight."

"No, look." Sanjay lifted one hand to sight at a far ridge. "We'll have moonlight soon enough. I wonder if that will end these—these hauntings."

"I sincerely hope so." Julian ran a hand down the rough surface of the stones. "It's an impressive structure. Nothing like it farther out. I wonder how they built it."

"Your lordship!" The workman's low shocked voice came from the other side of the wall. "Monsieur."

The wall ended in what might have been a gateway some twenty feet from where Julian and Sanjay stood. They hurried around and were brought up short by the sight of the two workmen peering at a huge shivered stone lying in three great pieces at their feet.

"Look how this is fallen," said one of the men. "See this flower here." By lantern light he poked with one boot at a half-crushed stem, a few petals peeping out from beneath stone. "This stone weren't here yesterday."

"And I were working in this area last week," said the other. "I didn't see nothing as overbalanced as this must ha' been to fall so—we would ha' marked it, for safety's sake."

One of the workmen crossed himself. The other looked at Julian and Sanjay, as if they could explain it.

"Do you suppose—" began Sanjay, crouching to examine the shattered stone.

"Lady!" swore Julian abruptly. "That damned—"

Sanjay looked up. The moonlight was beginning to invest the air with the barest of contrasts, a lightening only perceivable by the appearance of shadows and dim forms. Julian was staring off at some sight to his left.

"There! Do you see—" he grabbed the lantern out of Sanjay's hand and broke abruptly into a jog, heading for a low mound. "That damned child slipped her keeper. I could have told Kate—"

Sanjay was up and after him. "Julian! What—"

"There—" Julian pointed with his free hand. "What other goblin child have we with us? She went in there, where they've been excavating this past week—" He stopped talking as they came to a jumble of rubble, saving his breath to negotiate the scatter of rocks that led to the base

of the tiny hill. It rose like a swelling in the midst of a
tight group of walls and curving ruins.

"Wait." Sanjay came to a halt by a heap of grass-grown
stones. "Isn't this—"

A scrape sounded from above, shoe on rock. Julian
expelled his breath on a sigh of deep disgust, and climbed.

Sanjay, for a moment, could only stare about himself.
"I'm sure this is the centralmost portion of—"

"Sanjay!" Julian's shout startled him out of his reverie.

Julian stood at the summit of the little mound, lantern
held high, peering down. As Sanjay began to climb up to
him, he heard another voice, fainter, sounding as if from a
distance, then Julian again.

"Hold tight where you are," Julian was saying. "But
how in Heaven's name did you end up down there?"

Sanjay stopped just in time, finding his boots poised at the
edge of a precipice. An abrupt slope, broken and still loose
from recent collapse, gaped open before him. It was black as
the earl's eyes below, but for the barest oval paling that revealed itself in the lantern glow as a face staring up at them.

"We was just out for a stroll, my lord," said a light
woman's voice, taut with concern and relief but not at all
wild. "Come up here, an' it was as if the ground opened
up of its own and swallowed Billy. He screamed something
awful, he was that surprised—hush, dear, don't speak—
and I climbed down after, careful as I could be, it were so
very dark. An' it looks to both of us as if his leg is broke,
so I sat down here to bide with him 'til help might come,
shouting out now an' again, which must be what you heard."

Sanjay and Julian exchanged glances. Behind, the two
workers had reached the base of the mound and now
began to clamber up it.

"But you must have a stout heart indeed," said Julian.

"Whyever for?" she asked, matter-of-fact as only a country girl can be in such wilderness. "Sure, an' it's dark, an' I
fancy now an' again there's some o' them pictures her
ladyship does like down here, a-staring at me, but—" Her
pause was as eloquent as any shrug might have been.

"But surely with all the—the sounds we've been hearing—"

"Sounds?" The dim suggestion of her face moved some
thirty feet below them. "Just our breathing, my lord,
an' what little talk we had, Billy being in such pain. But
we ha' heard naught else."

Chapter 17:

THE GATE

"Absolutely not," said Kate, by this time annoyed with Julian's insistence. "And I can't imagine why you would think I would lie to you. They were both with us the whole time. In fact the only time we let go of them was to run after Lucias, and then they were with Mistress Workman—whatever the woman's name is. They couldn't have gone so far in so little time *and* gotten back to us in less."

"You say you thought you saw Flu—" Chryse's considering gaze rested on that child where she huddled against Mog on a blanket at Charity's feet. "But I wonder—did the child you saw wear a little cap?"

Julian only shrugged. "I don't remember. Why do you ask?"

"Just a hunch," replied Chryse cryptically.

The bonfire was alight again, a more sober flame now, damped still by remnants of wet brush. Someone had removed the effigy, or buried it in the stack. In the fire's dull light, augmented by the illumination of the moon at its height, the slow activity of late night could be seen like the shadowed stage of a play.

Thomas Southern stood remonstrating with the worker Hawthorpe, a brash young man who had, it transpired, wagered with another fellow that he could climb to the Evening Palace at night unaided by light or companionship. A search party had interrupted the bet and brought him back.

A makeshift litter sat close by the fire. Four stout workers had carried Billy back to camp on it, after another ten had dug a rough stairway down and hoisted the injured man out of the hole. The solicitous Daisy knelt now at Billy's side as Cook, who also served as the camp wise-woman and healer, inspected his leg.

Charity sat swathed in blankets, the children beside her, the professor behind her, absorbed in his own thoughts. Next to her stood Lucias, who was speaking with Maretha. At a comment from her, he frowned, giving the angelic mien of his face an uncharacteristically mulish look in the fire's flickering glow.

Chryse felt Sanjay approach from behind, even before he spoke.

"All accounted for." He rested a hand familiarly on the small of her back. "That last fellow, Tagmoss—evidently he was in his tent all along and the initial search missed him." He shrugged. "I'd say we got off light enough. Considering."

"Not all accounted for," began Julian, but a movement in the shadows interrupted his words. With a low mutter-ing, like the sudden withdrawal of water from beach, the workers dispersed back into their camp, leaving only South-ern in the circle of bare ground surrounding the fire.

The glow seemed to increase slightly, as though touched by fresh fuel, and the earl walked into the ring of light. There was uncanny animation in his face, as any combusti-ble substance ignites when brought to flame. He wore the same black evening clothes he had worn to supper, im-maculate still except for a single fold in his cravat that now bore a small blot: in this light it seemed impossible that it be anything but a tiny oval stain of blood. His gaze came to rest on his wife.

"You tried to murder me!" Lucias's voice cracked, lanc-ing high above its usual light tenor.

The earl's expression, stiff as ice, did not change, but his gaze lowered to examine the boy. "I beg your pardon?" His voice was soft.

"Lucias." Sanjay moved to stand in the space between the two. "You said yourself you never saw the man's face."

"And the only voice you heard," added Julian with a hint of a smile, "you took to be mine."

Lucias's expression stiffened and he flung himself away abruptly, running to the laborers' camp.

"I'll go." Kate hurried off after him.

"Undoubtedly," said the earl smoothly as he walked over to Maretha, "I provide the most convenient suspect, as well as the favored one." He extended a hand towards the fire, as if warming it, then lay it on Maretha's sleeve, a gesture possessive rather than affectionate. She did not move, but her expression tightened. "An interesting turn of events," he continued. He seemed amused, knowing, perhaps, some piece to the puzzle that the others had not yet seen. "The place where the man fell—" His gaze shifted to Sanjay. "Did you recognize it?"

"Oh, yes," said Sanjay. "If my sketches are correct, I believe that mound marks the center of the city."

"I feel sure they are correct."

Professor Farr, who had been standing quietly all the while, came forward now. "But this is marvelous! We'll bring in the blasting powder tomorrow and blast out the dirt—this must surely be a major structure of the city—a central temple, perhaps, or the marketplace."

Maretha slipped her arm out of the earl's grasp and crossed over to Farr. "Father." Her voice was quiet. "Surely you wanted to dig more slowly in such a potentially vital place. If only to preserve the frescos that the young woman saw there."

He blinked and adjusted his spectacles. "So I did, my dear. I had quite forgotten in the excitement."

"But I don't understand," continued Maretha, "how we can have been digging in that area these past weeks and found nothing, when this fellow fell through so easily."

"Perhaps it was not wanting to be found," said the earl. "It is High Summer's Eve, after all."

"Why would that be important?" asked Chryse.

The lift of his eyebrows was so close a copy of Julian imitating him that it seemed a terribly sophisticated double parody, except that the earl did not joke. "I forget, Madame, that you may not be as familiar with the ancient customs as a native of our land would be."

Chryse looked at Maretha.

"I suppose," said Maretha slowly, "that a correspondence could be seen. Of course it is the longest day of the year—but in the ancient stories it is referred to as the imprisonment of the sun, the days getting shorter from then on, you understand." She clasped her hands in front of her as if they were cold.

"Imprisonment below," finished the earl, with an unreadable glance at his wife, "in the depths—in the night—is the fate decreed for the sun, and for the person representing the sun. Or so one might deduce, studying old customs and older legends."

"And if one believed such tales—" Maretha considered the earl, looking strangely disturbed. "That might explain why we had such strange manifestations tonight." She shook her head. "No, you can scarcely expect me to believe that the city itself revealed its secrets only when it attempted to fulfill some ancient ritual—" She trailed off, shifting her gaze to the fire: a more comfortable, and safer, resting place than his eyes.

"Believe what you will," said the earl in the tone of one who already knows the answer.

"Aren't those the same legends that tell of a treasure hidden here?" asked Chryse. As she spoke, Sanjay moved back to stand by her again, and they exchanged speculative glances.

Much to their surprise, the earl lifted a hand to touch the stained fold of his cravat. "Never doubt there is treasure here. It is the form it takes that will prove unexpected to those whose only idea of treasure is gold."

"So one must know not only *where* to look, but how," said Sanjay, musing.

The earl's lips curved, giving a chill to his face that in another person would have been a smile. "You have the gift of sight," he said. "An advantage that even the most adept sorcerer does not possess. You must use it wisely." He turned away, raising one hand in an imperious gesture toward his wife. "Maretha." It was a command, but one tinted by the excitement that the night had seemed to arouse in him.

Her face was still of emotion except for a paling in her lips, pressed tight. But as she walked across to take his arm, she looked in her turn at the professor.

"Father? Charity? Are you coming with us?" The professor helped Charity up and, with the two children hanging on her skirts, they followed. If the earl was amused by this gambit, he did not show it. The party faded into the night, heading back to their tents.

"Not at all surprised, was he," said Julian, "by any of our interesting events tonight."

"Should he have been?" Thomas Southern's comment startled the other three because they had forgotten he was there. "Your lordship," he added as an afterthought, as he always did. He was looking after the group that had just left, a frown creasing the usual undisturbed clarity of his face. "His is a godless soul, undismayed by manifestations of the Daughter."

Julian chuckled. "Tell me, Southern, do you believe our precious earl is damned?"

Southern at last shifted to look at the others. His expression was perfectly serious. "We have all sinned. But we have hope of Our Lady's mercy. *He* does not believe in the salvation of Our Blessed Mother and Her Son. For that he is doubly damned. If you will excuse me." His hands clasped behind him, lost in some rumination none of the other three could guess, he walked slowly out of the dwindling circle of firelight towards the laborers' camp.

"Speak for yourself." Julian laughed. "Lady knows we Haldanes will burn as hot as any."

"I'm cold," said Chryse, tugging her cloak a little tighter around her shoulders.

Sanjay was staring at the fire as if he saw something there. "Why do I have the feeling that he was challenging me?" he said in a low voice.

"Thomas?"

He shook his head. "The earl."

Chryse looked at Julian. They both shrugged. "But Sanjay," she continued, turning back to her husband, "he's saying that the city itself is in some way aware, isn't he? As if it holds power, as a person might."

"The treasure might hold power," said Julian. "Even if it *is* only gold and jewels, it holds power in some fashion over men's minds."

"But that's not what he means, or not entirely it. You know that." She stared out; in the moonglow she could see the faintest outlines of the ruins, speckled close by with the handful of lanterns that now illuminated the two camps. "As if it had some kind of life of its own. And after tonight . . . Sanjay, do you believe that?"

Sanjay still gazed at the fire, but his eyes were on a vague height he could see beyond, through the lick of flame and curl of smoke. A figure stood there, too sharply defined at such distance for the available light and with a

nebulosity that made him realize that no one but he could
see it. A human figure, perhaps, or at least humanlike;
more than that he could not make out, except for the stark
and obvious shape of a bow held with complete confidence
in its hands. Inevitably, he thought of the three arrows
that had saved Lucias.

"Yes," he replied. "I believe it." He clasped her hand in
his, gave Julian a brief smile. "Let's go back. I think the
rest of the night will be quiet." They began to walk.

"It makes you wonder, though," said Chryse in a soft
voice, "about what the other holidays will be like."

Maretha had to restrain her father a second time from
bringing out the blasting powder when the initial excavations into the central mound revealed two walls of incomplete frescos that led into solidly-packed earth on all sides.
Once she had reminded him that he had meant to use
more precise and careful methods, he lapsed back into his
usual routine of mornings spent bothering the laborers
with pointless details and confused directions, which
Maretha would later countermand, and afternoons scribbling in an unreadable scrawl his observations and conclusions, at such great length that only his daughter had the
patience to decipher and then recopy them.

There was some muttering amongst the workers about
hauntings and black magic and the earl, but the weather
kept so fine and clear, and Thomas Southern so piously
determined to maintain order in the work force he was
hired to supervise, that the doomsayers found little support.

The edifice in the center of the valley emerged slowly,
long curves of frescoed wall that averaged a man's height
but in places rose even higher. Intermittent tiling marked
the floor of the structure. The work progressed at a sedate
pace out of Maretha's concern for the delicate paintings
that covered the stone.

As the weeks passed, no further incidents disturbed the
site. The grumbling and complaining of the workers sub-
sided until only a few remnants—warding spells and charms
to protect from ghosts and the evil eye, a short swell of
agitation when it became apparent they might have to dig
underground—remained to interrupt the progress of the
excavation.

Late in the month of Tew, when the weather might

reasonably be expected to be at its hottest, a cool spell
descended suddenly. The day dawned cloudy, and eventually a slight drizzle wet the hard ground, damping the
laborers' clothing. Chryse and Maretha, caught out without cloaks, had come inside to change and now sat in easy
camaraderie in the big tent cataloguing glyphs with the aid
of Sanjay's recent sketches.

In one corner of the tent Charity lay half sitting on a
couch, dozing over the weekly menu that she was prepar-
ing for Mistress Cook. In sleep she looked even more
beautiful. The fresh air had given her cheeks heightened
color, and the abundance of food to be had at an earl's
table, even in such conditions as this, had filled her out,
adding a lusciousness to the suggestion of her figure beneath her gown.

"What do you suppose it represents?" asked Chryse as
she smoothed out a crease in one of the sketches. A host of
figures, a procession, perhaps, filled the page: the hind-
quarters of hounds, a trio of bare-bosomed, full-skirted
women, five men attired for war or for hunting, all traced
in two colors: one a frequently-interrupted line of the
actual remains, one a light continuous line of Sanjay's
superimposed reconstruction. On a page next to it, she
could compare it with an exact rendering of the find, a
fragmented picture obscured by large gaps of worn-away
stone that an observer who was not also an artist might
have difficulty making sense of.

Maretha raised her head. She had grown more relaxed
as the dig progressed, free of her father's constant presence, seeing little of her husband, engaged in work she
found stimulating. The smile that lit her features now
made her face quite handsome, unmarked by worry or by
that disquieting sense of confinement and foreboding that
sometimes came over her.

"What I suppose it represents would certainly be more a
reflection of my thoughts than any accurate explanation of
its real meaning, don't you think?" she asked.

"But Maretha, if you aren't qualified to guess, then who
is?"

"No one, I think. No one but one who has lived in that
time and seen the hand that painted these frescos." She
paused to compare two glyphs, made a little sound of
satisfaction under her breath, and quickly penciled in the

new glyph below the other in her catalog. "Once I've studied this material for as many years as my father has, I might be willing to write a paper on my theories."

Chryse, watching her face, was struck by the lack of resemblance between Maretha and her father; one could see the Farr blood more readily in Charity. She had never seen a picture of Maretha's mother. "Would you agree with your father?"

"I don't know." She looked troubled, as if the admission was blasphemous. "I think ritual must have been of primary importance in the life of this city, and this culture, but how to interpret that ritual—" She set down her pen and examined her fingers. "My father and the earl are certainly more knowledgeable than I am, so one must give serious consideration to their theories."

"Even if one doesn't find human sacrifice palatable?"

"Who are we to judge? Think back to the circumstances in which we found Mog and Pin. Were the ancients necessarily any more cruel?"

In the silence Chryse carefully penned three glyphs onto a clean sheet of parchment, double-checking them several times from Sanjay's drawing. "You might check this top one against number sixty-two." She lifted the paper to survey it in a different angle of light. "I wish that these people had had the forethought to standardize their notational system. They're making it difficult for us." She set down the paper to take a sip of tea, then leaned back in her chair, stretching, unclosing and closing her right hand. "We should have brought a piano along. I'm getting out of practice."

Maretha chuckled. "Perhaps I can ask my husband to have one sent up here."

"Do you think he would?" Chryse's reply was more jest than serious, so it surprised her when that shuttered look descended on Maretha's face, like the closing of windows in a house.

"He might. He treats me very well."

"You sound as if you can't understand why he should. Aren't you being a little hard on yourself? It was no easy bargain on your side. I think you deserve far more than you've received from it so far."

But Maretha only shook her head, her eyes dropped, her shoulders bowing in a way Chryse hadn't seen since before her wedding. "I told him I wouldn't—" Her left hand toyed nervously with her pen. "That I didn't believe he married me because he needed an heir."

"I'm not sure—"

"I haven't— We haven't— I couldn't bring myself to—" Maretha flushed. "He hasn't touched me, in *that* way."

"Oh." Chryse's voice was as soft, if less impassioned. "But isn't that what you wanted? To be free of him?"

"I wanted my freedom," said Maretha fiercely. "But I feel the bargain has not been paid in full on my part. What can he want of me, Chryse? What can he want?"

"I don't know. He wanted to come here, after all." Maretha did not respond. "I'm sorry, Maretha."

Maretha lifted her gaze finally to look at the blonde woman. "I agreed to it. I could have refused to marry him."

On the couch, Charity stirred and yawned and sighed deep from her chest. Her hands shifted to rest on her belly.

"Easy to say now," said Chryse. "I'm not so sure it would have been so easy then."

Maretha glanced away from her, towards her cousin, not in any furtive way, or as if she were avoiding the unspoken question, but as if she were distracted by the sight of Charity asleep. "I still wonder why he chose me when he could have had Charity."

"Oh, Maretha." Chryse sounded a little disgusted. "Humility is all very well, but too much humility is as much a vice as too much vanity."

Maretha laughed. The sound startled Charity out of her doze; she blinked slowly and all at once lost her grip on the menu. It fluttered to the floor just as the tent flap stirred, a larger echo of the sound, and Sanjay came into the tent.

Charity made a little *oh* of surprise and sat up quickly, straightening her dress. Sanjay kissed Chryse on the forehead and smiled at Maretha, proffered a short bow in Charity's direction. His face shone with excitement.

"Sanjay!" Chryse stood up. "What is it?"

He sat down in the third chair, laughed, and stood up again. "Come on." He extended a hand and lifted Maretha to her feet. "We've got to go down to the excavation."

"What have you found?"

"The treasure!" Charity started up with an animation she had not shown in days.

"A whole room of gold and jewels!" Sanjay laughed again. "No, nothing so mundane. This is much better: I think we've found some kind of cache, beneath the floor. There's a loose stone slab that can be moved, but we thought you should be there, Maretha." As he said this one hand drifted back to clasp Chryse's.

"I'll come too," said Charity. She followed her cousin out the entrance.

Chryse pulled on Sanjay's hand, holding him back for a moment. "What if it is the treasure, hidden under there? What do we do?"

In his look she could see the same lack of answers that she felt in herself, but he merely shrugged. "Let's not count our bridges until we come to them." When she chuckled, he grinned. "Isn't that right? You Occidentals have the most peculiar sayings. There might be trouble, though."

"Why?" They went outside, catching up to Charity and Maretha.

"The workers refuse to dig underground. Some kind of superstition."

"Oh dear." Maretha frowned. "That will make it difficult. I don't suppose anyone thought there might be underground levels to this city."

"I wonder whether their technology was sophisticated enough to manage such construction," said Sanjay.

"But wouldn't that depend on—" began Chryse.

"—on what kind of technology they used?" finished Sanjay. He lifted one dark hand to touch the coat pocket where he carried, as always, half of their deck of cards, and his gaze shifted quickly to the little pouch dangling from the waistband of Chryse's gown, where she carried the other half. He turned his attention back to Maretha as they hurried along the well-worn path that led through the ruins to the central excavation. "I'm afraid this refusal is quite serious. Not a single worker has dissented."

"Not even Thomas?"

"Mr. Southern crossed himself, and said he was sure you would make the right decision."

For an instant Maretha's expression fixed in a look the more surprising for its bitterness. "Don't I always? But no, it would do no good to antagonize the workers now. There is quite enough to do aboveground. By the Lady! Has everyone gathered here?"

They had walked up to the excavation from the high side, a low height that looked out over this portion of the site. Beyond, on the far side the dug-out area sloped smoothly into undisturbed ground. The mound Billy had fallen through was obliterated, its remnants half carted off and half heaped in a haphazard pattern across the building revealed by its absence.

The centralmost portion was about half uncovered. Frescoed walls curved in on themselves, and it was clear from the arc of their curve that they met under the rubbled ridge on which Sanjay, Chryse, Maretha, and Charity now stood. Pillars dotted the ground, some still twice a man's height, others broken off halfway down, still others shattered into splintered pieces that littered the tile floor. The tiling was stark: one dark and one light color that interwove as it curled into the center, following the slightly off center line of the pillars to a low circular platform that had just two days before been uncovered in the very middle of the building. From their vantage point, they could guess that the edifice itself was built on the pattern of a spiral.

On the central platform stood Professor Farr, Kate, Julian, and, to no one's surprise, the earl. Kate was crouched at the base of a great pillar, twice the diameter of any of the others, that stood in the middle of the platform. With one hand she brushed at something on the stone floor, but as swiftly as if Chryse or Maretha had called out to her, she looked up at the party standing above on the ridge and waved.

"We'd better go down," said Sanjay. "Before they get impatient."

They circled about a third of the way around the site before climbing down to the building remains. The workers, clustered at the edges of the dug-out area, separated to let them pass.

"Ain't right, your ladyship," said one as they reached the platform, "to ask us to go unnerground, not in any wise, and certain not in a place like this."

Maretha turned. Thomas Southern had stepped forward to speak to the worker, but she forestalled him with a lift

of her hand. "I can assure you that Professor Farr respects
your feelings on such matters."

"Regent don't," a lighter voice muttered, meant to be
heard only by its neighbor, but a trick of the hollow
amplified it.

"In any case," continued Maretha, ignoring the comment, "there is no guarantee that there is any underground work to be done here at all."

"The flooring all looks the same to me," said Chryse to
Sanjay as they went to stand by Julian. The floor of the
platform was made of plain fitted stone, unadorned by
carving or paint. "How did you find the loose slab?"

Kate rose from her crouch and stepped aside to let
Sanjay kneel where she had been. "See here." He brushed
with his fingers at a series of small holes, no more than
three fingerwidths across, that pierced in two lines a large
section of the stone. "It occurred to me that those holes
could be used as a means to shift the slab, and with the
help of a few fellows, we found we could. So I called
everyone together. Who knows what we might find."

"You have a keen eye," said the earl from directly
behind Sanjay, "to have seen such a delicate clue. Who
knows what we might find?"

Sanjay tilted his head to give the earl a speculative
glance, as if to say, *You might.* The earl smiled, a frosty
cordiality, and, much to the surprise of the others, Sanjay
smiled back, as if he and the earl shared some secret, or
recognized some likeness between them.

"How do you think it worked?" asked Chryse into the
pause.

"Rope handles." Kate looked at Sanjay for confirmation.

"That's what I was thinking." He stood up and beckoned
to Thomas Southern. "Did you get the crowbars and rope?"

Southern brought several burly laborers, each armed
with a heavy iron crowbar, and they set their backs to
levering up the great slab. It was slow work. The earl
stepped off the platform, brushing unseen dust from his
white cuffs. Professor Farr ventured too close in his excitement and had to be drawn back by his daughter.

At last they shifted the slab enough that ropes could be
slipped through the holes in the stone, and with a grating
that echoed across the hollow like the rumbling of a dis-

tant avalanche, heard after it is seen, they dragged it to one side.

Only the earl did not crowd forward to see what lay beneath. There was silence.

"Oh dear," said Maretha.

The top of a staircase lay revealed in the afternoon sun. A single step, alone; the rest was buried in rubble and debris.

"A little dynamite," began the professor.

"Uncle, I'm not feeling well," said Charity with what was apparently an unexpected rush of common sense. "Could you take me back to my tent." She was, indeed, pale, in distinct contrast to the rose that had flushed her cheeks while she slept.

Professor Farr blinked in his vague way. "Not feeling well, my dear?" He looked uncertainly at Maretha.

"This can wait, Father." Maretha cast a glance both grateful and concerned at her cousin. "Perhaps—" She turned to Southern. "Perhaps you could assist the professor, Thomas."

"If you wish, your ladyship." His acquiescence seemed disapproving, but of what it could not be told. He offered Charity his arm with what appeared to be great reserve, quite in contrast to his usual manner. Charity seemed not to notice as she took it and let him escort her out of the site. The professor followed.

Maretha turned to face the earl, who had come up on the platform to examine the buried stairwell. Behind, the workers were muttering, their voices swelling with discontent.

"My lord," she said in a soft voice that scarcely carried to Chryse and Sanjay's ears. He met her gaze. His face bore no discernible expression. "Don't force this." She made an infinitesimal gesture toward the stairwell, and a second toward the tide of revolt stirring in the laborers.

His gaze, drifting with lazy arrogance over the crowd of workers, stilled their talk as if he had spelled them to silence. "Do you suppose," he said on a slow, exaggerated drawl, "that they would dare to resist me?" Her expression darkened, fire rising in her eyes to match the chill in his, but he spoke again before she could reply. "Not yet," he said, with the barest bow to her. "Not yet." He scrutinized the opening, stair peeping from rubble, for a few more silent moments, then strode away abruptly into the ruins beyond.

"It's late enough that we can safely call off work for today." Maretha pitched her voice to carry to everyone left in the hollow. "Be assured that there will be no digging for the time being below this floor level. You may go."

The workers dispersed quickly.

"Do you know what strikes me," said Sanjay into the lull.

Kate stood one step down into the stairwell, poking at the debris with a crowbar. "Hell. Give me a shovel and I'll dig it out. I'd wager my fortune that our treasure is buried somewhere down here."

"Good winnings for someone," said Julian drily. "What strikes you, Sanjay?"

"I don't know much about the science of digging," he replied, "but *I'd* wager that there's only one layer to this city—that it was never built up over an older city, and that over an older one yet again, as you'd find in, say—" he paused.

"Heffield?"

"How much would you wager?" asked Kate. "If we don't find this treasure soon I won't have a penny left to my name."

Sanjay chuckled. "I'm hardly the one to wager with."

"Father!" Maretha's exclamation interrupted them. She stepped down from the platform to meet the professor, who was peering through his spectacles at the dim outline of frescos on one of the excavated walls.

"Arguments. Arguments," he muttered as he stared at the wall. "Don't understand 'em."

"How is Charity, Father?"

"Incredible." He moved closer to the pictures, until his nose practically touched the wall. "Just as I predicted."

By now the others had come up beside them. The fresco was faded and worn; all that could be discerned was a kind of bed or flat couch on which a figure, probably female, lay reclined, a second figure leaning over the first, arms stretched over the female's chest or shoulders, hands rubbed away until they were little more than a suggestion about her neck.

"Now where was that other fresco?" The professor wandered along the wall, Maretha hurrying after. "Bad day," he mumbled as he walked and peered. "Bad day tomorrow."

"I know what was so strange," said Chryse abruptly to her audience of three, watching Maretha and the professor walk away from them. "He was *baiting* her."

Kate nodded with swift understanding. "You're right."

"Am I simply obtuse," asked Julian, "or—"

"Obtuse," said Kate. "The earl. He baited Maretha, back there. He said that bit about the workers resisting him just to get a reaction from her. Interesting."

"What do you suppose he means, 'bad day,'" asked Sanjay.

Julian looked thoughtful, staring at the fresco. "Haven't you noticed the weather? It should be the heat of the summer coming on. The last day of the month is—I can't remember what the holiday was called anciently—"

"Hunter's Run," said Kate. "Remember your cards."

"Of course. First day of the season—dove and such. Usually I take my dogs out, dry run for October, you know, when the really good hunting starts. Isn't much of a holiday anymore. I suppose the church couldn't find a holy day to merge with it."

"And tomorrow is the last day of the month, isn't it?" asked Chryse.

"Maybe he was referring to something else." Sanjay reached out to touch a fresco farther down the wall. A few faint lines showed the forequarters of, perhaps, a stag—in any case, some antlered beast.

"I hope so," said Kate. "At least it isn't too hot for digging."

CHAPTER 18:

DAWN

That night the wind rose. The noise of it filled the distant forest and scattered ruins until it drowned out the other senses, like the constant rushing of falls to a blind man. The canvas of the tents flapped and shuddered until Chryse, huddling against Sanjay in their bed, felt impelled to wake him so that he could reassure her. Half asleep, he managed to enfold her tightly enough in his arms that she could sleep.

When he woke completely, the wind had ceased and the bed was empty beside him. He slipped on a pair of trousers and a shirt and stepped outside. It was just dawn. The haze of light that heralds sunrise was brightening to day. He saw her figure silhouetted against a dark height, edged in silver by the rising sun. He climbed up to stand beside her. She had put on her kid boots, but only a robe over her nightshift.

"Do you hear them?" she asked without looking at him, then lapsed into a silence so intent that he did not reply.

"There," she said again. And listened. "There."

Like a sound blown so far on the breeze that the current of wind itself had shredded it almost beyond substance, he heard the belling of hounds.

"Horns," she said. "And that melody. How perfectly the harmony complements it." She stood rapt. He could not break her quiet to tell her that he heard nothing now, certainly not music. "Lord, it's beautiful," she breathed. He took her hand. A tear slid down her cheek, and as he watched it, he saw out of the corner of his eye a movement far beyond, in the distant forest.

He snapped his head to look, but it was gone, no more than the suggestion of some antlered beast, perhaps, bounding away through the distant trees.

And then, sudden and clear, the voice of hounds, belling and barking. He shuddered at their tone, for it was a killing run, with death as its goal. Chryse started suddenly, her hand convulsing in his, and she took a step back.

"Someone is hunting over there. The music is gone."

From below, a shout carried up to them.

"Oh Christ, I'm still in my robe," said Chryse.

"Fire!" cried Sanjay. "Look!" A haze of smoke, like an echo of the lightening horizon, swelled up from the center of the ruins.

They ran down to the cluster of tents. Thomas Southern was talking to Maretha, who also had had time only to put on a robe over her nightshift. Julian emerged from his tent, bleary-eyed and, though fully dressed, a bit rumpled. He shook his head as Sanjay and Chryse came up beside him, and they hurried over to Southern and Maretha.

"— we don't know how the fire got started," Southern was saying, "but it's spreading in this direction. I have every hand digging trenches to protect our camp. I'll send a group down here as well, though it appears to me that you'll be well out of it. And we're missing that—" he paused on an aspirative, as if he had been about to swear and caught himself "—that fool Hawthorpe. Evidently he got drunk with some of his mates last night and boasted that he could swim across the lake to the north shore. Hasn't been seen since."

"Is anyone else missing?" asked Maretha.

"I don't know. I haven't had time to take a count, but—"

"Bloody hell." Kate's voice cut into their conversation. She ran up to them, fully dressed, from the direction of the stables. "He's gone again."

"Not—"

"Yes. Lucias. He's early up to the stables in the mornings, so I've taken to trailing him, not trusting to luck like last time, in case that murder attempt wasn't a fluke." She lifted a hand to tug her cravat back into position. Dirt smeared her fingers, as if she had been digging. "And now he's disappeared."

"Again," said Sanjay.

"We are not," said Maretha decisively, "sending any search parties across the lake."

"Lady bless us." Charity had appeared at the entrance to her tent, looking bemused and quite lovely in her robe, which was belted so loosely about her that one could not make out even the barest outlines of her figure.

"Prim of her," muttered Kate. She grinned as Chryse looked self-consciously down at the revealing fit of her own robe.

There was a rush of energy about Charity's skirts, and Mog and Pin came charging out of the tent.

"Fire! Fire!" shrieked Pin, while Mog simply bellowed like an ogre.

"Back!" Julian lifted a hand. The children halted stock still. "Into the tent," he ordered, "and stay there." Meek as worshippers, they went.

"What about Lucias?" asked Kate.

"Send what men you can spare to dig trenches around this camp," said Maretha to Southern. "the rest of us will have to look for the boy. But I—" She directed a challenging look at the men present. "—am going to change first."

"Yes," agreed Chryse.

They returned in short order. By this time Professor Farr had come out of his tent, pen in one hand, journal in the other. "Maretha? Are we starting so early today?" He did not seem to notice the pall of smoke that rose behind them.

"Nothing important, Father. Why don't you finish what you're writing and then Charity will bring you breakfast." He nodded and retreated back to his tent. Southern had already left.

"I would suggest we investigate the fire first," said Sanjay, "and then split into search groups. Is the earl—"

"No." Maretha's voice was shadowed by an emotion that her face disguised. "He's gone, too."

Without further comment they set out for the other camp. Soon enough the first drift of smoke began to permeate the air as they walked. It grew heavier, and by the time they reached the other camp the smoke had gathered so thickly that it had begun to obscure the sun. A line of workers labored on a deep trench; like ghosts, they flickered in and out of view as the breeze shifted. All wore shirts tied about their noses and mouths.

Thomas Southern approached them, lowering a dirty white cloth from his face. His skin was red, mottled by heat, and soot dappled the hollows of his eyes. "If you're going out there, I'd advise covering your face with wet cloth. The worst of it is northwards, but there's a front burning down this way, and another headed straight for the center."

"Any sign of Lucias?" asked Kate.

He shook his head, called a worker over, and sent him off to get handkerchiefs for Maretha and the others. Julian, with an expressive grimace, retrieved his own mono-grammed handkerchief from his waistcoat pocket and re-fused the one offered him by Southern.

"Let's walk towards the center," suggested Maretha.

"You had best be careful, my lady," said Southern. "It's a fierce blaze, though it's mostly burning east and north now."

"I have to find my husband," Maretha murmured. She set off so quickly that the others had no choice but to follow. The smoke lightened as they headed west from the laborer's camp, but as the path wound north, heading for the central excavation, a trick of the breeze brought the sound of fire to them.

"I don't like this," said Sanjay. "I suggest we head back."

"We can go up," said Maretha. "At the Evening Palace we'll have a clear view."

They agreed, but by the time they negotiated the switch-back trail that led up to the western ridge and its half-excavated edifice, they were all as hot and sweaty as if they had been fighting the fire. The panorama was spec-tacular: fire raced and burned below, blanketing half the valley, licking and racing and smoldering across stone and grass alike. Smoke hid the reaches of the forest beyond the northern river and lake; to the south a thin layer of ash hung lazily in the air. Even at this height, the light of the rising sun was dimmed.

"Look!" cried Maretha, pointing down.

At the closer camp, the earl's, a single line of workers could be seen digging. Farther east, mostly obscured by smoke, three longer lines labored to save the larger camp.

There were five of them on the height: each saw something different, as clear across the distance as if their sight was telescoped.

The earl stood on the central platform in the shadow of the central pillar in the very heart of the dig. As Maretha watched, a wave of flame circled the excavated area and flowed along the bare dirt towards him. Perhaps she cried out—she was not sure later—but the fire arced and leaped as if it were alive, and washed forward to engulf her husband. And he laughed, truly laughed, as if its presence brought him joy rather than destruction. A sudden faintness as strong as any wind-whipped blaze drained her until she could barely stand, had to catch at a waist-high wall, as her knees buckled and she fell forward onto them. Far below, the earl blazed like a star might, thrown to earth, as beautiful and as deadly.

Julian had turned to look west at Maretha's comment, and he saw, running away into the height above the Evening Palace, a snout-faced, whiskered child, a little cap askew on its head. "Pin! Damn it." He split away from the others and climbed after the retreating figure.

The first moment Chryse thought they were instruments; the second she realized that she was seeing figures in or of the flames themselves, and that they were indeed using musical instruments, playing music atonal and wild. As the fire roared and spread, more liquid figures joined the flickering orchestra until, with a spitting crescendo, the entire vision vanished and she saw only flame again.

Smoke shivered Sanjay's view of the forest, like mist sunk in trees. He saw the hounds first, in a pack as they ran along the river and disappeared into the forest again. Mounted riders followed on brilliantly arrayed horses; their faces were unclear in the smoke, their clothing unlike any he had ever seen, supple and golden. Of their quarry he saw no sign: only, solitary and small at the tail end of the hunt, a single man who seemed to be naked, running at a tireless pace, spear hefted and ready in one hand.

Kate saw Lucias. Hands bound, he was being driven by a man she did not recognize at this distance toward the eastern end of the valley, into the very center of the maelstrom. Their trail led into such thick billowing clouds of smoke that she was amazed she could see him at all. Then he and his captor vanished into the gloom.

"Come on," she cried, grabbing the nearest person, who happened to be Chryse. "We've got to save Lucias."

"Lucias?" Chryse hesitated, still bemused.

"Where?" asked Sanjay, quicker to register the comment.

"In trouble. If we run—" She faltered. "Lady," she swore, paling. "How could I have seen him? He must be over two miles away. We'll never reach him in time."

"Point me where," said Chryse with a sudden burst of decision. "Sanjay, your cards. Which one—"

"I know," said Sanjay. "Kate, you'll have to help us. Maretha. Where's Julian?"

Maretha had recovered enough to hide her weakness, and in any case the faintness was ebbing now. She could no longer make out anything but flame and smoke where she had seen her husband. "I don't know. What do we do?"

"Here." Sanjay handed his cards to Chryse. On the top of his pack he had set the final face card: a woman tied to a stake, engulfed in flame, her mouth open in agony, or ecstasy.

Chryse tucked the rest of the cards into her pouch, keeping out one other from her half: a man bound and chained to stone in a closed cell. Holding them together in one hand, she knelt. Sanjay rested a hand on her right shoulder, Kate on her left.

"Kate," she said. "Think of where you last saw him. Sanjay, think of fire."

In the hush of their concentration, only the distant spit and roar of the fire could be heard, and once a chorus of barks that cut off abruptly. Chryse thought of Lucias, of his hands bound behind him, of his hair, golden as the sun. Of the sun, brilliant in its fiery high seat, of heat, of the lick of flame, of smoke, thick and choking and hot to the breath—

"—I can't breathe," she gasped. Heat seared her lungs as she reflexively took in air. Beside her, Kate choked, coughing and swearing.

"Put the cloth in front of your face." Sanjay's voice was muffled.

Chryse lifted one hand to her face, felt a cooling moisture on her skin as the cloth settled against her mouth and nose. Immediately her lungs breathed easier, but her eyes stung now. Smoke surrounded them; there was no sign of fire. Kate tugged at her sleeve, and she groped up to stand and stumbled after her.

"Where is Sanjay?" she gasped. Her foot caught on a rock and she tripped, but a strong arm gripped her and held her up. "Thank God," she said to him. "Where's Maretha?"

"I don't think she came through."

"Where are we?"

Sanjay paused to peer through the smoke. "At the eastern end of the valley, I think. It's hard to tell."

Kate dragged on them. "Come on!" Her voice was urgent.

They came out of the thickest smoke abruptly, straight into a blast of heat so fierce that she felt as if her face had caught on fire. Flame shot at least twice their height into the sky. What it fed on was inexplicable to her, here in this corridor of stone and dirt and scrub grass.

"There!" shouted Kate. Her yank on Chryse's arm almost unbalanced the blonde woman, but Sanjay was still beside her.

Fire crackled and rumbled by turns about them, advancing at so slow a pace that it seemed deliberate, branching out to surround them. In a little sink of ground that was slowly filling with smoke, a figure lay heaped like any bundle thrown to earth, topped with a light crowning of hair. It was Lucias, bound both hand and foot now, struggling feebly to free himself.

They stumbled down a litter of sharp rocks to crouch beside him. Kate and Sanjay worked furiously to release him from the ropes. Chryse stood and stepped back to get a vantage point. Started back, fear like a vise in her chest. Flame surged up to cast a circle around them. They were surrounded.

Terror streaked through her. She did not realize that she had taken another step back until the ground gave beneath her boots. With a "whoosh" like fire leaping a great gap to kindle fresh fuel on the far side, her footing vanished and she fell. She tried to cry a warning, but smoke choked her throat.

The impact of landing jarred her through her body. She scrabbled at the dirt, found herself neck deep in a hole. Kate, Sanjay, and Lucias were almost lost in smoke above.

"Here! Down here!" she gasped.

A spark landed, sizzling, on Sanjay's trousers. He slapped

it, in the action of slapping saw Chryse, and grabbed Kate. Together they dragged Lucias over and threw him in beside Chryse, squirmed in beside her themselves.

"Farther down." Kate's voice was ragged, torn by the heat and smoke inhalation.

They slid back, down, found stone beneath their feet, felt with their hands a damp stairwell. Hunkered down as the fire roared above. Debris and sparks sprayed down on them like the offal of fireworks. They were filthy with dirt, patting each other free of embers.

From far off, a shuddering crack splintered the monotone rustle of fire. A flash of light too brilliant to be natural scorched the entire sky for a blinding instant, and following immediately upon it a second grinding clap of thunder. And rain.

Abrupt, tearing out of the sky that had been free of clouds the last time they had seen it. They turned their heads down to avoid choking on the rain, it came so hard. It pounded the dirt around them, peppered their shoulders and backs and hair, churned the dirt on which they lay into mud. The fire whuffed and steamed and vanished, as though it had never been. The rain faltered and ceased, and sunlight lanced across their faces through the dispersing smoke.

For a long time they just breathed.

"Hell," said Kate at last, savoring the flow of the word and the hoarse flavor her strained throat gave it.

A dry coughing racked Lucias's body.

"Are you all right?" Chryse laid a hand on his head. "Who did this?"

"Don't know," he rasped.

"I was afraid of that," she replied.

"Holy Lady!" Kate's voice was still thick with smoke, but her tone was clear. "It's a stairwell. We've found another stairwell. There *must* be an entire lower level below the ruins." She shook her head, wondering, and crawled up the slope to help Lucias find an unsteady foothold on a stone step.

Above, Sanjay crawled up to peer over the top at the destruction wrought by the fire. His body stiffened as he looked, and he climbed out of the hole and simply stood, staring, silent.

"Sanjay?" Chryse scrambled up beside him. "What is it—" Her voice died away, and she stared as well.

There was no sign at all that a fire had raged across the ruins like an inferno. The valley looked as it always did, but for thin trails of mist that separated into ragged streams, dissolving into nothing as they watched.

"Look, the sun has just come up."

No one replied to Chryse's comment. She turned finally to help Kate hoist Lucias out of the stairwell. The youth was filthy, his hair matted with soot and dirt, his wrists marred by a pink rope burn, but he was otherwise unharmed.

"You're not going anywhere by yourself anymore," said Sanjay.

Lucias merely wiped a tear from one dirty cheek.

"Rescued," said Kate, her voice thick with irony. She waved an arm, and a group of searchers, Julian and Maretha among them, waved back and hurried over to them.

"We thought we'd lost you," cried Maretha as they reached them. "Thank the Lady you're safe." She hugged Chryse, weeping a little, and from her shoulder Chryse saw Julian, without a word, grab Kate into a tight embrace.

"I don't understand," said Lucias. "How can the sun have just come up? Hours and hours have passed since I got up before dawn. It should be at least noon."

"Don't try to understand it," said Sanjay in an undertone.

"Kate." Julian broke away from her and stepped forward to gaze down the stairwell. "What do you suppose I found west and above the Evening Palace? I thought that child had gotten loose again—" He paused, and Kate came up to stand beside him, looking down as well.

The stairwell ended, they could now see, in a blank, featureless wall of stone some fifteen steps below ground level.

"Exactly the same," murmured Julian. "West and east." He and Kate looked at each other and, as if with one thought, at the pickaxes and shovels carried by the workmen in their party.

"Lucias," agreed Maretha. "Go back with the workmen and wait for us at my tent." The tone of her voice did not encourage protest.

"I'll go with him," said Kate quickly.

"Yes," said Maretha. "But you three—" She paused,

and Chryse, Sanjay, and Julian waited, curious, until the others had walked out of earshot, heading back to camp across the eerily intact grass and brush that flourished in the rubble. "We've got worse," she said. "Thomas is waiting for us at the shoreline. But we've got to keep it to ourselves, I'm afraid."

"I want a bath." Chryse dragged her fingers through the matted tangle of her hair.

"It can wait. Follow me."

It was a long hike to the shore of the northern lake, and all four were dragging their feet by the time they breasted a low rise and saw the dark water spread out before them, the darker forest beyond. No trees reflected in the lake, though the first spears of morning light lanced out across the still waters.

Thomas Southern knelt on the grassy beach, praying. His lips moved in some litany, and his hands were clasped at his chest. Now and again he crossed himself, for him a deeply devout gesture.

On the shore, water lapped gently at the body of a man. His clothes, rough-spun laborer's garb, rippled in the tiny swells. His lips were open, his eyes shut. It was the worker Hawthorpe, the brash fool, as Southern had once named him. His left hand lay gripped as if it held a final message.

"If he had simply drowned," said Maretha, "it would be no great disaster, under the circumstances of his boast. But the earl will not give up this valley yet, so you see why we must keep this incident secret."

Peaceful enough, the scene: a dead man rolled on a calm lakeshore at dawn—except for the bloody stain on his back, drying now, but irrevocable. The broken haft of a spear protruded from between his shoulder blades.

Chapter 19:

THE DROWNED MAN

" 'It was easy enough to let the laborers think that he had drowned trying to swim across the lake—a foolhardy venture in any case, whatever the outcome. By shrouding him immediately, and carrying him back into camp that way, we managed to keep hidden the fact that he had actually been killed by a spear thrust to the back. The broken spear we flung back into the lake, after examining its point: you will undoubtedly be interested to know that it was a fine chipped-stone implement, primitive and razor sharp. Quite effective, as you might imagine.' "

Aunt Laetitia paused to take a sip of tea, moistening her throat, and looked up from the letter at her visitor. "Although why he expects," she added with asperity, "that I might imagine such a thing at all is quite beyond *my* powers of understanding." Her guest merely chuckled. "Henry," she said in a warning tone, and with a disapproving sniff returned to reading aloud.

" 'Nevertheless, the events of the morning resulted in an unanimous vote by the workers to strike. Our weeks of effort were salvaged only by the quick work of her ladyship and the foreman Southern: it was agreed to move the laborers' camp out of the valley and to limit working hours to daylight, together with a promise to expect no underground digging from anyone. I fear that this might be setting a dangerous precedent, giving workers such say in their laboring conditions, but Elen is uninterested in matters so far below his station, and the countess is I fear entirely too sympathetic to the plight of the downtrodden, as those temperance pamphlets love to term the indigent

206

classes. But in all fairness I must add that only some handful of the fellows left when previously the entire group had threatened an exodus *en masse*, so one must show some respect for her ladyship's methods.' "

Here Lady Trent interrupted herself again, taking another sip of tea. "I must say, Henry, that I did not read this to apprise you of my nephew's political leanings. There was a reference here that reminded me of something you mentioned in our previous conversation—"

"No, no, Laetitia." Henry, Lord Felton, leaned forward to choose a slice of cake and transfer it with the smoothness of long practice to his plate. "I find the letter quite interesting. Please read on."

"Ah, well, Henry," replied Laetitia with an air of tolerance that would have shocked any of her grand-nieces and -nephews, "you were always an easygoing man."

He sighed ostentatiously. "But not so easygoing that you could ever be persuaded to accept me as your husband."

The mischief that lit in Lady Trent's eyes at this remark revealed as nothing else could have the spirited boldness that had made her the most celebrated beauty of her time. "And a great disappointment it is to you, too, Henry," she scolded, with affection, "as I know with some certainty that the only reason you propose to me regularly is because you are tolerably sure that I will refuse you. You and I do very well as widower and widow."

"I refuse to be discouraged." He settled back comfortably in his chair, crossing his hands over the pleasant round of his belly as he waited for her to continue.

She coughed first, clearing her throat. " oxodus . . . methods . . . Here. 'Our camp remains where it has always stood, only Miss Farr and the boy Lucias voicing any desire that it be moved. The children of course wish simply to run wild through as much danger as possible. The arrangement has settled out nicely, and work progresses only a little slower than before. The central building, which Professor Farr has now titled "The Grand Marketplace," is almost completely uncovered. The three stairwells, middle, west, and east, have been partially dug out by Miss Cathcart, working entirely on her own since none of the laborers will help her and the rest of us are too busy with the other business of the excavation. However, any further work in the depths will have to wait: all of our lanterns were shattered by an unknown person or persons one week after the fire, and we are waiting for replacements. The only other incident of comparable interest was the arrival one week ago of a regiment of Horse Guards in the area, led by one Colonel Witless. He is evidently one of the undistinguished litter produced by that Sir Alfred Witless who was I believe commonly known to have lost trousers, shoes, and estates for the dubious pleasure of a single night with Lady Broadlands. I had the tale from my father.'

"And a fine education Julian got from that wastrel of a father," Laetitia interposed, turning her head to glare at Lord Felton. "Why are you laughing? Don't you believe it?"

"Oh, I know the tale," Lord Felton said quickly. "One of the great scandals of twenty years past, but I believe the principals were Sir Alfred Whitmore and Lady Smallfields, although the other name does her—ah—considerable charms more justice. Left his family penniless, forced the daughters into trade and the sons into the army, although the whole lot of them is I understand as dissolute as their father when it comes to the pleasures of the flesh." He coughed discreetly here, casting a sly look toward his companion. "Though I am sure it is little enough you would know of such things, my dear Laetitia."

"We will ignore your insinuations, Henry, as any gentlewoman ought, and continue with Julian's letter. It is this section that I thought might interest you. Let me see. Broadlands—" She coughed abruptly, covering some other reaction. "Vulgar woman. And dressed the part, too. Ah, yes, his father. 'The regiment has encamped less than a day's ride from our valley, and Miss Cathcart and I rode over one day to investigate—' Although what Miss Cathcart was investigating I won't presume to discuss here. '—and it seemed to me that Colonel Witless—and a more self-satisfied, overweening, vain bore I have never before had the misfortune to meet—had little beyond some vague explanation of "maneuvers" to justify the arrival of his regiment in this Lady-forsaken region. You might ask a few questions, Aunt. It does not look now as if we will be leaving for another month or even two, and I confess myself a trifle suspicious of his motives.' And the rest is gossip of mutual acquaintances whom you do not know,

Henry." She set the letter down on the side table at her right. "There. What do you make of that?"

"When was the letter written?"

She turned it over to look for the date. "Some five weeks ago. All his letters have taken four to six weeks to get here. I find it marvelous how swiftly one can correspond these days with the northern shires."

Lord Felton considered his teacup thoughtfully. "It was a cursed strange marriage for Elen to make. I've said it before, and I shall certainly say it again ere long. But this business of wall paintings and notions of sacrificing young women—one might well suppose our Pariam ancestors had no artists who painted as they pleased without a notion of copying stiff old rituals to the order of some stuffed-shirt minister of ceremonies."

"Why, Henry, I had no idea that you believed in the Pariam legends. It is not a *conventional* belief."

"My dear Laetitia. Please do not accuse me of that particular attribute. If I am a *careful* man, it is due entirely to my mother's gambling habits, which left me with an inheritance of one ramshackle estate, a host of debts, and no chance whatsoever of being admitted as a suitor to this very parlor when it hosted the debut season of the Incomparable Letty. But I appreciate you sending for me today with such news." He reached for another slice of cake, thought better of it, and sat back. "This movement of troops disturbs me indeed. It implies to me that there is something in the north that the Regent wishes to safeguard. Or gain. But what, and for what purpose, I cannot imagine."

In the silence that followed this remark, Lady Trent rang for a servant to refill the teapot, and she and Lord Felton waited out the interval in a companionable silence until fresh tea was served and the housemaid gone again. Laetitia poured.

"Never a day's illness in her life," said Lord Felton. "Georgiana has always had a remarkably strong constitution. The only thing, dare I say, that she inherited from her mother that is of any use to her. But let us not speak ill of the dead. And furthermore, I have been forbidden to go to her at this 'ocean retreat.' "

"Forbidden!"

"I have always distrusted Blessa. She was not an open

child, always had secrets, and at a far younger age than I thought fitting. A sly girl, with, shall we say, precocious appetites. I do not trust her, Laetitia, but I have no proof, and only suspicions to link this regiment suddenly gone north and Georgiana's illness."

He reached into the pocket of his coat and removed a pair of spectacles. "It is no secret," he continued, "that Blessa has long dabbled in the arts of the mage, but how long and how deep I have never before attempted to discover. I am neither curious about nor any kind of intimate with the means of sorcery. I feel that it is now time to investigate the full range of her ambitions. But that is a matter for another day. For now, I must excuse myself." He fit his spectacles carefully over his nose and got to his feet.

Laetitia rose as well and extended one hand. "Then I will see you tomorrow, Henry."

He took her hand and kissed it with a fond and playful reverence. "Nine o'clock, my dear. Have we ever missed a Harvest Fair celebration together?"

She let him retain her hand in his grasp. "The art of the fan is sadly lost in these callow times," she said severely, "else I would rap you smartly on the knuckles for your impertinence. One does not remind a lady of her indiscretions. And certainly not at our age."

"The pleasure of such a reminder must be greatest at our age, don't you think?"

"Out," she said as he relinquished her hand, but she smiled. "And be careful."

"What do you mean, he walked all the way into my inner suite before anyone stopped him?" The Regent's voice snapped with the force of a blow across the breadth of the room. The servant who had brought the message recoiled a full two steps before the door brought his retreat up short. "I hope that you had the sense to detain him there," she continued in a tone that boded ill for that man who had not.

"Yes, highness," he murmured, bowing deeply.

She removed her gloves, straightened her skirts with a brisk shake, and strode out past him to the hallway that led to her private rooms. The servant followed ten paces behind. She could feel his trembling, his fear, as if he were actually touching her.

In the outermost room of her private suite she found Lord Felton tied tightly to a chair. He surveyed her calmly as she entered and halted before him. Her face was impassive, betraying no emotion at all.

"I fear I thought you had left the palace for the afternoon," he said in an even voice. "Or else I can assure you that you would not have caught me here."

"Do you think I leave my most private places unguarded?" she replied, at once coy as a flirting woman and firm as a general interrogating the enemy. She crossed back to the door, where the servant waited. "Go to your quarters." She did not lower her voice. "Bring me back the razor you shave yourself with. Make sure it is sharp. And be quick about it."

He scarcely bowed before he was out the door.

"My dear Blessa," said Lord Felton smoothly. "You know that at my age death holds no especial fear. I will be quite blunt about my purpose in coming here."

"I have no intention of threatening you or torturing you." She walked past him into the second room. Two drawers had been opened in her vast desk. She went on into the farthest chamber, but its precise arrangement of strangely angled furniture and carefully placed cards, plant clippings, and animal skins had not been disturbed. Satisfied, she returned to the outer chamber, where Lord Felton waited with the patience of a crafty old politician.

There were no windows in any of these rooms. The Regent took her place next to a painting of her mother, in which the old queen had posed in a pantomime recalling St. Maretha as the Harrower of the Infidels. After contemplating the painting for a long, silent moment, she turned slowly to regard Lord Felton with equally careful scrutiny. She said nothing.

"I do not care," said Lord Felton, "what practices you choose to engage in, your highness. My concern is for Princess Georgiana." He waited politely for her response. She did not make one. "Then I will be frank. I suspect you of some collusion with the Earl of Elen."

"I am well aware of your suspicions."

"Then you also know that I will do everything in my

power to insure the safe, whole, and undisturbed ascension of the princess to the throne of Anglia."

The Regent paced with deliberation twice across the room, halted behind his chair, and turned it so that its back, and thus Lord Felton's, now faced the door to the hall. "I wonder," she said in a musing tone, "if you ever felt any reservations about the inheritance passing through the male line, Lord Felton."

"I obey the law of the land, your highness. I am an administrator, not a lawmaker. That job I leave to those Our Lady ordained for such tasks, and mind in my stead those for which I was ordained."

"Ah," she said. Turning, she watched as the door opened and the servant entered. With a bow he handed her his shaving razor, a long, sharp blade.

"You might at least tell me," said Lord Felton evenly, facing away from this exchange, "what you mean to do with Georgiana."

Blessa, princess of the realm, was a deft woman. With a movement so swift and controlled that Lord Felton perhaps did not perceive its coming, she slit his throat.

Blood sprayed onto the carpet, but she had positioned herself in such a way that none of the blood touched her. After a moment he slumped over in his bonds, dead.

She got no pleasure from the act; neither did it revolt her. She was above all a practical woman. Lord Felton's suspicions endangered her plans—but she was never one to pass off a distasteful job to others, especially when it was vital that the task be accomplished successfully.

She tossed the razor onto the blood-soaked carpet and turned to the servant. His face was pale.

"Send for two of my women to clean this up," she ordered. "The carpet will have to be discarded. And the three soldiers the colonel left here can dispose of the body after I have finished with it. In the river, I think." She nodded and was about to dismiss him when another thought occurred to her. "And I must contact Nastagmas." She went abruptly into the second room and took from one of the open drawers a written report detailing Lord Felton's movements in past months. Bringing it back into the outer room, she set it on a side table. "I will have further use for the soldiers," she said, as much to herself as to her servant. "No news of this must carry to any of those in the earl's party. They are the only real threat left to me."

The servant shuffled slightly, his shoes scuffing the floor, and the Regent's eyes rose to scrutinize him with more interest than before. He was, like all her male servants, well formed, fair of face, and young.

"And when you have done with these tasks, you will return to the inner chamber. You know what is expected of you."

He bowed, quivering with some emotion he could not put into words.

"You, and a woman attendant as well. Now go."

He left quickly. She went into the inner room, retrieved her deck of Gates, and returned to kneel by Lord Felton's body.

"Now," she said, "we will prepare to set the illusion."

At ten o'clock on Harvest Fair night, Lady Trent sat in her parlour flipping through a deck of old and well-worn cards. When the door to the room opened, she laid down the cards expectantly and looked up. A footman entered.

"My lady." He inclined his head respectfully.

"You have been quick, James," she said. "For that I thank you. You reached Felton House, then? Any news?"

"Lord Felton left at half past ten this morning with instructions that tea was to be laid at five, my lady. Tea was laid, but his lordship did not, and has not, returned."

"Ah," she replied. Her voice quavered a little on the sound, but she controlled it. "Have Master Coachman bring the carriage round. You will attend me."

He bowed and left.

Now she turned her attention with real intensity to the cards, picking them up with reverence. Her hands were pale with age, patterned with veins blue and prominent under her skin, but they did not tremble as she began to lay out the Telling known as The Directions: six cards surrounding the center, which is the seventh.

"The east." Her voice was low with concentration and full with the power that seeks only self-knowledge, not domination. She laid down a card, and smiled. "The Harvest Fair. Yes, that is the place he and I first met.

"To the south, the Lover." The faintest of flushes edged her cheeks, giving her an air of youth that echoed the innocence of a blushing girl who, leaning from a high window to smile down at her paramour standing below, marked the card. "His companion. A long time ago." She shook her head and continued.

"In the heavens, the Heiress, aiding. And below, attacking—" she frowned, placing the card. "The Midwife? Yes, I see. Laboring to birth an unholy scheme from the womb of the Daughter. And then north."

She breathed out sharply as she laid the card down. "The Labyrinth. It turns back in upon itself. And to the west," a pause, "the River. And last, the center."

The pause here was longer, as if she was reluctant to reveal the card to herself, but at last she turned it onto its place.

The Drowned Man.

"Oh, Henry," she whispered, and even the calmness of great age, the experience of the many strange, horrible, and wonderful events that life had cast in her way, could not prevent her voice from cracking with sorrow now. She sat quietly with hands folded on the table, and she mourned him. A few tears slipped down her aged face.

When the door opened to admit the footman James, she swept the cards into a neat stack, fastened her hat on her head and, as she rose, pulled its black lace veil over her face. He escorted her to the carriage and helped her in.

"River Street," she commanded.

"So late, my lady? It will be dangerous."

"Then bring two more footmen, and arm yourselves and Master Coachman with pistols."

As they travelled, carriage rattling over the cobbled paving of Heffield streets, Lady Trent could hear the thanksgiving hymns and calls of the almsgivers, dance music and rousing drinking songs, that marked the Harvest Fair celebrations. The sounds of festivity faded as they reached the dockside districts. She rapped with her cane and the carriage halted, and footman James appeared at the window.

"We will proceed carefully now," she ordered, "with all lanterns lit. We are looking for a man thrown on the river's edge."

"My lady." He looked a little shocked, but schooled his expression quickly to impassivity. The carriage moved along River Street slowly, looking in the darkness like some ponderous animal attended by fireflies that swooped and rose and circled in and out around it. Water, smelling not so sweet, lapped here the street's edge and there the rotting pilings of an old wharf. A snout-faced loiterer hurried away into the safety of a black alley as they passed, its footsteps pattering wetly over the damp stones. A gentle misting rain began to fall.

The first body they found was that of an emaciated woman who had obviously been adrift many days before the tide threw her high on the shore. Her face was unrecognizable. The second was of a young man profusely scarred in the face and dead from stab wounds in the back. The third was Lord Felton.

"He must ha' drowned, your ladyship," said footman James as she knelt, heedless of her fancy gown and furlined cloak, on the muddy bank. "There's not a mark on him."

"Nonsense." She reached out with a hand to touch the slack face tenderly. When her fingers met the water-pale skin, her own skin took on a kind of nimbus, a faint, luminous glow. The unscarred throat of the corpse shimmered slightly, like a heat mirage rippling in the distance, and steadied back to whiteness.

In a neat line around the curve of his neck, the skin was parted as a piece of meat parts to the cut of a butcher knife. It was as clean as immersion in the river could leave it; all the blood had drained out.

The footmen gathered above gasped and muttered to each other. Lady Trent withdrew her hand, and the corpse's neck appeared clear and unmarked again. She rose, leaning on her cane. In that movement her years sat clearly on her, and footman James had to help her up, one hand solicitous on her elbow as he escorted her back to the carriage.

"We will bring him to Vole House," she ordered. "Have Mistress Housekeeper lay him out as is proper, and Master Butler to inform his heir and relatives of his death. By drowning."

It was a silent trip back, with Lady Trent seated on one side of the carriage, Lord Felton's body propped up by a footman on the other. When they arrived at the entrance of Vole House, the initial flurry of activity—summoning Mistress Housekeeper, calling for housemaids to open the back parlour for the laying out of the body, sending a kitchen boy out to Felton House—kept Lady Trent separated from her butler for some minutes, so that when a footman opened the door into her front parlour so that she could sit for a time in quiet, she was unprepared for her visitor.

She stopped on the threshold of the room. For an instant, like a hallucination, she seemed to blaze with a luminosity that bathed the dim room in a suffusion of light. As quickly it was gone, and she appeared a frail old woman who has seen the death of too many of the dearest companions of her youth.

"Your highness," she said, curt. She sketched the merest fragment of a curtsy.

The Regent turned from her contemplation of the fire and the painting above the mantel of Our Lady and Her Son. "Lady Trent." She too wore a lace veil. She swept it aside with one hand. "I will be brief. By the powers vested in me as regent in this realm, I confine you to the walls of Vole House for the rest of this year. You may have correspondence with no one, may receive no visitors, none of your peers or relatives or acquaintances."

Lady Trent waited a moment to speak. In that time she set her cane firmly against a chair, removed her cloak and hat with neat preciseness, and inspected the stained hem of her gown with what appeared to be disapproval. "And in three months, at the Festival of Lights, you will lift this ban?" Her voice showed no sign of weakness.

"It is likely," replied the Regent.

Lady Trent smiled, with irony. "How carefully you phrase it. If your work progresses and, I assume, succeeds. But meanwhile, how am I to be expected to live under such circumstances?"

"You can spread it about that you are quite ill. As for day-to-day living, your servants of course can attend to tradespeople and those of their own class as needed. I do not intend to deprive you of your supper, Lady Trent, nor your servants of their no doubt well-deserved half day off." Her tone was halfway between sarcasm and amusement. "I believe you understand the limits of what I intend."

For the first time Aunt Laetitia met the Regent's gaze, and neither woman looked away. 'I understand quite well, your highness. Should I be grateful that you have spared me?"

"It is a pity," said the Regent in a ruminative tone, "that you never followed your gifts as far as you could have. I have no intention of attempting a struggle against them now. You might have been an unparalleled mistress of the arts, Lady Trent."

"I might have been," she conceded, "but I did not have such a lust for power that I was willing to cut out my heart to achieve it."

"A great loss." The Regent lifted her hand to her veil, and paused with her fingers poised in the act of drawing it across her face.

"I should think that would depend on what you valued," replied Aunt Laetitia. She reached for the bell pull and eased it down. "Master Butler will show you out."

The Regent veiled her face. "Remember, Lady Trent, this house will be watched, and the movements of your servants as well. Do not attempt to send them to the home of some relative or friend. I cannot be duped by such stratagems."

The butler appeared, bowing, and Regent left, her skirts sweeping the floor as she went.

"Don't be so sure," murmured Lady Trent as the door shut behind her. She rang again. "Ah, yes, Master Butler. Do any of the people in my employ ever frequent the Crusader Inn? It is in—" She hesitated.

"The Hutment district, my lady," he supplied. "Be assured, my lady, that no one under my supervision is allowed to harbor any radical leanings . . ." He hesitated in his turn.

"But one, or two, have been known to go there? Good." She smiled. "I have surprised you. But it is always a mistake to discount that class which provides the foundation on which ours lives. I have learned that much in my life. I have a number of orders for you, but foremost among them, when next it is likely that these 'one or two' might go to that inn on their half-day off, they must come to see me first."

"Yes, madam."

"Very well. I will need Miss Botherwell to bring my mourning blacks to me, and then I will attend Lord Felton's body in the back parlour until his people arrive to take him." Her eyes shone with the temper of best steel. "Your death will be avenged, Henry. I promise that."

CHAPTER 20:

THE LOVER

Only two incidents marred the Harvest Fair holiday. When the members of the earl's party rose that morning, they found the entire valley in bloom: an unseasonable flowering of white climbing roses, spread across the rubble and slopes of the ruins in such profusion that it could have been the welcoming decorations set out in preparation for the visit of the queen.

When they gathered at midday for the mile walk to festivities at the laborer's camp, just south over the containing ridge, Kate was discovered missing. The children found her at the Marketplace. She had, it transpired, gone out early with a lantern to dig deeper down the central stairwell, and had slipped on a damp corner of loose dirt, spraining her ankle. Cursing all the while, she endured without much grace Julian's sardonic commiserations as he carried her back to camp. In the end they put her on the gentlest mare and Lucias led her along the trail that led to the other camp. She went with as much dignity as she could muster, and sat meekly in her chair throughout the festivities.

"We're no match for her, Kate," said Chryse with a mock sigh as, late in the day, they watched Charity crowned Harvest Queen. A very self-conscious and reluctant Thomas Southern was voted King by the unanimous vote of the workers. They crowned him with a wreath of wheat and berries and seated him in a chair next to Charity.

"What do you mean?" Kate sat with her foot propped up on a stool. Chryse had sat next to her throughout the afternoon's games and feasting, and now, as dusk lowered, they chatted softly as the Harvest Sovereigns were invested and a large circle of lanterns lit and hung about the dancing area.

"They look well together, don't they?"

Kate nodded. Charity's fair, pliant beauty set off the obstinate handsomeness of Thomas Southern's face to perfection.

"Just that with Charity here, none of the rest of us could ever hope to win such a contest."

Kate chuckled. "Do I detect a note of envy? You're well-looking enough, but you don't carry the expectation of beauty around with you like she does. Personally, I think her hair is a rather insipid blonde, whereas yours is like real gold. Almost," she added with another grin, "as beautiful as the earl's hair."

"Flatterer. She must be hot bundled up in all those clothes. She looks positively rotund."

"You *are* in a cat's mood today, aren't you?"

Chryse smiled, looking smug in her trim, tailored gown and matching military-style jacket, the legacy of the treaty of Amynn, the signing of which had caused military fashions to go out of style and Julian's sister to consign the outfit to her closet.

Kate's eye wandered back to Thomas Southern. "Wouldn't have me, you know," she added conversationally.

"What?" Chryse laughed. "You didn't proposition him?"

Kate looked offended. "Of course I did. Just look at him. There's something about an abstentious man that attracts me. I suppose it's the challenge. But damn me if he isn't as staid as he makes himself out to be." Chryse was still laughing, pausing only to brush a tear from the corner of one eye. "It's all very well for you," continued Kate, "having Sanjay, but what am I to do? His Blackness is obviously quite out of the question. And Lucias—well, even *I* have some compunction about despoiling innocent young virgins."

"What about Julian?" asked Chryse, suddenly acutely curious.

"Julian?" Kate's expression bore honest surprise. "Why would I proposition Julian? Lady, but we've known each other since we were babes-in-arms."

"Haven't you ever— I mean, ever even been attracted to him?"

Kate shrugged. "We grew up together, as close as two foals in a paddock, having no one else to play with. So of course it fell out that the spring we both turned sixteen—" She smiled. It was an expression that softened her face to a remarkable degree. "That was a happy time, that spring and summer. Then in the fall Julian was sent off to university, and I was banished to my grandfather's estate for expressing a desire to study medicine. We saw each other next—" She shook her head. "—six years later. By that time I was well on my way to being disinherited, and Julian was . . . well on his way to having a reputation as a cicisbeo of married ladies."

"Tell me, Kate," said Chryse slowly, turning her face away to hide her expression, "does Julian often take married women as his lovers?"

"He *only* takes married lovers. I don't know why. Baste me and burn me—" Her tone altered abruptly. "The earl is dancing with his wife!"

"To a waltz!" exclaimed Chryse, as startled by the familiar dance as by the sight of Maretha gliding past in her husband's arms. "I can dance this!" She got to her feet. 'I'm deserting you, Kate. This is too good of an opportunity to pass up. Have you seen—there he is."

She hurried over to Sanjay. He was standing to one side, smiling as he watched Julian attempting to teach Pin how to waltz, an effort hampered by Pin's hiccoughs of excitement at this attention from her hero. Mog glowered jealously at them from his seat next to Lucias.

"Shall we dance?" Chryse asked, and Sanjay accepted.

At first they waltzed in silence. The laborers had cobbled together a quintet of amateur musicians from their ranks, and the music was a little rough, but sincere.

"I should have offered to play with them," said Chryse, and fell silent again, watching the earl and Maretha through the other couples.

The earl stared down at his wife, and the only word Chryse could think of to describe his expression was "hungry." Maretha danced with her eyes lowered, but now and again, as if she could not help herself, she glanced up, then down again as quickly. At those moments, the earl's hand would shift at her waist, Maretha's at his shoulder, in a way that somehow combined the standoffishness of strangers and the intimacy of lovers.

As the dance ended, Chryse followed Sanjay off into the shadows beyond the light of fire and lanterns.

"How long do you suppose a marriage can go on without being consummated?" she asked as they strolled through the quiet of the laborers' camp, the sounds of dancing and laughing and festivity fading behind them.

"It's too late now," said Sanjay quickly. "But if I'd known how you felt, I wouldn't have insisted."

She made a face at him. "Where are we going?"

"I have a fancy to hike up the ridge and see how the valley looks in the moonlight."

"What did I do to deserve you? That's a mile away!" Nevertheless she did not halt or even slacken her pace. "Good thing it's a temperate night."

"What makes you think that the earl and Maretha haven't consummated their marriage?"

"Because she told me."

"They don't act like lovers," he said, thoughtful, "but then, Julian and Kate often interact in such an intimate way that you might suspect they're lovers, but they aren't."

"I worry," said Chryse in a subdued voice. "I worry about what he really wants of her."

"I wonder." He lapsed into a silence made deep by his contemplation.

The trail led into a light scattering of trees. The first fallen leaves rustled under their feet, and they walked for a long time just listening to the rhythm of their strides on the path.

"Sometimes," said Sanjay at last, taking her hand, "I feel that I wouldn't care if we never went back."

The height of the ridge opened before them, and they scrambled up the slope and arrived gasping to look out over the valley called the labyrinth gate. Gasping, now, not just from being out of breath. In the twilight of Harvest Fair evening, the city had come to life below them.

Chryse did not see so much as hear it; festival music, bright songs of thanksgiving, but also solemn music that inspired dread as well as glory. And from another direction, festive dance music. She slipped her hand out of Sanjay's and, slowly at first, tried a few, tentative steps, as if by finding the dance she could understand the music.

Sanjay scarcely noticed her separating from him. The entire city was laid out before him: the simplicity of its

structure, its architecture, as profoundly beautiful as any
natural object's, formed to nature's laws, magnificent and
cruel. The buildings, the thoroughfares, were suffused by
light, glowing from within like a translucent, whorled shell.
They stood for a long timeless space.

"It's a beautiful place," said Sanjay at last, "and a terrible one."

As if triggered by his words, the vision faded, and they
saw only shadow in the great hollow below, the dull mirror of the pair of lakes that surrounded the valley reflecting a strange pattern of stars.

Chryse shivered. "Let's go back."

They walked for a time before they spoke again.

"Do you think," asked Chryse finally, "that a treasure
hidden in such a place as that, whatever it proved to be, is
a safe thing to possess?"

Sanjay did not need to reply for her to know his answer.

At the laborers' camp, no one seemed to have noticed
their defection. Chryse went to stand by the musicians;
soon enough one offered her his extra hornpipe, and she
played with them for the rest of the evening while, under
the light of dim lanterns, Sanjay sketched, on paper bor-
rowed from Thomas Southern, a rendering of the city he
had seen, one quite at odds with the professor's interpretation of the ruins.

The weeks passed. Julian waited for a letter, some message, from his great-aunt, but none came. In fact, all
correspondence from Heffield ceased. Colonel Whitmore's
regiment remained encamped some fifteen miles away,
but even Kate's infrequent visits there stopped as the
weather turned more and more to rain and blustery winds.

Autumn grew towards winter, but still the earl refused
to call a halt to the dig for the season. At last, under
pressure even from Professor Farr, whose enthusiasm was
daunted only by his arthritis, the earl agreed to set a date
for departure. He settled on St. Maretha's March, the
church holy day commemorating the legendary knight's
rescue of a thousand doomed children from a valley cursed
by the Daughter with the Black Death.

The morning of Marching Eve dawned clear and still.
The laborers from Heffield set off in a compact train just
after sunrise. Most of the local workers had gone the day

THE LABYRINTH GATE 223

before; a handful remained—Mistress Cook and four or five brawny lads to take down the expeditionary tents, as well as the four coachmen and grooms for the trip back. The day passed quickly to afternoon as the members of the earl's party readied themselves to leave the next morning.

"It is cold." Chryse emphasized each word as she rubbed her hands together before attempting to latch the handles on her trunk. "There. Everything is packed. Now we have time to walk over the whole site in what's left of the day—a sort of farewell." She blew on her hands and pulled on a pair of dark gloves.

Sanjay sat at the table, bare now of its usual scattering of papers. He flipped through his last sketchbook; the others had been packed away together with their clothing and sundry goods. "Farewell? We haven't found anything Madame Sosostris would call a treasure, my love. And neither has the earl. We may very well be back here next spring."

She sat down on the trunk. "You say neither we nor the earl has. What about Professor Farr?" She answered herself before he could reply. "I suppose this place is treasure enough for him. The excavations, the frescos, the catalog of glyphs Maretha has collected. He can write monographs for years just on what we've done this past season. And next year—"

She broke off at the sound of shouting. They rose together and went out. Kate stood in the cleared space between the tents, her audience Julian, Maretha, and Thomas Southern. Mog and Pin jumped up and down behind her.

"It's incredible!" In her excitement she was gesticulating wildly. "The central stairwell is completely excavated—clear, all the way down. I went down as far as I could, but without a lantern—" She shrugged eloquently. "I was there yesterday and I know it was only cleared to the seventh step. I just walked there today with the children and—" She broke off. "Where is Lucias?" Her voice was uncharacteristically sharp.

"I'm here." He appeared from around the corner of Julian's tent, looking a little embarrassed.

"I *told* you not to go out of sight," snapped Kate. "Do I have to remind you again that on every one of the old holidays someone has attempted to murder you?"

"They didn't Harvest Fair."

"Only because you were in our sight every second of the day. Bloody hell!"

"I thought tomorrow was the holiday," said Sanjay as he and Chryse joined the circle.

"It's a churchday," explained Maretha. "After—" She blushed a little. "—after St. Maretha. But isn't Marching Day Eve really one of the ancient holydays disguised?"

"I know which one," said Chryse abruptly. "Lord Death's Progress. You remember the card, Sanjay. Death riding a fine horse with a procession of the—ah—unfortunate trailing behind."

"Oh, yes. I remember that one. Kate is right, Lucias. You'd better stick with one of us."

Lucias paled and moved to stand close to Kate.

"You found the treasure?" Charity's soft voice barely stirred the air. She had pushed aside the entrance to her tent and stood under the awning so wrapped in clothes and cloak that she had no shape at all.

"Lady bless us," said Kate. "What if the treasure is down there?"

"Let's go look! Let's go look!" shrieked Mog and Pin.

Maretha turned to Thomas Southern. "Thomas, we'll need lanterns besides those we have here. Are any of the wagons still here?"

He nodded. "Some of the local lads are coming back up tonight to drive them out in the morning. I can get half a dozen more, I believe." He glanced at Charity as she came forward. She had developed an awkward walk, a little off-balance: the result, she had told Chryse, of back pain. "Will you need assistance, Miss Farr?" he asked in his most reserved voice, but even as he said it, she walked past him to Julian.

"Perhaps you would escort me, Lord Vole?" The full rosiness of her cheeks belied the lassitude of her voice. Julian bowed and offered her his arm. Southern left to get the lanterns.

They went as a procession to the central excavation: Kate and the children first; Lucias next, alone, frowning like an angel perplexed by some high moral question; Chryse and Sanjay, thoughtful; Julian with Charity; and Maretha last of all, her face expressionless as she walked with a lantern in one hand and a journal in the other.

Southern had arrived before them, with a number of

lanterns. With him stood Professor Farr: he had lit one of
the lanterns and was about to descend. As the others
hurried up to crowd around the stairwell, they saw another light below, growing smaller. It had a strange wild
quality to it that was clearly magical in source.

"Just following the earl down," said the professor.

"Wait a moment, Father. I'll go with you."

Below, the flickering light vanished. Maretha and the
professor started down as the rest hurriedly lit lanterns
and went singly behind them, all except Charity, who kept
hold of Julian's arm. Thomas Southern descended last, his
lips set tight as if only by keeping them closed could he
prevent himself from delivering a sharp rebuke.

Inconstant figures accompanied them in the dimness,
following along the walls, suggestions of shapes and long-
forgotten events rubbed away by centuries of elemental
erosion. Chryse, going down one tentative step at a time,
was halted more than once by Sanjay's back as he stopped
to peer at the indistinct tracery of lines along the wall.
Ahead, the excited chattering of Mog and Pin reverberated up and down the stairwell. Gloom and rock closed in
above, and abruptly the floor was level and they ducked
under a low lintel and came into a small, square room.

A kind of collective gasp caught in their throats. Thomas
Southern stopped in the lintel opening and crossed himself.

The frescos in the room were brilliant, even by lantern
glow, beautiful in execution, but macabre in detail. Directly opposite the door a fine horse walked, golden and
proud, and on its back sat a fine, golden-haired man
dressed in some ancient costume, heavy sword in one
hand, the other cupped around a shimmering ball of light,
or fire. A beautiful young woman, sorrow etched on her
face, babe at her breast, walked alongside, holding onto
the fine hem of his trailing robe. Behind her another
figure walked, and another, each detailed, each progressively closer to death, and then passing beyond it, deteriorating, rotting, wasted to bone, until the final figure, as in
an unending circle, walking just in front of the horse, was
a capering, empty-eyed skeleton.

And in the center of the room, on a thin pillar of white
stone, stood a cup, a golden chalice. It had no decoration
whatsoever, but from it emanated a force that both attracted and repelled the eye.

"The treasure," whispered Charity, gaze locked on the cup.

Chryse, too, stared at it, just as fascinated, sure that at any moment the plain burnished gold of its surface would shift to reveal in simple patterns the secret of the city. Sanjay nudged her.

"Almost too like to be coincidence," he said in an undertone into her ear. The warmth of his breath on her skin broke her from her hypnotized stare. She followed the touch of his arm to look beyond the golden cup.

The earl stood just below the figure of Lord Death. In the light his hair shone like the gold of the chalice, and in one hand, extended before him, he cupped a shimmering ball of sorcerous fire. He could just have dismounted from the fine horse painted on the wall behind him. His gaze, unlike almost everyone else's, was not on the cup. Instead, he watched Maretha as she slowly circled the room, lantern lifted high to illuminate as much of the detail of the frescos as possible. His gaze could have been death's, it was so piercing.

Then she reached the end of the procession and passed back by her husband to stand before the chalice. Professor Farr was scribbling hasty notes in the journal she had bought for him.

"Lift it up for me, Maretha," he said in a distracted tone. "I need to see if there is any mark at its base."

She extended her hand and touched the cup.

Every light in the little room vanished. Someone swore. It was so black that Chryse could not discern her own hand in front of her face until her breath brushed it.

A soft grating echoed in the chamber, like the scraping of stone. Laughter sounded, as if from the walls, from the very air, from the depths, but it was neither crazed nor mocking; it was the laughter of young women sharing sweet secrets about their admirers.

Then a snap, like the first spark of fire, and light blossomed at the earl's hands, casting their shadows high on the painted walls. Mog and Pin yelped with fear and cast themselves on Julian.

"Where is Maretha?" asked Sanjay sharply.

"She couldn't have come past me," said Southern from his stand in the doorway. "There isn't room, and I didn't move."

"Damnation." The earl's tone fairly dripped fury. Fire blazed in his hands. Maretha was gone. "I *knew* there was another level." He moved so abruptly that no one could react until it was too late. "She will be mine," he said, and he charged out past Thomas Southern and raced up the stairs, plunging the room into darkness again.

"Bloody hell," said Kate. "I don't know what happened to her, but we'd better find her before he does. Got any matches?"

Julian felt Charity remove her hand from his arm and move away from him. Cloth rustled against cloth. Chryse grabbed for Sanjay, found his belt, and gripped there. She started violently when a hand touched her back, relaxed when Lucias breathed her name and huddled in under her arm. Professor Farr was mumbling indistinguishably. A match snapped and hissed, and a second later Thomas Southern's lantern flared to life.

"Hell in a basket," said Kate in the gloom. "The treasure is gone, too."

Sanjay's lantern flickered and caught. In the double light the white pillar could be seen; there was no cup. It might as well have been an apparition that had dissolved into the air.

"I feel ill," said Charity abruptly. She was hunched forward next to the pillar, arms crossed over her abdomen. Sanjay and Thomas Southern stepped forward at the same moment. There was an instant's hesitation, and then Southern turned and retreated up the steps, his lantern held as a beacon for the rest, while Sanjay went to aid her.

"Wasn't Maretha the one who—" Chryse was surprised to discover that her voice was unsteady. "—who didn't believe that the city itself had magic?"

"She can't simply have vanished," said Julian. "There's got to be another way down."

"Can't she?" muttered Kate. "And why Maretha? Was it something to do with the cup?" She shook her head. "This is pointless, Julian. If this stairwell was miraculously cleared out, the others might be, too." She had gotten her lantern lit and now scoured the floor and walls for some sign of a seam. "We'll never find anything here. I feel sure of it."

"Then we'd better go," said Chryse. "I don't like the way the earl ran out of here any better than you do."

Lucias shrank away from her, into the center of the glow

generated by Kate's lantern. His eyes were wide, half dazed. " 'The labyrinth.' " His voice held fear and the hypnotic dullness of one reciting at the behest of some stronger will. " 'The hunter seeks the labyrinth as well.' " He backed up, away from a sight the others could not see. Kate put out a hand, touched him, and he jerked as if he had been shot and shuddered and began to cry. "Don't go," he muttered under his ragged sobs. "Don't go there."

"Something very strange—" murmured Kate, holding him against her with one arm. She looked at the others as if for confirmation.

"We don't have any choice," said Chryse. "We have to find Maretha. And we'll have to take the children."

"I've got to take Charity back to camp," said Sanjay. Charity was leaning against him; she moaned and tightened her grip around her belly.

Julian rose. Mog and Pin clung each to one of his legs. "Kate. You and I and those three can go to the western entrance, beyond the evening palace—"

"Sanjay and I will go to the western stairwell," interrupted Chryse. "It's too hard a climb for the children. You go to the east."

Julian nodded.

"I'll meet you there," Sanjay said to his wife. "And I'll bring more lanterns. We'll leave Thomas at camp—he'll have to handle any problems with the workers who are left."

"I say." Professor Farr looked up from the scribbled notes in his journal. "Where did the chalice get to? Did Maretha take it back to the tent for cataloging and packing?" He slipped his pen into his coat pocket and closed the journal. "Always anticipating me, that child. Always has." He harrumphed once or twice, clearing his throat, and walked back to the stairs. "I trust you are all coming," he continued as he began to climb. "It must be about suppertime."

It was quite the strangest thing that had ever happened to Maretha. As she touched the cup she felt, not metal, but a hand clasping hers: a soft, feminine hand, warm and reassuring. Her surroundings were dim and hazy and seemed unimportant.

A woman stood before her. She was young, no older

than Maretha, with hair so black that it seemed painted. Her face had a slightly alien cast, high-cheeked, deep eyes rimmed by black coloring, a striking cosmetic touch. Her lips, by contrast, were so pale as to be almost bloodless, insubstantial. Jewels studded the lobes of her ears like a dual sickle of stars. Huge skirts of yellow-and-green-striped, stiff cloth belled out from her slender waist; her yellow jacket was tight and close-fitting and exposed her beasts. Each nipple was startlingly red—daubed with some deep textured color. At her throat hung a pendant. Maretha could not quite make it out.

"Set the cup back on its pedestal," said the priestess in a low voice full of music.

"Will it be safe?"

The priestess smiled. "Only a virgin's touch opens this door." She turned her head and chimes tinkled in her hair as she moved. "Come with me."

Maretha followed as if in a glamour, but the priestess's hand was firm. Lord Death fell away before them to reveal a staircase curving down into darkness. They descended step by step, feet a light scuff on the stone. The curve of the stairwell was tight at first, on her left, but expanded gradually as if they walked down on an opening spiral. On her right lay only air, so profoundly still that the gulf beyond might have been bottomless. All was black.

Eventually they passed through an arch and the curve of the stair began to compress again, the wall on her right now, the air on her left close and confined, until at last they came to a deep end, a tiny, circular chamber with a single door. Maretha lifted her lantern and saw on that door a picture. A young woman dressed much as the priestess sat before a mirror, pots of rouge and black kohl and fine bits of jewelry on a table beside her; roses were woven through her dress. In the mirror was reflected a passageway, bright with frescos, that led into some torchlit mystery.

—Except that it was not reflected in the mirror, it was beyond the painting itself, and the priestess drew Maretha forward and they passed through the place the painting had been and walked down the passageway itself. Smaller, darker ways branched off at intervals that seemed to have some pattern.

"That was The Heiress," said Maretha. "It is one of the

Gates, the—" She faltered. The priestess turned to look at her with a high echo of chimes.

"She is the Chosen One," said the priestess. "Have you not guessed?"

Maretha shook her head.

"You are she."

At that moment they came out into a large circular chamber. The light of the lantern was too dim for Maretha to see more than the vague tracery of wall paintings around her and a low slab of stone in the very center of the room.

"What is this place?" she asked. She passed a hand along one side of her neck; it was hot down here. The slight stirring of air did not cool her.

The priestess disengaged her hand from Maretha's. "Here is the very center." She took one smooth step back. "Here you will receive the treasure of the labyrinth."

And she was gone, vanished, as if she had never been.

Maretha lifted her lantern higher—at first to look for the priestess, but then to study more closely the frescos that decorated the walls.

A young woman dressed in an elaborate version of the priestess's garb, head crowned by a wreath of blazing white roses, crowned in her turn a young man with a circlet of lit candles. Contiguous with it ran a line of glyphs. As Maretha stared, moving slowly along as the fresco unfolded in a long sequence, she began to see a pattern emerge in the writing.

"Lady," she breathed, feeling understanding rise until it was about to break to the surface, "how great a treasure, indeed."

She had to pause, it was so hot, to remove her jacket and, a little later, her kid boots, and on to an extended tableau of a great fair of artists and craftsmen rendered in loving detail, where she felt impelled to unbutton the neck of her dress; removed her stockings as she studied the rite of spring sowing. It grew ever more stifling as she reached the feast of the goddess of the flowering, bride and groom resplendent at high table, surrounded by celebrants. As she at last slipped out of her gown to stand clad only in her shift, she found herself looking at the bedding ceremony of the newlywed couple.

A sound behind her, something dropped. She turned, lantern held out in front of herself, so that it illuminated her more than the person beyond. But she knew who it would be. It seemed inevitable.

She walked across the chamber. Her hair came unbound, falling loose down around her shoulders. They met at the low slab of stone, she and her husband. She did not know how he had found her. He, too, had lost his jacket, his waistcoat, his boots, his gloves. His white shirt was unbuttoned halfway down, and she could see the fine down of light hair across his chest.

His was a beauty made finer by the dimness; the shadows lent tiny imperfections to a face otherwise too cold and pure of feature. His expression was not cold now; neither was it warm—it was anticipatory.

She stretched out a hand to touch his lips, to be sure that he was real and not a vision. There was a kind of desire in him that woke the desire in her she had tried to suppress. He was the treasure she longed for—golden and dangerous. The very stone beneath her seemed to throb with it, as if it was at one with her, this room, this labyrinth, this entire city.

His lips parted under her fingers, and she felt their moistness. She took, he took, a step forward; the lantern set down; a shifting; a sinking; and they lay together on the couch of stone, unaware of anything but each other. They made love by the indistinct light casting shadow over all but the glow on their faces, a ring of light around their necks and chests, the fading in and out of their hands as they moved.

At the moment of consummation she saw his face, the widening of his eyes, the shock, and she felt, she *knew*—as if the stone, being one with her, could communicate of him to her because his flesh also touched it—that he had been, like her, a virgin.

At first she thought it was she, trembling with astonishment. Until she felt power welling up, from the walls, from the floor, the air, from the stone itself so strongly she felt as if it were heating around her, melting into her flesh—

It was this act that the city had been waiting for. Gold, jewels, chalices, frescos, writing and rituals; all this was nothing. The city, the labyrinth, had been waiting for long centuries, patient in its sessile way, until two would come to reenact the ritual that gave it life, renewed its life.

There was no treasure here that one could hold in one's hands, unless it were the body, the warm flesh, of the beloved.

He kissed her, like a consecration, and she stared at him in sudden wonder, and sudden fear.

"You're a virgin," she breathed. "You're never done this before either."

His eyes bore a disturbing glow in the wavering gleam of lantern light. "What do you think is the source of my power?" His voice was almost inaudible. He shifted with her, and for a long moment she could not speak or even think.

But when she could, she lifted a hand to brush at the gilded line of his hair. "But if it—if it was—then where will you get your power now?"

"From the sacrifice," he whispered.

When he put his hands on her throat, she thought at first that it was a caress.

CHAPTER 21:

THE MADMAN

When he saw that Maretha had disappeared from the square chamber at the base of the stairs, he felt such a swell of hard, cold fury that he knew he could immolate the very stone if he did not contain himself. The golden cup still stood on its white pillar, but Maretha was gone. He pushed past the others and fled up into the late afternoon light.

Three workers stood at the excavation, drawn by some inexplicable instinct, but they scattered before him as he ran. He knew there had to be another open entrance. He knew it as he knew his soul, but the key to the city had eluded him all these months, tantalizing, close, but always just out of his grasp. If magic was his language, then here a dialect was spoken that he could not quite understand.

He returned to his tent, paced there a time among the bits and pieces of his art: a deck of Gates, seldom used, a small stove always lit, and burning within, the tiny creatures, half dragon, half fire salamander, that attended him. Somehow Maretha had gone below, through an entrance closed to him—

But there were other entrances. And if there were entrances east and west, then there must be one north, far away in the forest, and one south. With this thought he left his tent and set out to search.

Whether by scent, or good fortune, or some other force, it did not take long. The trenches the workers had dug partially around the little camp to protect it from that dawn fire had never been filled in. The stairwell had evidently never been noticed, but now, as he walked, it seemed abruptly to be there, gaping open at his feet.

He descended. When the light grew too dim, he called fire to his hands. Eyes of flame winked at him and curled into a ball at his bidding. He had learned when quite young that emotion can be channeled into power, separated and distilled until it coalesces into a source for the magical arts. Leaving, of course, its practitioners quite free of the impediments of joy and fear, hate and sorrow. Only one thing threatened him, as he got older—a stirring so insidious and compulsive that he recognized at once its danger and its promise.

He embraced chastity not with enthusiasm, since by the age of fifteen he had pretty much destroyed that capacity within himself, but with ruthless purpose, and felt his power grow hotter, and his heart grow colder. To protect himself from a temptation stronger than he cared to admit, he let rumors and gossip spread, fueled them himself by providing the material on which other men and women, prisoners of their basest instincts, could act out their twisted desires and then blame the damage and horror on him. It sometimes shocked even him, with what ability was left him to be shocked, what such people were capable of. But the subterfuge kept women away from him, even the most fortune-hungry. Only the discovery that at heart he was a bit of a prude had enough force to make him smile at the irony of it all. He was content, and very powerful.

Until he began at last to feel the drain, just after turning thirty, and had to face the unpleasant truth: virginity is not a circle; in and of itself it produces nothing, but only uses itself up at the last. A source of great power, used wisely, but not infinite.

That was when he came across Professor Farr's monograph. There were other options open to him, it was true. The prospect of draining the life from thousands of children he found distasteful. The unfettered use of sexuality and arousal to power magic, which he suspected of the Regent, offended his fastidious soul. But Professor Farr's monograph promised one act, one death, and the power would be sealed within him. Vast power, strong power, a veritable treasure—he had made his plans swiftly and mercilessly. And he had chosen Maretha as the sacrifice.

He frowned now as he halted at the base of the stairs in

a small, square room that mirrored the first one. It was decorated with the feast of the bride and groom, and the light in his hand dimmed as he recalled how she had looked at Harvest Fair when he had danced with her—deep-eyed with intelligence and courage and passion, a face strong in line, but weak with a capacity to give and forgive too much—or was that its strength?

He stood almost in blackness, cursed, and erased her image from his mind. As the fire boiled back in his hands, he saw a spear embedded haft down in the middle of the stone floor. When he closed his hand around it and lifted, the wall opened to reveal another staircase, going down. For an instant he thought he saw a woman, black rimming her eyes, broad-skirted, in a yellow jacket that exposed—but it was just a lingering vision and it faded. He hefted the spear in his right hand and descended.

It grew hot as he went down. When he reached the deepest level at last, he had to unbutton his coat. He stood in a small circular chamber with a single door. On that door a picture: through late-summer woods ran a loin-clothed hunter carrying a spear. Dogs ran and nipped at his heels. Just beyond the trees one could see what he pursued, almost— As he walked forward, he walked through the picture and immediately found himself lost in a maze of tunnels.

The fire in his hands was dying, shrinking slowly. It was so hot that he had to remove his coat, then his waistcoat, his boots. He was unbuttoning his shirt when he came into a huge room and saw, by the lantern light coming from the opposite wall, Marctha.

She was taking off her dress. He stared, finding that he could scarcely breathe. The dress slipped to the floor and she stood wearing only the thin material of her shift. He was seized by a compulsion so fierce that he let go of the spear. It clattered to the stone and she turned and saw him. They crossed to each other and she touched him and he was flooded by feelings so intense that he did not even notice that the light in his hands was extinguished.

She was sweet, infinitely sweet; he found her so. His power became lost in her, lost by the very act of finding her, but he did not care: it was clear to him now that love is the infinite source of power, having neither beginning nor end, having no limit. Love begets love, and so creates itself, on and forever. With such loving as this, they could create a child, the only true immortality for humanity, a child, if he had not stripped himself barren in the years before, that they could share and love, and then—

Then she spoke to him. He returned to himself out of this hallucination and realized that his power was trembling as if on the edge of an abyss, and that in one more instant he would lose it forever. He put his hands on her throat and began to strangle her.

For a moment there was no resistance, and he settled into his task with grim determination, in order to finish it quickly.

Then she fought. She fought with a strength that he could feel was augmented. The very stones struggled with her, shook and heaved. His grip slackened, slipped, and she was free, and running.

He had to dress. He even had enough rational thought left to pick up the spear and the lantern before he followed her. *That* corridor, he thought, but enclosed by stone he searched and searched and at last was hopelessly lost. He felt the weight of earth, of centuries, pressing down around him, stifling the air. The lantern guttered out and he stood in utter blackness. He could not call the least of his fires—his power was gone, as lost as he was. His only hope was to find her and complete the sacrifice that would release the power of the city into the chosen vessel.

Women's voices whispered down along the walls, seeping through the tunnels from a great distance. He listened carefully, but none were *her* voice. As he stood he realized that a faint nimbus of light rose like mist off the stone and rolled away down a dank tunnel. He went cautiously, but the luminous mist merely grew brighter and thicker, until it led him into a small circular chamber out of which opened a staircase.

He climbed, accompanied by a swell of mist. The stairs ended abruptly in a door. The mist framed the painting that decorated the door in eerie mystery: it was She, the Daughter, the Temptress, the Evil One, the Princess of Darkness, in her aspect of the Mistress of the Underworld, the Bringer of Nightmares. Blindfolded, dressed in a simple shift, she ran wildly through a forest of horrors—he did not wait to examine the scene in more detail, but started up the last step. The door opened out of its own accord, silent on unseen hinges, light as if it was not stone at all.

He found himself in forest. Utterly still, uncannily still, as if it was not just windless but airless. Behind, the doorway closed with a low grating. He whirled, pushing at the heavy stone, but it was firm under his hand, unmoving, and even as he stood with his palm against the stone, the door dissolved under his fingers into nothing.

He stood alone in the unbroken forest. He looked at his palm, curled the hand into a fist, and walked cautiously forward. He could not even hear his feet on the low grass. The leaves of the trees seemed pinioned there, motionless, heavy with moisture.

It was a thickly-grown forest, so that he could not see much around. The light was not quite day, not quite night, still yet neither dusk nor dawn but some suspension of both.

A sound: the drip of water through leaves to the rich earth. He moved in that direction, listening, alert.

The jingle of a horse's harness stopped him. He gripped his spear tight, hefting it to throw, and watched. Through a gap in the trees he saw a clearing. Sun shone there, lancing through leaves to cast a brilliant shower of light on the grass. A young woman, scarcely more than a girl, pulled up her horse and dismounted, looking about herself with an expression composed of stubbornness, fear, and excitement all melded into one. Her clothing was of an old-fashioned style, one he did not even remember from his youth. She looked strangely familiar to him, but he could not place her.

She started around, seeing someone—but not him—and in the turn of her head he recognized the face from a portrait: his grandmother, soon after she married. Her defiant expression dissolved into a more vulnerable one, wonder and passion mingled, and she walked as if asleep out of his sight towards some person, and spoke a name.

He ran forward, but when he reached the edge of the clearing, it was empty. Stillness shuttered the forest once again. He went on. The trees shifted in kind, as from a spring forest to a summer one. Tiny flowers bloomed out of the loam. Ferns spread out from dim corners.

A scream. He saw Maretha, a hazy figure running frantically away; perhaps she had seen him. He chased her, stumbled and fell to his knees over a thick tree root, and saw her real pursuers.

Three lions, huge, golden creatures, converged on her. They nipped at her heels until she tripped and went down beneath them. Snarling and a horrible ripping and chewing filled the air. He groped up a tree to his feet and ran forward, shouting. The lions scattered, fleeing, leaving behind them a thing of sinew and bone and mangled flesh.

He took halting steps until he stood beside her remains, but it was not a woman, bloody and torn; a half-eaten deer lay before him. Its black eyes stared sightlessly up at him as he poked at it with the point of his spear. Wings fluttered down beside him, and a kite settled onto the ground a stone's throw away, waiting for its chance at the kill. He shuddered, wiped the spear point on grass, and walked on into silence.

Summer passed to autumn. Leaves littered the ground but not the slightest scuffing or rustling sounded as he passed.

Laughter, wafted on the breeze. *Her* laughter. He halted, cast for the direction of the sound like a hound casting for scent. Followed it.

Coming out into a glade made picturesque by half-bare trees and a warm, sweet breeze, he saw her, seated on a couch of branches and late flowers. But she was not alone. A man sat with her, hair black as his own was golden, a man with a face as gentle and loving as his own was cold. And they were making love, the two of them, with a tenderness, with delight and pleasure. Her body moved in the sunlight, and the sight of it, the sight of her face made beautiful by joy, burned a heat into him that obliterated what vestiges of his old power still lay hidden in his last secret places. And with that heat, an absolute rage consumed him in fire. Flame pulsed up along his skin as if escaping at last from its confines.

He ran forward and before she or the lover could react he thrust with the spear. Thrust again, stabbed again, and again, heedless of cries or blood or gaping wounds until he was bathed in their blood and they lay scarcely recognizable below him.

He began to shake. Trembled uncontrollably, and dropped the spear. It rustled in leaves and undergrowth—

there were no bodies at all, merely a tumble of rotting leaves and old branches.

His breath came ragged and gasping. He backed away from the spot as if from an abomination, grabbed for the spear, and with it in his hand, he ran blindly away through the forest.

CHAPTER 22:

THE DREAMER

His hands were strong. As they closed on her throat, she was at first so astonished that it wasn't until the air was cut off that she started to struggle.

At first it seemed hopeless. His grip was like the grip of iron, and he had pinned her beneath him. His expression was emptied of emotion. It was all the more terrifying for that. Her fists beat feebly at his arms; her legs shifted and kicked uselessly.

Then her anger rose. It all came clear: he had indeed never intended to have an heir. That had been his excuse to allay her distrust so that she would agree to marry him. All along he had intended this, had studied her father's writings and theories, had believed them, and had chosen this route to augment his power. To gain the power of the labyrinth by her sacrifice.

In that instant, she found her anger. It seemed to her that the stone she lay on rose with her and tore at his grasp, and with the strength of stone she pushed him aside, flung him off her, and ran.

She had no idea where she was going. Her shift tangled in her knees, and she pulled it free and straightened it so that it would not impede her. At first she ran wildly, without any thought but to escape him. Slowly, as she began to think, she realized that she traversed this maze of tunnels without light, without map, and yet she was going somewhere. Some instinct, some knowledge rising out of the stone itself, led her. The labyrinth was of incredible complexity, corridor branching off corridor, but she was mistress of it; she could not lose herself here.

When her steps brought her to a stairwell that disappeared up into rock, she was not surprised or relieved. She paused to catch her breath, caught instead the sound of a voice. The turning in and out of the corridors disguised its distance: it could have been a mile away, or a corner away. With renewed energy, she fled up the stairs. At the top a figure waited, but it was only a painting. She rushed through it out into the night and ran.

Halted, panting, she finally looked about herself. Immediately she wished she had not. She stood in forest illuminated only by moon and stars. At first glance the woods seemed a beautiful cathedral of limb and branch and leaf, arching up into the sky, closed buds and low undergrowth padding the forest floor. But an ominous undertone grew around her, not as a sound, but as a feeling, an instinct of malignance.

She moved forward slowly. Ground cover rustled under her feet like sinister voices. Vines trailing off of low-hanging branches opened needle-point eyes, transforming them into vipers that stared at her, hissing sibilant messages to each other as she passed. Dark things slithered away into the undergrowth. Deformed gnome faces peered around branches, jeering and chittering. Heavy steps padded along parallel to her, but the creature itself was too far away or too dark in coloring for her to see. Once a low growl rumbled from an unseen throat. An owl too-whit-too-whooed. A smaller voice shrieked in terror, and there was a scuffling, and a snap, like a neck breaking.

"Maretha."

The voice stopped her stockstill.

"Maretha. Little saint, where are you?"

She took one hesitant step forward, "Mother?"

Trees parted to reveal a moonlit glade. Three figures stood there. Their pale faces turned to her, and she recognized them: her mother and her young brother and sister. Her mother held out her arms. With a faint cry Maretha ran into them.

"Have you kept well, little saint?" Her mother's voice held the warmth of comfort and safety. Small hands clutched at her legs and arms, the familiar grasp of her young siblings. "Have you kept care of your father as I asked you? Helped him with all your heart and soul? Done what he asked of you without complaint? That is the duty I passed to you, little saint, to support your father in all things."

"I have, Mother," she cried, "I have." She began to reach up to touch her mother's face, but her hands were pinioned to her sides. She tried to move her legs, could not. Thick vines like ropes were growing up her, twining around her, trapping her. The familiar, loved faces had vanished; growth snaked around her, ragged-edged leaves like giants' mouths smothering, enclosing her, tightening around her throat.

"No!" She could not break loose of the twisting vegetation. Terrified, she struggled wildly to free herself. A great wind swept down on them, scattering leaves and branches and vine into nothing, and she stood alone in a silent glade.

A branch snapped in the forest behind. She fled on.

She ran for a while heedless of the little horrors inhabiting the trees until shortness of breath forced her to pause. Under her bare feet the ground felt moist, almost slimy. A rustling, some movement through the undergrowth, and she turned—but it was only Professor Farr.

"Father! Father! Thank the Lady!" He started at her voice and looked vaguely about himself. She rushed over to him. "Oh, Father! You came to look for me."

He clasped the hands she proffered, tucked one under his elbow and drew her away through the forest. "Of course, my dear," he said with the characteristic absent-mindedness that always underlay his words. "I need you. You seem to have run away from your responsibilities."

"Not from you, Father," she protested, secure in his grip.

"Not from me," he agreed. "From your husband." He pulled her along and ahead she saw the earl, waiting. As they neared, that veneer of handsomeness with which his sorcery endowed him began to peel away. It sloughed off him like skin, revealing a hideous old man with festering sores on his face and bony hands riddled with maggots and living, writhing things. He opened his mouth to speak but a long red thing more like a tentacle curled out, reaching for her.

She jerked away from her father, but his grasp did not give at all. The creature that was her husband slithered closer, wheezing and choking, and fire began to rim it, in preparation for her immolation, the sacrifice that would bring it her power.

Thunder shook the air above, followed hard by a shaking in the earth itself, so violent that she was thrown to the ground as the abomination before her shattered into pieces. Her father's grip tore away from her arm.

The trembling ceased abruptly. When she could raise her head, both were gone. She sat back on the thick loam and buried her head in her hands, uncaring of what might creep up behind her.

"Maretha." *His* voice.

She looked up.

He stood some ten paces from her, his hands held out, palms open to her in the eternal posture of the supplicant. His shirt was torn and dirty, his hair disordered, his boots scuffed and marked by his passage through the wood.

"I have been a fool, Maretha," he said. If his voice was soft, almost entreating, it still had at its core that hardness that he had so long cultivated. It was true that he was severe, self-absorbed, difficult, but did that mean that he could not change? He had become angry with her once— was that not a sure sign of regard? And once, that once when he had danced with her, she had caught him looking at her in a strange, questioning way, as if he had just realized that there was an answer in her for him, to a question he had never before thought to ask.

"Forgive me," he said.

He was beautiful. He might have been the avatar of her heart's desire, created whole out of the elements and the very soul of the forest. And in any case, she had loved him since the day she had first met him in the library.

She rose and went to him. He enfolded her in his arms, and as she embraced him, she felt more than saw him draw the knife and stab her through the heart.

CHAPTER 23:

THE SEEKER

"Sanjay! Thank God you're here." Chryse ran to hug her husband as he came up the last slope to the little hollow that hid the western stairwell. "As I was hiking up here I saw two people go down the central staircase, and I would swear it was Professor Farr and Thomas Southern. They didn't come back up. Was it them?"

Sanjay extricated himself from her grip and looked thoughtfully back at the valley, laid out below them in the lowering dusk. "I haven't seen the professor," he admitted, "but I left Thomas back at camp. Charity was really feeling poorly and he was talking with Mistress Cook and two of her people when I left." He shook his head, then handed her two unlit lanterns. "But there's worse. Evidently there's one of these entrances south as well, just outside our camp. I saw the earl go down it, but I still had Charity, and by the time I could follow I found the room below empty. I don't know if he found a way in or not."

She knelt to light a lantern. "We can't afford to assume that he's not down there chasing her. If he didn't really want an heir, then what *does* he want her for?"

"Good question. Let's go."

"I'll go first. I'm more afraid of what's behind me than what's in front. This way, it'll grab you first."

"Thank you," said her husband as he followed her down the steps.

The entrance was laid out just as the other had been, this one decorated with an elaborate fresco of the Harvest Fair celebrations, but all in such an antique, ancient style that they could both see it was centuries old, and of a

society quite alien from the one they lived in now. There
was an object set on a pillar of stone here, too, and Chryse
gasped with pleased surprise to see it.

"A pipe!" She picked it up. It was some kind of bone,
pierced with holes, carved with a filigree of intertwined
animals along its length. She put it to her mouth and
blew. The tone was pure as water, and as she moved her
fingers, creating a tentative melody, the wall dropped
away to reveal a further staircase.

Sanjay laughed. "I wish your music professor could have
seen that. They'd have begged you to stay for a doctorate."

"And what makes you think they didn't?" she asked with
hauteur. "Lady, it's dark in there. Maybe I'll allow you to
go first."

He kissed her. "For luck. Better bring the pipe. We
may need it."

"And it isn't even my best instrument," she replied, but
he was already descending.

It was a long, slow, cautious climb down, circling, but at
last they reached a small, round chamber.

"It's hot down here," said Chryse.

Sanjay had lifted his lantern high to get the broadest
circle of light, but he looked back over his shoulder at her
and grinned. "I'll take off mine if you'll take off yours."

"You must be joking. I'm not afraid of a little sweat."
She advanced several steps across the chamber. "But don't
let that stop *you*."

He came up beside her, laying a hand at her waist.
"Whatever's down here, my sweet, I'm don't plan on
meeting it clad only in my underwear."

"Oh, Sanjay. It's terrible to laugh when Maretha could
be in danger."

"Do you have your half of the deck?"

"Of course. Pouch tied at my waist."

He nodded and patted the coat pocket in which he
carried the other half. "But how do we get out of here?"

"Look!" she breathed. "There's a picture on that wall.
It's like it's forming out of nothing. It's—why, it's one of
the Gates—one of the ones Madame Sosostris read for me,
The Seeker."

"No," said Sanjay, puzzled. "It's the one with the young
knight, the—" He broke off. "There's nothing behind that
painting at all. That's a tunnel!"

He walked forward, and Chryse hurried after. They passed through a cold wall of air and then into the stifling heat of the tunnels.

"Slow down, slow down," she called. "Hold my hand."

Sanjay did not reply, but he took her hand, and they went on. Their two lanterns illuminated the passing walls. They were of smooth stone broken with the barest of seams at intervals, but it was impossible to tell if the tunnels had been hewn out of rock or built with such skill that the seaming of stone was almost imperceptible. There was an impression of great age sealed into the very air, caught in the stone itself.

"Hold on." Sanjay stopped to peer down a side tunnel. "There's got to be a pattern to this—there must be a center to all this."

"Do you suppose the entire city sits above tunnels? My God, Sanjay." He turned to look at her. His face blended half into the darkness. "This is the labyrinth." She began to laugh, a little nervously. "It isn't a myth at all. It's true."

He waited, patient, until she stopped. She coughed, self-conscious, and he gave her hand a squeeze and they went on. She was soon utterly lost, but he paused by every branching corridor and seemed to taste or measure the air in some way, and eventually they came to a huge circular chamber in the middle of which lay a low stone slab.

Sanjay walked forward and knelt beside the stone. "Look." He picked up a scrap of cloth. "The earl's handkerchief."

Chryse had wandered away to the walls, attracted by the dim shapes of frescos along the wall. They sprang into brilliant life as she neared with the light.

"Maretha's dress!" She crouched to touch it. "I guess she found it too hot, too—but if they were both here . . ." Her words trailed off as her eyes lifted to examine the painting in front of her. She felt a slight heat creep into her cheeks. "No wonder she took off her dress," she muttered. "Sanjay, you should come see this."

He made some reply she could not quite hear.

"Talk about a graphic—" She backtracked a little on the wall. "Oh, I see. It's the wedding night, and before that the wedding feast, and before that—the planting, the sowing of the seeds. . . . Wait." She followed slowly back along the wall to return to the place she had started, folding Maretha's dress into an easily carried bundle, and stared at the ritual that unfolded as she walked. "This is the scene Professor Farr thought was the sacrifice of the young priestess, but in context you can see that it's really the consummation of the marriage. And then, this next one must be High Summer Eve. I don't understand this. It seems the groom, or king, or whatever, is being chained and led away to a dungeon—probably down here—and this must be the Hunter's Run holiday— Good Lord." She halted. Her voice shook with amazement. "Now I see. Sanjay. Sanjay, come look at this. The ritual is the wheel of the year, like the Gates, like the city, turning in and out. Each holiday is one aspect, and in a way it never ends, just repeats itself. The professor was right about that much, about the ritual being central to the life of the city, although I'm not sure he knew why. And do you remember that old folk song about two lovers, a hunt, and a sacrifice? The one I sang to you? There is a sacrifice, but everyone was wrong. Completely wrong—it's so clear in this picture. It's so terrible. Sanjay."

She turned. Silence, and complete blackness in the room except for her lantern. "Sanjay? Sanjay!" She knew by feeling that she was alone in the chamber.

"Oh, bloody hell!" she swore. Darkness clustered near the glow of her lantern like shadow moths engulfing light. "I hate the dark. I hate it, I hate it. Oh damn damn damn." She stood staring into black. Her hand trembled on the lantern handle. The room lay hot and still and silent around her.

"Chryse," she said, keeping her voice even. "Don't be an idiot. Just think about what to do. Wait here, or go exploring, but you know your sense of direction—"

One hand, straying, touched the smooth bone of the pipe. She shut her eyes briefly, letting out a long, tight breath. It took a few minutes to rig a way to hang the two lanterns from her belt, using Maretha's dress as a pad between the warm glass and her dress, but once her hands were free she lifted the pipe to her lips and played the same set of notes she had at the western entrance.

In the hush that followed she heard an answer: five liquid notes caught on a rising interval, like a question. She pursued them into a corridor, trading melody for

melody until she and the unseen piper had an elaborate
improvisation going, variations on a theme. She was so lost
in the pleasure and challenge of it that she had almost
forgotten where she was when she found herself at the
base of a stairwell that led up. High, high above, she saw a
faint shaft of light, and a small figure turned in the light,
framed against it, in silhouette. Small, no bigger than a
child, its face bore the weasel-snout of goblinkind and a
cap at an angle on its head. Even at such distance, she felt
she could see its bright eyes.

"Wait!" she called, but it disappeared through the opening. She took the steps two at a time and arrived out of
breath at the top to step out into a beautiful spring dawn.

The soft green of young leaves dappled the trees around
her. It was a forest of light—birches, aspen, and alder. A
bird sang, and she recognized its song as the five-note
melody that had brought her here. She felt more than saw
movement to her right, turned to see a beautiful, majestic
black horse pause between distant trees and stare at her
with such intelligence that she almost expected it to speak.
Then it broke to its left and cantered away into the forest.

She blew out the lantern and set it and its companion
down beside the gaping hole that admitted the staircase to
the light.

On the breeze, the music carried like a thought just
entering her head. She wandered in its direction, still
caught by the beauty of the forest, but pulled inexorably
by the lure of the song.

A single pipe, first, elaborating on that five-note phrase;
a second instrument joined, plucked strings, and a third,
which she did not recognize. Voices added harmony, breath-
taking in their perfection. Despite her yearning to find the
players, she had to stop more than once to fully listen, to
absorb the sound and the timbre, the peculiar twists of
harmony, the instruments blending and separating with
precise craft and felicitous art.

She discovered them in a glade, these musicians. She
was not aware of what they wore, nor really even what
they looked like, but she gazed raptly at the way they
played, their technique, their breathing.

There was an empty chair, so she took it. Next to her sat
a woman holding a reeded instrument. She lowered it
from her mouth and sat waiting for her part to enter again.

Chryse leaned across to her. "Who wrote this?" she whispered. "It's so beautiful."

The woman's mouth quirked up in an expression not quite human. "Don't you recognize it?" Her voice was as musical as the wind through spring leaves. Her hair shone like the sun through blossoms. "You wrote this."

"But I've never composed anything half this good."

"You can," said the soft voice, "if you choose to." She cocked her head as if listening for her cue and began to play again.

Chryse realized abruptly that a part was missing, leaving the piece incomplete, and she lifted the pipe to her lips and joined them.

They played. She had no idea how long it went on. As she played she listened. She would lower her pipe when it seemed appropriate, lift it when it was needed. At times it seemed that she anticipated the way the music should flow, and it would indeed flow that way. A phrase would occur to her, and then, like an echo of her thought, occur in the music.

A few times the music meandered, as if it had lost its focus, though its lines and melody never lost their enchanting clarity. But she at length began to sense a climax to the piece, a given, inevitable end, and the music began to build towards that place.

Until a scream shattered it, abrupt as a wrong note, destroying her concentration. She dropped her pipe, it was so unexpected.

Dull, thick silence shuttered the woods. She sat alone in a glade that the first rays of the sun were just beginning to warm. Lowering her hand, she almost leapt up when she felt a damp softness on her skin. She was sitting on an old rotting stump. She stood quickly and brushed off her dress. As she turned to survey the clearing, she heard sobbing.

With pipe in hand she listened this way and that until she found the direction, and then walked cautiously through the woods.

Another clearing opened amongst the trees, and in a single shaft of sunlight a figure knelt in grass, trembling and sobbing.

"Holy Lady," breathed Chryse. And louder, but not too loud, so as not to startle her. "Maretha."

Maretha's head jerked up and she scrambled backwards to her feet, ready to run. She looked terrified.

Chryse put out her hands and did not try to approach any closer. "Maretha. It's Chryse. I don't know what has happened to you, but this really is Chryse. Do you remember the time—I sent Kate into the village pond with the cards?"

Maretha froze in mid-run, like a deer suspended between paralysis and flight. Her white shift was stained with grass and dirt around the knees, torn at the hem where it brushed one calf. Her hair was wildly disordered, her feet bare.

"Maretha," said Chryse again, soft.

"Chryse." Maretha's voice broke, but she stumbled forward into Chryse's arms. "This place is full of nightmares. Nightmares, hidden as beautiful dreams." She did not weep, just clung there for a bit. "He tried to kill me. He tried to kill me just as we were—were—finally—how can a person be so close, so intimate, and then just—" She had to catch herself to collect her voice. "And it was—we—I'm pregnant, Chryse."

"But if you just—how could you possibly know so soon?"

Maretha shook her head, unable to explain.

"Well, you're safe now."

"No. He's still out here. He means to re-create the old rituals. He has to sacrifice me to gain the power of the labyrinth."

"Now I understand. That's what he thought the treasure was all along," said Chryse slowly. "Not an object at all, but the city's power."

Maretha lifted her head. "What do you mean, *thought?* He isn't—dead, is he?" Her voice faded on the last words.

"I don't know. But I don't understand *why* he needs the labyrinth's power. I would have thought he had power enough."

"Maretha!" The third voice broke into their conversation like an arrow, and the two woman spun around to see Professor Farr standing at the edge of the glade, looking, as usual, perplexed. "My dear girl." His gaze was fixed with unnerving lucidity on his daughter. "You can't mean that the earl tried to kill you."

"Of course I can mean it." She broke away from Chryse. "You were the one who gave him the idea. You were the one who was willing to sacrifice *me*, to marry me to him, to finance this expedition."

"Maretha, my dear child—" He took a step towards her. "You can't mean that."

"Of course I can mean it," she continued, reckless now. "He would have strangled me if he could have, but I escaped. And he has to find me now, because he's lost the source of his old power. He can't get it back. Just here, he tried to—" She broke off. Her father extended a hand, but she flung herself away from him. "No, no. It was my own dream." Her tone was almost scornful. "My nightmare. Much you cared."

"But—Maretha . . . I never—"

"You're a selfish old man," Maretha cried. "You never cared about anything but your work." She moved abruptly past him, as if to run on into the forest again.

And was brought up short with a frightened cry by the sight of the earl advancing on them through the trees.

"Maretha," said Chryse in a firm voice. "Come back by me."

Maretha retreated.

The earl looked so different a man that Chryse would almost not have recognized him: his clothes in disorder, without coat or waistcoat, without boots or cravat; his hair mussed and a smudge on his cheek; but more than that the look of desperate passion on his face, so entirely removed from the chilly hauteur that characterized him. The inconsequential thought crossed her mind that at least he had never used sorcery to enhance his looks: he was still a handsome man, not some repulsive horror as she had often imagined.

"Stop right there," she said.

He had a spear in one hand, but he stopped. "Let me through. You don't understand. I must kill her. The ritual has to be completed."

"I understand." With a push she moved Maretha behind her, so that her body stood between the spear and the earl's wife. "You're the one who doesn't understand. I understand that you were willing to murder Maretha to gain power for your sorcery. You *tried* to kill her. You'd still do it, given the chance. I understand that both you and Professor Farr completely mis-read the ritual of the labyrinth."

"Impossible," protested Professor Farr. "I have studied the remains of this civilization for decades."

The earl kept his spear hefted, point towards Chryse. "What do you mean?"

"How did you get here, Professor? Was it with Thomas Southern?"

The professor shook his head, confused. "No. No, it was one of the workers. He'd found a way to get below. What was his name— Tagness, I think. Somehow below we got separated, and I found myself here. I fail to see what this has to do with my years of careful research."

"Did you come through the central chamber below? Did you?" She turned to the earl again. The slightest blush colored his cheeks, matching the one that flushed Maretha's face at the question. "Did you look at the frescos there? An entire set, the whole year, unbroken, and very clear. They depict the same eight holidays that are on the Gates. The old legends are true, in some sense: the Gates do descend from ancient Pariam. And you were right on one count, Professor. If the frescoes are a true reconstruction of an ancient ritual and not just some artist's fancy, then there was a sacrifice. A—coronation beginning the year, I suppose, followed by a—craft's fair, and then the sowing in early spring. There *was* a sacred marriage, as you theorized, which was indeed followed by a sacrifice to fulfill the ritual of the labyrinth." Her voice rang in the glade. "But it wasn't the bride, at all, who was sacrificed. It's the man."

Maretha gasped.

The earl's expression did not change, but there was a kind of whitening around his eyes as the shock of her statement hit him.

"You've thrown the year off a little, I think," Chryse continued, so furious that she felt the last shred of mercy or sympathy drain from her. "I didn't get to see the whole thing, but the Gates tell it anyway. And if it's been as long as centuries, I don't think the city cares what season it is, as long as it gets the blood it wants. I finally understood why the day is called Hunter's Run. The wedding takes place, and then the groom is imprisoned and then released, into the forest—like any wild animal. They're hunting the bridegroom. Men, hunting a man. He's the sacrifice."

Into the silence left by the effect of her words, a wind came up suddenly and rushed through leaves, rattling the undergrowth. As if a cloud had covered the sun, the light dimmed abruptly and quickly, like a reversal of the dawn that Chryse had just experienced.

Faint, far in the distance, a horn sounded, and hounds belled.

The professor and Maretha both started at the sound, and turned to look around. Only the earl's gaze remained fixed on Chryse, and hers on him.

"I'd start running if I were you," she said.

CHAPTER 24:

THE PALADIN

Sanjay was leaning over the slab of stone that lay in the center of the great circular chamber, examining it with both eye and touch, when a wisp of a breeze stirred the close air of the room and his lantern flame wavered, guttered, and went out. He sighed, a little exasperated, and crouched to re-light it just as his gaze caught on a faint pattern glowing on the stone floor. He stretched out his arm and brushed at it with two fingers.

"Chryse. Come look at this. I could swear these are footprints leading away. It's as if—I don't know—each step left a tiny bit of life energy that marked the stone. I feel sure that this is Maretha's trail."

Chryse made some reply, but he did not really hear it, he was so intent on following the track. It was like a pale dusting, barely discernible, but unmistakable once the eye caught it. He traced it out of the chamber and down one corridor, turning into another and another before he realized that he was lost and that the trail of footprints was fading behind him, so that he could not follow it back to his wife. He had no choice but to go on.

He was not entirely surprised when the traces led him to a straight length of stairs that led up into the rock. He looked back once, into the dark tunnel behind, and then climbed.

The transition from under to above ground was almost imperceptible, until he realized that of course it was now night. There was no moon, only the brilliant scattering of stars above to illuminate the forest.

It was warm, for autumn. He found a smooth bole of a

tree and sat against it, yawning. To his right he could
barely discern the opening of the stairway set into a low
rise. After all, he reasoned, Chryse was surely as likely to
be drawn out this way as he had been.

He could see by the nature of the forest around him that
it was as much a labyrinth as the maze of tunnels below.
At first, sitting quietly, he let his eyes adjust to the way
the dim light fell among the trees. Though it was night,
his sight penetrated farther than it should have in such
conditions. A quality of uncanny shifting permeated the
woods. It was as if no thing or no point in the forest was
ever entirely at rest, as if some force sifted randomly
through it, changing its aspect from one moment to the
next.

A double-trunked oak that grew some meters in front of
him, when he looked again, had shifted position a good
ten feet to the right. Later, looking a third time, the oak
had shifted back, but now bore three trunks. A glade
opened out to his left. Its boundaries altered when his
attention strayed to other areas. None of this was abrupt,
or even, he felt, conscious on the part of some unseen
manipulator, but rather the natural result of a power that,
loose in the forest, manifested itself by these constant
transformations.

Above, he heard the quick beat of wings and a bird's
cry. Out of the brush loped a light blur that materialized
into a white wolf. It stopped dead in its tracks and stared
at Sanjay as if surprised to see him there. Some creature
made a faint *chuff*ing noise out in the gloom, and the wolf
flicked its ears and vanished into the woods behind. An
insubstantial form that could as likely have been a wisp of
smoke settled into the nook of a branch and coiled itself
around the limb.

Wind rose from far away, fluttering the last leaves,
talking in the branches. Its timbre changed as it grew
stronger until it sounded like the snap and rush of a sail in
steady wind, and Sanjay felt it push at his back and then
subside abruptly. A thick, rumbling sigh shook the air
behind him, followed by a hot gust of sulphurous breeze
that brushed his cheek and made the hair on the back of
his neck tingle as if someone was touching it. He turned
his head to look.

And stood up, one hand on the tree to stop himself falling over from sheer amazement.

The most beautiful creature he had ever seen had settled into the glade. As he watched, it folded its wings against its body, an action incongruously graceful in so huge a creature. Light shimmered along its skin. It might have been moonlight trapped in the lustrous silver of its scales, running like water along the lines of least resistance as the creature shifted position, then flowing back again.

Sanjay came as close as he ever had in his life to swearing, except that he was too staggered to speak, never having expected, even here, to see a dragon.

As if he *had* spoken aloud, it turned its great horned head about and fastened its gaze on him. Unalloyed power radiated from it. Its eyes held both sheer terror and utter fascination, so that as he stared he felt progressively less that he had any will of his own and more an inchoate yearning, some longing buried deep that had surfaced only now. Like a famished man finding golden apples, he desired this thing more than anything and was yet afraid of the effect it had on him.

It spoke. Not a voice, pushed by air through vocal cords, but a melisma of sound that could yet be understood as words.

>Thou art known, child< said the dragon, not so much examining Sanjay as encompassing him. Its sinuous neck arched in a move as smooth as the flow of water.

"How do you know me?" asked Sanjay, finding speech at last. After the sonority of the dragon, his voice sounded thin, one-dimensional.

>That which has already passed, is yet to be< it said, a rising and falling of tones on one syllable. >It is thy task to see the truth and let it therefore be known<

It gathered itself, claws pulling at the turf like a cat pulls at a rug, tail sweeping and curling as it unfurled its wings. It had a fluid beauty, never complete, never imprisoned in any one aspect.

Unlike mortal humans, thought Sanjay, trapped in time.

Than it sprang. Up—the force of the air displaced by its wings brought him to his knees and sent gusts of leaves scattering over the ground. He remained kneeling as he stared up, following its path with his eyes until the trees hid it.

As if the dragon had pulled all sound up with it, the night was covered with utter silence. Even his own breathing did not sound, or the rustle of undergrowth as he stood.

A hound bayed, then a chorus of hounds. A horn-call lifted on the breeze just after it, as if in pursuit. Sanjay brushed at the last dirt clinging to his trousers. The barking grew in volume, and under it he could hear the noise of horses passing through undergrowth. He stepped to one side so that his back was protected by the tree trunk, and waited.

The dogs came first, a pack of red-eared, brindle hounds that moved forward like some many-limbed, exciteable creature. They barked and bayed and bellowed and, spotting Sanjay, thronged to him and sniffed at a safe distance. They had huge, brown, weeping eyes and a look of such doleful exuberance that Sanjay had to laugh and crouch and put out a hand. The hounds swarmed over him, licking and snuffling as if he was their long-lost master.

The horn sounded again. The hounds, whining, retreated into a great quivering mass of dog. From out of the forest swept a phalanx of hunters. They pulled up their horses and the hounds crowded around them.

Sanjay tried not to stare until he realized that the hunters had evidently not noticed him. The horses had coats of burnished white, some shading to grey or gold. Each was arrayed with a spun-gold saddle blanket, fringed with strands of black pearls and brilliant feathers. Jewels blazed in their braided manes and tails.

The riders wore the same spun-gold fabric fashioned into clothing rich with interlaced patterns that seemed to expand and contract like an unbroken path of spirals through unfamiliar countryside, unending motion, unending change. Belts of intense red bounded their waists, and each bore an elaborately hafted knife in a sheath stitched with gold thread. All the riders carried spears.

Sanjay could get no clear idea of their faces. They had a kind of blurring focus about them, as if they existed on a different plane of time than he did. He only knew that they were not human.

One raised a horn to her lips. Before the high call rose on the wind, a riderless, grey horse cantered into the glade and halted before Sanjay. He felt a sudden shifting

of focus so strong it was disorienting, had to put his hand
on the horse's neck to steady himself. When he looked up,
he saw that all the riders were now gazing at him in a
half-curious, rather flat way.

He could see their faces now. They were not beautiful,
but splendid, graceful faces too exotic to be handsome to a
human eye. He understood that they expected him to
mount, so he did.

The horn sounded. The hounds belled and set off again
on the scent. A strong sense not of antiquity but of time-
lessness settled on Sanjay as the air rushed past and they
galloped through the trees. He felt caught up in some
archaic sacrament that he did not understand. There was a
relentless purpose to this chase; the trees themselves
seemed to create a path where none had been before. He
did not even attempt to guide the horse, but knew rather
that he was being carried along toward a consecration far
older than he was or could ever hope to become.

The baying of the hounds intensified. They had sighted
their prey. Sanjay felt a surge of blood-taste in his mouth
and his emotions, as he too sighted a single figure fleeing
the inexorable pursuit. Beside him, the riders lowered
their spears.

The hounds coursed alongside their prey, closing and
nipping at its heels to drive it out into the open. Not until
it turned did Sanjay register that the distant figure was a
man.

Golden-haired. His white shirt had been pulled free in
his run and now hung over the top of his black trousers.
He had a spear; as the hunt neared, Sanjay watched him
thrust at the hounds, who were merely harrying him. He
had a sharp eye, this trapped man, but each spear-thrust,
however well-placed, dug into turf, not flesh, though a
hound had been in that spot an instant before. His steps
slowed as he tired, and at last, when he thrust, two of the
hounds slipped inside his guard and nipped and yanked
and he fell, sprawling on the ground, his spear slipping
from his grasp.

The hunt pulled up, and at a piercing whistle from one
of the riders the hounds retreated to form a circle about
their hapless prisoner. They yapped and panted and wagged
their tails as one by one the riders dismounted with preternatural grace from their white and golden steeds.

The hunted man lifted his head. His gaze still had force, even under such circumstances: arrogant and resigned, feverish, desperate, and, most shocking to Sanjay, familiar. Familiar, and human, in that most ordinary and yet deepest level of humanity that is the most binding of all connections. It was the earl, but reduced, trying at once to get to his knees and also to reach the spear, which one of the hunters lazily pulled out of his grasp with the point of his own. All around the fallen man, more spears lowered to surround him.

Sanjay swung down from his horse with more haste than skill and ran forward, wading through the hounds. They slavered at his legs but let him pass. He could feel the imminence of the kill like the press of a hand closing around a haft. From the ground he scooped up the loose spear and placed himself squarely between the earl and the nearest hunter.

"I won't let you kill him," he said.

Attention focussed swiftly and penetratingly on him. All the hounds sat, seemingly perplexed by this turn of events. The only sound was the rasp of the earl's breathing, ragged and irregular.

Far in the distance a woman's voice called out unintelligible words, ending on a question. Like a spell, it broke through the paralysis of action that had frozen the scene of the hunt.

"Do not interfere," said the foremost hunter. His hair had the blaze of fire in it, shining like a beacon for benighted travellers in the darkness. "Once begun, this hunt must end in blood. This man called us back to the old ways that your kind have long forsworn, and ours used only in greatest need. Chosen of the chosen one, he has awakened the power of the heiress, and thus becomes the sacrifice to seal her power."

"It is all true," said the earl in a low voice that Sanjay could barely hear. "I knew there was treasure here for the taking. But I misread its agent." His tone might have borne the faintest hint of irony. He was still breathing hard.

"Nevertheless," said Sanjay, standing firm. "I cannot simply stand by and let it happen."

"You do not understand." The hunter lifted one hand and the hounds and his companions all moved back to form a still greater circle around the three in the center. "These are forces that once raised will run their course. You cannot *will* it to cease, any more than *will* can halt the wind or corrupt the purity of one of the Great Ones. Let us through."

After the last words, Sanjay could hear clearly the resonance of the hunter's voice, an uncanny echo that faded in on itself. The other hunters hefted spears. The hounds edged forward. Closer now, he heard a woman calling, and the faint thrash and rustle of disturbance in the undergrowth.

"Nevertheless." He did not move.

"So be it," said the hunter. "We will have blood." He lowered his spear.

"Sanjay!"

Sanjay had time only to register Chryse's voice, rising with surprise and confusion, before the hunter thrust with his spear. Sanjay dodged, felt the point sigh past his ear. He knocked the haft aside and switched his grip on his spear, dipping it and coming up underneath the other. But the hunter met and parried it, a hard snap, dipped and circled his own point and thrust for Sanjay's belly.

Sanjay barely deflected the point, driving it down. It tore at the fabric of his coat, catching in a pocket. The hunter jerked it back just as Sanjay riposted; as the pocket ripped, the hunter stepped left and with ready instinct pushed the point of Sanjay's spear past himself and on the same stroke drove his point down and into Sanjay's left thigh.

Someone cried out; Sanjay knew only that it was not his own voice. The searing pain in his thigh enflamed his reason and narrowed the focus of his concentration.

He saw the undefended chest of his opponent and thrust for it. For an instant he had an hallucination that the hunter was dancing with him, turning sideways with a lift of one arm, until he realized that his leg was free and that the point of the hunter's spear, yanked abruptly and desperately out of his thigh so that the haft could deflect Sanjay's thrust, now lay on the ground.

The hunter was grasping the very end of his spearshaft with his right hand, and Sanjay, his spear point knocked wide of its target but still controlled, stepped right and forward to straddle the grounded point of his opponent's weapon. As Sanjay advanced he felt the haft of the hunter's spear, now trapped, pressing against the inside of his thigh.

With a sweeping motion, Sanjay struck for the hunter's head with the haft. The hunter ducked, and the spear passed over his head. Sanjay began a backswing, but the hunter turned into him and, grappling at his waist, tried to throw him down. Sanjay braced, lifting his spear high, and brought the haft down square onto the hunter's back.

The hunter collapsed flat on his chest. His spear lay tangled beneath him. Sanjay had followed him down and was now on one knee, the haft of his spear pressed hard along the hunter's back.

With more instinct than thought he drew the hunter's knife and laid the edge against the man's throat. A thin line of blood welled up along the pale skin.

He felt a haze lift from him, and with its passing a steady throbbing in his left thigh. With a move like disgust he flung the knife away and stood up slowly, finding that his leg barely supported his weight. Blood trailed down the cloth of his trousers. The hunter lay still.

"Is that enough blood?" Sanjay asked. His voice was hoarse. He glanced about himself, at the golden-clad riders, the hounds. It seemed to him that three faint shades stood among them, but they were almost impossible to see.

The wind rose. Leaves fluttered and lifted, skittering across the earl's hands as he lay, still half stunned, on the forest floor. The hounds whined and slunk into a close pack. The hunter raised his head and, when Sanjay offered him a hand, took it and with Sanjay's help got to his feet.

"There are greater forces even than ours," the hunter said. The rising wind tugged at his voice, giving it a soft reverberation. He lifted a hand and his companions mounted. "Ones you cannot fight." His face was taking on that peculiar blur again, as if he were somehow retreating from Sanjay without actual physical motion. His horse stood beside him and he mounted. Sanjay could barely distinguish the line of blood at his throat. "But you may wear your scar with pride." His voice was so resonant that it was almost impossible to understand. He reined his horse away from Sanjay and with an incomprehensible command led the riders into the forest, the hounds racing out in front.

Sanjay stared after them. Wind whipped at his back. Above, it tore through the branches until they slapped at each other, a sound that blended into a vibrant humming punctuated now and again by the snap of a breaking limb.

"Sanjay!" He turned to see Chryse running to him across the dim, starlit sward. Maretha was beside her; behind her, Professor Farr. And behind the professor—

It was nebulous at first. It was the power that stirred these branches, or the embodiment of it, and he understood the hunter's words with such piercing clarity that for a moment he could not act.

A human figure, or at least human-like. Female, he thought, but neither clothed nor naked in any sense he knew. She held a bow, and with the fixed, unalterable expression of a justice sentencing death she drew and steadied her aim.

"Chryse!" Sanjay dived for his wife, tackling her, and they fell tangled onto the ground.

Maretha, hearing his shout, followed the line of his gaze. With a cry she flung herself on top of her husband, shielding him.

The arrow had already been loosed.

Professor Farr, looking a trifle confused, began to turn. The arrow impaled him through the chest.

A sudden, blanketing stillness dropped over the woods, permeating each leaf, each blade of grass, the air itself, even in a remote way the stars far above. Mist roiled in the distant gaps between trees, illuminated by the now-risen moon so that it seemed that an assembly of mute ghosts had gathered there. The hush was so complete that there might only have been the five of them in the entire land.

Out of the forest, appearing out of the mist with the eerie abruptness of an unnatural creature, came a stag, imperious in its silence. It paused on the edge of the glade, surveying them as if passing judgement. It lifted its head. In a nearby tree, a bird chirruped and broke into song. The stag turned and bounded away into the trees, soon lost to sight in the uncanny fog. An owl hooted.

"Father!" cried Maretha. She rose and ran to the professor, knelt beside him. "Father."

He moaned a little. His eyes did not open, but his hand groped along the ground until he found hers. "I did love you, Maretha," he breathed. It was his last breath.

She began to weep. "He did love me," she said in a low voice, to anyone and to no one. "As much as he was capable of love."

"It's starting to rain." Chryse rolled to one side to get off her husband. "Oh, Sanjay. You're hurt!"

He sat up, winced. "It's not bad. It will heal, love."

"Here." She ripped at her dress until she had torn off several strips. "Wrap this around it." She kissed him. "You idiot. What were you doing? It was—it was like there was a curtain between you and us, all a blur."

"I must be attracted to hopeless causes. I couldn't just stand by and let them kill him." He had to stop a moment. "Good thing it didn't hurt like this when it happened," he muttered in a voice made ragged by pain.

Chryse laid a hand on his arm, but her gaze lifted to the earl. He was sitting now, elbows on his knees, head in his hands. He looked completely drained of emotion, energy, and resolve. "I would have," she said in an undertone, and she looked away from him, from her husband, ashamed.

"What did you say, Chryse?" Sanjay asked.

She hugged him fiercely. "Nothing. Nothing. You *will* be all right?"

He smiled, a bit wanly, but with gentle obstinacy. Around them, the light rain misted down, a low hush through leaves, dissipating the fog. "Of course I will. I may be sweet, but I'm stubborn."

CHAPTER 25:

THE HEALER

Maretha knelt by her father for a long while, weeping with quiet dignity as she prayed to Our Lady, Healer of Sorrows. Chryse knelt beside her for some time, rose finally and went back to help Sanjay bind his wound. The earl did not move.

Eventually the rain slowed and ceased. The moon had risen high above the trees, its light diffused through the last autumn leaves, giving the forest floor a grey sheen. Chryse pulled Sanjay to his feet and supported him as he hobbled over to Maretha. But she had already stood and was wiping the last tears from her cheeks with her fingers. Her father's body had vanished.

For a moment Sanjay and Chryse just gaped. The place he had lain was apparent: crushed grass, a stain of blood.

"The forest took him," said Maretha. Her voice was calm but there was a disturbing quality about her eyes as she turned to look at them. "We may as well go back." Chryse handed her her dress and, wordlessly, she put it on, then looked past them toward her husband.

Sanjay, watching her, wondered at the intensity of her gaze—he could not read what emotion lay behind it. "You saw the figure, too." It was more statement than question.

"Yes." She walked away from them, over to her husband.

"Was that what it was?" asked Chryse. "I just remember hearing—" She shook her head. "I'm not sure it was even a sound, only that for an instant I knew something was behind me."

"I wonder." Sanjay shifted. His weight was heavy on Chryse's shoulders. The two of them stared at Maretha as she stopped beside the earl but did not speak or touch him. "I wonder if she had an instant to decide whether to save her father or her husband—and now regrets the choice."

"Pierced by an arrow." Chryse shuddered. "Do you remember the bonfire at High Summer's Eve? And the effigy they burned on it?" She examined the dark forest and the thin globe of moon above. "How are we going to get out of here? I'm completely lost."

Maretha had still not spoken, but now the earl stood and followed her when she walked back to Chryse and Sanjay.

"I think we had better go back," Maretha said. She appeared far too matter-of-fact. Her face had a tight, over-controlled tautness. "It will be dawn soon."

"How will we find the entrance?" asked Chryse. "And how can we possibly find our way back through that labyrinth?"

"I know the way," said Maretha.

The earl stood so meekly behind her that it seemed a charade until one saw the look of stunned despair on his face, panic suppressed only by the knowledge of the complete devastation this place had wreaked upon him and his powers.

They went slowly through the forest. Sanjay used the spear like a cane, but his progress was slow. The first filtering of light had just begun to penetrate the deep of night when they came to a low hillock where gaped a dark opening, blacker even than the night sky. Two lanterns sat on the turf outside it.

Maretha, picking up the lights, led them down the steps with complete confidence. Chryse had to support Sanjay. At the bottom, Maretha halted. She stood still in intense concentration, as if she was tasting the air.

"I'd like to sit down for a moment," said Sanjay. Chryse helped him lower himself to the cold stone floor. She knelt beside him, resting her head against his right shoulder. The earl had moved away from them to stand in the darkest corner. He had not yet spoken a single word.

"There's someone else down here," said Maretha.

Chryse got up and went to stand beside her. "What do you mean? Who?"

Maretha did not answer immediately. She listened, and Chryse laid a hand on her arm and listened with her.

Sanjay sighed and put a hand on the floor to push himself up. His palm touched cloth, closed around a hand-sized object. He picked it up, found himself holding the velvet pouch in which they had first discovered their cards. He could feel the shape of cards inside.

"Chryse." His voice was low as he slipped the pouch into the pocket of his coat next to his half of the cards. "You must have dropped this."

Her attention was elsewhere; she did not respond.

As he began to push himself up, he felt a hand at his waist; the earl had returned to help him.

"Thank you," said Sanjay once he had gotten himself balanced with the main part of his weight on his un-wounded leg. He leaned back against the cold stone wall.

The earl's expression was an astonishing mix of fierce pride and utter hopelessness. "Thank you," he murmured, as if the words offended him. "You saved my life, and now you thank me for such a trivial—" He halted, perhaps as much surprised by the raggedness of his voice as lost for words.

"—kindness?" supplied Sanjay, smiling in the dimness.

The earl looked at him as if he had no idea of the meaning of such a word.

"There!" Maretha clutched Chryse's free hand in a tight grip, starting forward abruptly.

Chryse held on to her and dragged her to a stop. Out of the dark recesses of the maze echoed a gunshot.

"Evidently we're not done yet," said Sanjay with all the dry humor of an old campaigner. He hobbled forward, the earl at his side.

"This way," said Maretha.

Julian thought it prudent to stop back at camp to get his pistol before they went down the eastern entrance. Kate got extra lanterns for herself and the children to carry. Dusk was gathering as they started down.

Kate went first, followed closely by an unnaturally sub-dued Mog and Pin; Lucias came after them. He walked in a kind of stupor, his eyes wide and staring. Julian, behind him, guided him easily enough with brief words and the occasional pressure of his hand, but he never responded directly to questions. As they descended, he muttered words under his breath that no one else could quite make out, although once he said, quite distinctly, "He is not of this land."

In the square room at the base of the staircase they found a fresco that, winding around all four walls, depicted the crowning of the young king by the young queen at the Midwinter Festival of Lights.

"Looks like you, Lucias." Kate held her lantern close to the central figures: a black-haired young woman in a bell-shaped flounced skirt and a tight, revealing jacket and a fair young man dressed in stiff leggings and laced sandals.

"I cannot see him," said Lucias clearly. His face showed white in the lantern light. His eyes seemed unfocused.

"Can't see 'oo?" demanded Mog.

"Shh, stupid," hissed Pin. "Can't you see he's spelled?"

"Pin," said Julian severely, "a young lady does not use the epithet 'stupid' when speaking in public."

"Cor!" breathed Mog at the same moment that Pin shrieked. Neither reaction was in response to Julian's admonition.

In the center of the room stood a slim pillar of white stone. A small, straight, thin-bladed knife of finely-chipped obsidian rested on it.

Mog and Pin reached for it simultaneously.

"Don't touch that!" shouted Julian, coming forward from the doorway. He held onto Lucias with one arm as he walked to the middle of the room.

"What is it?" asked Mog. He had clasped his hands behind his back as if it was the only way he knew to resist the temptation. Pin had both her thumbs in her mouth.

Julian reached out tentatively and touched it. It felt smooth and cold, a perfect blend of primitive materials and sophisticated worksmanship. He picked it up. "I don't know. Some kind of knife." He licked his thumb and tested the edge. "Quite sharp."

"Nothing," said Kate. She had walked the entire perimeter. "No entrance. What have you got?"

Julian held it out for her to examine.

"Holy Son. If I didn't know better I'd call that a scalpel. Here." She put out a hand to take it. "Let me see. It's a curious design, but no less effective for that, I'd wager—"

"Look!" shouted Mog and Pin at the same moment. Kate and Julian glanced up to see the wall fall away to reveal a staircase that led down into black depths.

Lucias pulled free of Julian and moved like a sleep-walker towards the stairs. "She is veiled." His voice was a strangled whisper. "Veiled, or not here yet. But all power is hers."

He was on the third step before anyone moved. Kate ran after him, and Julian grabbed the children's hands and tugged them along. It was dark, quite dark, even with Kate's lantern a soft beacon before them, illuminating the light shock of Lucias's hair as he led the way down. It was also still, stifling hot air untouched by freshness, and si-lent. Only Lucias's muttering broke the hush. They reached at last a small circular chamber at the base of the stairs.

Kate paused, wiping her brow, to let Julian and the children catch up with her. "It's empty, except for that painting. I don't see a door. That looks like a very ancient version of the Physician card of the Gates."

"No, it doesn't," began Julian. "It looks like the man on the ice—I can't remember—"

Lucias had hesitated only a brief moment. Now he kept moving forward, straight into the wall.

"—it's not a wall at all," finished Julian, and he and Kate and the children hurried after Lucias.

They let Lucias lead them through dark corridors, Kate directly behind the youth, Julian at the rear sheparding Mog and Pin before him. Once Julian thought he heard the rustle of heavy cloth behind him. Kate paused, twice, at side corridors, but the soft noise of low, agreeable feminine laughter was, she decided, only her imagination. Mog and Pin whispered furtively to each other. Only Lucias seemed undisturbed, oblivious to the darkness, intent on some path he alone could detect.

They went further and further in, wandering a maze of tunnels until finally, as they rounded the curve of a long bend and found themselves at a branching of four corri-dors, Julian halted. "Do you know, Kate, I'm thoroughly lost. I sincerely pray that you are not in a similar case."

Kate laughed, a low chuckle. "And as you are an unre-pentant sinner, Julian, I fear that your prayers are unlikely to be—"

Mog screamed. Pin darted past Kate and knocked into Lucias.

A flicker of a shadow moved in one of the corridors just as the shattering explosion of a pistol shot rang in the closed space, deafening. Pin, with the instinct of a child brought up in gutters and back alleys, threw herself flat. Lucias was already off balance and now he reeled backwards from the force of some impact and collapsed against the wall.

Kate yelled and raced forward, swinging her lantern like a weapon. The steel blaze of a pistol muzzle glittered in lantern light as it came down hard on Kate's head. She dropped as swiftly as Pin, but as a dead weight.

A second shot sounded, followed by a muffled cry that gurgled to silence. A body fell to stone and tumbled out into the light of Kate's fallen lantern. Blood leaked out along the cracks between the stones on the floor.

"Bloody hell," swore Julian. A barest waft of smoke drifted up from his pistol.

"Cor, guvnor," said Mog with awe. "You took him right o' the throat."

"Kate!" cried Julian, propelled forward by some utterly compelling emotion. He let his pistol fall as he sank to his knees beside her. "Kate! Son's mercy, Katie, answer me!"

She stirred, making a sound halfway between a curse and a groan, and began to push herself up, slowly.

Julian embraced her, pulling her into his chest. "Oh, Katie my love," he murmured into her hair. "Thank the Mother."

Kate was unsure whether she was hallucinating or simply suffering the after-effects of a blow to the head. Julian held her as tightly and tenderly as any lover might, and he trembled as he held her, as if in the throes of a fever.

"Julian," she said in a weak voice. Her head throbbed.

He tilted her back enough that he could look into her face. With a sense of disorientation, as if the ground had dropped away from beneath her and yet she did not fall, she recognized the look of concentration melded with brilliancy in his eyes as he gazed at her for what it was: the look of a man in love.

A moment later he had controlled his expression and composed himself to look at her with cool concern. "I trust

you will live," he said. She knew him well enough to hear
the effort it took for him to keep his voice calm.

"I daresay," she replied, and was shocked by the shaki-
ness of her voice.

"Lucias been shot," said Pin in a fascinated undertone.
"Come look, Mog. 'Spose he'll die?"

"Bloody hell." Kate jerked up.

"Let me help," said Julian solicitously. He lifted her up
and set her on her feet gently.

"Thank you," she replied, a little constrained. She released herself from his grip with a delicacy brought on as
much by her own confusion as by the sudden look of
vulnerability about him. "We'd better see to Lucias."

"Of course." He toed the corpse with a fastidious nudge
of one boot. "Do you know this man? He's in typical
laborer's garb, but he's much older than any of our people."

Kate was already beside Lucias, one hand on the youth's
wrist. "He's alive. I can't tell whether the bullet went into
his chest or— Do you have a knife, Julian?"

Before he could reply she grasped at her coat pocket
and removed the obsidian scalpel. Carefully she cut Lucias's
shirt away from his body and peeled it, matted with blood,
back from the skin. Lucias gasped and his head moved,
but he did not open his eyes. The wound opened below
his collarbone.

Kate touched the torn skin cautiously.

"He ain't goin' to die, is he?" asked Mog. His voice
broke on the word "die" and he suppressed a sniffle.

"I don't think so. Julian, come hold him down. I don't
like the look of this ball, but I think I can get it out easily
enough, and then we'll take him back to camp and wash
the wound out properly."

Julian did as he was told, and Kate, using the scalpel
with a deft hand, parted the muscle just enough to slip an
edge in and lift out the ball so swiftly and gently that there
was scarcely any more bleeding.

"Give me your cravat," she said, not really aware in her
concentration of her tone of voice.

Julian smiled slightly, but the elegant folds were quickly
destroyed and Kate used the linen to bind the wound.

"You're really very good, Kate," he said as she sat back
on her heels to survey her work. Lucias stirred, opened
his eyes, and closed them again. The deep hush, the

darkness beyond, seemed to foster intimacy within the dim circumference of illumination. "I always wondered why, after your parents disinherited you, that you didn't just study to be a physician—there was nothing to stop you then."

She did not look up at him. Her hand cupped the light curls of Lucias's hair. "I suppose at first I was resigned to losing it." She shrugged. "Later, I never had the means to pay for my education and live at the same time."

"You might have come to me, Kate," he said, a little reproachful.

"Always as your debtor, Julian?" she asked, softly. "Is that always the only course left me?"

Silence lowered down on them like a heaviness emanating from the ceiling. Mog and Pin crept ever closer to Julian, huddling against each other. Lucias breathed evenly. On either side of him knelt Kate and Julian, each with head bowed. The flame of the lantern cast constantly moving highlights across their faces.

Julian reached out slowly and laid his hand palm open against the soft flush of her cheek. "As my wife, Kate."

She did not even react at first, merely stared into his long-familiar eyes. His hand remained, warm, on her skin.

"Told you he love her," said Pin in one of her hissed whispers that penetrated easily to every ear.

"*Loves* her, Pin," said Julian in a voice so quiet that it seemed almost absorbed in the rock. His gaze did not waver from Kate. "Never stopped loving her, after that summer half a lifetime ago."

She pulled away finally, not with any rejection, but with the tiniest shake of her head, the only gesture of her real bewilderment that she could trust herself to make.

"We're lost here, aren't we " she asked instead, walking to the farthest reaches of the light.

"Oh, very," he replied, fully aware of the irony.

"Do you recognize him, our assassin?" When he shook his head, she picked up a lantern and examined the corpse more closely. "I don't either. Do you suppose he's the one who's been trying to kill Lucias all along? I wonder why."

"Someone's coming," cried Pin abruptly. She grabbed hold of Julian as if she had no intention of ever letting him go.

"My pistol." He stood up, prying her loose.

"It's Monsieur and Madame," said Pin. An instant later Mog cried, "It's 'er Ladyship."

"Kate! Lord Vole!" Maretha's voice.

Light showed at the deep recess of one of the corridors, bobbed towards them.

"Kate!" cried Chryse. She came forward through the gap of darkness into the circle of their light, her golden hair like a touch of the sun. "Thank Heaven." She stopped short and gaped at the body. "What happened?"

Neither Kate or Julian replied immediately. Instead, they stared at the unlikely procession that greeted them: Maretha in a rumpled dress, Sanjay wounded, and, most of all, the trailing, subdued figure of the earl.

Kate shook her head. "We found our assassin. Do any of you recognize him?"

One by one they shook their heads until Sanjay frowned. "I'm sure— I remember. This is the man who came to me before we left Heffield. I think he was trying to bribe me to give him information on the expedition."

"That doesn't explain," said Julian, "what happened to your leg. I hope the wound isn't serious."

" 'No, 'tis not so deep as a well, nor so wide as a church door,' " said Sanjay with an infinitesimal grin.

" 'Courage, man,' " replied Julian gravely, " 'The hurt cannot be much.' Another aficionado of Shakespeare, I see. Old Anne is coming back into vogue these days."

"But that still doesn't explain—" began Chryse, at the same time as Kate said, "We've got to get Lucias back to—" They both stopped.

Maretha stood with her head cocked to one side, as if she was listening. "We must go. The door will close with full sunrise, and there are already the uninvited walking on my lands."

At the sound of her voice, Lucias stirred. "The treasure," he muttered, rolling his head from one side to the other. "She means to have it, to use the power to rid herself of the heiress." His head lolled back as he lapsed into unconsciousness.

Maretha had already started forward.

"Come on," said Chryse, a little urgent. "She won't wait."

Julian picked up Lucias and carried him. They followed Maretha in a close line; the earl trailed along at the rear. Maretha's lead was swift and sure—soon enough they came to the base of a stairwell and ascended it. They halted in the small, square room at its end for Sanjay to catch his breath and Julian to rest his arms.

"Chryse." Sanjay reached into his coat pocket. "You dropped this." He drew out the velvet pouch.

She gasped and reached in her turn for her belt. Stopped. "No, I didn't. I still have it."

"Then what— No, you're right. This has a funny little monogram on the other side—I didn't notice it before."

Into the silence left by the quiet of their companions and the sudden realization shared by both of them, Madame Sosostris's words echoing as along a dark tunnel— "the one thing in the city of the Queen that will be familiar to you"—they heard from far above a command called out and a reply.

"Quick," ordered Maretha.

They all filed up the steps after her to find themselves at the edge of their camp, surrounded by soldiers. There was a flurry of movement among the troops, and a moment later out of the ranks appeared Colonel Whitmore.

"My lord." He addressed himself to the Earl. His tone was not at all conciliatory. "I apologize for this intrusion, but we have been forced to take over your camp and belongings and to detain you and your people. You possess certain items that we have been ordered to obtain. Give them to us, and you will be allowed to leave."

It was Maretha who replied. Her entire aspect was fierce, strong, and completely self-confident. "What items?" she demanded.

"That boy." He pointed at Lucias, who still lay unconscious in Julian's grasp. "The treasure." He returned his gaze to the disheveled earl. His tone was mocking. "My orders are to obtain them, or to execute every member of this expedition."

Behind him, like the embodiment of his threat, rose a woman's anguished cry.

CHAPTER 26:

THE INVALID

"Bring her in here," commanded the Regent.

Four servants bearing a litter followed her into the inner room of her suite and set their burden down carefully. None looked up, or evinced any curiosity at all about their surroundings.

The Regent paced around the chamber. It was obvious by her expression and her taut, quick movements that she was furious.

"Go!" she ordered, and they were quick to comply. "No, you!" She pointed at the youngest of them. "You stay."

The designated man cast a look of desperate appeal towards his retreating comrades, but there was nothing they could do. "Send Doctor Wrackwell to me." In a moment she was alone with the litter and the young servant. She examined him minutely, as if he were a piece of livestock she were considering buying. After a bit, while he stood perfectly still, too frightened to move, she said, "You will do."

There was a knock on the door and a tall man with an emaciated face and ill-fitting clothes entered.

"Doctor!" Her voice was sharp as any good steel blade. She walked across the room to the litter and whipped aside the curtains to reveal the unconscious figure of Princess Georgiana. The girl's lips were slightly parted, still pink with life, though scarcely any breath escaped them. Her eyes were closed, unmoving under the lids. "When did this happen? How?"

Facing her anger, the doctor seemed remarkably unafraid. "Dawn, your highness. I had her brought here immediately."

"Was there any warning? Any sign?"

"None, your highness," he replied, unruffled. "Her deterioration has been remarkably gradual, very like her father's gradual illness. Her fainting spells never too severe, her loss of appetite never too pronounced, her fatigue never too debilitating. But all worsening slowly, so imperceptible a change day by day that this lapse into a coma I knew was no part of your—ah—handiwork."

The Regent laid a hand on Georgiana's brow, looking thoughtful. "Is it your opinion that she will die?"

"On the contrary, I believe that hers is a state akin to suspended animation, but with some indefinable healing properties about it rather than, shall we say, draining properties."

The Regent removed her hand from the princess's forehead. "Very well. You will report to the Council of Ministers that her state of health is quite delicate at this time. Add a few assurances that you feel certain that it is nothing like the disease that carried off my brother. That ought to set the seal on their hopes. It shall be proclaimed to the government and the populace that unless a quick recovery comes about, the coronation will have to be postponed. I suppose preparations should continue, and Prince Frederick may as well arrive for a visit. It would not do to appear too pessimistic." She paused, surveying Georgiana and the servant. "It is too bad," she continued, more to herself than to any of those present, "that Nastagmas died so close to the goal. We must hope that Colonel Whitmore accomplishes what Nastagmas could not. Nevertheless." Her gaze centered on the doctor as if she had forgotten that he was there. "You may go, doctor," she ordered, brusque.

"The princess?" he asked, bowing.

"She will remain here. Do I understand from what you have told me that this is a condition imposed by arts other than mine?"

"That is my belief, your highness."

"Then you do not expect the condition to lift in the near future?"

"No, your highness."

She pressed her lips tight. "I feel the mark of another

mage on her. She will stay here. You will attend her as usual once a day, to see that all is well. I will have put an illusion about her so that she appears to be something else." She smiled, some secret irony that pleased her, and continued. "But a touch of my hand will reveal her to you when it is necessary that you examine her. Come tomorrow morning. That is all."

He bowed. "If I may be so bold, your highness."

She nodded.

"I am a physician, and skilled at my work. I have my suspicions about your purposes, and I wonder, why do you not simply kill her outright?"

The Regent laughed. She had not a cruel laugh, nor a clever one, but one of simple amusement. "You *are* a bold man, Doctor. I admire that. But not subtle. You must know that an adept can trace certain lingerings, certain lines of magic, and to kill for power leaves traces another mage might follow, if they had the skill and cared to. And in any case, I will have to swear I did not kill her, so I cannot risk having her death on my account. I do not *wish* to have it on my conscience. After all, I have nothing against the girl personally."

"What guarantee do you have of my loyalty, your highness?"

"I could kill you in a moment, doctor. Or discredit you. I know a great deal about your past, and specifically about your relationship to my dear departed brother Prince William and *his* unsavory activities, some of which I know for a certainty contributed to his early death." She shuddered. "I detest that sort of—sloppiness. But you are a neat and efficient worker. Therefore, I use you."

"Your highness." He bowed again, precise in angle and placement of his hands, and left.

"And come the Festival of Lights," she said, hands clasped at her waist, like a medieval portrait of a saintly queen, "come the colonel with the treasure and the youth to be buried in her place, my oath taken on my blood as a churchwoman and a sorceress will be true enough and not affect my power or my position—since it will not be Georgiana dead and buried but a simulacrum bearing her face and her virginity—and I shall be free to keep the throne, as I should have all along."

She walked over to her servant. "You have been here before, I think." She put out a hand to caress his neck.

"Yes, your highness." He trembled.

"Then you know what I require."

They were taken, each one, and searched. The handling was circumspect, but the search thorough. The soldiers took Julian's pistol, Kate's scalpel, the spear; found the hornpipe and, worst, took the pouch of cards Chryse wore, the half a deck Sanjay carried, and the little velvet pouch, match to the one they had received so long ago, that Sanjay had found at the north gate of the labyrinth. Neither he nor Chryse even had time to see what was inside it.

They did not search the earl, did not even approach him, but regarded him with wary glances. Thomas Southern appeared, escorted by two soldiers, and spoke quietly and briefly to Maretha. She paled visibly and went away with him, disappearing inside the tent Charity shared with Kate.

"Now," Colonel Whitmore's eye roved over Kate and Chryse with the belligerent stare of an unrepentant womanizer. "We will take the boy and leave you."

Immediately Julian and Kate stepped back to stand over Lucias where Julian had been forced to set him down on a blanket before being searched.

"He's been wounded," began Kate, angry. "You may very well kill him if he isn't treated correctly."

"That would be a shame," replied Colonel Whitmore without a trace of compassion. He made a gesture with one hand and his soldiers moved out to surround them. "I must warn you that it has been left to my discretion whether or not to leave anyone alive in this camp." As he said this his gaze strayed briefly to the earl, as if he were gauging his reaction.

Julian caught the glance. "My lord Elen. Surely you do not intend to tolerate this—"

But the earl merely turned aside and went without a word into his tent.

"Stand aside from the youth," ordered Colonel Whitmore. "You see that you are surrounded."

The tent flap to Charity's tent was pushed aside with

unceremonious haste and Maretha appeared. She shook with anger.

"How dare you!" she cried. She strode forward to stand directly in front of the colonel. "How dare you treat a woman so." Her voice was low, but no less furious for that. "And in her condition."

"Heaven above, your ladyship," drawled the colonel in a lazy and insulting voice. "How were we to know that *Miss* Farr was pregnant?"

"Pregnant!" Chryse heard Kate utter the word at the exact instant she did. Sanjay and Julian exchanged knowing looks.

"How were *you* to have the decency," Maretha cried, full in her stride now, "to search her tent, her belongings, and most of all, her *self* gently enough that you would not force her into premature labor? Now she will likely die, and the child with her."

As if to echo her angry words, a low, ragged sobbing began in the tent behind, dissolving into a distressed moan.

"Animal!" Maretha slapped the colonel.

He caught her wrist, hard, and twisted it. "Bitch!" he hissed. "No one does that to me." With his other hand he forced her to her knees. "I could have you executed for that, countess or no. Beg me for mercy."

She stared up at him, her eyes blazing. Heat emanated from her. The sun rose in a full glory that spread like wildfire along the heights.

"Holy blood!" swore Kate. "It's burning!"

Chryse followed her shocked gaze and gasped. It was not sunlight—it *was* fire, running along the heights as if it was racing along a clear path. Sparks caught and flared up through the grass, and then the flat area where the regiment's horses waited erupted into waves of flame.

Chaos erupted. Horses neighed in fear, bolted and scattered. Soldiers ran frantically after them, as much to escape as to catch their mounts. The circle of troops that surrounded the camp fragmented quickly as lines of wildfire licked into their midst. The cook's tent burst into flame, billowing sheets of burning canvas as the wind tugged at it.

"Take your hands off me." Maretha's voice was thick with rage. She seemed oblivious to the inferno growing around her.

Colonel Whitmore twisted harder on her arm. He had paled, but his lips were still set in a vicious grimace. "Tell your husband to stop this, or I will shoot you, my *lady*." His voice was harsh, and he reached for his pistol. Around him, soldiers cried out, panicking when they had to run through flame as high as themselves to get out of the inferno.

Colonel Whitmore did not even touch the handle of his gun. The entire sleeve of the arm holding her caught fire as easily and quickly as if it had been soaked in kerosene and thrust into a raging bonfire. He screamed. The flames licked up and down his arm, skidding off Maretha as if she were invulnerable.

For a long moment he could not let go of her, but only suffer. When he could get free, his retreat was hasty and utterly undignified. His face was seared with agony.

Those of his men who could catch a horse rode out; the others fled on foot. Fire spread and smoldered and erupted again all over the valley. Julian had to hoist Lucias and haul him out of the path of a trail of flame, Sanjay shepherding Mog and Pin.

"Sanjay," Chryse called over the crack and spit of fire. "They've got our Gates. We've got to—"

"Bloody hell!" shouted Kate. "I think the whole damn camp's going to go."

At the entrance of his tent, the earl appeared, like a visitation of a fallen angel come to view the apocalypse.

"Tell him to stop," Kate called. The heat of the fire reddened her cheeks. Flame gushed up in great sheets a man's height or higher.

"It isn't him!" cried Sanjay. Sweat dotted his forehead. "It's Maretha. I don't think she has any control over it." Fire shot up along the central path that led between the tents. A spark caught in the canvas of Charity's tent.

Above the noise, a tiny, weak wail caught and held. Maretha started up to her feet, her rage dissolving instantly. The fire guttered abruptly and vanished as if it had never been. Maretha whirled and ran into Charity's tent.

There was a hush, broken at last by a low, soft sound that none of them recognized. They stared around until Sanjay found its source: the earl was chuckling.

He stopped when he discovered that they were all looking at him. "You don't see the joke, I take it," he said

with dry, self-mocking despair. "*She* gained the treasure of
the labyrinth, the power I meant to sacrifice her for in
order to get it for myself." He stood a moment longer. The
baby's wailing faltered and ceased, started up again. It was
a thin, feeble sound.

"Bloody hell," swore Kate. "Was that it?"

No one answered her. The ash that covered the area
surrounding the camp, still warm and smoldering, seemed
answer enough.

"Now what?" asked Chryse into the silence.

"I suppose we wait," said Julian.

The earl turned away and went back inside his tent at
the same time that Thomas Southern, looking drawn and
exhausted, came out of Charity's tent. He was coatless,
shirt sleeves rolled up, shirt partially unbuttoned as if he
had been hard at work.

"It's a boy," he said, voice caught between awe and
relief. "A tiny, tiny boy."

"What in hell's name were you doing in there?" demanded Kate.

"I have a son," he added, in a tone so casual that it was
clear that he was overwhelmed by this discovery. Against
his shock of black hair his face looked doubly pale.

In the stunned silence that followed this remark, he
blinked, recalling something, and reached into the disheveled coat hanging over one arm to draw out a battered,
dirt-stained letter. "Here." He came forward to Julian. "I
believe this is for you. It came from a Lady Laetitia Trent,
through rather strange channels—from the Greater Heffield
Correspondence Society to the Birwick Correspondence
Society to the Endelby Tailors Guild and then through
Felthorpe by way of the Cobbler's Union to the Little
Wrent Miners Letters Workshop who sent it on to Arrow-
root Correspondents for Free Labor North, who sent a lass
on a pony up here. You'd better read it." He was so
entirely discomposed by his new position in life that he was
oblivious to the amazed stares directed at him. "She makes
some quite serious allegations concerning the Regent." As
Julian, bemused, took the letter from him, he retreated.
"Now if you will excuse me." He paused. "What was it I
was supposed to get?" He turned and disappeared back
into the tent.

"Angel of death," swore Kate after a suitable interval.

"And I thought he was a bleeding saint—pure as the driven snow, as they say. It just goes to show—" She shook her head. "Hadn't we better put Lucias down in one of the beds?"

"Use mine," offered Julian.

"I have any number of questions," said Julian after they had deposited Lucias gently on the bed, left the children to sit beside him, gotten a chair for Sanjay, and returned outside to sit impatiently in front of Charity's tent. Paths of blackened grass scored patterns in the ground all around them. Smoke trailed up to shroud the morning sun. "Any number. But foremost among them is *why* Miss Farr would be searched so ruthlessly that she would— And for that matter, when in hell did this affair *start*, for the Lord's sake?"

"Your language, Julian," admonished Kate.

His gaze rested on her for a moment too long. Both Chryse and Sanjay caught a glimpse of his expression before he recovered himself and looked away.

Kate frowned abruptly and broke away from the group, walking ten steps up, ten steps back, between the rows of tents. Her boots quickly acquired a sheen of ash.

"I'd better read this letter," Julian said with a carelessness that was transparently an effort. He unfolded the sheets and began to read. Chryse rested her hands on Sanjay's shoulders. Kate paced.

After some time Maretha emerged from the tent. "She'll be fine." Her voice was husky with relief. "Mistress Cook says she did very well, under the circumstances. But the baby is so very small. At least two months early, Mistress Cook says, and she's been midwifing upwards of thirty years. But she says it's strong for its—for *his* size." She paused, aware of the expectant gaze of her four listeners. "Am I babbling?"

"No, no, not at all," Julian assured her quickly.

"Yes, you are," said Chryse at the same time.

"I suppose I am," said Maretha with a weak smile. "But I had *no idea*. None. *Charity*, after all. And Thomas Southern—I would never have believed it of him."

"Why was she searched?" asked Kate. "Why so roughly?"

Maretha frowned. "Do you remember the golden cup, in the room at the bottom of the central staircase? It seems—" She faltered. "It seems Charity took it. How the colonel guessed she was hiding it I can't imagine. Evidently there was a bit of a struggle."

"But why would Charity take the cup?"

"I don't know," said Maretha. "She's sleeping now. I'll ask her later, if she feels well enough."

"Mother and Son!" swore Julian, looking up from his letter. "We've got to get to Heffield!"

"Quick! Quick!" It was Mog, jumping up and down outside Julian's tent. "He's awaked. He's awaked. He says they goings to kill 'er Highness!"

For a moment they all simply stared at each other. Then Julian stuffed the letter into his coat pocket and strode across to the tent. Kate and Chryse followed.

"I think," said Sanjay, "that I'll just sit here a bit longer."

"You ought to have that looked at," said Maretha severely. "Here." She beckoned to Mistress Cook as that individual came out of Charity's tent. "Mistress Cook," she called. "I have two more patients for you."

"We'd best be getting you laid down." Mistress Cook frowned with a decided air of disapproval as she peered through spectacles at the stained white cloth that bound Sanjay's thigh. "Then I'll have a look."

"I would be grateful," he replied.

"Sanjay!" Chryse had come back. "Are you really all right? Let me help you."

He limped into their tent, leaning heavily on his wife. Inside they found chaos—their trunks open, clothes scattered, Chryse's music paper strewn across the floor.

"My sketchbooks," Sanjay gasped. He sank down onto the bed, looking for the first time as if he was in intolerable pain. "They took my sketchbooks."

"Oh, sweetheart." Chryse embraced him, eased him down onto his back as Mistress Cook came up to the bedside.

"Barbarians," she said succinctly with a glance around the tent. "We'll have to have those trousers off, now."

"Do you want me to stay?" Chryse asked.

"Actually," said Sanjay in a faint voice, wincing, "I'd rather you left."

She frowned, but kissed him and went outside. Maretha was gone. Next to Julian's tent, Kate and Julian stood arguing.

"I fail to see," Kate was saying, "what purpose it will

serve for you to ride off now alone. The colonel's men could easily pick you up and then where would you be?"

"You can scarcely expect me to forget that my aunt is in danger—" He broke off, seeing Chryse.

"Chryse." Kate waved her over. "Perhaps you can talk sense into him."

"I don't know," said Chryse judiciously. "How is Lucias?"

"Incoherent," answered Julian. "Rambling on about the treasure of the labyrinth and a plot by the Regent to do away with Princess Georgiana and claim the throne for herself on the princess's birthday, which I believe is the Festival of Lights. Which would seem perfectly ridiculous, ravings brought on by the shock he sustained, except that I have confirmation of the whole story here—" He patted his pocket. "—in this letter from Aunt Laetitia. Including the fact that Colonel Whitmore's regiment was sent north by the Regent to claim the treasure if it was found."

"How did they find us?"

"Our trail can't have been so hard to follow. And in any case, I can only suppose that the Regent must have had an agent planted among us, to report to her or to the colonel."

"But if she wanted the treasure, why didn't *she* just finance the expedition, instead of the Earl?"

Julian shrugged. "I don't know that she has the resources, at least so readily available. And if this talk of a plot is true—and I have no reason to doubt my aunt—it would scarcely have behooved her to advertise her intentions so clearly. She has not ever been a popular figure, you know."

"She must have been worried, then," said Kate, "to send the colonel and one hundred men. Hardly a discreet act."

"To so isolated a place as this? They'll be back, Kate."

"But how does Lucias fit in?" asked Kate.

Julian shook his head.

"I see," said Chryse slowly. "Just as the earl sought this treasure, thinking it part of the ritual, to enhance his power, so did—does—the Regent, except that she believes, like the rest of us did, that the treasure is an object. So does—" She halted abruptly, flushing as she recalled that only she and Sanjay knew of their mission for Madame Sosostris. But both Julian and Kate were frowning pensively at the tent.

"I've heard rumors," said Julian thoughtfully, "of the means by which the Regent—ah—channels her sorcery. But it still doesn't make sense. How would he know about her plot?"

"It explains why he was shut up in that factory," answered Kate.

"Just what I was about to say."

Chryse caught the look he exchanged with Kate, surprised by the intimacy it suggested—and equally surprised by Kate's quick, dismissive gesture.

Julian turned away abruptly. At the same moment, Thomas Southern emerged from Charity's tent. "I'd better talk to Southern about this." Julian bowed to the two women and walked away.

"Kate," said Chryse in a suspicious tone, "I thought you said that Julian had never propositioned you."

Kate responded with a quite uncharacteristic reaction: she blushed. "I'm afraid," she said, barely above a whisper, "that I've—ah—mis-read Julian all these years." She looked a little ashamed, and a little apprehensive.

Chryse hid a grin and laid a sympathetic hand on Kate's arm. "We'd better go discuss this with Maretha and the earl."

"Julian's proposition?" Kate demanded. "I don't think so!"

Chryse could not help but laugh. "I meant this business about the Regent. Remember, Kate, they took our Gates. Without them, Sanjay and I haven't a hope of getting home. I agree with Julian—we'd better go as soon as we can."

"Bloody hell," said Kate without heat. "I'm touchy, ain't I? You're right—let's see what the earl has to say. But I'll let you ask him. He probably doesn't much care who rules, and won't take kindly to interruptions. You saw how mad he was." She scuffed at a black patch of grass, still warm from the fire.

"You don't know what happened yet, do you?" said Chryse as they walked across to the earl's tent. "He meant it, when he said Maretha got the power. You saw it. I think you'll find that things have changed."

CHAPTER 27:

THE PRISONER

"I see no need for such haste," said the earl to his wife after Chryse and Kate had left the tent. He had declined to read Lady Trent's letter. Maretha had suggested in the end that those who could ride would leave within the hour, while Charity, the baby, Lucias, and the children would be escorted to the nearest safe manor by slow stages along back paths the locals knew, and wait there until they could be safely sent for. But none of this could be accomplished unless the earl agreed to it, since he owned the horses and carriages that made travel possible. Only Julian had brought his own mount.

"How can you mean that?" Maretha stood amidst the disorder left by the troops. The earl reclined in a chair, still maintaining the air of studied indifference that he had held throughout the conference. "It will take us at least five weeks to return, perhaps more with the weather as it is now. And after the turn of the year and the Festival of Lights, it will be too late."

'Mother and Son, Maretha," he swore, abruptly losing his temper and standing up. "These matters of succession have never made any difference to me. I fail to see why they should now. Or do you suppose they must, since I am now bereft of any other purpose?" His expression bore the old hauteur, but flushed with the heat of anger rather than pale and chill.

Maretha held her ground. "Do you care so little for the concerns of others? Lady help us if you will not even assist Sanjay, who saved your life, and now needs to recover his deck of Gates. Are you really so selfish?"

For a moment the earl froze, his expression as hard and unfeeling and cold as it had ever been. "You would not have dared speak like this to me *before*."

"Not only selfish," she cried, "but full of self-pity. I cannot believe that after so many years learning the arts that they can have utterly vanished beyond any hope of retrieval. And do you suppose that I have any idea at all how to control all the power I received? Do you even suppose I *want* it? I didn't ask for it. If you will remember, you forced it on me, and quite by accident." A hard gust of wind shook the tent, echoed by a tremor in the ground whose rumbling was felt rather than heard. "I would gladly give it to you if I could. Gladly." Her voice caught. Spatterings of rain sounded on the canvas over their heads. One of the lanterns, unlit, sparked and began to blaze brightly.

The earl took three steps forward and grasped her by the arms. "Control it, Maretha! The entire place reflects you. You could destroy this whole camp."

So close, she could see tiny lines at the corners of his eyes. His expression was utterly, strangely human: anger, a trace of fear, perhaps, even some concern. Only twice before had she stood so intimately with him: once dancing at the Harvest Fair celebration, the second—

As if the same thought occurred to him, he released her precipitously just as she jerked away. "How dare you ever touch me," she breathed, "after what you did to me?" The wind died; the lantern guttered out.

"What do you want of me?" He sounded tired.

"You know we need the horses and carriages."

"Then take them."

"And you, to go with us," she added, softly.

"Why? How can it matter if I go as well?"

She turned her face away and did not reply.

After a bit, he coughed in a way she would have described in any other person as self-conscious. "If we need leave so soon," he said at last, "we had better prepare. There's little enough to salvage here in any case. The colonel has apparently no respect for either law or rank."

"I've had no time to check," said Maretha, "but I suppose that my father's journals and all my notes and catalogs were taken as well."

"I'm sorry," he said, a little stiffly, as if compassion did not come easily to him.

Maretha shrugged. "It doesn't matter. My father's theories were basically wrong, and in any case, I can read the hieroglyphs now. I'll simply come back next year, if we aren't all dead by then."

"*Dead?*"

She met his gaze. "I mean, my lord, that I intend to stop the Regent. If she is as powerful a mage as I have heard it rumored, I don't know if I will be able to."

"There is no doubt that you have the power. It is the mastery of it that you lack."

"Well then," she replied, "I will have to do what I can. It can hardly matter to you if I die trying." She waited, staring at him until he looked away. Then, as if the victory had been hollow, she sighed and frowned. "And I have to do *something* with Charity before we can leave."

The earl had moved to stand by his table, where his papers and books lay as neatly as they ever had, the only objects in the camp not ransacked. "Isn't it usual in such cases to have the—sinning parties marry?"

"But he's a common laborer!" She paused. "You don't suppose," she said slowly, "that he's the least bit ambitious. He seems so austere, so—I don't know, so above such things. After all, if he married Charity, it would be a great step up in the world for him, and especially for his children."

"One might well suppose it. Even clergymen have their vanities."

"But he isn't a clergyman."

"He could be made one. I still have power enough, of position, at least, to do that much." His voice was bitter, but he looked at her as he spoke. "But don't be so foolish as to mistake it for a—a kindness, for Miss Farr or Southern. If you mean to meet the Regent, I cannot let you be burdened by such concerns."

"You cannot let me . . ." Her voice trailed away in astonishment. She merely stared as he rummaged in one of his trunks, lifting out a coat, and in a few efficient minutes made himself more or less presentable. He was, she realized, vain of person—it would never have occurred to her before to ascribe any such human failings to him.

When he had done, he offered her his arm. "We shall go to see Miss Farr."

Outside, they saw Kate, Julian, and Chryse standing in the entrance of Julian's tent in intent conference with Mistress Cook. In Charity's tent, it was dim. A tiny, bundled shape lay on Kate's bed, stirring now and again in infant sleep. Charity lay on white sheets, her hair spread out around her head like a halo. She looked tired, but still beautiful. Thomas Southern sat in a plain wooden chair beside her, reading in a low voice a passage from an old, worn copy of the scriptures.

" 'Turn thee unto me, and have mercy upon me; for I *am* desolate and afflicted. The troubles of my heart are enlarged; *O* bring thou me out of my distresses. Look upon mine affliction and my pain; and forgive all my sins.' "

" 'Consider mine enemies,' " said the earl, " 'for they are many; and they hate me with cruel hatred.' "

Charity moved her head on her pillow, her eyes widening. Southern stopped reading and stood up.

"My lord," he said. "My lady." He inclined his head.

The earl escorted Maretha to a chair, returned to stand at the foot of the bed.

"I am not remotely interested," he began in a cool voice, "in the particulars that led to this turn of events. But in the interest of Miss Farr, and for the sake of my wife's peace of mind, I am prepared to settle a sizeable dowry on Miss Farr—" At this, Charity's face lit with an expression of mingled hope and triumph. "—contingent on her marriage to Mr. Southern."

Like an alchemical transmutation, Charity's expression changed to shocked outrage, while Southern's face took on the look hers had previously held.

He knelt beside her, grasping one of her hands in his. "It's what we always wanted, my love."

Charity was not even looking at him. "You must be mad! He's a common laborer! I am a gentlewoman's daughter."

"Such dowry," continued the earl, "to be used for the necessities of life and upkeep, and to provide the where-withal to buy Mr. Southern an education and a position in the church. In which case, Miss Farr, you will not be married to a common laborer but a respectable clergyman."

Southern was so stunned that he released Charity's hand and stood up. "My . . . my lord!" he breathed.

"I take it your great wish is to become a minister in the church," said the earl drily. "It is as well you have made some effort to educate yourself, because with your background you will not be easily accepted in such a position. However, if you are diligent, I feel sure you will succeed."

"My lord," said Southern, a little hoarse with emotion. "I do not deserve such a blessing, or such generosity."

The earl examined him with a combination of skepticism, amusement, and straightforward appraisal. "I shall not even attempt to make *that* judgment."

"I refuse," said Charity. When everyone looked at her, she repeated it, louder. "I refuse. Completely. Maretha, surely you cannot expect me to marry him."

"But Charity. How can you say that? Why else would you—" She faltered, blushed.

"It is my fault," said Southern quickly. "I am weak. The sins of the flesh held too much temptation for me. I ruined you, Charity. It is only right that you let me bear the responsibility."

The earl spoke before Charity could reply. "Ruined her? I think it more likely she ruined you. She was certainly no virgin when I met her last spring."

The silence this statement produced was so profound that they could all hear the infant's snuffling and panting on the other bed.

"Charity—" Maretha began.

"Very well," said Charity in a tight voice entirely uncharacteristic of her. "I may as well admit that it is true. I don't know how you found out."

"Like recognizes like," said the earl, cold and cryptic, "and unlike, as well. I have—had—certain gifts."

"Charity—" Maretha shook her head, unable to go on. Southern was evidently too stunned to attempt speech.

Charity was quite pale, but her eyes bore the intensity of an old and deep anger. "Don't think I wasn't grateful for your and your father's charity, Maretha. Lady, how I learned to hate that word—'charity.' Uncle always thought his sister was a saint, but the truth is my mother isn't dead, as far as I know. She ran off with a discharged navy captain when I was fourteen, leaving me with Father, who for all I ever knew was not my father at all. At any rate, he had no compunction about using my beauty to make a living for himself. I must have been sold as a virgin ten or twelve times before Uncle traced us, and Father, thank the Lady, died in that carriage accident, and I came to live with you. I'm not proud of it. I meant to live cleanly and decently, but without any dowry at all what hope had I of a good marriage? I thought I might at least have some pleasure out of my life." Her eyes strayed to Thomas Southern, who was, Maretha saw clearly, the kind of man who is most handsome when he is suffering. But there was a calculation in Charity's eyes that Maretha had never seen there before, meek and gentle as she had always seemed at Farr House and throughout their travels, and it gave her cause to wonder.

"Why did you take the cup?" she asked.

Charity hesitated, came to a decision. "To buy a dowry for myself."

"I wonder," said the earl, "where you expected to sell such a thing, Miss Farr. Or how Colonel Whitmore came to suspect that you had it in your possession. And whether it was a struggle that sent you into labor, or the simple act of taking the cup—which is, indeed, a thing of magical value, and thus tends to act upon its possessors in ways they cannot necessarily predict."

"Wait a moment, my lord," said Southern. "What are you accusing Miss Farr of?"

"Collusion. How do you think the Regent found us so easily?"

"That's ridiculous," said Maretha. "There were over one hundred laborers, a good half of whom were hired in Heffield."

"Few of whom can write. And none but Mr. Southern knew our destination."

"Is this true, Miss Farr?" said Southern in a stiff, distant voice.

"I told her nothing but unimportant things," said Charity recklessly. "How was she to know the difference? She could have had us followed easily enough in any case. I never saw that that was any great secret. And she had a man amongst the laborers. I can't remember his name—Tagmill, or something. I would give him messages."

"Oh, Charity." Maretha clutched the arms of her chair

tight in her distress. "How could you have done it? It's terrible."

"So is poverty." Charity's voice was heavy with exhaustion, her face drawn and lined with it. "The treasure and a little information, and she would provide me with a dowry and the means to marry well. What other way had I to provide that security for myself, having no other resources? You would never have understood, Maretha. You always had your father's work."

"I would have helped you."

"I suppose you would. I never meant to hurt you. But I've no choice now, have I?" Her gaze shifted to rest with loathing on the earl. "You've trapped me."

"You have trapped yourself," replied the earl. "I believe that is what most of us do." He looked at Thomas Southern, who stood at the opposite end of the bed, one hand so tight around the bedpost that it seemed that his grip was the only thing holding him there. "Do we not, Mr. Southern?"

"The Son is merciful," said Southern, "and forgives us even as we sin. I would ask a boon of you, my lord."

"You may ask."

"For your—your generosity," he continued, very formally, "we would ask that you allow us to name our son after you."

"No!" cried Charity. "I will not—"

"Charity. You will." He did not look at her, but his tone silenced her. "My lord." He waited respectfully.

"I am not used to receiving compliments," said the earl, a trifle aloof. He put out his arm for Maretha to take, and pushed aside the tent flap. "But if you wish it, you may call your son John." Behind, as they left, Thomas Southern sank to his knees beside the bed and began to pray.

Outside, Maretha had to blink several times until her eyes adjusted to the bright late-morning light. Across the way, Julian had crouched to bid farewell to a tearful Mog and Pin, had even gone so far as to hug each in turn, for once heedless of his cravat.

"John," Maretha said, musing.

The earl began to answer, stopped, perhaps self-conscious, perhaps offended.

She risked a glance at him, but he was impossible even now to read, and she reflected that his eyes were still black—enchanter's eyes. She shuddered. "It just seems so ordinary and common a name."

His smile, in answer, was cool and ironic. "Have I never told you? I too am named after a saint. St. John, the Martyr, who gave his life that another might live."

Sanjay had fallen asleep on the parlor's only couch when the innkeeper brought the tea trays in and poured tea for his guests. Julian stood by the window, staring out at the lowering dusk. In the three chairs that surrounded the table on which the tea was laid out sat the three women, talking, a low, soothing sound that, like rain, seemed to blend into the background.

"I wish," said Kate, not for the first time, "that your Gates hadn't been taken as well. We could have at least tried to use them to get to Heffield in one magnificent jump."

"Using you to test the idea? *I* wouldn't have tried it." Chryse frowned, took a sip of tea to hide her real worry over the loss of their cards. She and Sanjay had discussed it only once on the journey, and that discussion had ended in an argument—not because either blamed the other, but precisely because neither was to blame.

"But you know that they are capable of transporting over greater distance—you yourself came over the ocean from Vesputia with those cards."

"Oh, Kate. Please."

"Sorry. Just like me to keep reminding you of it. What are you dreaming about, Maretha?"

Maretha had been watching the fire with a distant, considering expression. She started, smiled self-consciously as she picked up her tea. "Nothing important. I was remembering just that—what I was dreaming about last night. It's that strange dream I've been having this entire trip."

"What, the one about turning into a rose bush?"

"A climbing rose, actually," said Maretha. There had been a slowly perceptible change about her since that last day on the site: she had grown more subtly attractive, not so much in looks but in magnetism, as any person does who has gained inner self-confidence. "Leaves and shoots budding out of my limbs, my body slowly turning to wood. Except," and here she looked puzzled, "that it wasn't me,

but someone else. I don't know who. Someone like me,
but the connection—" She shrugged. "It's gotten more
vivid, stronger, as we've gotten closer to Heffield, and last
night—" She trailed off.

"Last night we had quite a windstorm." Kate grinned.
"And we're only a half-day's ride from the city tonight.
Well then, Maretha. You'd better stay up all night with
me, gambling. I'll take some of your husband's fortune off
your hands. I'm destitute."

"But Kate," said Chryse. She glanced at Sanjay. He was
dozing lightly, mouth a little open. "But I thought there
was a remedy for that." She looked across the room at
Julian, but he was now gazing at Kate's back with a look
both pensive and slightly angry.

Kate made an impatient gesture with one hand. "Bloody
hell, Chryse. Give me some time to get used to the idea."

"She's had about seven weeks, hasn't she?" said Chryse
to Maretha. "I can't believe how bad the roads have been."

"And you haven't been forced to ride next to old prim
and proper for all that time, either," retorted Kate. "Lady!
You'd never guess someone could change so fast overnight."

Chryse shared a smile with Maretha. "Oh, I rather
think he's always had a tendency that way."

"Is that so?" asked Kate with a dangerous gleam in her
eye. "Did you know that he's decided to adopt the children? Not as legally his, obviously, but he's going to give
them a home, educate them for a good trade. Can you
imagine? Julian, after all!"

Chryse chuckled. "Are you raising your voice so that he
can hear you? It's no use, he's gone back to looking outside."

"Are you laughing at me?"

"Of course. For the last seven weeks I've had Sanjay on
one side, being stoic about how long it's taking his leg to
heal, the earl on another, speaking two words a day if
we're lucky, Thomas Southern being stiff and worried
about Charity and the baby back north, Julian doing his
imitation of Thomas and the earl combined, and you being
annoyed about Julian. The only fit company around here is
Maretha, probably because everyone is afraid to annoy
her. And you know very well, Kate, that you wouldn't be
angry if you didn't care."

"Sometimes," said Kate ominously, "I don't like you."

Chryse smiled. "You're just like me, you know. Contrary. As soon as someone tells you to do something, you immediately decide not to."

"And furthermore," added Maretha. "You haven't been such fit company either, Chryse, brooding over music most evenings and breaking off in the middle of conversations to scribble down pieces of compositions."

"There!" Kate grinned. "Have some of your own back."

"This is unfair," protested Chryse.

"And you've been fussy about food the last couple of weeks," continued Maretha with a wink at Kate.

"That's true." Kate nodded wisely. "Usually you eat like a horse."

"Thank you," said Chryse. "It's such an—evocative phrase. I guess I'm simply not used to riding all day, every day, whether in or out of a carriage. It's caught up to me. I get tired so easily."

"Sweetheart," said a sleepy voice from the couch. "Could you hand me some tea?" He yawned as Chryse brought him a cup.

"Had a good nap?" she asked, enough concern in her voice that she sounded worried. "How is your leg?"

"Fine," he answered. "A little sore today, but I think that's the rain. I was dreaming that I was back in the forest."

"No wonder you looked content."

He shrugged, looking over at Kate. "Have you—" He hesitated, took a sip of tea, looked at Maretha, at Julian across the room, back at Kate. "Have you ever seen a dragon?"

Kate laughed. "Have *I*? Lady, no. Only saints, simpletons, and madmen can see dragons."

"I was afraid of that," said Sanjay softly. Chryse took his hand in hers, but said nothing.

"It strikes me," said Maretha slowly, looking thoughtful, "that none of us left that place unchanged." She stood up. "If you'll excuse me, I'm going to go see if John would like tea." She left the parlor.

"*John.*" Kate dwelled expressively on the syllable. "How very familiar of our Maretha. Do you suppose—but no. He's been so reclusive since we left, as much to her as to anyone. But I've long suspected she harbors a certain affection for him. Much good it will do her."

"How unfortunate for her," said Julian from the window.

Kate blushed, but managed to ignore him.

"I have wondered," said Chryse quickly, filling the breach, "why you never noticed that Charity was pregnant. You did share a tent with her."

"She always dressed behind a screen. And like everyone else, it simply never occurred to me."

In the lull generated by this remark, Julian walked over from the window and sat down in the chair Maretha had vacated, helping himself to some tea. Chryse left Sanjay and went back to her chair. The lull stretched into an uncomfortable silence.

"It certainly seems that we've seen a large number of people on the road today," said Sanjay. "Going away from Heffield. You would think folk would be going *in*, to see the coronation."

This remark fared no better. Julian sipped his tea, looking, as he lounged in the chair, elegant and disdainful. Kate looked as though she was about to say something everyone would regret.

"Perhaps there are some celebrations out in the country tonight," said Chryse valiantly, exchanging an exasperated glance with Sanjay. "Isn't this New Year's Eve? And the Festival of Lights is the first day of the new year, but there's a day in between, tomorrow. What's it called?"

"St. Austin's Day," said Julian. "The day all your sins are forgiven." He looked pointedly at Kate. She was examining the chipped rim of her teacup as if it were a great work of art. "It isn't in one year or the other, just—out of time, as it were. It used to be a solemn holiday. Now it's rather characterized by more—ah—energetic activities."

"Bloody riots," said Kate. "Once a year the lower classes combine to trumpet their grievances. That's how we met you, last year. It had spilled over onto Lightsmass."

"You ought to temper your language, Kate," said Julian.

"With what?" cried Kate, jumping to her feet. "Your damned officiousness? I'm going out to the stables to see how Mr. Southern is getting on. At least if he reads me sermons they'll be from the scriptures." She slammed the door behind her. A moment later the innkeeper appeared, enquiring anxiously if all was well. Chryse assured him that it was, and he left.

"You know, Julian," said Sanjay finally, "it isn't any of

my business, but—ah—that isn't usually considered the most successful method of courtship."

Julian stood up as abruptly as Kate. "I know it. I know it." He paced to the window, returned. "I knew it would be a disaster if I ever admitted my—my feelings. I don't know what got into me."

"I do," said Sanjay softly. "The same thing that got into the rest of us."

"But you can't simply have been willing to go on forever like you were, could you?" asked Chryse.

"Kate was living in my house, wasn't she? Now what can I expect? I've lost her."

"Julian." Something in Sanjay's tone caught Julian's attention, and he halted at one end of the couch and waited. "I suspect the direct approach is the very worst tack to take with Kate. She's a little like Chryse."

Julian looked at Chryse with the barest of smiles, back at Sanjay. "Then what do you suggest, since you have had, I presume, a certain degree of success?"

"Be patient," Sanjay replied. "And be subtle."

"I'll try." He gave them both a sketch of a bow. "If you will excuse me." He left quietly.

"I don't know about subtle," said Chryse.

"Of course you don't. If you'd noticed, it wouldn't have been subtle."

Chryse laughed and, sitting on the rug beside the couch, kissed him. "It's hard to believe we've been here an entire year."

He put a hand on her hair and stroked it gently. "I feel as though we found things out about ourselves that we wouldn't have otherwise." He shook his head. "That does sound trite."

"It reminds me of a quote I read once—about the real treasure being in your own home—that is, yourself—but that you have to go to a new land to understand it, that it can only be revealed to you by a stranger of . . . of another belief and race. Only said much better than that, of course."

"What are you going to do, Chryse? If we get home."

She laid her head against his. "When. We have to. I love this place, just like I loved the year we met, when we studied in Scotland, but there's so much unfinished business at home right now. I've got to go back to school. I need more tools to compose—there's just so much music waiting there."

"Going to make me rich?"

She laughed again. "I doubt it. What will you do, Sanjay?"

"Quit school," he said, decided. His hand, stroking her, paused on her neck. "I don't know. I guess I have to work at seeing the truth. I've always had a fancy to—I don't know—save the world."

"Oh, Sanjay." She got on her knees in order to embrace him. "I do love you."

Marctha pushed open the connecting door that led from her room into her husband's. They had chosen to stop at this inn a little early in the afternoon for the same reason they had chosen most of the others: it had a suite that the earl and his wife could share. He had insisted on it, as if to advertise some fiction about their marriage to a world which he refused to tell the truth. Even so, he had become so remote from her, from the others, that it was as if he was not traveling with them at all.

He treated her with aloof courtesy. That flash of what *he* did not choose to call kindness which he had shown in solving the matter of Charity had come and gone. She doubted if he regretted his original intent to kill her, but there was a quality to his studious avoidance of her that made her believe he was ashamed of the act, having been shown to be so bitterly and incontrovertibly wrong. At those times when she was feeling hopeful, she thought there might be another emotion behind his avoidance. She had not dreamed that brief time of passion, back in the labyrinth, and because he had since then not attempted by the least word or action to remind her of it, she wondered if perhaps he felt he had no right to approach her. Or even if, she sometimes thought with a wild touch of fancy, after his lifetime of abstinence, he did not know how to.

She stopped just inside his room. Her step was silent; he did not look up. Only a single dim candle lit the chamber. He sat brooding in a chair in the darkest corner, but as she watched, she realized that he could as well have been a statue. Not even his lips moved, or his eyes.

He stared at his right hand, extended before him. His palpable effort was like a third presence in the room. As she watched, the barest nimbus of light, a tiny, tiny flame, appeared at his fingertips. He seemed almost to shudder with the exertion.

She walked across the room to him. He did not look up or even seem to notice her. She stopped beside him, and on an impulse she could not resist she leaned down to kiss his cheek. He started just as she touched his face, turning his head, and their lips met.

The shock was like a flash, a flare, of lightning. She grabbed hold of him to stop herself from falling, knelt, but that only prolonged the kiss. His hand settled, tightened, on her waist. She knew then that she would forgive him, if they could replace everything that had gone before with this.

He broke away from her abruptly, stumbled up, and flung himself forward to the window, opening it with the fumbling desperation of a suffocating man.

There were four lamps hung from the walls; all of them were lit, and the hearth fire burned fiercely, that had been cold ashes before.

"*We* did that," breathed Maretha, wondering. She followed him, halting three steps behind.

"Leave me alone." His voice was hoarse, his back to her as he leaned outside. "I never wanted this."

Torches from the stables illuminated his face, giving it a phantom's gleam. His eyes were shut, so he did not see the gathering of men at the stable entrance, did not see Thomas Southern, and then Kate, speaking with them. Maretha saw it, saw first Kate, and after her Southern, break away from the group and hurry back to the inn, meeting Julian on the way. From the way they moved, she could tell it was urgent. She left the room quickly and soundlessly.

A moment after, the earl relaxed his grip on the windowsill, seeming to come to some momentous decision. "Maretha," he whispered, and he opened his eyes and turned, but she was gone.

He followed her trail through her room and to the top of the stairs, stood watching what transpired below with an inner tumult that at last, by dint of sheer cold will, resolved itself into detachment.

Below, the scene was not so composed.

"What is it, Thomas?" Maretha asked as she came down

the stairs. The door to the parlor opened to reveal a puzzled Chryse and Sanjay.

"Riot in Heffield," said Southern. "The Regent has issued a proclamation that Princess Georgiana is seriously ill and cannot be expected to live. The coronation has been postponed indefinitely."

"Why is there riot?" asked Chryse.

"We have never trusted Princess Blessa," he replied. "She would as soon we were serfs again, or slaves. They're crying 'murder' in the streets, and demanding to see Princess Georgiana in person. The army has been called out. It will be bloody tomorrow."

"We'll have to ride on tonight," said Maretha. "If we wait until morning we won't be there until afternoon, and that may be too late."

"You would be fools to go now," said the earl from the top of the stairs. His coolness hit the group below like a blast of winter wind. "Whatever the Regent does, she will wait until St. Austin's Day to begin it. Being a day out of time, as it were, it is particularly auspicious for sorcery And she will necessarily have to spend the morning setting her bounds, if the spell is to be powerful—which it must be, given the trouble she has gone to. She will have the advantage of rest and stillness. We will have to ride nevertheless; if we ride half the night we will be exhausted on top of all else." In the silence that followed, he turned and went back down the hall.

Supper was a subdued occasion that evening. By a kind of mutual unspoken assent they afterwards filtered away to their rooms without further conversation. Maretha walked slowly upstairs to her chamber and sat on her bed.

Then, as she had done every night for the last seven weeks, she tried the only way she knew to calm the wild forces that now permeated her entire being. Her father had taught her how to catalog and order things; she sat with as much stillness as she could find within herself and used all her concentration to channel the power into what she imagined as a library full of journals, each neatly numbered and labeled. Whether it worked to contain and to control she did not know, only that far fewer earth tremors and unnatural fires, hard rains and sudden winds had manifested along their road in recent days.

When she grew tired, she rose, quiet, and pushed open

the connecting door a crack. The earl sat in his chair, completely concentrated on his right hand. The barest nimbus of light shone around it. He seemed oblivious to her.

She let the door shut, sighed, and went to bed.

CHAPTER 28:

THE ANGEL OF WAR

The morning of St. Austin's Day dawned clear and unseasonably warm. Outside Blackstone Palace, a mob ranged restlessly over the grounds, more gathering as each hour passed. A troop of horse soldiers stood at alert at every entrance. Inside it was far too quiet. The halls and rooms were empty. There might have been no one there at all, except for a hush of activity in the very depths of the palace, in the Regent's most private suite.

Colonel Whitmore had brought the treasure in about midnight. Now he stood in the outermost of the three chambers, burning the journals and notebooks and sketchbooks in the great hearth. He kept as far away from the fire as possible. What she was doing farther within, with only one ancient waiting woman in attendance, he did not know, but he was willing to be patient a little longer, since this was the day he was to receive *his* reward for services rendered.

There was a rustling at the door and he looked up to see the Regent standing under the lintel. She watched not him, but the flames licking at the pages, and this annoyed him.

"It is a shame," she said, musing, "to burn so much knowledge, but I cannot afford to leave any evidence." She came over to the fire, flipped through one of the sketchbooks. "A remarkably talented eye, this one has. A—a purity of vision." She paused as if the words awoke some resonance in her. "A true pity to destroy it." She laid it carefully, almost reverently, in the flames. It browned, blackened, and caught, reduced to thick ashes in minutes.

"I sense the pattern turning in on itself," she murmured. "And now I wonder if I read it right."

"Can't even read this one." The colonel eyed the scrawl of Professor Farr's handwriting with distaste. He tossed it into the fire, turned to stare boldly at the Regent. "Your highness," he added.

She smiled, amused and a little scornful. "Are you impatient, colonel? I assure you, you will get more than enough of what you desire."

"Do not underestimate me, your highness."

She laughed. "So like a man. But I will have plain speaking here, Colonel. I dislike secrecy, though I often must resort to it to rule this country as it ought to be ruled."

"And the heiress?"

"I am quite pleased with the treasure you brought me." She lifted a hand to touch his cheek. "It is not quite what I expected—nothing of the power I thought they must find—but it will suffice."

He lifted a hand as if to touch hers, thought better of the gesture. "I had thought you were very powerful."

"I am." She lowered her hand. "But transubstantiation is beyond even my resources." Picking up the last of the sketchbooks, she looked through it, musing, and finally put it on the fire. "I will change her into something that no one, not even her siblings, will ever suspect is her."

"If I may be so bold, what is that, your highess?"

"You intend to be bold." She perused the neat catalog of glyphs. "Into a climbing rose, of course, to ornament my balcony." At his bewildered expression, she smiled, secretive and gloating. "You would not appreciate the subtlety of it unless you understood the Gates."

"But you must explain her disappearance somehow."

"Had you brought me the youth as you were supposed to, it would have been much easier. Cast an illusion on his body, let the physicians examine him thinking he is Georgiana, all agreeing that she had succumbed to the same illness that took her father, and then have him buried. He was excellent material for holding illusions. No one would have suspected."

She picked up the last journal and cast it into the fire with a force that sent ashes up in a cloud and the fire sputtering and, a moment later, bursting into flame like temper.

"You were a fool, Colonel. I wanted circumspection in recovering the treasures. I had two agents, one of whom failed, one of whom evidently did not. Now there are any number of people who suspect my complicity, and getting rid of them will tax *my* ability to be circumspect to its limit. It is well, Colonel, that I have use for you now. Otherwise let me assure you that you would be dead."

His face changed from ruddy, to pale, to ruddy again in the course of her tirade. "You wouldn't dare kill me," he said with all the bluster of the terminally vain.

"Doubly a fool if you believe that. In any case, once I am done with you today you may well be dead, or wish you were."

He whirled and strode to the door that led into the hall. It was locked. He turned back, cheeks flushed with anger and a growing fear. "Let me out, or you will regret it."

"Surely, Colonel," she replied, still calm, "you realize that you are too far gone in my plans to be allowed to leave."

He took three stiff, menacing steps towards her.

She laughed, mocking him. "My wards are far too strong. Or do you think I walk about unprotected?"

"You cannot force me to—to your will."

From the bodice of her gown she removed three cards. "You brought me a remarkable set of Gates, colonel. Let me show you three of them. The Lover, to enflame desire. The Angel of War, to channel it down a furious path without hope of breaking free. And here, the Midwife, whom I choose in this case to represent myself, birthing a new order in this land."

He had fallen to his knees, caught between uncontrollable desire and the last ebbing of his will to break free of her power.

"There is a place for you to recline," she said, "in the farthest room. I will be in shortly."

He was breathing hard, fighting it, but he went.

She watched the fire as it reduced the last written trace of the expedition to ash. It was a pity, she considered, that she had to use so much power to transform Georgiana before she would be able to deal with the expeditionary members. And more of a pity that Colonel Whitmore had proved less ruthless than he had claimed, with so much blustering bravado. Once he had shown his hand, he should have simply killed them all.

The fire sank to a few red gleams in ash. Of course, the Earl of Elen had been there and, according to the colonel's account, had routed the entire troop with ease. Although there was also the possibility that he was leaving some minor, but important, fact out of his report. She shrugged. It had always been her belief that there was no use worrying about something that had to be dealt with later. She went into her innermost chamber.

The colonel was on his knees beside the backless couch he would soon be lying on. He was fumbling with the buttons of his jacket. On a high table next to the couch the objects from the ruins were arranged at the points of the compass, with the cup in the center. Princess Georgiana lay on a pallet at the far end of the room. The ancient waiting-woman sat on a chair at the foot of the pallet, loosening the soil in a large ceramic flowerpot.

Georgiana stirred and moaned as the Regent halted beside her.

"Has she been like this long?" asked the Regent.

The waiting-woman nodded.

"This healing trance was cast on her with a light touch, but a strong one for all that. We must be careful to channel it properly into the new spell. We will have to go slowly with this." Georgiana moved her head and breathed a single, incomprehensible word. "All is ready?" asked the Regent. "Good. Let us waste no more time."

Lady Trent was sitting in her morning room leafing through a novel when her attention was drawn to the window by a rag-tag procession of two travel-stained carriages bearing the crest of the Earl of Elen and what appeared at first glance to be a mob of riders. She had barely enough time to set down the book and stand up before the door to the morning room burst open and her nephew strode in.

"Good heavens, Julian," she began, but by that time he had kissed her dutifully on the cheek, taken her arm, and escorted her to the door.

"I beg pardon for being so abrupt, Aunt Laetitia." He had not even removed his hat. "And for coming in in all my dirt, but we are in a bit of a hurry. We are on our way to Blackstone Palace."

"My coat," said Aunt Laetitia to the nearest footman,

and to Julian: "I see you received my letter. I had my
doubts about the channels I sent it through."

"Quite efficient, let me assure you." He led her out to
one of the carriages. He handed her in and she settled
onto the seat opposite Maretha, who was the only other
occupant.

"Good heavens," Lady Trent exclaimed again. She passed
a hand across her eyes, but the blinding swirl of power
radiating off Maretha was not just a trick of the light.

"I hope you are not feeling poorly, Lady Trent." Maretha
leaned forward solicitously.

"No, no, dear girl. Just adjusting my sight." She found a
set of spectacles in her handbag and used the moments of
fussing with them to moderate her perception of Maretha.
When she finally sat back she regarded the young woman
with keen interest. "You have had," she said, "a quite—
ah—singular experience in the north, I see."

"Is it so obvious?" Maretha's voice was plaintive.

"Only to those with some knowledge of these matters, I
assure you."

"You have—" Maretha halted in some confusion. "I had
no idea you were a mage, Lady Trent, but now it seems
quite obvious to me. You have a certain—gleam."

Lady Trent chuckled. "That is a very pretty compliment
to a woman of my years, countess. My years of serious
study in the arts are long past. But I see we are to go to
the palace."

"We have reason to believe that today is the day the
Regent will act."

"St. Austin's Day—yes, it would be an auspicious time
to cast on a large scale, unbound as one is by the wheel of
the year and its waxing and waning."

"You must know a great deal."

"I know a few things. None of us understands more than
the tiniest fraction of these mysteries, my dear. Else they
would engulf us."

Maretha shuddered. "I know that feeling," she whispered.

A sound like the rush of wind carried in to them. Three
raps sounded on their shutters; when Maretha opened
them, they heard clearly the mutter and growl of an angry
mob in the distance. Julian rode alongside.

"We're coming in to the palace grounds." He looked
annoyed. "Brace yourselves. We've a mob out here, but

we sent Southern on ahead—he has reason to believe that
his sister, the orator, is out there. We'll have to get
through this crowd somehow to reach the palace entrance."

"And through guards there, no doubt," added Lady
Trent.

Julian inclined his head in agreement. "We're sending
Madame et Monsieur in with you. We can't trust their
riding through such a crowd."

He rode away as Maretha closed the shutters. A moment
later the carriage halted and Chryse and Sanjay got in.

"Aunt Laetitia!" Chryse gave the older woman a kiss on
the cheek. Sanjay kissed her hand as gracefully as he could
as the carriage lumbered forward. Both of them were
chuckling with the nervous energy that precedes an anticipated conflict.

"Oh, his face," Chryse said, laughing. "Forgive us," she
said to the other two women. "Julian was trying to convince Kate to ride in the carriage as well, for her safety,
and she answered with a string of swearing that shocked
even me. I had no idea such concepts existed."

Lady Trent looked thoughtful. "Julian is not usually so
protective."

"I think you will find Julian changed," said Sanjay.

Lady Trent examined all three of her companions with
an astute and careful eye. "I have no doubt of it."

Like a peal of thunder, a volley of shots cracked above
the loud voice of the crowd. Screaming shattered the air,
followed by a roar of anger that seemed to come from all
about them. The carriage lurched forward as if it was
being pushed by many hands. A moment later they heard,
above the clamor, a woman's strong voice, and realized
that the speaker must have climbed on top of the carriage.

"—get me forward, lads!" Her words cut with effortless
potency through the general ruckus. "I'll give the Regent
a piece of my mind!"

The mob howled in approval. The carriage shuddered
and shook and rolled on.

"Are we not ten thousand here together? Will we suffer
from tyranny as well as poverty?"

The answering roar of the mob was deafening. Through
it, they could barely discern a tapping on the closed shutters and a quiet voice.

"That's Thomas." Before the others could react, Maretha leaned over and unlatched the shutters.

Southern's face and shoulders filled most of the opening. Beyond him they saw the seething disorder of the crowd. He was pale, and his voice was ragged. "You had best prepare yourselves. They're for blood today—nothing we can do but stem the flow enough for you to get inside. You're our hope, my lady."

Maretha laid a hand on his, a brief touch. "Take care, Thomas."

He heaved himself away and she slammed shut the shutters.

"How long will you suffer yourselves to be beaten and strangled? How long will you suffer the bloody soldiers and their bloodier mistress while your children cry for bread? Rise against the oppressor! Restore our beloved Princess Georgiana!"

A round of musket fire peppered the air at the same moment that the carriage jerked to an abrupt halt, almost throwing Maretha and Chryse from their seats. Frantic pounding sounded on the door. As Maretha unlocked it, it was flung open and Thomas Southern reached inside and grabbed Maretha's arm.

"It's hell out here," he gasped, barely audible over the rage of the mob. "You've got to get inside the palace. There's—"

Screams and shots mingled. Chryse followed Maretha out, Lady Trent and Sanjay behind her, to see Julian, Kate, and the Earl, still mounted, urging their horses up the steps towards one of the huge entrances to the palace. They were surrounded by a swarm of rioters, who surged forward toward the contingent of soldiers guarding the entrance. A few gripped at the riders' legs. The earl was beating them off with his whip, but before those around him could turn their anger on him, the first rush of the crowd reached the soldiers.

The troops were set in formation, but their firing made little difference. For each person shot down, three more flooded forward. A few of the mob had firearms. More had various implements: pitchforks, boathooks from the docks, old, rusted swords, long knives, heavy staves. When the mob hit, the soldiers scrambled for the great doors, still ajar.

Some did not make it, and the work with pitchforks and staves was enthusiastic and bloody. The other soldiers began to close the portal, but through sheer determination a few foolhardy or berserked souls wedged themselves into the gap until their comrades could pry the doors back and trample over the bodies into the entranceway inside.

But here the troops had formed to better advantage. They shot with scathing accuracy, and bodies, most alive and moving weakly, littered the beautiful tiling of the entry floor. Blood leaked in thin streams to the walls. The press at the doorway did not cease. The soldiers, giving up their position, began to retreat up the wide hallway that led to the ceremonial chambers.

On the steps, squeezed in among the advancing crowd, Lady Trent had calmly picked two muskets off of two dead soldiers and handed one to Chryse and the other to Sanjay. They pushed their way to the edge against the doors, clinging to each other. As they were forced on into the entryway by the pressure of the crowd, they could see clearly the three horses and their riders, and hear the inconstant volleying of shots receding up the widest hallway. The crowd streamed after the sound.

Kate had Southern's sister on the back of her horse and Julian rode directly beside her, whether for her protection or his own it was impossible to tell. The earl fought his way back through the crowd, and, coming up to the five huddled against one wall, leaned down and grasped Maretha around the waist. She was too surprised to resist as he pulled her up behind him on the horse.

A moment later she had her bearings.

"To the left," she cried, her voice scarcely carrying over the shouts and screams and distant firing, and there was indeed a small branch hallway leading to the left down which poured a thin stream of people from the crowd.

Behind, on the other side of the entry, Kate and Julian saw them and sent their horses into the mob. As if they were forcing a torrential river, they drove their animals across the flood of bodies, losing ground bit by bit but at last coming to rest against the opposite wall some meters up from the left hallway. When they reached Maretha, and the other four trailing behind on foot, Kate dismounted.

"Take the horse," she said to Southern's sister, and

went to stand beside Chryse. She had two pistols strapped at her side.

Thomas Southern moved to take the horse's halter. "I've got to stay here with her," he said to Maretha. When she nodded, he pulled the horse aside.

Maretha did not look back as she led them down the hall. It quickly emptied into a large courtyard where a few groups of rioters were dancing wildly on the cobblestones. Julian offered to let his aunt ride; she refused. Maretha paused only a moment before she pointed to a small door set under an arch.

Lady Trent nodded to herself as they hurried in that direction. "It's spreading, the force of her spell," she said to Chryse.

"Whose spell? Maretha's?"

"No. The Regent's. It is that which Maretha is following. We must hurry."

Sanjay had to break the lock with a blast from the musket he carried. The shot splintered wood, but the door opened. This hallway, decorated with fine hand-painted gold leaf in a scalloped pattern, seemed hushed after the tumult of the mob. They walked alone down it until, reaching a branching, they turned directly into a group of about a dozen soldiers.

Julian shot two before the others had time to react. The earl spurred his horse forward and drove it into them, scattering them, while Kate handed her two pistols to Julian and reloaded his spent ones. He shot again at the same time Chryse raised her musket and fired. The recoil sent her stumbling backwards and she caught her balance only to find herself looking down the barrel of a musket held by a fierce-faced soldier. She gasped.

Several shots fired all at once behind her. Someone spoke beside her, and she felt a sudden disorientation at the same time as the soldier whirled sideways and fired harmlessly into the ceiling. A calming hand settled on her arm.

"Dear me," said Lady Trent softly. "This sort of conflict is always so messy."

Chryse reversed her gun and clubbed the soldier on the back of the head. He went down hard. She stepped past him to see Sanjay clubbing one soldier and two others escaping at a run back the way they had come.

Lady Trent was matter-of-factly looting the bodies of their
guns as she picked a delicate path across the carnage.
Ahead, the earl reined in his horse impatiently. Kate and
Julian traded pistols again.

"How can you do that?" asked Chryse as Lady Trent
handed her a musket gleaned from the body of a man
whose chest had been shattered by musket shot. "I think
I'm going to be sick."

"Necessity, my dear, is an unforgiving mistress," said
Lady Trent as she steered Chryse firmly past the bodies.
One fellow moaned and writhed on the floor. "I have seen
worse violence than this in my time."

Just in front, Sanjay was looking decidedly queasy as he
exchanged his musket for an unfired one still in the grip of
a soldier shot through the head. They were the last in line.
Julian turned to speak to them, but his expression flooded
with alarm.

Chryse stood confused a moment. Sanjay was still un-
bending. But Lady Trent spun and, raising the musket she
held to sight with remarkable precision, shot a soldier
rising to his knees behind them before Julian could even
aim his pistol.

"Bloody hell," breathed Kate with awe. "Where did you
learn to shoot?"

"We must hurry," cried Maretha from the front, and
they all turned and hastened after her.

She led them along a maze of corridors higher up and
further into the palace. On one staircase a swarm of
soldiers lined up and aimed their guns, but Maretha and
Sanjay shouted at the same time, "They're not real," and
they passed through them as through a cold draft of fog,
which dissolved into nothingness about them.

Higher up the air got heavier and difficult to breathe.
Julian had to dismount first and let his horse go. Soon
after, the earl did as well. Both animals fled back the way
they had come as if driven by unseen sticks. Maretha and
Lady Trent began to gleam. It was just a dull tinge at first,
but as the hallways grew darker, despite the occasional
window revealing sun outside, the glow emanating from
them waxed in strength until it alone illuminated their way.

Chryse was, by this time, holding tightly to Sanjay's free
hand, and Kate and Julian, differences forgotten for the
time, walked close as lovers, side by side.

"Here," said Maretha at last, like a portent. As the earl reached for the door handle, she quickly jerked his hand back. "Don't touch it!"

He pulled his hand free of her grasp with icy disdain. "I may have been stripped of my powers," he said coldly, "but that does not mean I am entirely bereft of gifts." He made two passes above the door handle with his open palm, speaking five incomprehensible words. When he put his hand on the handle, light sparked and raced like lightning up his arm. If it hurt, he did not show it. "Clever," he said under his breath, "but too hastily prepared." He opened the door.

A blast of wind took him off his feet and hurled him back against the opposite wall. The others were flung back as well. Only Lady Trent remained upright, both arms lifted, crossed across each other. Maretha struggled to rise beside her, but could not gain her feet.

The wind lessened slowly. Lady Trent's face grew pale with the strain of controlling it.

"One chance," she gasped. "To go through. When I say."

Wind keened and tore at their clothing. Sanjay felt as if he was pinned to the wall by a huge hand. Beside him, Chryse's hair was blown free of its tight bun and swirled madly about her face. Kate shielded herself with her hands and arms. Next to her, Julian tried hopelessly to pull himself up along the wall.

Like a window closed on it, the gale abruptly lessened.

"Now," whispered Lady Trent, unable to muster anything louder.

They scrambled up like one being and hurried through the doorway. Chryse and Julian had to hoist the earl up between them and help him through. Just as Lady Trent stepped past the opening, the door slammed shut as if thrown.

Lady Trent sank down onto a nearby chair. She looked exhausted, and very old.

"Aunt Laetitia!" Julian exclaimed, letting go of the earl and moving towards her.

"Hurry on!" she said, urgent. "I just need a moment."

Maretha had already passed into the next room, and as the other five came up behind her, she opened the final door and stepped through.

The room was dark, more shadow than light, and dim shapes moved in a slow rhythm, murmuring words in a monotone chant. Only the far end of the chamber had any illumination. In the glow of three candles Princess Georgiana could be seen, propped up in a ghoulish fashion by stakes attached to a latticework that stood against the wall. She was entirely limp, head lolling, and, quite incongruously, her feet were set into a large ceramic pot.

The sight was incongruous only for a moment. As the seven crowded into the room, they all froze in amazement for one long moment.

The princess changed. Her skin took on a sickly hue. Her fingers and toes budded with new spring leaves, her limbs and trunk shaded with the suggestion of stalks and reaching vines. The scent of roses pervaded the chamber, subtle and sweet.

In the center of the room a figure sat surrounded by huge, rustling skirts, her hands poised over a high table on which the five objects from the labyrinth had been carefully laid out. The golden cup, in the center, gleamed with an unnatural light that lent the barest cast of light to the Regent's features as she turned her head to regard these intruders. Her expression was a remarkable blend of ecstatic calm and resolute intelligence that in that instant shifted purpose quickly and without hesitation to meet this new threat.

The earl laid a hand on Maretha's arm and began to speak, but the Regent struck too swiftly.

The first blow hit like a shock wave, hammering all but Maretha to their knees, filling them with chaotic visions of violence and desire and fear, weighing on them like a massive burden. Following hard upon it came absolute cold so deep and abrupt that it froze the ability of the lungs to expand and contract.

Julian attempted to support his aunt and breathe at the same time. Lady Trent looked half dead, pale, skin tight against bone, but her lips moved.

"Move out," she whispered. "Directions. Counter her boundaries."

Flashes of intense burning heat began to alternate with the cold in time to the Regent's back-and-forth swaying on the couch. Her face had a peculiar out-of-breath cast to it, but her eyes were direct and murderous. Maretha reflected the changes like a chameleon: with the cold she grew pallid, with the heat a luster shone from her. Her lips were tight with concentration, but her only action was to remain upright.

At the far end of the room, Georgiana slowly reverted to her flesh color as the force of the spell slanted off her onto the others.

Julian at last comprehended his aunt's words and crawled forward, whispering as loudly as he could her words. Chryse tried to reach Kate's hand, as if the simple act of touching another person would free her from the weight that gripped her. Her hand inched forward in infinitesimal pushes along the wood floor, but her feet felt rooted, as if she, like the princess, were transforming into some arboreal being. She heard Julian's hissed words and with every gathered iota of will she possessed, she changed direction and crept for the wall opposite Georgiana.

Sanjay attempted to follow her, but his vision was distorted and his body caught in a paralysis the more horrifying for the alertness of his mind. Nothing responded but his panting gasps for breath. Then a hand brushed him in passing and he started as if awakened and could crawl, however slowly. Waves of heat and cold and paralysis beat down over him, unceasing in their succession one to the next, but he kept moving. Each motion was painful, but with each motion the pain grew more bearable.

Kate crept away from him towards Georgiana. Lady Trent lay beside the door unmoving. Julian and Chryse were ahead.

Beside Maretha the earl still knelt, but his face was drawn in agony with the effort of remaining on his knees. He seemed unable to move at all, even to turn his head, but he was nevertheless aware of the motion of the others. Sanjay saw his lips move with anguished concentration, though he could not hear his words, and Maretha lifted her hands in front of her face.

As if she were pushing through snow, she began to clear a way forward for herself toward the Regent, the earl following in her wake. As she neared the Regent, the heat and cold and pressure on the others slackened. Fire sparked and guttered in her hair. Her dress whipped and snapped in some unfelt wind, once flicking the earl in the throat as he inched forward behind her, leaving a welt.

As Sanjay reached the top of the couch on which the Regent sat, he felt suddenly the lifting of the spells on him, as if he had reached a tiny cocoon of safety. He looked around. Maretha's radiance lent more light to the chamber, and he saw the seven members of their party spread around the room in a pattern that abruptly and eerily reminded him of Madame Sosostris and her daughters: Lady Trent at the door, Julian opposite her at the other wall; Kate by Georgiana, and Chryse at the far wall from her; himself between Chryse and the couch; Maretha almost at the couch, and the earl three feet behind her in the direction of Kate.

Somehow he could also see the Regent's face: handsome in a feminine way, pervaded now by a concentration so intense that her features seemed obliterated by the potent force of her will. Sanjay knew instinctively that if he moved he would once again be subject to her spells, so he knelt quietly in the envelopment of still air.

In that same light he began to perceive the lines of the Regent's magic. Like a thin rope of luminescence they trailed out to Georgiana, to all the corners of the room. But now, building, massing, her power coalesced into a single strand that arced and lanced at Maretha.

Everyone else was strangely silent, as if they saw nothing unusual. Sanjay tried to cry out, but the force of the Regent's heightened power slammed into Maretha like a bolt of lightning.

Maretha knew the moment she entered the room that the Regent's attention was inexorably drawn to her. She felt herself the palpable attraction she radiated, focus of so much unleashed and uncontrolled power, like the golden cup or any of the treasures of the ancient city. She felt, too, the shift in the tide of the spell, and saw Georgiana transform fully to her human state at the same moment the full strength of all the Regent's stored power, channeled through her years of experience in wielding it, struck her.

Like the obliteration of all the senses, the attack left her blind and deaf, mute and staggering. She did not even know she fell until hands touched her, grasped her, pulled her tight against warm flesh. That was the entire scope of her universe: a body against hers, whispered words she could not discern, and pain. She sank, struggling against her collapse but unable to do more than wish it onto her opponent. A void consumed her, and she acceded to the grip of her captor.

Felt, instead of annihilation, a new force gathering in the hands that held her, skill unlocking the neat mental shelves of books that were her only means of controlling the power of the labyrinth. Recognized *his* touch, somehow, clean and cold.

And unleashed it, sending the force of the Regent's attack back on her, twice over.

The shock of its impact was as much explosion as earthquake, as much hurricane as inferno, and it was followed hard upon by utter silence as absolute as death.

She knew that her body still existed, felt a second presence embracing her, a face pressed against the back of her neck. Emboldened by this knowledge, she opened her eyes.

At first she could see no more than her companions surrounding her: Chryse to her north, Sanjay above, Julian to the east and Lady Trent to the west, Kate to the south.

The sight of Kate clasping the ceramic pot that held Princess Georgiana restored her perspective. The princess was slumped over like one dead, but her chest rose and fell in the slow regularity of sleep. For an instant, panicking, she thought she had lost her husband, until she realized that he was the person holding on to her.

She took a deep breath. Gently disengaging the earl, she stood up. The others, all but the princess, followed suit.

Blackstone Palace no longer existed. They stood alone in a flattened ruin of smoke and a scattering of small fires that blazed at intermittent intervals amongst the rubble. Beside Maretha the shattered and blackened remains of a couch were littered with ash, fragmented bones, and a jumble of burnt objects.

A tremor shook the ground beneath their feet. The doorway behind, still intact, swayed and cracked and collapsed into a heap of dust and debris. A mist of rain swept over them like damp spray and went on, blown before a brisk wind that smelled of sea wrack.

"Julian." Kate's voice rang distinct in the hollow silence. "Help me get her highness free of this. How in bloody hell did we end up here on the ground from the upper stories?"

Julian did not answer. He was already moving over to his aunt. He lifted her gently, surprised at her lightness. Her eyelids fluttered and opened.

"I am quite tired, Julian," she said in a faint voice. Her eyes shut again, sunken in an aged, lined face.

Chryse and Sanjay walked, shaky, across to assist Kate, untying the princess and lowering her carefully to the ground. She looked a little pale but otherwise unharmed, and still breathed as if asleep.

"The cards!" said Chryse suddenly.

Sanjay rose and returned to the devastated couch to dig among the ashes. His hands covered with more and more fine gray dust, he unearthed first the chalice, dull in color now and cracked, then the hornpipe, broken into three pieces, the obsidian knife, split in two as if by a single, precise tapping blow, and last the spear, shaft burnt away and point melted into slag. Only the monogrammed pouch he had found by the northern entrance remained intact and, scattered throughout, their cards, unmarked, undamaged.

He counted them out with painstaking thoroughness as the earth trembled again and distant rumblings marked the further disintegration of the palace.

"Fifty-one." He leaned back onto his heels in his relief, glanced at all the others before meeting Chryse's gaze directly. "And the pouch. The one I found in the labyrinth."

She nodded.

"Gracious," said a slight, low voice. Princess Georgiana's eyes had opened. They widened as she saw first Kate, then Chryse, and then the devastation surrounding her.

No one spoke for a moment. A flood of emotions crossed the princess's face, controlled at last into the disinterested mask most often worn by a judicious ruler.

"Perhaps you would assist me to rise," she said softly but regally.

Kate and Chryse helped her up. A tremor passed under their feet. Fires blazed up to consume the last remains of walls and great piles of fallen tapestries and curtains. More stone archways buckled and crumpled, sending up clouds of dust and steam. An army ten thousand strong might have passed through the palace and not left such total destruction.

"I might suggest," said the princess in a calm and practical voice, "that we remove ourselves from this place. I will be happy to wait until later for an explanation."

CHAPTER 29:

THE HEIRESS

They discovered the magnitude of the devastation as they picked their way through the ruins of the palace. The edifice had collapsed to become a field of stone and debris. Only a few doorways and arches still stood, but nothing above ground level. They skirted the odd fires that flared up and scrambled for solid ground when the occasional tremor shook the rubble. Here and there marble statues or suits of medieval armor had melted into slag. Steam hissed and rose to create small pockets of fog. Now and again, in chasms produced by parallel heaps of fallen stone, one could see corpses. Some were bloody with wounds sustained in the fighting, but most were crushed and mangled by the palace's fall. Once they found a single, limp hand stretching out of a pile of debris like a drowning man reaches for help out of water; they passed with averted eyes. Chryse felt ill with the sight of it, of so much destruction.

They came at last to the edge of the great park surrounding the palace. At a considerable distance from the ruins a small crowd had gathered, perhaps what was left of the rioters, perhaps simply those curious enough and brave enough to come so close.

Once out of the palace the air took on a cooler, crisper bite. The sun had lowered near to the horizon, and a few wise souls were lighting torches or lanterns.

A carriage detached itself from the crowd and was driven toward them. At the same time, the characteristic rumble of a new tremor began to sound, and they all braced themselves, Julian even kneeling on the grass as he held his aunt. It was no tremor, however, but a troop of cavalry approaching from the left at a gallop. A man in captain's gear gestured to the riders to pull up, and he came forward alone and dismounted and knelt before the princess.

"Your highness. Captain Malroy, Queen's Lancers."

"Very good, Captain Malroy," she replied, composed despite the torn hem of her gown and the dirt patching her face and hands. "If you will lend me one of your horses, I can ride, and you and your men will escort me to St. John's Palace. Once I am arrived safely there, you will send out a picked group to summon my Council of Ministers to the Palace. There is a great deal to do if I am to be crowned tomorrow."

"Your highness."

The breeze played havoc with the loosening coil of her hair, but she maintained her air of placid command as though the smoking ruins behind her were a typical feature of her life. "You may rise, Captain. We had best make haste. There is little left of the day."

She turned to survey her companions with a clear gaze, pausing longest on the earl. "What I wish to say to you, as my rescuers, must wait until I am crowned and wed and in full possession of my throne. I trust that my lord Elen—" Here she paused to consider him with a gaze both curious and slightly apprehensive. He bowed, brief but respectful.

"—and his lady wife—" There was another pause as she looked at Kate, Chryse, and Maretha in turn, as if she was not quite sure which was the countess. "—will be able to assemble your companions when that time comes. And that you—" She turned to Julian.

"Lord Vole," he supplied quickly, unable to bow because of his aunt.

"Of course." Her face, though plain, was a wonderfully transparent conduit of emotion. It was obvious she had at last connected faces to names. "—that you, Lord Vole, will keep me informed as to Lady Trent's condition. Now, I must go. Will you be able to find conveyance home?"

The carriage that had pulled away from the crowd drove up next to them. It was filthy, but the Elen crest could be discerned on the door. Thomas Southern swung down from the seat beside the coachman. He was bloodstained and dirty, coat torn, but he seemed unhurt. When he saw the princess, he dropped to one knee.

"Yes, your highness." Maretha dipped a brief curtsy. "As you see."

Georgiana nodded and walked away to the troop of soldiers. The captain signaled and one of the men quickly dismounted and led his horse forward for the princess. She mounted, and the entire troop wheeled around and rode away.

"You're safe, Thomas?" Maretha asked.

He nodded. "It was a great inferno, my lady. Those of us who escaped it were sure all the others must have perished. It is a blessing you still live."

"Indeed." She glanced at her husband, but he looked away from her.

"Most of the crowd dispersed, those who were not killed outright," Southern continued. "Frightened of Our Lady's righteous wrath. My sister collected the rest and drew them away to a safe distance."

"You had best return to her, then," said Maretha. "And see to your family tomorrow. Day after next come to Elen House and we shall see to your and Charity's future. Be sure, Thomas, that the queen will know of your part in saving her."

"My lady." He bowed to her, inclined his head to the earl and Julian and, with a brief nod to the rest, set off on foot back across the park towards the crowd.

Lady Trent stirred in her nephew's arms and opened her eyes. "I see we succeeded." Her voice was weak, but her gaze, scanning the wreckage, was keen. "Might we go home now, Julian?"

He blinked back tears. "Yes, aunt. Of course."

After Vole House, where Julian and his aunt, Kate, Chryse, and Sanjay all disembarked, the carriage seemed quite empty. The two of them rode in silence to Elen House. Around them, the city lay in a hush of mingled shock and anticipation.

Elen House, too, was quiet. The earl opened the front door for Maretha himself. The act, so inconsequential, reminded her with bitter clarity of her first entrance into this house. Now, standing in the huge entry hall, she felt a strange lack in the walls, in the air, surrounding her.

She had grown used to having no human servants—or if not used to it, at least resigned. But the absence of spells, the damped-down aura of magic which once had filled the house, disturbed her. She could hear the coachman outside calling round for the groom at the attached stables.

It was dark indoors. None of the lamps were lit.

"Do you have any matches?" she asked in a low voice.

"No." His reply was curt. "You must be tired. I will escort you up."

He offered his arm. The gesture so astonished her that she hesitated, and when she did put her hand on his sleeve, she laid it there so lightly that it was almost no touch at all. His expression was shuttered and distant.

They mounted the side stairway in silence. He had to open the door into her chamber for her, left her there, abrupt, without a word. She sighed and went in. It was cold. The hearth sat with cold ash and empty grate.

She had to let herself into her bedchamber. The bed, at least, was neatly made, everything tidy and in its place, but she had to go to her dressing room for a nightgown, had to reach for all the buttons herself. She gave up halfway down her back, went over to the window that looked out over the garden.

Over rooftops, the moon rose low and full. Nothing moved along the neat paths laid out through the garden. Her dress slipped a little on her shoulder, and she had to hitch it up once, twice, before she finally turned and regarded the door that led into his rooms. The key still sat in the lock.

She unbound her hair and shook it out. Walked with deliberate steps to the door, unlocked it, and opened it.

His dressing room, lined with dark suits and white shirts, lay beyond. She passed through the narrow room, opened a second door, and found herself in his bedchamber.

It was starkly furnished: a four-posted bed, a small table with pitcher and basin, and a chair in front of the hearth. It was also quite dark, lit by neither fire nor lamp, and it took her a moment to realize that the dark figure brooding in the chair was the earl. Only his hair and face and hands showed like lighter shadow in the gloom.

"John." Her voice was so soft that the word barely stirred the air, but his head jerked around and he stood up as abruptly as if she had screamed.

She flushed, in darkness, but forced herself nevertheless to take three more steps towards him. "I can't reach all the buttons on my back." Her voice sounded false even to her own ears.

He started to lift a hand in a gesture clearly meant to summon, stopped, and turned his back on her to stare at the dead fire.

"What were you going to use the power for?" she asked, emboldened by his rejection. "To gain more wealth? To gain worldly power? A dukedom? The throne?"

His voice spoke out of darkness. "What use do I have for such things? With such power I could have uncovered deeper mysteries, found a new understanding of my art."

"Is it too late?"

In the silence, she knew he was thinking of that moment when the full force of her power had been unleashed onto the Regent—her power, it had been, but his knowledge.

"I don't know," he said.

"I'm pregnant." Her voice shook on the word. What impelled her to tell him she did not know, but the effect was electrifying. He spun to face her, came six steps across the room to stand before her. Even in the dimness she could read amazement on his face.

"Is it true?" he breathed. "I never imagined. All those years, pulling the source of my power out of myself." He shook his head. "I thought I must be sterile. But perhaps that is part of the mystery."

She felt suddenly colder. "Then it *was* never, not at any time, your intention to have an heir?"

"Never. I won't lie to you, Maretha. I always intended to sacrifice you. That I am sorry for it now does not change the fact." In the half-light the pallor of his face made him resemble a statue carved of hardest stone, etched with chisel into one fixed, unchangeable shape. "I turned away from such—desires long ago. They have no place in my life."

"Could they now?"

She put out her hand, found that he stood just at the limit of her reach. Her fingers brushed his pale hand.

A hiss, a breath of warmth, and the fire lit in the hearth. Looking past him, she saw a red-gold creature stir in its depths, sparks of eyes unblinking. Lamps lit the room. A hush descended, separating them as if with a great blanket from the world outside.

"I can't decide that for you," she said. She turned away

and walked back through his dressing room into her own
bedchamber, shutting the door but leaving it unlocked.
Fire snapped and whispered in the hearth, and when she
went to the window, she saw the familiar insubstantial
wraiths moving with unnatural grace along the paths in the
garden. They wavered, fading out, returning, as to the
pulse of some undecided will.

She stood a while there, feeling the warmth of the fire
flicker and fade and begin to die at her back, and abruptly
swell up again into flame. Then she heard a soft noise, a
footfall, and the door opened behind her.

Panels of morning light fell across the bed, illuminating
Sanjay's formal black tails and trousers as he sat on the
mattress. He examined the portrait of the Queen of Heaven
and Her Son that hung above the mantel while Chryse
talked to him from her dressing room.

"There's nothing here formal enough. And the gowns
that *are* formal enough don't quite fit." A pause, augmented by rustling. "I'll have to wear my wedding dress—a
little old-fashioned, but correct enough for coronations, I
should think. I hope it still fits." Another silence, followed
by more speech that was muffled by cloth. Eventually she
appeared at the door with the dress on but unfastened.
"Can you help me?"

He smiled and stood up. In a few minutes she stepped
back for him to admire her. "I'd forgotten how beautiful
you look in that dress." He shook his head. "Do you
realize we've been here an entire year?"

She hugged him tightly. "It seems somehow much shorter,
and yet other times I can hardly remember being anywhere else."

With a kiss, he disentangled himself. "We'd better go
down. We have to be there by midday."

On the stairs they paused, hearing an altercation in the
front parlor.

"The way I dress never bothered you before." Kate's
voice carried easily into the entry hall. "Bloody hell, did
you drink something with your coffee this morning that
turned you into a sanctimonious old—"

"Just for once, Kate. Just for once you might attempt to
look like a lady."

"Oh, *lady* is it now? You weren't so damned particular before in your companions, Lord Vole."

"You can give over this ridiculous lord-this-and-that. Kate. You know very well that for an event as important as this coronation—"

Lady Trent appeared in the doorway that led into the front parlor and, shutting the door behind her, advanced into the hall. Kate and Julian's voices went on, but the closed door muffled their words.

"Quite the wrong tack to take with Miss Cathcart, I fear," she said, smiling up at Chryse and Sanjay on the stairs. She looked less tired than she had the day before, but her years rested more heavily on her now.

"I don't suppose there has been time to tell you, that Julian—" Chryse hesitated.

"Oh, I've known that Julian was in love with her for these last eight years. But I read from this new state of affairs that he was at last pushed by circumstances to admit it."

"He asked Kate to marry him," said Sanjay.

"That explains it." Aunt Laetitia smiled again. Her expression was distinctly mischievous. "I expect they'll get along very well."

Through the door, they heard Kate's voice raised in a couple of choice, penetrating swear words.

"Like that?" Chryse laughed.

"My parents, as was customary in those times, arranged a good marriage for me, to a man I had never met. I rebelled and ran away from home. Found myself in the middle of a rather wild adventure where I met a young man and fell madly in love with him—only to discover that he was the very betrothed I had meant to escape." Her expression softened. "Oh, I married him, even took his title, which was less common in those days. We fought like cats and dogs until the day he died. The Haldane temper, you know. I'm glad to see that Julian has it in him. I was beginning to fear that he was too patient."

The door into the parlor was flung open. Kate poised on the brink, face flushed, oblivious to the three people in the hall.

"*Nevertheless*," Julian said, his tone so close to a shout that it seemed to echo around the stairs, "you *will* ride with me to Wellminster Cathedral and not with those rash, raking, insolent cardsharps that you choose to call friends."

Kate slammed the door, whirled, and stopped short, seeing her audience for the first time.

Chryse laughed. "Oh, Kate." She went over to her, taking her hand, and kissed her on the cheek. "Perhaps you'd better humor him this once."

Kate glanced at Sanjay, but he merely nodded, trying to look serious but failing. "I'll think about it," she replied in an ominous tone. Chryse let her go, and she left the house.

A moment later Julian appeared. "Where did she—"

Sanjay came forward and drew him to the door, one hand on his arm. "Remember what I told you, Julian," he said in a low voice.

Julian frowned, but he clasped Sanjay's hand briefly in his own. "I'll try." He followed Kate outside.

"Do you know," said Chryse slowly, pondering, "Julian once said that I was reckless to marry for love."

"He was quite right," replied Aunt Laetitia. "One is always reckless to marry for love. Ah, here is Master Coachman. We ought to go."

Once they had settled into the carriage, she opened the shutters so that they could see the houses pass. "I have asked Coachman to take us by Fenwych House." Her voice had a slight tremor. "I received a note this morning from Madame Sosostris. She wishes to see you."

"Oh." Chryse felt as if the seat had suddenly dropped out from beneath her. Her throat constricted. Then she remembered the cards, and the pouch, and she looked at Sanjay. He nodded, twice, to show that he had them.

"I thought," she continued when she could speak again, "that it took weeks to get an appointment."

But at Fenwych House Lady Trent disembarked with them and kissed them each on the cheek with a decided air of finality. Chryse paled, and Sanjay gripped her hand tightly.

"I'm not sure I'm ready to go," he said.

"The wheel of the year," murmured Aunt Laetitia. "It turns out, and it turns in, and leads you back to the place you started."

Chryse felt tears gathering in her eyes. "But we haven't said goodbye to anyone!"

Behind, the door to Fenwych House opened, and Madame Sosostris's eldest daughter, Ella, waited expectantly for them to enter.

"A quick goodbye is the best." Aunt Laetitia squeezed their hands in turn. Perhaps it was only the glint of the sun, but her eyes, too, were bright with tears. "I will write, if I can."

"Mama is expecting you." Ella's voice was soft behind them.

With a last kiss, they left Lady Trent and followed Ella into the house. She led them through the empty parlor, past the double doors and tiny anteroom, and into the half darkness of the chamber where Madame Sosostris sat before the single table just as she had before. She might not have moved at all, as if it was only a moment that they had been gone.

"Madame. Monsieur." Her voice had lost none of its resonance. In the dimness they saw her seven daughters standing or kneeling in the same positions, as Ella walked to her corner, as they had last seen them. It heightened the illusion that minutes rather than months had passed at Fenwych House since their last visit. "You have brought me something. Your Gates, first."

Sanjay hesitated a moment, then handed them to her.

She laid them out with deliberate, practiced precision, every card set into its place: hinge, wheel, journey, and face cards. "Fifty-one," she said. "But you are missing one."

"The Sinner," said Chryse.

"Properly called the Queen of the Underworld." The veiled form shifted forwards. "You have brought me something."

Sanjay held out the monogrammed velvet pouch. She laid it on the table with dark-complexioned hands and contemplated it in silence.

Chryse looked at Sanjay. "We haven't even looked in it yet," she whispered.

As if in response, Madame Sosostris deftly opened the pouch and extracted its contents: a single card, which she laid in the empty spot.

The Queen of the Underworld, running blindfolded through the haunted forest.

Chryse and Sanjay were too astonished to speak.

"The deck is complete," said Madame Sosostris.

"But—how did it get *there*?" Sanjay reached to touch it, pulled his hand back before he did. "It's ours, Chryse. It's the one we lost."

"I know." Her voice was almost inaudible. "I don't understand."

"I don't understand," Sanjay repeated. "Are you going to take our cards?"

"They are your Gates. I cannot take them."

"But then what is your reward if you give us back the card you said was the treasure?"

They felt that Madame Sosostris smiled, but the veil concealed all but her voice. "I brought you into your power. You came through the Gates and discovered the labyrinth. You can never be the same again."

She lifted her hands, crossed them in front of her throat, and lowered her head until the top of the veil was almost touching her palms. A faint, resonant drone vibrated the air around them.

"Wait!" Chryse gripped Sanjay's wrist, a little frantic. "Isn't there some way we can come back?"

"To come once across such distance to this land is a gift." Madame Sosostris' voice had taken on a slight blur, as if the vibration in the air came from her person. "To come here twice from *your* home is dangerous, for it can alter you past all recognition."

"But there must be some way," insisted Sanjay.

The room grew darker. He could no longer distinguish the faces or forms of Madame Sosostris's daughters.

"You must follow the path. But without a guide you could not know where you would end up, or how you might return. Skills such as mine are long sought and hard won." As her voice grew more distant, it grew also more familiar without becoming recognizable. "But the key to travel is the Gate."

Under their feet, the floor shuddered and fell.

"Oh, Sanjay!" Chryse clapped her free hand over her mouth. "I really feel sick."

Madame Sosostris spoke one last time, more an amused thought than a voice. "You will have a souvenir from your visit here. In a little over seven months' time."

"You're pregnant!"

The cards fluttered down around them. Lights came on,

and they found themselves in the elevator as it descended. They knelt and gathered up the cards that were now scattered across the carpeted floor, all fifty-two of them.

The elevator shuddered to a halt and its doors opened to reveal the grey concrete corridor that led to the parking garage of the hotel.

"I told you that this would happen," said Chryse, accusing.

Sanjay laughed. "Let's go home," he said, taking Chryse's hand.

EPILOGUE:

THE QUEEN OF HEAVEN

The sketch taking shape on the paper could have been a preliminary rendering for a painting to be entitled "The Queen of Heaven nurses Her Infant Son, Lord of Man, on Whose Cross shall all of our Sins be hung."

In fact, although Chryse *was* nursing their seven-week-old baby son, she was also, with her free hand, laying out cards on the table at her right. She examined each one before she placed it with a bemused expression. The movement of her hand and of her husband's as he sketched was the only motion in the room, except for the rhythmic suckling of the infant, Julian.

"Just think," said Chryse as she laid the last card, the Queen of the Underworld, into its place in the pattern: hinge, wheel, journey, and face cards. "Maretha must be holding a child of about this age. There are times now when I think it must have been a dream."

Sanjay paused. "Those compositions you did got you accepted into graduate school, didn't they?"

She smiled.

"And I have something to show you. I've been saving it as a surprise." He set down his sketchpad and went into the bedroom, returned with a bulky, manuscript-sized package. With great care, he withdrew the contents and sat at Chryse's feet.

"But those are—" She gaped at the title page of an over-sized manuscript: *Pictures From Another Land*. "Those are galleys. What is this?"

He began to turn them for her, and she saw their journey, and the excavation, come to life again before her eyes: Maretha cataloging hieroglyphs, Mog and Pin and Lucias hiding in the ruins behind; the earl sitting at table, aloof and frowning; Julian elegant in his town wear, Kate slouched in a seat, glass of ale in one hand; Charity looking prim and Thomas Southern looking solemn, Aunt Laetitia mischievously wise and Professor Farr simply confused; images from the factories, the ruins, the forest—all as she remembered them, yet with a clarity that she knew was the vision Sanjay brought to such sights.

"You know I'd been reconstructing all the sketches that were burned. But I didn't tell you that, on a lark, I suppose, I assembled them as if they were the record of one of those nineteenth-century artist-travellers who roamed the globe drawing various exotic locales and then publishing sets of lithographs. I was afraid nothing would come of it."

"But something did." She watched, rapt, as he flipped page by page through the galleys. "They're beautiful, Sanjay."

"Thank you." A small, secret grin quivered on the edge of his lips.

"There's something you're not telling me."

"They're so pleased with how this one turned out that they want me to do a series." He stopped trying to hide his smile—it touched, more than his mouth, his eyes, mirroring his delight and excitement. "Of different countries, here, to see—well, I suggested something like 'faces of humanity.' To show how we're all human on one level, all bonded by that link, despite our other differences."

"Oh, Sanjay." Chryse laughed, low. "How idealistic of you."

"Someone has to be."

She lowered her free hand to rest on his shoulder and together they looked again at the faces and scenes they had left behind. "Do you think I look different?" she asked as she considered an illustration of she and Maretha cataloging glyphs. "My aunt Emma didn't recognize me when we got back."

He shrugged. "You were pregnant."

"But still—" She hesitated, tilting her head. "What's that noise?"

"What noise?"

"Sort of a low drone—"

The next instant he, too, heard it; their eyes met with the same idea. On the table, the cards showed a faint blurring nimbus of light and a shadow above. The drone ended abruptly, and an envelope dropped one inch to land with a light smack on the tabletop.

"Well?" cried Chryse after a long moment of stunned silence. "Open it!"

He did so.

" 'My dear Chryse and Sanjay,' " he read. " 'I promised that I would write, and so I shall, having some expectation that this letter will be able to reach you, although little that any further communication will prove able to.'

" 'There is a great deal of news to impart. The coronation of Georgiana was a great success, and her wedding to young Prince Frederick, a rather plain, unassuming lad, I must say, went off to great acclaim by peer and populace alike. Thank Our Lady that that business is now settled.'

" 'As well as private meetings with the Earl and Countess of Elen, Julian, Miss Cathcart, and myself, the queen took the surprising step of granting a royal charter to the so-called correspondence societies of the working classes, as a tribute to the help they gave her in passing my letter on. Of course the charter itself means nothing if the government chooses to suppress what they consider to be seditious writings, but the recognition is doubtless worth twice its weight in gold to folk like Mr. Southern.'

" 'However, it is the more personal news that I expect will interest you the most. Maretha was delivered of a baby girl on the day of Hunter's Run, speaking in the ancient year—' "

"Wouldn't that be the exact same day as—"

"Shh, you're interrupting. '—and the child has been christened Elena. The earl continues as cold and aloof as ever, but there is a new quality tempering him now which I will not attempt to define, except that Maretha at least seems to be flourishing. She has a certain, shall we say, glow about her that has sustained itself without fail since the Festival of Lights.'

" 'Mr. Southern and Miss Charity Farr were wed some six months ago in a very quiet ceremony. She is, I understand, expecting again. One is constantly amazed at the fecundity of the lower classes, although one also wonders if Mr. Southern's rise in the world will doom his progeny to small families. He is progressing in his studies, as I hear it, but has refused a vicarage in a rich parish on lands the earl owns in favor of a Heffield parish in the midst of the worst slums. Ah, well, one reaps as one sows.' "

"He would, of course," said Chryse. "The better to incite the new generation of union agitators."

" 'The youth Lucias, having recovered from his injuries, has proven to have very common antecedents: he is the son of one of the grooms at Blackstone Palace. He has been given a position as an undergroom in the Queen's establishment, and by all reports is quite happy there.'

" 'The two urchins saved from the factory have, at Julian's insistence, been apprenticed out to respectable trades, a far cry better than they could have expected even had they not been sold to the factories. However, this social conscience sits strangely on Julian's shoulders—he is not to my mind of the reformer's cast of mind, but we all of us need one purpose or another in order to give some sense to our lives.'

" 'I had thought that your sudden departure might prove to be the catalyst on which Julian and Miss Cathcart would resolve their differences, but it did not prove so. After one very *long* month, Julian at last proposed a scheme to end the stalemate once and for all: He made her a wager, to a game of cards, where if he should win, she would marry him, and if he should lose he would never mention the subject again.'

" 'This seemed to me a clever enough ploy, since Julian has, like all the Voles, the devil's own luck with the cards. I was frankly surprised when Miss Cathcart accepted, until it occurred to me that perhaps she *wanted* to lose. Imagine my amazement when *Julian* lost!"

" 'I had not realized up to this time the subtlety of my nephew's plan, for of course now Miss Cathcart had what she had claimed to desire all along—freedom from Julian's importunities. But the result produced was quite the opposite. With a group of the most disreputable rakes and sharps you have ever met, she went on a spree of wild drinking, gambling, and carousing that quite scandalized polite society—only to disappear from sight the day after winning a handsome fortune at the tables. When she reappeared one month later (poor Julian left in ignorance of her whereabouts and cross as flinders the entire time), she was quite sober and enrolled as a student at the College of Surgeons. Whereupon she promptly seduced my nephew—so I hear—and then, claiming that she had compromised his reputation past redemption, said there was nothing to it but that he must marry her.'

" 'You may guess that I am pleased.' "

"I might at that," said Chryse, laughing.

" 'It all has fallen out exactly as I hoped it might years ago. You may also guess that I wish the very best for you and your son, and that I shall always remain, your fond aunt (if I may style myself so), Laetitia Haldane, Lady Trent.' "

"How did she know we had a son?" asked Chryse.

Sanjay did not reply. There was a little silence as they sat together. The baby had fallen asleep.

"What are you thinking of?" asked Chryse at last.

Sanjay took her hand and smiled at her. "Weddings and gifts and the fragmented remains of old paintings. I suppose the real treasure is in learning to connect the lines and isolated pieces into a coherent whole. The same picture is hidden there. We just each of us see it in a different fashion."

"One that makes sense depending on who you are?"

He reached past her to pick up the central card of the deck: the Gate. "I think it must be so," he said.

THE GATES

This is the deck as it usually
appeared in medieval times.
Many different permutations have appeared
in other places and other times.

I. THE HINGE

1. DAWN
Letter: C
Picture: Out of a cottage comes a little child, walking stick
and satchel in hand.
Meaning: Beginning; optimism, "a new day," setting out
on a new endeavor; inexperience, newness, development;
early understanding, origin of idea or activity.

2. DUSK
Letter: Ɔ
Picture: Same cottage—an old person, bent and weary,
returns to the hearth within.
Meaning: Ending; completion of a cycle, a task achieved;
pessimism, oldness, finish; rest and hope of shelter.

3. THE GATE
Letter: ∩
Picture: A gateway of stone.
Meaning: The path, road, or passage to another place or
state of being; the hinge on which all decisions and choices
are made, however large or small, changing the traveller
in the act of passage.

II. THE WHEEL OF THE YEAR

1. THE FESTIVAL OF LIGHTS
Letter: A
Season: Midwinter Solstice

Picture: A young woman, wearing a circlet of burning candles, crowns a young man with a circlet of unlit ones, soon to be lit.
Meaning: The birth of the new year, or of any venture or quest.

2. TWIN'S FAIRE

Letter: J
Season: The Thaw
Picture: Tents of a medieval crafts fair fill the background; in the foreground, a man works smithing over a hot fire while a woman weaves an elaborate tapestry on a loom beside him.
Meaning: Aspiration and inspiration; work and labor, individual and unique; expression of one's own self.

3. SOWER'S DAY

Letter: AE
Season: Spring Equinox
Picture: In a field, a woman and a man work side by side, the woman furrowing, the man sowing.
Meaning: Planting; sowing for a future project or for future use or harvest; planning ahead, working to purpose, worthwhile and effective labor; balance and harmony.

4. FEAST OF SOMORHAS

Letter: O
Season: The Flowering
Picture: At the high table, the bride and groom preside over a lavish feast. The bride is dressed in green, the groom in black; on the wall behind hangs a tapestry depicting the Harvest Faire—it is seen to be the same tapestry that the artist in Twin's Faire is working on.
Meaning: Marriage, unity, choice and renewal; fertility; desire.

5. HIGH SUMMER EVE

Letter: E
Season: Midsummer Solstice
Picture: An obviously pregnant woman kneels before a mature man. A "daisy chain" is looped around his wrists—it is impossible to tell if the woman is putting this chain on him, taking it off, or receiving it from him.
Meaning: Fruition and ripening; but also separation.

6. HUNTER'S RUN
Letter: W
Season: The Long Heat
Picture: A group of hunters hunts a stag (if one looks closely, it can be seen to be a man wearing a deerhide and antlers).
Meaning: Sacrifice; uncertain rewards; fear and the implacability of Death; but also the hope of harvesting all one has striven for.

7. HARVEST FAIRE
Letter: I
Season: Autumn Equinox
Picture: A young man and woman, the woman with a tiny babe in arms, seated at the assembly of the fruits of the harvest.
Meaning: Harvest, thanksgiving, joy; plenty balanced against barrenness to come; the ability to sustain oneself through difficult times; the seeds from which the next year's growth will spring.

8. LORD DEATH'S PROGRESS
Letter: U
Season: The Freeze
Picture: Lord Death, mounted on a stallion, leads the parade of the doomed: a weeping woman holding a child in her arms walks beside him, one hand gripping the trailing end of his fine robe; others walk behind her, each closer to death than the last until, at the end, walks a bleached skeleton.
Meaning: Death, but also conception; a sundering from old ways, but also the beginning of new; barrenness, but also the suspended power of growth.

III. THE MONTHS OF THE YEAR

The months of the year equate to the Journey—moving from the small self-absorbed circle of The Hut (the child's self) to the larger circle of the Village (the family), breaking away by means of The Road that leads to The Town Square (provincial life), through stages of introspection— The Temple representing collective, guided study, often of a religious bent, and The Tower true introspection, self examination in an isolated place or state, meditative and illuminating. Such study allows the traveller to then take leave of old boundaries, by way of The Harbor, for new horizons, represented by The City, where larger possibilities for social interaction and endeavors are available (The Hall). One still can separate oneself out, to contemplate in The Garden, but such contemplation leads to study of the deeper mysteries, which demands a descent through The Barrow, the separation of life from death, into the Labyrinth, the place of mysteries from which none emerges unchanged and in which many become irretrievably lost. It is here, if one survives the perils of the journey, that one can find The Castle, the center, or the heart, of life.

1. The Hut/The Meadow B
2. The Village/The Forest L
3. The Road/The River N
4. The Town Square/The Lake F
5. The Temple/The Marsh S
6. The Tower/The Mountain H
7. The Harbor/The Sea D
8. The City/The Shore T
9. The Hall/The Fields K
10. The Garden/The Waste M
11. The Barrow/The Ravine G
12. The Labyrinth/The Cave P
13. The Castle/The Spring R

IV. THE DAYS OF THE MONTH

1. THE MIDWIFE
Letter: A
Element: Earth
Direction: East
Rank: Queen
Animal: Snake
Plant: Mandrake
Picture: A mature woman in a wimple stands holding a newborn. Behind her we see part of a chamber with a window and part or all of a bed or birthing chair.

Meaning: Birth, creation; bringing something into being; a new direction, goal, endeavor; a propitious time to begin (a new venture, turn a new leaf).

2. THE HEIRESS
Letter: B
Element: Earth
Direction: South
Rank: Queen
Animal: Pig(s)
Plant: Climbing rose
Picture: A young woman sits at a dressing table, examining herself in a mirror, various bits of jewelry and makeup jars on the table before her. Reflected in the mirror, one can see doors opening to a balcony on which is a climbing rose.
Meaning: The mirror of knowledge; the heiress represents the priestess (the adept) who, seeing herself, sees knowledge—who knows herself; but also, worldly vanity, material fixations; love of luxury, prideful love of self; stagnation in selfishness and self absorption.

3. THE QUEEN OF HEAVEN
Letter: R
Element: Earth
Direction: Heaven
Rank: Queen
Animal: Bull
Plant: Lily
Picture: On a throne suspended in the air sits the crowned Queen of Heaven. Her expression is detached, her eyes raised to something beyond her, one hand across her chest, the other trailing down. At the hem of her voluminous skirts crouch three tiny supplicants—one man, one woman, and a calf.
Meaning: Forgiveness; selflessness—giving of one's substance to succor others; also, detachment.

4. THE EMPRESS OF BOUNTY
Letter: Λ
Element: Earth
Direction: Center
Rank: Queen

Animal: Cockatrice (basilisk)
Plant: Wheat
Picture: A richly robed matron with long, luxurious hair sits at a loom. At her feet sit four wild animals: a mouse, a wren, a toad, and a lizard. Around and beside her, the fruits of the earth.
Meaning: Plenty; mother of All Things; the bountiful.

5. THE DREAMER
Letter: P
Element: Earth
Direction: Underworld
Rank: Queen
Animal: Mare
Plant: Belladonna
Picture: A blindfolded young woman dressed only in a simple shift runs wildly through a forest of horrors: spiders, bugs, and weirdling creatures populate the branches. As she runs, she is (accidently) stepping on a snake.
Meaning: Unreasoning fear, terror, nightmare, lack of control, brutality; imagination, also its dark side; magnification of what you are at this moment—whether for good or bad; ability to harness the sheer power of the unconscious.

6. THE ARCHER
Letter: L
Element: Earth
Direction: North
Rank: Queen
Animal: Stag
Plant: Hemlock
Picture: In a winter forest, a naked woman draws her bow, aiming at an unseen target.
Meaning: Revenge; fixed unalterable purpose—purpose which must be carried out; justice; the "furies."

7. THE GATEKEEPER
Letter: E
Element: Earth
Direction: West
Rank: Queen
Animal: Worm

*Plant:*Dill
Picture: An old woman sits beside a stone archway. In her hands she holds knitting. At her feet sits a lantern.
Meaning: Knowledge of life and death, of passage from one state to another; wisdom of life and its processes; knowledge of the future.

8. THE TUTOR
Letter: J
Element: Air
Direction: East
Rank: King
Animal: Hawk
Plant: Fennel
Picture: In a library a man holds a book. He could be either offering it or receiving it.
Meaning: The dissemination of learning; the beginning of self-knowledge; curiosity about one's own inner processes.

9. THE PHILOSOPHER
Letter: T
Element: Air
Direction: South
Rank: King
Animal: Swan(s)
Plant: Pansy
Picture: In a marketplace, a man holds forth to a collection of listeners (male and female).
Meaning: Exchange of ideas, cross-fertilization of ideas on the stage of the marketplace, the square; stagnant, monopolizing pontificating.

10. THE PHYSICIAN
Letter: K
Element: Air
Direction: Heaven
Rank: King
Animal: Eagle
Plant: Foxglove
Picture: A robed man seated at a table holds the tools of a physician; behind him one sees the paraphernalia of the alchemist.

Meaning: Healing; the use of thought and rationality to have an impact on the material; helping others with no thought of one's own gain.

11. THE EMPEROR OF ORDER
Letter: --
Element: Air
Direction: Center
Rank: King
Animal: Gryphon
Plant: Iris
Picture: A man seated on a throne carved of living wood. His crown is vines and leaves. In one hand he holds a staff, in the other a flower.
Meaning: The melding of culture and nature; rationality, but also too much rationality, to the exclusion of mystery; the triumph of reason; necessity of order, but also, ordering without imagination or flexibility.

12. THE PRISONER
Letter: S
Element: Air
Direction: Underworld
Rank: King
Animal: Raven
Plant: Rue
Picture: A man in ragged clothing sits slumped in a cell. He is chained to a large block of stone, a tiny, barred window above him.
Meaning: Imprisonment; being caught in a closed place, idea, goal; being chained to a person, place, concept; prejudice; bias to a view that lacks perspective.

13. THE BEGGAR
Letter: ∩
Element: Air
Direction: North
Rank: King
Animal: Owl
Plant: Thistle
Picture: A thin, old man sits beneath a leafless tree, an empty bowl at his right knee, a lit lantern hung on the branches above him.

Meaning: Freedom from material burdens; wisdom brought by self-imposed isolation; self-knowledge, enlightenment, asceticism; without either home or possessions, a state either blessed or damned.

14: THE HUNTER
Letter: W
Element: Air
Direction: West
Rank: King
Animal: Kite
Plant: Mistletoe
Picture: Through late-summer woods runs a loinclothed hunter with a spear, dogs at his heels. What he pursues cannot be seen.
Meaning: Death, cruelty, fixed purpose without reason; when you are marked by the Hunter there is no recourse—unlike the Archer, he is not motivated by revenge or justice, but is rather on the blind scent of blood—no emotion is linked with the hunt except that it is inevitable and unstoppable.

15: THE PAGE
Letter: AE
Element: Water
Direction: East
Rank: Knight
Animal: Salmon
Plant: Daisy
Picture: In a room a boy is being fitted in new armor. Behind him the door opens to reveal a landscape beyond.
Meaning: Beginning of knowledge of the world, of life outside of oneself; beginning of independence; exploring, curiosity, initiative.

16: THE CRUSADER
Letter: D
Element: Water
Direction: South
Rank: Knight
Animal: Porpoise(s)
Plant: Laurel
Picture: A young man, mounted and in armor, armed with

a lance, sword and shield hung from his saddle, leads the charge at an unseen target. Others follow him.

Meaning: Being on "crusade": some larger purpose, outside of oneself, directing and informing one's actions—often with a group; can lead to prejudice; lending oneself as a participant in another's goals, ideas; being controlled by someone else's goals, opinions, or biases.

17: THE PALADIN

Letter: M
Element: Water
Direction: Heaven
Rank: Knight
Animal: Newt
Plant: Olive branch
Picture: Through a wasteland a young man rides, armed, his eyes uplifted to the sky in which shines a single, brilliant star.
Meaning: The noble quest; purpose—to aid others and deny oneself, usually undertaken as a solitary task; purity of purpose.

18: THE MASTER OF WATERS

Letter: ᚎ
Element: Water
Direction: Center
Rank: Knight
Animal: Sea-serpent
Plant: Vine
Picture: A naked man rises from the waves, in one hand a trident, in the other a twining snake. He is crowned by seaweed.
Meaning: Mutability; can change to fit any space, container; ability to adapt; master of the ever-changing processes of life.

19: THE MADMAN

Letter: G
Element: Water
Direction: Underworld.
Rank: Knight
Animal: Frog
Plant: Henbane

Picture: In an ominous forest, a man clothed only in tattered rags roams, obviously mad.
Meaning: Insanity; twisting of purpose; lack of control; madness.

20: THE WANDERER

Letter: N
Element: Water
Direction: North
Rank: Knight
Animal: Seal
Plant: Columbine
Picture: On a field of ice and snow, a hooded man lies half frozen, obscured by drifting snow.
Meaning: Lost purpose; wandering in circles; life's goals, purpose, frozen in indecision or from lack of goals; to try one thing after another with no set purpose.

21: THE DROWNED MAN

Letter: I
Element. Water
Direction: West
Rank: Knight
Animal: Crab
Plant: Water lily
Picture: On a shore, a dead man lies half in, half out of the surf.
Meaning: Dissolution; death; change from one state to another.

22: THE LOVER

Letter: O
Element: Fire
Direction: East
Rank: Magi
Animal: Salamander
Plant: Myrtle
Picture: In the window of a tower a girl leans out. Her hair is unbound. Far below stands the figure of a young man.
Meaning: Beginnings of desire, of interest in other people; infatuation; passage from child to adult, with adult's passions.

23: THE MERCHANT
Letter: T
Element: Fire
Direction: South
Rank: Magi
Animal: Fox(es)
Plant: Marigold
Picture: In a market stall stands the proprietor, a woman with carefully coiffed hair, displaying her wares.
Meaning: Desire for wealth and material goods; trading of all sorts, physical wants, economic, artistic, cultural, political; bargaining; cheating; competence, but also incompetence; deviousness.

24: THE MAGE
Letter: C
Element: Fire
Direction: Heaven
Rank: Magi
Animal: Lion
Plant: Vervain
Picture: A woman levitating.
Meaning: The serene levitator; nobility of desire, control of desire leads to mastery of the subject at hand; serenity; vanquishing of desires and emotional turmoil; mastery of one's profession.

25: THE ANGEL OF WAR
Letter: +
Element: Fire
Direction: Center
Rank: Magi
Animal: Dragon
Plant: Cinquefoil
Picture: An armed woman advancing to battle. Light blazes around her.
Meaning: Purity of desire, but also lust; violence; the conquest of passion; the power of pure emotion; all-out assault.

26: THE INVALID
Letter: ⊃
Element: Fire
Direction: Underworld

Rank: Magi
Animal: Cat
Plant: Poppy
Picture: On a couch in a shuttered room, a woman lies, passive, clearly ill, one hand cast up over her eyes, the other hanging limp, a book lying open on the floor.
Meaning: Passivity, debilitation; the diseased decay of inward-turned desire; wasting, usually from the inside out; helplessness, or not bestirring oneself to make any effort.

27: THE SEEKER

Letter: H
Element: Fire
Direction: North
Rank: Magi
Animal: White wolf
Plant: Heather
Picture: A cloaked figure turns away from the gates of a lighted city—it is dusk—about to take the road that leads into the mountains. High in the mountains one can see the suggestion of a dark castle.
Meaning: Desire for knowledge, so much so that one leaves all else behind; the search for answers; the quest that leads one away from human society; the restless need for understanding, to find the synthesis of what is known and what has yet to be known.

28: THE SACRIFICE

Letter: U
Element: Fire
Direction: West
Rank: Magi
Animal: Phoenix
Plant: Red rose
Picture: A woman tied to a stake, being burned alive. Her face is contorted, either in agony or in ecstasy—one cannot quite be sure.
Meaning: Sacrificing oneself for desire, for what one considers to be a greater purpose, goal, desire, or passion; passion—pain, but also ecstasy; complete immolation in one's passion of goal, usually voluntary; death, but a death that leads to rebirth, either of a new self or of a new purpose.